LIES THAT COMFORT
AND BETRAY

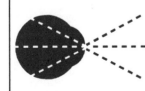

This Large Print Book carries the
Seal of Approval of N.A.V.H.

A GILDED AGE MYSTERY

LIES THAT COMFORT AND BETRAY

ROSEMARY SIMPSON

THORNDIKE PRESS
A part of Gale, a Cengage Company

GALE
A Cengage Company

Farmington Hills, Mich • San Francisco • New York • Waterville, Maine
Meriden, Conn • Mason, Ohio • Chicago

Copyright © 2018 by Rosemary Simpson.
A Gilded Age Mystery.
Thorndike Press, a part of Gale, a Cengage Company.

**LIBRARY OF CONGRESS CIP DATA ON FILE.
CATALOGUING IN PUBLICATION FOR THIS BOOK
IS AVAILABLE FROM THE LIBRARY OF CONGRESS**

ISBN-13: 978-1-4328-5365-5 (hardcover)

Published in 2018 by arrangement with Kensington Books, an imprint
of Kensington Publishing Corp.

Printed in Mexico
1 2 3 4 5 6 7 22 21 20 19 18

*To everyone who understands
that forging a new identity
is a necessary part of life.*

CHAPTER 1

"Jack the Ripper's killed number seven. An Irish girl this time, younger than the others. Only twenty-five. The detective in charge had photographs taken of the scene and the victim. I don't think I'll buy a newspaper next week." Josiah Gregory rattled the pages of the *New York Herald* of November 10, 1888. The shocking story of the mutilation of Mary Jane Kelly was graphic and unsettling.

"Have you ever been to London, Josiah?" Geoffrey Hunter set down the *New York Times,* which was running the same story, but in far less detail; its readership preferred to be informed and only inadvertently titillated. The lead story in the column cabled by their London correspondent was the partisan wrangling of the Parnell Commission. Politics as usual first, then the Ripper.

"I haven't, sir. Mr. Conkling went, of course. Twice. Once in 1875, then again two years later. He was a great one for seeing everything there was to be seen, but I doubt he ventured into Whitechapel."

"You still miss him, don't you, Josiah?"

"Every day. I always will. You can't spend that much of your life with someone and not regret his absence. I was the senator's personal secretary from his first swearing in at the House of Representatives in Washington until he died. Almost twenty-nine years."

"You could retire, if that would suit you."

"And do what with myself, Mr. Hunter? I'd rather stay on here with you. I'm used to working, and I'm used to this office."

"What else does the *Herald* say about Mary Jane Kelly?"

"So much that I'd be careful not to leave the paper lying around where Miss Prudence might pick it up. The Kelly woman was a lady of the evening like all the others the Ripper's killed, but this time he did more damage to the corpse. The doctor on the scene is quoted as saying it was worse than anything he's experienced in dissecting rooms. The Ripper cut the body open and took out all of the organs. He sliced her face so badly it didn't look like a face anymore and nearly severed her head when he slit the throat. Then he hacked off all of her private parts. That's the short version, Mr. Hunter, and about all I care to read." Josiah folded the newspaper four times into a neat rectangle that he handed to his employer. "As I say, it's nothing Miss Prudence should see."

"I've already read the story, Josiah." The young woman standing in the doorway to Geoffrey Hunter's office was tall and slender, dressed in black, but without the long, heavy veils of full mourning. It had been more than ten months since her father's death, nearly eight since her fiancé had been murdered in the worst blizzard the northeastern seaboard had ever known. "You shouldn't leave the outer office unattended if you don't want intruders coming in unchallenged." Prudence MacKenzie smiled to take the sting out of her words, and was immediately transformed from a pretty girl into the kind of delicate beauty men instinctively want to possess and protect.

"Let me take that," Hunter said, standing to reach for a rectangular package secured in brown paper and tied with butcher's twine. "What is this, Prudence?"

"It's the Hunter and MacKenzie stationery," she said. "I decided I couldn't wait for delivery. I went by the printer's on my way here." Using the scissors Josiah handed her, Prudence cut through the string and then the sturdy wrapping. "What do you think?"

The letter paper was a heavy, off-white bond, the firm's name engraved across the top of each sheet in a thick calligraphic script. *Hunter and MacKenzie, Investigative Law.*

Josiah Gregory ran his fingers lightly over the lettering. "Mr. Conkling would have liked this," he said. "It's what he hoped for when he made out his will that last time."

Like Prudence's fiancé, Roscoe Conkling had been among the 200 New York City casualties of the Great White Blizzard, though it had taken almost a month before the damage done to his body during a long walk up Broadway at the height of the storm finally killed him. When he knew without a doubt that he would not survive, the former senator from New York deeded his office and his law practice to Geoffrey Hunter and wrote a letter in which he urged him to follow a profession that would give meaning to his life. Josiah Gregory, now a man of independent means through his longtime employer's generosity, had been an unexpected and invaluable bonus.

"I'll put this away." Josiah gathered up the new stationery, the wrapping paper, the twine, and the scissors. Moving quickly and quietly, with a deft neatness that defined his every movement and gesture, he retreated to his desk in the outer office. He'd give Miss Prudence and Mr. Hunter a few minutes to themselves before he brought in the coffee tray. November was always cold and damp; nothing made a New York winter bearable like strong, sweet coffee with a good dollop of heavy cream.

"I did read the article about the Ripper's latest atrocity." Prudence unfolded the newspaper Josiah had placed on Geoffrey's desk, settling herself in one of the client chairs to look at the headline. "I cannot imagine what kind of monster would do something like this, not once, but seven separate times. They're calling him a lunatic and a homicidal maniac. For once I don't think the press is exaggerating. He has to be insane, Geoffrey. It's the only explanation that makes any sense. Thank God it's not happening here."

"We've had our share of killers. No country or society is immune from violence. Think about what we did to one another not very long ago. The war's been over for twenty-three years, but for some people it's as though it were still being fought."

Matthew Brady's photographs of Union

11

and Confederate dead on shell pocked battlefields had horrified and saddened a nation torn in two by irreconcilable beliefs and a warrior culture that enshrined blood sacrifice. Death had ridden the land for four long years, and when it was finally over, greed galloped in like a fifth horsemen of the Apocalypse.

There were more enormously wealthy men in America now than ever before, but there were also legions of hopelessly poor and homeless men, women, and children. Armies of exploited workers whose wages barely staved off starvation. Violence was commonplace in big city slums, but few of New York City's killings could match what Jack the Ripper was doing in the far away London cesspit of Whitechapel.

"How could he do what they say he's done? Especially this latest killing, this Mary Jane Kelly. The reporter writes that he carved her up as casually as a butcher does the carcass of a sheep hanging from a hook in a slaughterhouse. I don't think I'll ever be able to understand the man who did that."

"Would you be able to defend him, Prudence?"

"Women haven't been admitted to the bar in New York, Geoffrey. It's only been a few months since New York University finally allowed three women to enroll in their law courses. Whether they'll graduate with anything equivalent to a law degree is another matter entirely."

"You didn't answer my question."

"I'm not sure I can. My father taught me everything he knew about the law. Even though the lessons took place at home, I learned as much if not more than any intern in any law firm in the city. The Judge made sure of that. But since the bar is closed to women in this state, your question is moot."

"There was a killer in Austin, Texas, three years ago. He murdered eight people, seven of them women, mostly in service. Chopped them to death with an axe."

"Did someone defend him?"

"I don't think the murders have ever been solved."

"Like Jack the Ripper."

"One theory is that when a murderer leaves the area where he committed his crimes, he doesn't stop killing; he starts again in a different place. The Ripper is still somewhere in London; there's no telling how many more women he'll kill before something or someone forces him to leave."

"For an ex-Pinkerton, you don't sound very optimistic that the Austin killer or the

Ripper will ever be caught."

"I'm not. You can trace a *crime passionel* to a spurned lover, and a murder committed in the course of a burglary to the man who's foolish enough to pawn what he's stolen. You can even link a poisoner to the victim. But if someone kills for the sheer pleasure of killing, and there's no personal link to his prey, then he'll only be caught by accident, by some small, fortuitous mistake he doesn't realize he's made."

"At least we don't have a Ripper in New York City." Prudence refolded the newspaper, placed it headline down on her partner's desk.

"Not yet. It's only a matter of time before someone decides that London shouldn't have all the glory."

"Surely not."

"Sooner or later we'll have an American Ripper, Prudence. For all we know he's already at work; the newspapers just haven't discovered him yet."

"Can you manage, girl?" Brian Kenny handed his daughter a heavy wicker basket containing the freshly butchered bodies of four of his wife's finest stewing hens. Wrapped in saltwater soaked toweling, they'd keep nicely until she could hand

14

them over to the MacKenzie cook in the house on Fifth Avenue. "Mind you keep the lid on tight, now. Mrs. Hearne is that careful about what she puts in her soup pot."

Nora Kenny drew her small, slender self up to her full height of just over five feet. She'd bundled her black hair into a fisherman's knit cap for the cold, windy ride from Staten Island to Manhattan, but there was nothing she could do to keep the red from her cheeks. Chapped skin and lips were the price you paid in November for having a fair Irish complexion. "I'll be fine, Da. I've carried baskets heavier than this one many a time."

"Don't forget it's Sunday tomorrow. You don't want to miss Mass."

"I'll go to Saint Anselm's with Colleen." Nora had become good friends with Miss Prudence's maid, sharing a room with her whenever she worked at the Fifth Avenue house.

"One of your brothers will be here to meet the ferry next Saturday. Mind you're on time to catch it. Your ma will worry me to death if you don't."

She could feel a blush deepening the scarlet of her already cold reddened cheeks. It was always like that when she had something to hide.

"Go on then. The ferry's about to pull out."

A surge of passengers crowded across the dock toward the new paddle wheeler named the *Robert Garrett*. Nora slung the handle of the wicker basket over one arm, picked up her carpetbag with her free hand, and smiled up at her da. She was his only girl in a family of ten children, six of them still living, thank God. He worried about her more than he did any of the five lads. He'd been reluctant to let her go by herself to help get Miss Prudence's Fifth Avenue house ready for the Thanksgiving and Christmas holidays, but she'd reminded him of how welcome the extra wages would be and he'd given in. Brian had a terrible soft spot for his Nora.

As soon as the *Robert Garrett* pulled away from Staten Island into the choppy waters of the Hudson River, Nora found herself a comfortable seat in the portside saloon, the basket containing the plucked fowl sitting in an empty seat beside her, carpetbag at her feet. From this side of the ferry she could look out the windows that ran all along its side and see the enormous Statue of Liberty that had gone up on Bedloe's Island two years before. The weather on the day of the dedication had been bad enough to force cancellation of the planned fire-works. Nora remembered how disappointed they'd all been, crowded onto the family's two fishing boats to catch a glimpse of President Grover Cleveland, then forced to return to Staten Island in thick fog and heavy rain without having spied a single dignitary. The mist swirling up from the river today reminded her of that late October day in 1886. She and Tim Fahey had just begun walking out.

The ferry wasn't as crowded today as she'd thought it might be. Most of the seats were taken, but there were none of the weekday crowds pressed against the rails. Nora let her thoughts fly ahead to the mansion on Fifth Avenue where she'd be spending the coming week. She and her mother had both worked for the MacKenzie family since the Judge first built the Staten Island summer house named Windscape where he hoped his wife would recover from the tuberculosis. She didn't, of course. No one ever did, though sometimes the invalid coughed out bits of his lungs for years until the final hemorrhage.

Nora came to Windscape as a three-year-old, tied by a long rope looped around her waist and fastened to one of the thick wooden legs of the kitchen table so she

17

wouldn't wander and get into mischief. Agnes Kenny kept a watchful eye on her daughter as she peeled potatoes, polished silverware, or baked the Irish soda bread that Sarah McKenzie loved to nibble with her afternoon cup of tea. The child was four when she was first let loose to play with Miss Prudence, the two of them a lively, mischievous pair whose antics brought a smile and occasionally a laugh to Miss Sarah's lips. Then a cough. Laughter always exacted a price. Nora remembered the sound of that coughing, how it echoed through the rooms, getting worse and worse until Miss Prudence's mother stopped coughing and the house became empty and silent.

Once they'd grown out of childhood, which happened early in their young lives, Miss Prudence and Nora seldom met, though Nora continued to accompany her mother whenever Agnes went to Windscape to cook or to clean. The Judge never spoke of selling the house, but he was seldom there. When the summer air in the city was brutally hot and hard to breathe, Judge MacKenzie brought his daughter across the river to the white painted house on the hill, but the young miss was never alone. There was always a nurse or governess or tutor

18

beside her; she'd grown beyond the free, open play of the early years. She was being groomed to take her mother's place in a society from which Nora would forever be excluded.

That was the way of the world, her mother told her, reading the sadness in her daughter's expressive blue eyes. Miss Prudence didn't mean anything by it. She'd just moved deeper into the world she'd been born to, leaving her childhood playmate behind. Where she belonged. It was all about knowing your place and keeping to it. That was why her parents approved of Tim Fahey, why they'd pushed her in his direction and encouraged the engagement even when Nora herself was sure it was no longer what she wanted. Her ma said there wasn't a finer young man on Staten Island than Tim, and that Nora and Tim fit together as well as they did because they were so much alike. They lived in the same world.

She smiled at her da's caution to remember to go to Mass tomorrow. One of the reasons she was taking this early ferry was so she could stop by Saint Anselm's for Saturday confession on her way to Miss Prudence's house. She'd already confessed this particular sin to Father Devlin on the island more times than she cared to think about. She was sure he hadn't recognized her yet through the screen, but eventually he would and then there'd be hell to pay. Priests weren't allowed to reveal what they were told in confession, but she couldn't afford to take any chances.

She could walk in off the street to Saint Anselm's and be just another blue eyed, black haired Irish girl. Lost in the crowd. She'd been to Mass there many times with Colleen, but she didn't know any of the priests personally and they didn't know her. She'd whisper her sin through the grille, bow her head for absolution, gabble her penance at the altar rail, and be on her way. Ten or fifteen minutes at most. The hens wouldn't mind.

The other stop she had to make was more important. She decided to go there first, just in case it took longer than she had planned for. If she didn't make it to Saint Anselm's before confessions ended for the day she'd have to lie to her mother about receiving Communion on Sunday because you couldn't go to the altar with a mortal sin on your soul.

Then it would be back to Father Devlin again when she got home because she knew she wasn't going to stop. She was caught already, so what could it matter?

Unless something happened in the mean-time. Unless she was wrong.

She'd told so many lies by now that a few more wouldn't trouble her conscience at all.

CHAPTER 2

Weekly confessions at Saint Anselm's started at midafternoon during the winter months. The November sun usually set by five o'clock and even with snow on the ground to reflect the light from streetlamps, it was dark as well as cold. People wanted to get home.

This Saturday only one of the three priests assigned to the parish was on duty. Father Gerard Mahoney, Saint Anselm's sixty-year-old pastor, was confined to his bed with a mustard plaster on his chest. Father Kearns, the assistant pastor, had been called to the bedside of a dying child.

"I'll manage," Father Mark Brennan assured both his colleagues.

"Give them all five Our Fathers, five Hail Marys, and five Glory Bes," coughed Father Mahoney. "The faster you get them in and out, the more they'll thank you for it." The pastor had been known to say an entire

Mass from *Introíbo ad altáre Dei* to *Ite, Missa Est* in twenty minutes flat.

It wasn't Father Brennan's way to rush his flock along like sheep being herded to the shearing pen. He scrupulously matched each sin to its appropriate penance, not forgetting to accuse himself of the sin of pride for lacking humility in the doing of God's holy work.

The line outside his confessional box was long, stretching halfway down a side aisle. He took his time with each sinner, and as a result many would-be receivers of the sacrament gave up and went home, especially once four-thirty had come and gone. Parishioners popped their heads through the massive wooden central doors, took a look at the length of the line, lingered a moment to gauge how quickly, in this case how slowly, people were entering and emerging from the curtained side boxes. They dipped their fingers into the holy water font, made a sketchy sign of the cross, and were out again before their coats had finished steaming in the indoor air. They wished Father Brennan would learn to speed things up. This wasn't the old country; everyone in America was in a hurry.

It occurred to Nora Kenny that she ought to step out of line and be on her way to the

23

MacKenzie mansion, but once she made up her mind, she seldom changed it. Both the Kenny parents and all of the lads were like that, too. Obstinate, mulish, as immovable in their determination as an Irishman could be. And proud of it.

She reminded herself of the other reason she wouldn't give up today. Agnes Kenny expected all of her children to walk to the communion rail every Sunday, and God help the one who didn't. So if Nora was to allay any suspicions her mother might have about her recent excuses to slip away from the house on her own, she had to receive Communion next Sunday. Today was her last chance to confess to a priest who could be counted on not to recognize her. She hoped the hens weren't warming up too much. She couldn't smell them, so they must be all right.

When it was finally her turn, Nora stepped into the confessional, knelt, and made the sign of the cross. "Bless me, Father, for I have sinned. It's been one week since my last confession."

It wasn't as dark as in the church on Staten Island; Nora could see more than just a shadow on the other side of the curtained grille. This priest was young and handsome, his hair nearly as dark as hers,

24

the hand he raised in the blessing long fingered and finely sculpted. She wondered if he would look in her direction; most priests faced forward and only leaned sideways a bit toward the penitent.

She started with the venial sins, the way she always did, hoping that when she slipped in the great big embarrassing mortal sin of committing impure acts he might be busy with his own prayers and not notice. But he did.

"Did you commit the sin of impurity with yourself or with another?"

The question shocked her. The priest on Staten Island had never asked Nora Kenny for details. "With another, Father."

"Are either of you married?"

"No, Father."

"How many times did you commit this sin of impurity since your last confession?"

"Twice, Father." She could feel the sweat beading on her forehead. Her voice was shaky, and she thought she might cry. *Why couldn't he just give her a penance and absolution and be done with it?*

"Have you thought that a child might be conceived?"

She didn't answer, afraid her voice might penetrate the long dark red curtain that fell over the backs of her legs. Unwilling to risk losing the little control remaining to her.

She heard a deep sigh and knew he was finally finished.

"For your penance I want you to kneel before Our Lady's statue while you say five decades of the rosary. Ask Our Blessed Mother for the grace to stay chaste."

She was sure tears were making tracks down her cheeks.

"Now make a good Act of Contrition and tell Our Lady how sorry you are to have sinned against purity."

Just before Nora lowered her face into her cupped hands to whisper the Act of Contrition, she felt his eyes on her. Dark brown eyes in a stern face. One glimpse through the fan of her fingers, but it was enough. This was the kind of priest everyone tried to avoid, the kind who took things too seriously and could make life miserable. She supposed she deserved it, though. She'd tried to avoid Father Devlin and this was the punishment she got.

She asked a man leaving the church ahead of her what time it was. Quarter past five. Just enough time to drop the hens at the MacKenzie house and get herself back to Saint Anselm's by six to say her five decades of the rosary. She'd learned in First Holy Communion class that you had to do your penance to make the absolution stick. The nun teaching them hadn't used those exact words, but that was the gist of it. If she ran both ways and didn't stop for a gossip when she gave Cook the hens, she could just make it.

There would still be time afterwards to complete her other errand, the one she couldn't tell anyone about. Seven o'clock. That's when her things would be ready and she could pick them up.

It was early dusk. The lamplights hissed softly in the cold evening air. Nora was surprised how easy it was to navigate the sidewalk despite the heavy basket bumping against her hip. There was no smell of dead hen coming from it, and when she reached a hand in, the cloths in which they were wrapped were still damp and cool. Almost as good as keeping them on ice, she thought. She passed few women as she walked; it was mostly men striding along in a hurry to get out of the cold, faces muffled in wool scarves, gloved hands carrying parcels or leather briefcases. Horses clopped by, nostrils breathing out steam, drivers hunched over to catch a draft of warmth from their broad backs. She'd give anything to be in one of those hansom cabs, but even if she had the money, no one would stop for a girl out all alone after dark.

Nora breathed a sigh of relief when she recognized the MacKenzie mansion, a thick blanket of green ivy climbing over its deep redbrick facade. Quick now, down the areaway steps to the kitchen door.

But when she hauled on the bellpull, she heard no sound of ringing inside. No footsteps tapped their way to the door. She didn't have time to stand there and try to figure out where everybody was.

She thought about pounding on the door and calling out, but what if a policeman were passing by and heard her? He'd haul her off without waiting to listen to an explanation and then she'd really be in trouble. She yanked on the bellpull one more time, then set down her basket, turned on her heels, and sped up the concrete steps to the street. Moments later she was back on Fifth Avenue, dodging and ducking her way toward Saint Anselm's.

She didn't expect to be climbing the broad stone steps of the church alone. She had looked forward to the comfort of light streaming out into the darkness as the doors opened and closed behind parishioners stopping by for a quick prayer or to light a candle on their way home from work. Catholic churches were never entirely empty.

But the wide steps were barren and Saint Anselm's had the look of a church settling into locked emptiness for the night.

Nora scurried through the vestibule, her shoes clattering on the stone floor. It was warmer inside the church itself, with a comforting fustiness hanging in the air, as though the people who had stood in the aisle waiting to go to confession had left bits of themselves behind — the smell of damp wool and wet leather shoes, that tangy scent of unwashed winter clothing and skin, the tobacco smoked by the men, the cheap scent worn by the women. It reminded her of going into the parlor at home before her mother readied up the coal stove and sent the wonderful smells of supper wafting through the rooms.

The church was dim because no one had turned on the huge, newly electrified chandeliers hanging from the ceiling. Banks of votive candles flickered at the side altars and the blood red sanctuary lamp burned steadily beside the tabernacle to remind her that Christ was present. God was here.

Nora genuflected, made the sign of the cross, and crept into a pew close to the side altar where a larger than life Virgin Mary in blue robes and white veil looked down at her. The kneeler boomed against the floor as she pulled it out and it slipped from her cold fingers. She glanced around guiltily. No one had heard. There was no one kneeling behind or to either side of her. No matter. She needed to get started on the five decades of the rosary she had to say.

She heard a sound like a key turning in a lock, but muffled, as if it came from the vestibule. Not a lock, but the click of one of the switches that turned on the electric lights? She waited for brightness to flood down, and looked up to see the chandeliers come ablaze, but the dimness all around her did not change. She clung more tightly to the rosary beads she'd wound around her fingers, feeling the sharpness of the small silver crucifix digging into the palm of her hand. She'd never been by herself inside a church before. No matter that the sanctuary lamp proclaimed the presence of Christ, Nora felt very alone and now very frightened.

She made her mind up quickly. Intention was all important when it came to sin, and she'd intended to say her rosary at the Virgin's feet. She'd kneel beside her bed in Colleen's room tonight instead and tag on an extra decade for the absence of a statue.

Nora got to her feet and scrambled out into the aisle, shoving the rosary beads into her coat pocket, pulling out the warm mittens her mother had knitted for her. She bobbed awkwardly in the general direction of the altar, then turned and fled toward the vestibule, pushing open the swinging doors with both outstretched arms, feet flying across the stone floor. Her hands flattened themselves against the outer doors and her body followed, pushing desperately to make them open. Nothing. They didn't yield to her pounding fists or to the sobs that burst from her throat. Why were the doors locked? Why hadn't someone looked into the church to make sure it was empty before closing up for the night?

She turned to go back the way she had come. There was a small side door opening onto a narrow alley that ran the length of the church. She'd seen people ducking out that way after Mass when they were in a hurry and didn't want to have to stop and talk to the priest standing outside on the main steps.

But the door she had just run through wouldn't budge. She didn't remember hearing it happen, but somehow it must have locked itself behind her. She was trapped in the vestibule.

The only thing she could do was make so much noise that a passerby would hear something odd and stop at the rectory next door to tell the housekeeper or one of the priests. Nora pounded until her arms went numb and then flamed in pain; she yelled and screamed until her throat closed up and nothing came out but a hoarse croak. Finally, all strength and hope gone, she slid down onto the stone floor, back propped against the wooden door, legs stretched out in front of her, bruised hands lying slack and useless in her lap, too spent and tired even to cry.

She wondered if anyone would be surprised that she hadn't kept her seven o'clock appointment. No matter. As soon as the church was unlocked tomorrow morning she'd be on her way. Colleen would scold her for not showing up when she was supposed to, and then together they'd have a good laugh about it.

When she began to tremble with the cold, Nora crawled to the lost and found chest against the side wall and pulled out coats, scarves, and sweaters that smelled of dust and other people. She made a nest on the floor and curled up into the bits of clothing, singing and humming to herself to keep up her courage. She thought about the soup her mother made from hens like the ones she'd left in the MacKenzie areaway. Hot chicken broth with lovely chunks of meat and vegetables floating around in it. She could taste it on her tongue, feel the heat in her empty belly. And how nice it would be to close icy fingers around the warmth of the bowl.

Nora fell asleep, a ragamuffin huddled into lost and forgotten garments so worn that no one had bothered to retrieve them.

She was deep in her dreams when the man who had locked Saint Anselm's doors came to stand over her. The picture of innocence, someone else might have thought.

He knew better.

CHAPTER 3

Prudence MacKenzie slept hardly at all on Saturday night. She tossed and turned in her comfortable four poster, lighting, extinguishing, and then relighting the gas reading lamp on her bedside table. She tried to lose herself in a chapter of one of the half dozen books lying open atop the coverlet, but the words streamed meaninglessly past her tired eyes. She reread the same paragraphs over and over again, then finally climbed out of bed to stand and stare out the window at dark and quiet Fifth Avenue far below.

Josiah Gregory would say she shouldn't have read the Ripper story in the newspaper that morning, but what was haunting Prudence tonight was as much the events of eight months ago as the attacks taking place in far off London. On the surface she had nothing in common with the women whose lives the Ripper had stolen, but Prudence had once been the vulnerable target of someone's greed. She would never forget the fear and helpless desperation she'd felt as the victim.

Most of the time she managed to beat back nightmare memories of the stepmother who had schemed to steal her inheritance. Victoria had tried to turn her late husband's only child into a laudanum addict, one of a small legion of unwanted wives and daughters dozing away their empty lives in the opium stupor of an exclusive upstate rest home.

Geoffrey had saved her, Geoffrey and her own determination not to disappoint the father who had loved her so much. *"Never give up,"* he had urged when bleak loneliness settled over the pale oval face of his motherless daughter. *"I miss her, too, but we'll always have each other."* Then he, too, had died.

As the night wore on, the violent and confusing dreams developed into a pounding headache. Not even resting her forehead against the cold glass of her window brought relief. Prudence knew what her body craved, and what giving in to that fierce appetite would do to her. Even thinking about it brought a wave of passionate yearning that was as real as physical hunger. She had to beat it back with every ounce of strength she possessed. *Never give up, never give up.*

She had been introduced to the soothing oblivion of laudanum by the same well-meaning family doctor who'd tended her father in his last illness. For a time, the few drops a day he had recommended were enough to give the illusion of comfort. Like many women of her class, she carried a tiny brown glass bottle of the opium tincture in her reticule. It seemed harmless enough.

Then Victoria had begun adding laudanum to the cup of warm milk left beside her bed every night; additional bottles of the drug appeared without Prudence asking for them. The number of drops she required to survive each day's pain of loss increased. By the time she realized what was happening to her and began to fight back, Prudence MacKenzie knew the meaning of the word *addiction.* Laudanum would be her bête noire for the rest of her life.

Toward dawn Prudence wrapped herself in a cashmere shawl, slipped her bare feet into warm bed shoes, and made her way quietly down two flights of stairs to the basement kitchen. She would stir up the fire in the cook stove and heat some warm milk with honey. No laudanum, just the thickness of sweetened milk to coat the sick queasiness in her stomach.

It was too early for the servants to be up on a Sunday morning. No one need know about the private battles their mistress fought in the dark emptiness of the night.

Colleen Riordan was awake also, twisting restlessly beneath the quilts that brightened her tiny attic room.

Cook would say it served her right, reading those Ripper stories in the newspaper like she did. What business did a housemaid have scaring herself silly with killings that were an ocean away, not to mention happening to women who made their living in ways no respectable girl should know? All true and good, but the Ripper was the only thing everyone talked about for days after each victim was discovered. The attacks might be taking place across the Atlantic Ocean in London, but there were streets in New York City that were just as dangerous as the alleyways of Whitechapel. And it got dark so early in November.

Which was why it wasn't so much the London Ripper who was interfering with Colleen's sleep tonight as it was a nagging worry much closer to home.

Why hadn't Nora shown up yesterday afternoon as expected? Not knowing where her friend was or what might have happened to her was twisting Colleen's stomach into knots. She and Nora didn't often have the opportunity to work together, but when they did, the hours flew by; the mundane tasks they performed were quickly and easily accomplished. The Staten Island girl's energy and zest for life proved contagious.

Nora had such wonderful stories to tell about when she and Miss Prudence played together on the lawns of the Staten Island hilltop house called Windscape. Miss Prudence had let Nora ride her pony and shared her dolls as though they were cousins or sisters instead of young mistress and servant's child. Even now, though the closeness had ended years ago, Nora maintained there was a tie between them that would never be broken. She'd be there if Miss Prudence ever needed her, and she didn't doubt that the loyalty would be reciprocated.

Too bad the Kennys didn't have one of the new telephones. Miss Prudence treated the instrument she'd had installed in the library as casually as if it were an everyday tool like the shovel used to rake out fireplace coals. But it wasn't. Not yet. Voices traveling across wires was too magical to be taken for granted. Colleen had only held the earpiece to her head twice, thunderstruck at the sounds coming out of it. But it would have been nice to have heard Nora's pert voice saying she'd missed the ferry and would come tomorrow. There'd be a lot less worry in the world if people could talk to one another across the great distances that separated them. Where had that idea come from?

By five o'clock in the morning Colleen was up and on her feet for good, face washed, hair twisted into a respectable bun, teeth cleaned, and fingernails inspected for any bit of lingering dirt from yesterday. She'd go to the early Mass at Saint Anselm's, she decided, even though Sunday was the one day in the week when she could have stayed an extra hour in her bed. She'd go by herself and be back before the first cups of tea and coffee had been poured downstairs.

Saint Anselm's was a working class parish, so there was a daily six o'clock Mass for the nuns who taught at the school, the elderly widows in need of companionship, and the men on their way to the docks and slaughterhouses. Even on Sunday, people had to get up before the sun to earn the few coins that put a bit of bread and dripping in their mouths. Later in the day you saw well dressed men and women kneeling in Saint

Anselm's pews, but for the most part it was their servants who dropped the occasional penny into the early morning collection baskets. There weren't any tenements within the parish boundaries, but just beyond the immediate vicinity of Fifth Avenue stretched blocks of narrow buildings crowded cheek by jowl on lots no wider than they had to be. The wage earners who lived in them were one uncertain step up from the disaster of no work at all.

Colleen picked up her prayer book and rosary, made sure she had a clean handkerchief, and tiptoed quietly down four flights of uncarpeted wooden stairs to the basement kitchen. She hadn't had so much as a sip of water since midnight, so yes, she could go to Communion. She checked the state of her soul; nothing but a few venial sins of the kind everybody committed every single day of their lives. It was only the mortal sins you had to confess and get absolution for before you could approach the altar.

As hard as she worked and as little as she stepped out, Colleen rarely had the opportunity to sin. *More's the pity.* She made a quick sign of the cross because she didn't really mean it. Her mother would have rapped her knuckles against the side of her daughter's head for even thinking such a thought.

She'd wear her new navy blue wool coat faced with shiny brass buttons, an early Christmas gift from Miss Prudence. She was a good mistress; no one who worked for her went cold or sick or hungry. The same couldn't be said for every employer. Other maids wore thin shawls against the wintry air and shivered in the damp New York City chill. Not Colleen. In her fancy new coat she'd catch every envious eye in Saint Anselm's.

"I didn't see you there, Miss," Colleen apologized. She'd shrieked loud enough to wake the dead and dropped her prayer book and rosary onto the stone floor. The last person she'd expected to see in the kitchen was the young mistress of the house, especially at this time of the morning. It wasn't even daylight yet.

"I came down to make myself some warm milk," Prudence explained. She held a small copper pot in one hand. "I'm afraid I'm not very good at this. I meant to stir up the fire, but I couldn't get the door to the stove open, and I have no idea where Cook keeps the milk."

Colleen picked up her prayer book, set it

41

on the small writing desk where Mrs. Hearne worked out her menus, and slipped her rosary beads into her skirt pocket. Then she scooped up kindling from the stack beside the stove and pried the lid off the firebox. A whoosh of flame flared out as the slender sticks of split wood caught fire.

"A lady like yourself has no business fiddling about with stoves and firewood, Miss Prudence. I'll have your milk warm in a few minutes and I'll bring it upstairs to you."

"There's no need to make you late for church," Prudence said, surrendering the empty copper pot.

"There's another Mass at seven that'll do me just as well."

Miss Prudence had saved Colleen's life when the second Mrs. MacKenzie paid someone to push her down the servants' staircase to this very kitchen not so long ago. Colleen knew too much about how Judge MacKenzie had died. She'd spent nearly a month in bed before she got back on her feet again. Any other mistress would have fired her or docked her wages, but not Miss Prudence. Colleen had gotten her full earnings packet just as though she'd been working. Never a word was said to her that wasn't kind. She'd do anything for Miss Prudence, anything at all.

"I'll see if the milkman has delivered yet. You'll have a nice cup of fresh milk with a good bit of cream on top."

Colleen unlocked and opened the kitchen door on a predawn darkness that was beginning to lighten to gray. No milk bottles stood in their wooden crate on the cold stone slab. She supposed that on Sunday even the milkman had the luxury of a later delivery. Still, she'd have a closer look outside just to be sure.

One step into the areaway, and she nearly fell. Over a basket, of all things. Surely a delivery man wouldn't have left supplies outside without ringing the bell, without being certain someone accepted them. Colleen bent to pick up the basket. It was heavy, the contents protected against the elements by a once clean cloth now spotted with the soot no one who lived in New York City ever escaped.

"Colleen?" Miss Prudence approached the doorway, one hand clutching the cashmere shawl tightly around her. "Are you all right?"

"I'm fine, Miss. I tripped over something."

"What was it?"

Colleen lifted off the soot spotted cloth that had been folded over the basket's contents. Four plucked and gutted hens, each wrapped in its own napkin, were neatly

43

bedded down side by side, two below, two on top. Fowl gone bad emitted a smell no one could mistake; these birds were still fresh, though she wondered how long they'd sat by the kitchen door. And where they'd come from. And why Cook hadn't looked outside for them if she'd missed the bell. Mrs. Hearne ran a very tight kitchen, every penny tallied, every bite of meat and morsel of bread accounted for. It wasn't like her to order provisions and then forget them. Not like her at all.

"You'd better bring them inside. I can't imagine who could have left them there. Or why." Prudence stepped out into the areaway then back into the kitchen while Colleen carried the basket to the long wooden work table that ran nearly the length of the room.

One by one Colleen unwrapped the stewing hens. She stared at them as though she'd never seen plucked poultry before, then her face paled and she leaned forward as though she were about to collapse, both hands grasping the edge of the table.

"That's Agnes Kenny's basket, Miss," she said. "See where the handle's been repaired? She always sends Cook her best whenever someone makes the trip into Manhattan, so she must have packed it for Nora to bring

44

with her yesterday. But Nora never arrived. We all thought she must have missed the ferry."

"Are you sure, Colleen?"

"Nora's not here, Miss Prudence. She was coming to help with the holiday cleaning, so I made up the extra bed in my room for her. She wasn't in it last night and she's not there this morning." Colleen turned toward the kitchen door. "You don't suppose she's hurt herself? Slipped on the steps outside and knocked her head? She'll be frozen stiff if she's been out there all night."

"There's no one in the areaway. I looked," Prudence said. "But we'll search again, just to be sure."

"Shall I go up to the street, Miss?" Colleen asked.

"Go ahead, but be careful. Hold on to the railing."

"Nora," Colleen hissed as loudly as she dared, climbing the outside steps and opening the iron gate of the areaway. This was still Fifth Avenue; the toffs who owned the houses on either side of the street were sound asleep in their feather beds and wouldn't appreciate being waked up.

Nothing. No sign of her Staten Island friend on the sidewalk, the steps, or in any of the small sunken area's four corners.

"She's not here, Miss Prudence."

"Someone left these hens outside the kitchen door. It had to have been Nora. No one else would be carrying Agnes's basket," Prudence said. "If she took the last ferry and got here late, she might have gone around to the stables. Kincaid could have seen or talked to her."

"I'll find out, Miss." Colleen scurried through the kitchen and out the back downstairs entrance that gave onto the stable yard, leaving the door open in her haste.

Prudence could hear the rapid tapping of her heels on the cobblestones. Moments later a light flared in the coachman's quarters above the stable. She watched as a lantern was carried from stall to stall and then across the yard. James Kincaid walked rapidly toward the house, Colleen following in his wake.

"There's no one out there who shouldn't be, Miss Prudence," the coachman said. Every button of his dark green uniform jacket was properly buttoned; his boots shone with polish. "The horses would have woken me if anyone had gotten into the stable. No one slips past them."

"We thought Nora Kenny might have tried to wake you when she couldn't get into the house."

"Nora Kenny?" Ian Cameron had come down the servants' staircase and into the kitchen so quietly that Prudence hadn't heard him. The butler who had been like a second father to her had come back to the MacKenzie household out of forced retirement with a promise to stay as long as Miss Prudence needed him. He had no plans to leave. "What's this about Nora?"

"She never came up to my room last night." Colleen's fingers moved rapidly along the rosary beads in her skirt pocket. "I worried, but I thought she'd just missed the ferry. Then I stumbled over her basket when I went out the door to bring in the milk."

Prudence was speaking quietly to Kincaid, who nodded his head and left the kitchen without another word.

"You're sure she's not outside somewhere? Injured? Maybe from a fall on the steps?"

"I went up to the street and looked in both directions, Mr. Cameron. There's no sign of her," Colleen said.

"I've sent Kincaid in the carriage to bring Mr. Hunter from his hotel," Prudence told them. "He was a Pinkerton. They find missing people all the time."

"You're positive she's not upstairs in some other room?" Cameron asked Colleen.

47

Privately he thought the maid was probably making a fuss about nothing. Young girls in service had a tendency to skittishness. It was a shame she had bothered Miss Prudence with what was undoubtedly a misunderstanding. The wrong date or the wrong ferry.

"I didn't look. I didn't want to wake up any of the others when I was just on my way out to early Mass. She was supposed to share my room with me, like she's done before. There's no other place for her to be." Colleen reached for the clean apron and cap lying folded in the cubbyhole beneath her coat hook, then remembered that she wasn't wearing her morning uniform. Nothing was as it should be; the safe world of the MacKenzie household was all topsy-turvy.

"Nora must have brought those hens yesterday and left them when nobody answered the door." Prudence pointed at the four plump birds sitting on the scrubbed wooden table. "If she's not in the house, then something's happened to her."

"I wonder if we shouldn't take a look into all of the servants' bedrooms before we think the worst," Cameron said quietly. Tall, silver haired, and immensely dignified, he was also the soul of authoritative calm. "She might have come much later than expected, and been let in by one of the staff who hadn't gone up to bed yet. She could have been so tired she didn't realize she'd put the basket down and not picked it up again."

"She'd never leave her mother's hens sitting outside, Mr. Cameron," Colleen protested indignantly.

"It will only take a few minutes," Cameron insisted. "Nora may not have wanted to open your door and chance waking you up. She could be sleeping soundly in someone else's bed or on a pallet on the floor."

"She won't be," predicted Colleen, unshed tears glittering in her eyes.

"I'll be in the library, Cameron," Prudence said, "waiting by the telephone. I'd like to forewarn Mr. Hunter before Kincaid knocks on his door, but I won't call until you can report back to me."

Cameron was nothing if not thorough and meticulous, qualities that served him well as a butler, but Prudence doubted that Nora Kenny would be found safely ensconced in one of the empty servants' rooms upstairs. She hadn't forgotten a word of the Ripper article she'd read this morning. Respectable girls in New York City could be just as vulnerable as Whitechapel's ladies of the night. No city street was safe after dark.

"Nora Kenny is missing, Mrs. Hearne," Prudence explained to the heavyset woman who lumbered into the kitchen, tying on a fresh Sunday apron and adjusting her traditional cook's mobcap. "We don't know yet what may have happened to her."

Cook stared at her mistress, looked intently at the four hens glistening on her worktable beside their wicker basket, then turned toward the stove. If the world was coming to an end, at least they'd have coffee before it collapsed around them. "That's Agnes Kenny's basket for sure," she said. "The one with the mended handle. I'd know it anywhere."

As Prudence left the kitchen, she could hear Cook filling her largest kettle and hauling out the wooden grinder for the coffee beans, muttering under her breath as she worked.

Colleen accompanied Cameron with one hand on the rosary in her pocket; Cook was saying the prayers aloud, counting them off on her fingers.

"We'll send someone to meet the Staten Island ferries as they dock," Geoffrey Hunter said, mapping out the strategy they would use in their search for Nora Kenny.

"Frank can go. He's the boot boy." Prudence pushed aside her empty coffee cup. "He can stay on the dock either until Nora arrives or we find her."

"You're sure he knows what she looks like?"

"She was here in September. He's not likely to have forgotten. I can't bear to think what it will do to her parents if something has happened to her. Nora is their only daughter, Geoffrey. She's supposed to be getting married after Christmas. I was planning to go to the wedding."

"We'll find her, Prudence. There could be a dozen reasons why she didn't turn up last night."

"Or one horrible one."

"The stables have been searched again?"

"Kincaid checked every stall and behind every hay bale. It would have been such a logical thing to do if Nora got delayed somehow and then no one answered the kitchen door. We thought she might have gone to the stables looking for Kincaid and then stayed there to get warm and fallen asleep."

"But she didn't."

"No, she didn't. He said there was no sign anyone had ever been there last night."

"The Kennys don't have a telephone?"

"There's service on the island, but Brian

Kenny said he'd wait for fish to talk before he'd have one in his house. Brian is Nora's father; he's a fisherman. There is a telegraph office, though."

"It's too early to send a telegram. We'd only alarm them unnecessarily."

"At least we'd know." Prudence crossed out what she'd just written on the list she was composing. "You're right, though. We can't tell them anything yet except that she's not here."

"You said Brian Kenny isn't on the telephone line. But he knows you are?"

"Yes."

"Then if Nora went back to Staten Island for some reason, if she caught the last ferry, her father would have asked if she'd told you. And if she said she hadn't, he'd go to wherever there was a telephone to let you know. Or he would have sent a telegram."

"We've known the Kennys for years. Most of the sons worked for my father at one time or another, whenever the fish weren't running or Brian could spare them from the boat. Odd jobs. Painting, carpentry, pruning, keeping the lawns seeded and cut. Agnes worked for my mother. Nora and I played together when we were children. She was like the sister I never had. You're right, Geoffrey. Brian Kenny would have telephoned or sent a wire." Prudence capped her pen and laid it on the table. "So Nora didn't go home."

"I don't think so."

"Yes, Cameron?" Prudence had been aware of approaching footsteps before she saw the butler materialize in the doorway. Very unlike Cameron to warn of his arrival. He was usually as silent as a ghost.

"There's a policeman at the kitchen door, Miss. He brought this." Cameron had placed a blood-stained envelope on the silver letter tray.

Through the stains Prudence could make out her name and address. She reached out a hand, but her fingers hovered above the ruined stationery and would not descend to pick it up. She nodded at Geoffrey, who took both tray and envelope from Cameron and set them on the table.

"He said it was in the coat pocket of a young woman found in Colonial Park. One of the Marlowe footmen was taking Mrs. Marlowe's dog for its morning walk. They called the police."

"Nora?"

"The Marlowe footman didn't recognize the girl as working in any of the houses facing onto the park. The police thought we might know who she is since the letter was found in her pocket."

"Had it been opened?" Geoffrey asked.

"I didn't ask, sir. The patrol officer said the detective in charge of the case handed him the envelope and told him to find out whether anyone here had gone missing."

"Dear God." Prudence felt the blood drain from her face.

Cameron decided not to repeat what else the policeman had told him. It didn't bear thinking about.

"I'm afraid Nora Kenny has been found, Miss Prudence."

CHAPTER 4

Nora Kenny's body lay hidden in a bed of pine boughs within the gated enclosure of a small private park to which only the residents of nearby houses had keys. Less than half the size of Gramercy Park, it was a nod toward the landscape gardens of English country houses, but too small for statuary or a miniature lake. A narrow path meandered through sculpted hollies toward one tall Japanese pine; strategically placed benches provided quiet retreats for tired nannies and aged dog walkers. It had never before been desecrated by violence or invaded by city policemen.

New York Metropolitan Police Detective Steven Phelan stood with hands in his pockets, hat brim pulled down low over his face. All he'd been after when he sent a beat cop to the MacKenzie mansion with the envelope found in the victim's pocket was a quick identification. Instead an ex-

Pinkerton and a society belle had come poking their noses into his case.

Coppers and Pinkertons rarely got along well with each other, and Phelan didn't expect Geoffrey Hunter would be an exception. They'd met two or three years ago, on a case that never made it to court because of what Hunter uncovered and the police missed. Now a private investigator out on his own, Hunter might not be part of the world's most famous detective agency any longer, but once a Pinkerton, always a Pinkerton.

Prudence MacKenzie had been in all the papers last spring, some sort of family scandal Phelan hadn't paid much attention to at the time, but he recognized the name. He also remembered the rumor he'd heard that Hunter and Miss MacKenzie were partners in a private inquiry firm. Which meant they'd be asking questions and demanding answers.

Nobody needed to know that within minutes of viewing the body Phelan dispatched a patrolman to bring the city's senior investigative officer to the crime scene. He had a bad feeling about this one, and Chief Byrnes agreed with him. What had been done to the victim's corpse was so out of the ordinary way of killings that anyone with half a brain would make a connection to the bloody remains Jack the Ripper was leaving on London's streets. The worst of it was they'd have to wait for more killings if what they feared possible proved to be true.

For the time being, they'd deny any attempt by the newspapers to conjure up a Ripper copycat. The city didn't need to be plunged into the kind of panic that sort of speculation would cause. Chief of Detectives Tom Byrnes stayed at Colonial Park only long enough to satisfy himself that Phelan understood what was at stake. Nothing less than the reputation of the department. Consider what was happening to the police in the London slum of Whitechapel. The elusive Ripper had made Scotland Yard a laughingstock.

Byrnes and only Byrnes would talk to reporters. No one else. The public would get just enough information to put their minds at ease. Not a word more. There was no copycat Ripper in New York City and there never would be. Period.

Geoffrey Hunter tried to block Prudence from the sight of what lay on the ground, but he should have known better. She'd insisted on coming to identify the body instead of sending Cameron or the house-keeper, and now she stepped around him.

"Is it your maid?" Detective Phelan asked.

Hunter and Miss MacKenzie weren't the general public, but they weren't coppers either. Private investigators occupied some middle ground that made each side uncomfortable with the other. Hunter had a reputation for being a valuable asset if he was working with you and an implacable obstacle if he wasn't. The girl's father had been one of New York's most influential judges; she was female, but she had connections.

Phelan would have to humor both of them. It was an awkward position to be in. He didn't like it one bit. "Can you identify her, Miss MacKenzie?" he repeated. "Is it your maid?"

Only the victim's head was visible. The rest of the body was loosely covered in hessian as though a cocoon of rough burlap had been painstakingly peeled away and then draped back over what it contained.

"It is. She looks like she's sleeping." Prudence would have bent down to stroke the alabaster cheek, but Phelan shook his head and Hunter held her arm. "I don't see any marks on her face."

Phelan hesitated, then shrugged his shoulders. "The coroner did his examination, then he laid the burlap over her again for the removal. She was tightly wrapped when we found her." He'd seen Hunter stop and talk to the Bellevue coroner while the policeman at the gate fumbled with the latch to let him out. The ex-Pinkerton probably already knew the details that would be spelled out in the autopsy report as soon as it was written. That was the kind of investigator he was. Miss MacKenzie would have to learn the hard way that victims of violence were seldom a pretty sight.

"Her throat's been cut." Phelan twitched back a corner of the burlap wrapping. The single deep slash that had nearly decapitated Nora Kenny was dry and crusty in the morning light, dark red and black with congealed blood.

"What else?" Prudence's voice was tense but steady.

"Are you sure, Prudence?" Geoffrey asked. "Once you've heard and seen what was done to her, you'll never be able to forget it."

She had turned away before the coroner finished answering Geoffrey's questions and taken a few steps along the path to distance herself from what they were discussing, not ready to hear all of the horror of Nora's death. The young doctor had glanced at her sympathetically and lowered his voice, recognizing the effort she was making to steel herself for the identification.

"I need to know what the family will have to face." *Agnes Kenny's daughter had once been able to run like the wind,* Prudence thought. *How still she lies now.*

"Nora Kenny was gutted," Phelan said.

It was the kind of blunt description one copper might give another over too many beers at the end of a shift. It was, Prudence recalled, exactly the phrase the coroner had used, though he hadn't realized she'd heard him. These men, Geoffrey included, lived in a world she had only recently become aware of, a place where ugliness and cruelty were common, where a woman's life could be taken as easily as that of a steer in one of the slaughterhouses.

Prudence had to do it herself; neither of the men looking down at Nora's body would subject a lady to what lay hidden beneath the burlap. Phelan had seen the damage done to Nora when the coroner examined her; Geoffrey knew from the doctor's brief description that more than a life had been taken. Before she could change her mind, Prudence stooped over her childhood friend and pulled the hessian from her body.

She felt Phelan's eyes on her face, sensed that Geoffrey had moved closer, as if to protect her. *Never let them know what you're thinking or feeling.* The Judge used to say that about sparring lawyers and juries, but it could be applied just as easily to policemen and partners. Was Phelan an adversary? Would Geoffrey think less of her if he knew how hard she was struggling not to remember how much Nora had once meant to her?

Nora's coat stuck to the burlap so that when Prudence pulled it back from the body, the two front panels of the woolen fabric came with it. From the neck up, it was Nora; below the neck stretched a carcass that had been emptied of the organs that gave it life. One look and Prudence closed her eyes. Geoffrey had been right. She would never be able to forget her first sight of what one crazed human could do to another.

Detective Phelan waited only until he was sure Miss MacKenzie would not faint, then he covered Nora decently again, hiding even the gaping neck wound that looked like a bloody smile. He gestured toward the stretcher bearers leaning against the fence, motioning them forward.

"You're having photographs taken?" Hunter asked. He knew Prudence was testing herself, but he was determined to distract her from the worst of what had been done to the girl lying at their feet. He'd seen wrappings fall off bodies as they were lifted onto the canvas slings used by mortuary attendants; it was not something he wanted Prudence to have to experience. She had already stretched her courage to its limits. Now she needed time to recover.

"His name is Jacob Riis," Phelan said, nodding toward the young man balancing a tripod on the uneven ground. A small box camera had been screwed onto the faceplate of the tripod.

Riis held a magnesium flash pan in one hand, reaching for the lens of the camera with the other. When the powder ignited he moved quickly and dexterously, capturing the images on glass plates he handled as deftly as if they were pasteboard playing cards.

"He knows what he's doing. He'll have the pictures printed up for me by the end of the day."

"Scotland Yard photographed the Ripper's victims in London," Geoffrey commented.

Phelan didn't seem to have heard him.

"Riis is an odd bird, part newspaperman,

part reformer," the detective said. "He tells me he spends his nights in the tenements taking his flash pictures wherever and whenever he can. He works the Mulberry Street beat as a police reporter for the *Tribune* and does extra commissions like this one to earn money for his tenement supplies. I didn't ask him when he sleeps."

"The Scotland Yard photographs were printed in all the London papers," Geoffrey continued. "I don't imagine your Chief of Detectives Tom Byrnes wants to chance being left behind if this turns out to be the biggest murder investigation New York City has ever had. I'll lay odds that one of those reporters standing in the street over there compares this murder to the ones in Whitechapel we've been reading about. He'll christen your killer the American Ripper. All holy hell will break loose."

That was it then. Hunter had zeroed in immediately on what Phelan and Byrnes planned to keep from the press. Phelan wondered uneasily what his superior would have to say when he found out that the ex-Pinkerton and his female companion also knew about the throat cutting and the evisceration, the Ripper's signature modus operandi. Hunter and MacKenzie weren't press reporters, so technically Phelan had kept to the letter of Byrnes's restriction against talking to the newspapers, but he might have stepped over one of the chief of detectives' invisible lines when he allowed them to linger over the body. You never knew what might tick him off.

The morgue workers lifted Nora onto their stretcher and began carrying her toward the entrance to the park and the death wagon waiting in the street.

Geoffrey's eyes swept the ground around the spot where the body had lain. Unless Jacob Riis had managed to take photographs of the way it looked before being churned up by heavy policemen's boots, whatever evidence might have been there was now lost. "Whoever killed her had to have had a key to get in through the gate."

"Or he was a skilled lock picker. No scratches that my man could detect around the keyhole, but that could just mean our killer is good with his hands." Phelan answered Geoffrey's next question before he could ask it. "I've had patrolmen checking every foot of the fence for a place where a section could have been lifted out. Nothing. It's as solid as the day it was put up."

He knew what Hunter was doing, and he was willing to go along with it. Miss Mac-Kenzie looked better already. She was listening intently again. Somehow she had managed to banish from her conscious mind — for the moment, at least — what must have burned itself into her memory. She was concentrating on getting the job done. Maybe Allan Pinkerton had known what he was doing after all when he recruited a certain type of woman to serve with his male operatives.

Just before they reached the entrance to the park, the Bellevue attendants stopped and lowered the stretcher to the ground. They stepped back to allow another man to approach and then kneel down beside the corpse. His right arm made the sign of the cross over the remains of Nora Kenny. A faint scent of oil wafted through the clear winter air.

"That's Father Brennan from Saint Anselm's. It's the closest Catholic church," Detective Phelan told them. "I recognize him. There's three of them at Saint Anselm's; they take it in turns. He must be the one on call today."

Prudence watched Geoffrey study the priest, mentally filing away Father Brennan's every gesture and even the curve of his back as he bent over Nora's body. *It's the Pinkerton training,* she thought. *Nothing is unimportant.* She felt as though she were a student learning a valuable lesson. Her father had instructed her in case law; now she was absorbing the rituals of detecting in the same way. Suddenly she wasn't thinking of the burlap covered mound on the stretcher as her childhood friend. It had become a victim, the object of an inquiry.

The priest got to his feet and walked beside the stretcher bearers to the morgue wagon. He rested one hand on the remains as if loathe to let them go. Once the body was loaded into the dark interior of the van, Father Brennan disappeared amongst the crowd of onlookers.

It was time to get rid of Hunter and his society girlfriend. Let them know their interference would not be welcomed. The body had been identified. They weren't needed any longer. Phelan had no particular grudge against the pair except that he wanted them and their questions out from under his feet. He had a feeling they could cause him more trouble than they were worth. The patrolman guarding the park gate held it open so they could pass through.

"Since it's one of Miss MacKenzie's servants who's been killed, I'm sure the police will understand that our firm will be looking into the matter." Geoffrey Hunter's smile was brief and grim.

"Just so long as you don't get in the way," Phelan said. He tipped his hat to the young woman whose poised demeanor had surprised him, shook hands with Hunter, and turned back toward where Jacob Riis was packing up his camera. Phelan thought he'd handled the situation as well as could be expected under the circumstances. The important thing, as far as Chief Byrnes was concerned, was that the Metropolitan Police find the Irish maid's killer before a couple of private investigators did. And one of them a woman. The department would never live down the embarrassment of it.

In Phelan's experience, husbands, fiancés, and lovers killed the women they claimed to cherish. Nora Kenny wasn't married, but according to Miss MacKenzie, she had been engaged. Open and shut case, he decided. The fiancé followed her to the city, caught her with another man, bided his time, then killed her. Carved her up like the Ripper he'd read about in the papers. He was smart enough to want to shift suspicion elsewhere, but not clever enough to outwit Steven Phelan.

Two or three days and the detective would have the case wrapped up. Byrnes would be satisfied and the women of New York City could sleep safely in their beds again. Until the killing was repeated. He devoutly hoped it would not be, but he'd seen too much not to believe anything was possible.

"Chief of Detectives Tom Byrnes is a tough cop," Geoffrey said as he and Prudence made their way through the park gate. "And smart. He's the one who came up with what he calls the Rogues Gallery, photographs of everyone his men bring into the stations. He published a book a couple of years back, *Professional Criminals of America*. Looking at some of those faces is guaranteed to rob you of a night's sleep. Byrnes doesn't think much of the way London is handling their Ripper, and he hasn't bothered to keep his opinions to himself. If New York City has its own Ripper, he'll have to prove he can do better than Scotland Yard."

"And we'll have to do better than Chief Byrnes and Detective Phelan," Prudence declared. "This is what you were talking about the other day, Geoffrey, isn't it? The copycat. I can't bear that it's Nora he chose for his first victim. She didn't deserve to die like this."

"No one does, Prudence." Geoffrey looked across the street where a burly policeman in a dark blue uniform frock coat was keeping a small group of reporters and the curious at bay. "The reporters beat the morgue wagon," he said. "They always do."

"Do we know when she died?" Prudence asked.

"The coroner said she was well into rigor. He estimated time of death at close to midnight. And she wasn't killed here. She was rolled up in that hessian somewhere else and carried here. That's all he could tell me."

"I can't imagine that Nora had any enemies, Geoffrey. The only time she left her family on Staten Island was to come into the city to work for me, usually not for longer than a few days or a week at most."

"More often than not people end up dead because somebody they know wants them that way. That's the direction Phelan's investigation will take. In this instance, I think he's wrong, but I can't say I'd do any differently if I were in his place. He doesn't know Nora Kenny and her family the way you do."

"He'll want a quick resolution of the case, won't he?" Prudence mused. "He'll say that since Nora was out by herself in the city streets well after dark, she was probably the type of girl who liked to take chances. He'll insinuate that she brought it on herself. Blame her for her own death. I've heard that kind of argument before, Geoffrey, when someone's maid was discovered to be in the family way. The woman is always at fault." Prudence had yet to learn that anger never got you anywhere with the police.

"I'd like to have seen what was in the envelope Phelan found in Nora's coat pocket," Geoffrey said.

"It was probably a bill for the stewing hens," Prudence said. "Why didn't Nora leave it in the basket? If she meant for Cook to find the birds before she got back, surely she would have slipped the envelope in with them. To be sure Mrs. Hearne knew who they were from."

They'd reached the carriage where Kincaid had fastened feed bags over the horses' heads to distract them from the smells of death as the morgue wagon drove by.

"She might have been in too big a hurry to remember to do it," Geoffrey reasoned. "We don't know why no one answered the bell. Or even if she rang it."

"Begging your pardon, sir, but it wasn't working," Kincaid said. "I looked at the bellpull before we left. The cord was badly frayed. It could have snapped yesterday or the day before. No one noticed because deliverymen usually pound on the door to get attention if they don't hear a ring. They're always in too much of a hurry to wait." He opened the carriage door and pulled down the mounting step. A wave of warmth flowed out at them from hot bricks wrapped in wool.

Prudence settled herself inside the carriage, grateful for the heat. November was always a cold month, and she'd rushed out of the house without changing into outdoor boots. Her trained lawyer's mind had begun to treat Nora's murder as if it were one of the Judge's cases laid out for her consideration. Facts. She was reaching for and organizing the few facts they knew.

Geoffrey climbed in and sat beside her, silent, abstracted. He was going through the same mental exercise.

"I can't help but wonder what would have happened if someone had heard her," she said. "If Cook or Brigid had opened the door, Nora might not have gone wherever it was she went. Wherever it was she was killed."

"If it even was Nora who brought the hens. We can't forget that we don't know for sure who it was, Prudence," Geoffrey reminded her. "Her killer might have been bold enough to want to send a message. He could have read your address on the envelope if he searched Nora's pockets. It was bloody and crumpled, but we don't know how it got that way. You don't want to build a case on a false premise."

Most of the reporters had left, either to follow the death wagon on its way to the morgue at Bellevue or to race back to their newspaper offices with whatever information they'd been able to glean before deadline. The small crowd of bystanders curious enough to brave the early morning cold had begun drifting away. With the corpse gone, there was nothing left to see.

"I'll have to go to Staten Island this morning," Prudence said. "I can't let anyone else tell Nora's family."

"I'll come with you," Geoffrey volunteered. "They may have information that will help."

"Can't that wait? The questioning?"

"I wish it could, but we need to know if Nora intended on going anywhere except to your house. The only ones she's likely to have told would be family members or the young man she was engaged to. Phelan will send someone out to tell them the official identification of the body will have to take place at Bellevue. He'll probably want to conduct his interrogation there or at the Mulberry Street headquarters."

"How horrible for them." Prudence had

seen sketches in the newspaper of sobbing women identifying their sons or husbands laid out on hard tables in the Bellevue mortuary. In one illustration a young woman lay atop the table, a wrinkled sheet pulled to just above her breasts, long hair spilling over her shoulders.

She pictured Agnes Kenny's work-worn hands clasped together, her face contorted with the effort not to break down and weep in front of strangers. Brian Kenny standing stoically beside his wife, brothers fanned out around the bereaved parents, the fiancé mute with the horror of what his beloved had suffered. They wouldn't ask, but Prudence would send Kincaid to meet them at the ferry landing and take them in her carriage to Bellevue. Danny Dennis and his hansom cab were on retainer to the firm. She'd send him, too, because the entire family wouldn't fit in a single vehicle.

"Phelan never showed us the note," she remarked, her mind turning away from the grief she could not assuage to the murder she was determined to solve. "The bill for the hens. Do you suppose he didn't have it? Could Nora's killer have kept it, Geoffrey? As some sort of macabre keepsake?"

Geoffrey didn't remind her of what else was missing from the scene.

CHAPTER 5

On the Tuesday morning after Nora died Prudence went to the Wall Street offices of Hunter and MacKenzie at the same time that thousands of workers who thronged the streets of lower Manhattan reported to their jobs. She wore a trim black suit devoid of the elaborately draped skirt and wasp waist that had lately become fashionable. The tightly corseted waist made it impossible to walk quickly without feeling faint and the draped skirt was heavy and cumbersome. It seemed that the higher a woman's rank in society, the less practical and comfortable was the clothing she was obliged to wear, and the more restricted her movements.

Prudence was angry and determined. She had stood with the Kenny family in Bellevue's morgue yesterday as the attendant rolled down the sheet covering Nora's naked body. It would have been enough for the identification to reveal only her face, but before she could prevent it, the terrible wound encircling Nora's neck and the beginning of the incision that had mutilated her breasts and belly lay revealed to her family's eyes.

Agnes had not fainted, but she had clung so hard to Brian's arm that her fingers stiffened. The brothers remained stonefaced and silent, but in each young man's eyes could be read the resolve to wreak a terrible vengeance on the man who had done this appalling damage to their sister. Tim Fahey wept openly, streams of tears plowing his cheeks.

Prudence arranged with the undertaker who had buried both her father and her fiancé to take Nora home to Staten Island in the finest mahogany casket Maurice Warneke's mortuary parlor could supply. She would be laid to rest in Saint Brendan's hilltop cemetery where the view of New York Harbor and Lady Liberty was unsurpassed.

The funeral was tomorrow, Wednesday, but for today at least, Prudence was determined to turn her mind toward the future. The laudanum craving that almost overpowered her the night of Nora's death had frightened her into a cold examination of the life she was living. And she didn't like what she discovered. She was going to make changes. When the hunger for laudanum came again, as she knew it would, Prudence would repeat what her father had told her after Sarah MacKenzie's death nearly crushed the two of them. *"Hold on. Never give up, never give up. Hold on."* The refrain was like a drumbeat in her head.

No one was in the office when she let herself in with the key she was using for the first time since Josiah Gregory handed it to her. She had played at the game of investigative law, enjoying the idea of uncovering secrets and the excitement of doing what few women of her class ever dreamed of. Their homes were as much silk lined prisons as they were jewel boxes to showcase their beauty and accomplishments. Work, real work, when it was spoken of at all, was rarely mentioned without a disdainful curl of the lips. But that was precisely what Prudence had determined she would do. She would work. As hard and as steadily as any man. Work with the talent she knew she possessed for seeing to the simple core of a complex problem. It only remained to convince others of her sincerity.

Standing in Josiah Gregory's small kingdom, the impeccably neat outer office that was the gateway to Hunter and MacKenzie,

Investigative Law, Prudence decided she needed her own private place to work. She wanted a separate office with a desk and file drawers, comfortable chairs, and a table on which to spread out documents. A door that could be closed against interruptions. As long as she drifted from the library in the house on Fifth Avenue to the large office that was Geoffrey's domain, she would be more a visitor than a partner in the business to which she had given her name. The Mac-Kenzie name. She remembered with what enthusiasm she had embarked on the new adventure, and admitted to herself now how difficult it had been to maintain that level of zeal when she had precious little to do.

Part of the problem had been the untangling of her affairs after the death of her late and unmourned stepmother. Victoria Morley MacKenzie had blackmailed Prudence's father into a loveless second marriage and almost certainly connived at his early death. The Judge had thought to protect his only child with a complicated trust arrangement, but as soon as he was safely laid in the family mausoleum, his widow began manipulating the financial interests he thought he had safeguarded. It had taken months and far too much of Prudence's attention to undo the damage.

Geoffrey had offered to help, but he had also had to retitle the assets Roscoe Conkling left him in his will and meet with the late senator's clients. That too, had taken more time than either of them had expected.

The problem was not so much the complexity of the situation as the lack of any real need for haste. Geoffrey was a gentleman born and bred, happily without the need to support himself that afflicted so many of his impoverished fellow Southerners. He was a wealthy man with a tendency to drift into indolence until an intriguing problem was tossed into his lap. For several years Charles Linwood, Prudence's fiancé, had kept his former school and college friend amply supplied with challenges. After Charles was killed, it had been Prudence herself who'd roused Geoffrey from his lethargy. He had saved her life and fortune from Victoria, but in the months since then there had been nothing comparable to engage his considerable talents. Until now.

Like Geoffrey, Prudence had been born into a class that asked very little of its members except adherence to the social codes governing all but business behavior. A man could steal his competitors blind and no one would think the less of him. But let that same man breach a single one of the many odd customs of society, and the resultant buzz might very well ostracize him. Women, too, were bound by rigid codes of deportment. For all the independence Prudence's fortune should have bought her, she was on as tight a rein as any other woman who had a care for her reputation.

War and the deaths of more than six hundred thousand men had changed America, but real freedom for women outside their homes was a distant dream. Delegates to the Seneca Falls Convention of 1848 had debated female roles and even a woman's right to vote, but then war had intervened, profiteering had risen to staggering heights, and the imperatives of social change were pushed aside.

Prudence turned her attention to the problem of how to create a space that would be entirely hers, and by the time Josiah Gregory arrived, she had a plan. Hunter and MacKenzie would rent the adjoining and currently vacant offices.

"We'll cut a door through," she instructed him, "renovate and furnish one of the offices for me, designate the other as a permanent conference room. No more huddling around Mr. Hunter's desk every time we need to consult with each other. Can that be done?"

"Easily enough, I think. I'll contact the firm Mr. Conkling used when he first moved in here."

"I didn't realize he'd made changes."

"Everyone does. Nobody wants it said that someone else's office is good enough for him." Josiah's eyes lit up as he poured fresh coffee for Miss MacKenzie. He was something of an amateur architect cum decorator; the renovations his late employer enjoyed had originally been Josiah's idea.

"How soon can you get this finished?"

"I'll call today, Miss. Martin Parish works fast once a customer signs off on the specifications. He's a small operation, but the result is always high quality."

"I'll tell Mr. Hunter about the new arrangements." Prudence stood beside Josiah's desk, one hand on her hip, the other drawing sketches in the air. "We'll probably need to do more than cut one door. Walls may have to come down."

"Not today, I hope," Geoffrey Hunter said from the open doorway. He thought Prudence had never looked more alive and confident than she did at that moment. He hadn't liked the bleak, strained face she'd been wearing since Nora's body was discovered. Strong though she believed herself to be, Geoffrey knew that her core was still fragile. Laudanum would always beckon to Prudence; she would have to prove to herself over and over again that she could resist its lure. He wished she would lean on him more often.

She turned from her contemplation of the space to be transformed, smiling broadly at his teasing. "Soon," she said. "Josiah has a man coming to plan it all out and give us an estimate."

"Josiah always has a man." Geoffrey shrugged off his overcoat, accepted gratefully the steaming cup his secretary handed him. "Now tell me what this is about."

"I've decided to become a working woman," Prudence said.

"Like Hetty Green?"

Scornful of any male advice or attempt to interfere with her financial speculations, the woman known as the Witch of Wall Street had inherited money and then amassed an enormous fortune entirely on her own. And was still doing it, if the rumors of her deals could be believed.

"Not exactly. I won't be buying and selling stocks and bonds, Geoffrey. We have a crime to solve," Prudence said resolutely. "I don't think Nora's family has much trust in what the police will accomplish. I certainly don't." Unshed tears pricked at her eyelids.

She'd have to learn to control that, she thought, blinking furiously. A weeping private investigator wouldn't be of much use to anyone.

Josiah cleared his throat. Any display of emotion embarrassed him. "I'll send word to Mr. Parish," the secretary said. He smiled as he watched Miss MacKenzie walk into Mr. Hunter's office. He'd only observed her father the Judge a few times, when he'd come as a client to consult Roscoe Conkling, but Josiah thought the man's daughter just might be a match for him.

She had that look about her.

Nora Kenny's funeral was the first Catholic service Prudence had attended. She found the soaring gothic interior of the small Staten Island church awe-inspiring and grand for its size, given the humble station of most of its parishioners. Sunshine lit up narrow stained glass windows, casting vivid red, blue, and yellow shafts of color across the pews. The smell of incense and melting candle wax from the altar wafted over the congregation; a mournful tolling of muffled bells filled everyone's ears and touched every heart.

The same thoughts were in all of the mourners' minds. *Nora was too young to have died. There would be no more children for Agnes and Brian Kenny. They had lost forever the only daughter they would ever have.*

The coffin was carried down the central aisle of St. Brendan's Church by Nora's father and five brothers, all of them stone-faced with rigidly repressed emotion. Agnes Kenny walked behind her daughter's remains, veiled head to foot in black, gloved hands tightly clasped around her rosary. She paused for a moment before filing into the family pew, reaching out to lightly touch Prudence MacKenzie's arm. It was as though she needed to draw comfort from the young woman who had played with Nora when both were children. Perhaps she was reminding her that the relationship did not end with death; there was work still to be done.

The funeral Mass was said in Latin, the ageless, sonorous syllables soothing if incomprehensible to the congregation. Geoffrey Hunter, whose classical education at Phillips Academy and Harvard had included extensive study of both Latin and Greek, nodded his head from time to time. Whether your loss was new or far in the past, there was something very consoling in the measured cadences of the ancient language and the centuries old prayers.

As non-Catholics, Prudence and Geoffrey stayed in their pew while nearly everyone else in the congregation filed up to the altar to receive Communion. Prudence felt the intensity of her partner's gaze on every man who walked past where they sat; it was the Pinkerton in him scrutinizing faces and postures, looking for anything that betrayed guilt or anxiety. It was a truism among homicide investigators that murderers often attended their victims' funerals.

"Watch for signs of edginess," he'd instructed her. "Tension that seems misplaced, eyes shifting for no good reason, an unguarded smile. Whatever makes a man different from those around him is what we want to find."

None of the faces Prudence saw streaming past her seemed to fit Geoffrey's description of suspicious characteristics. There was something else about them she wasn't sure of at first, but that gradually made an indelible impression. No matter the color of hair or eye, tone of skin, height or body build, the men, women, and children gathered to bid Nora Kenny good-bye all shared some indefinable sameness that marked them as Irish. She turned to Geoffrey to ask if he had noticed the same thing. He bent his head so she could whisper her inquiry, and nodded in agreement.

Immigrants sharing the same language and religion tended to create neighborhoods of their own ethnicity. Staten Island was home to substantial populations of German, Italian, and Irish newcomers who had flocked to join earlier arrivals. The hodge-podge of villages in its hills and along its shores were as divided one from the other as though national boundaries had been wrapped around each one.

Prudence remembered the Judge commenting on how separate the groups held themselves. *"God forbid a young man or woman should cross one of those borders,"* he had said. *"You'd have a modern day* Romeo and Juliet *on the island. It would probably put the tragedy of Shakespeare's play to shame. There would certainly be more bloodshed."*

As she was remembering that conversation, the last of the communicants passed the pew in which Prudence was sitting. She turned to see if anyone else was coming down the aisle. As she looked toward the rear of the church she saw a man whose differentness was too obvious to ignore. She felt Geoffrey stiffen beside her, and knew they were both looking at the same person.

Young, perhaps in his mid to late twenties, tall and lean. Heavily muscled shoulders. His hair was no blacker than some of the so called Black Irish, but this man's eyes were the deep brown of a Mediterranean heritage and his skin had been kissed a rich tan by generations of sun drenched ancestors. Plainly not a member of this Irish parish, he stood close to the door leading from the nave of the church into its outer vestibule, nearly invisible in his dark clothes, poised to make a quick exit should anyone notice or challenge him.

"Geoffrey." Prudence spoke softly under cover of the organ music.

"I see him."

"He must have come in after the coffin was carried down the aisle. I could swear he wasn't there when we all stood as the Kennys were bringing her in."

"He wasn't there until later."

"You saw him enter?"

"I felt him."

A strange thing to say, but Prudence didn't question it. Geoffrey's natural instincts of discovery had been sharpened by years of Pinkerton training.

"What's he doing here?" Prudence whispered.

"I don't know. But he's grieving as deeply

as any of Nora's brothers. Perhaps even more so. Look at him."

Prudence knew the face of deep sorrow and loss. She had seen it reflected in her mirror often enough. An anguished emptiness in the young man's dark eyes proclaimed the stark absence of joy. Lines had carved themselves into his cheeks and across his forehead; it was plain he had slept badly if at all during the past few days. He seemed to yearn to touch the polished wood of Nora's coffin; one hand had begun to reach out toward where she lay, so far away, so hidden. As they watched, he caught himself, arrested the gesture in midair, made a sign of the cross across his chest with a quick, sketchy motion.

"Who could he be, Geoffrey?" Prudence breathed.

As if he had heard her, the young man's empty, despairing eyes met hers, boring into them with all the strength and power of a desperate passion.

The congregation stood as the final strains of "Panis Angelicus" gave way to the opening chords of the solemn recessional hymn.

Then the priest descended the altar steps, swinging an incense laden gold thurible before him. Before he finished blessing the coffin, the stranger slipped out of sight as unobtrusively as he had appeared.

"We'll have to let him go," Geoffrey said.

"But we can ask questions. Find out who he is."

"Not yet. Not today."

"We may never have as good a chance again," Prudence protested.

"He isn't going anywhere that we can't find him. He's an islander. I'm sure of it. But he isn't Irish, Prudence. If I had to guess, I'd lay odds he's from one of the Italian villages."

"*Romeo and Juliet.* My father used to speculate about what would happen if boundaries were crossed that had been put up to keep people apart."

"And what did he say?"

"That Staten Island would be bathed in blood."

"That's why we have to let him go. Whoever he is. We'll find him when the time comes. When we need him."

Detective Steven Phelan stood in the shadow of one of the side altars. He watched Nora Kenny's brothers and father shoulder the coffin to the altar, raking his eyes over every pew as they passed it. He heard not a word of the priest's eulogy, nor did he bother with the Latin Mass responses he knew by heart from years of altar boy service. He was looking for a murderer.

He had expected to see Prudence Mac-Kenzie seated near the Kenny family, and wasn't surprised that Geoffrey Hunter accompanied her. They'd warned him, after all, that the firm would be investigating the case. Idly, he wondered if the two private investigators might not serve the interests of the Metropolitan Police more than they intended. If he appeared to cooperate with them, hell, if he really did extend some cooperation, they might end up doing some of his work for him.

Maybe he shouldn't have said that Nora Kenny had been *gutted.* He knew the word had gotten Miss MacKenzie's back up. He never meant to imply that he wouldn't do his damnedest to find the man who killed her maid; cracking and solving a case was a point of pride. But the girl shouldn't have been out on the street alone in the first place. That's all he and every other cop believed.

What was it Miss MacKenzie was staring at? She'd gotten Hunter's attention and was whispering something to him.

Phelan turned in the direction they were looking. He saw a handsome young man who definitely wasn't Irish, as out of place in this crowd as it was possible to be. Three days ago in Colonial Park, Phelan had decided that Nora Kenny very likely caused her own death. It was a common story, but he'd kept an open mind. He'd come to Staten Island in case he was wrong, on the off chance the murder hadn't been committed by the girl's fiancé. Who happened to be a fisherman. Who used a gutting knife with the ease and skill of long years of practice.

He ran the scenario over in his mind again, liking it even more now. Nora's fiancé had caught her with another man and killed her in a jealous rage. The proof was standing at the rear of the church, drawn irresistibly to the funeral, but ready to bolt as soon as it was over.

Whoever he was slipped out the door as soon as he sensed he was being watched. Phelan would find out his name after the girl was safely in the ground. The priest would know. And if he didn't, Staten Island had its own police force. They'd hardly refuse to provide information to a fellow detective.

CHAPTER 6

"Tell Geoffrey Hunter the Kenny murderer is in custody." Detective Steven Phelan's voice faded in and out over the phone lines that had been hurriedly restrung after the Great Blizzard. "We arrested Tim Fahey yesterday. The case is closed."

"Is there anything else I should let him know, Detective?" Josiah Gregory reached for a pencil and his stenographer's notebook.

"That's all. Chief Byrnes will be making a statement to the press. He can read about it in the afternoon papers." Phelan didn't trouble to hide the gloat of quick success.

Josiah sat for a moment staring at the earpiece through which he'd clearly heard a snort of derision before the connection was broken. The door to Mr. Hunter's office stood open, as he always left it when Miss Prudence was with him.

"Josiah?"

91

"That was Detective Phelan. He called to inform you and Miss Prudence that the police have caught Nora Kenny's killer."

"Did he give you a name?"

"Tim Fahey. Wasn't he the fiancé?"

"I don't believe it for a moment," Prudence said. "I watched him at Bellevue. No one could have pretended to that kind of grief. Agnes told me they'd known each other since they were children. She said the only thing surprising about the courtship was that it took Tim so long to propose marriage."

"He's a fisherman, like Nora's father," Geoffrey remarked. "Nora was gutted."

"That sounds like something Detective Phelan would say." Prudence walked to the window overlooking Wall Street. It was a bright, crisp November morning, but wherever Tim Fahey was being held would be dark and dank.

"It's the way Phelan would think," Geoffrey explained. "Fishermen have to be as good with knives as they are with nets. Fahey has the skill to do what Nora's killer did. Phelan has to provide motivation and opportunity to make his case."

Prudence paced from the window to her partner's desk, heels tapping her outrage that an innocent man had been arrested.

"Why did he call us, Geoffrey?"

"It's a warning not to dig any deeper into the case. We're supposed to drop it on his word alone." Geoffrey tented his fingers and leaned back in his chair. "He wants us out of his way while he puts together evidence and charges are brought. Was there anything else, Josiah?"

"Just that Chief Byrnes would be talking to reporters and you could read what he says in this afternoon's papers."

"Byrnes doesn't want speculation about a Ripper copycat to surface. I'll lay you odds he'll suppress the autopsy report so the public won't know about the mutilation. He probably pressured Phelan to find a likely suspect before reporters started asking questions he doesn't want to answer."

"*Find* a likely suspect, Geoffrey?"

"It's been known to happen, Prudence. Wall Street might love him for drawing lines around the financial district that the underworld doesn't dare cross, and there's no doubt he's transformed the detective division. But Byrnes can be brought down just as quickly as any of his predecessors if he makes a big enough mistake. Admitting to the possibility of a copycat when he's boasted that a killer like Jack the Ripper would be no match for the New York Metropolitan Police could be that mistake. Especially if the murderer strikes a second or a third time. He needs to put the Kenny killing behind him, declare it a case of lover's jealousy that's been solved, and bury it in the police archives."

"He won't get away with it. Nora came from a respectable working-class family."

"That's why it's so important to solve the case quickly. Nora's death could remind New Yorkers how vulnerable they are. Society matrons all over the city won't want their maids going out for their half days if there's a chance they won't come back. So the killer has to be found, tried, and speedily executed. It's the only way the city can have any kind of confidence in its police force."

"What about your theory of a copycat?"

"It's only a theory. Based on the type of mutilation Nora suffered. I might be wrong."

"How do we find out? Where do we start?"

"We set Josiah to using his connections in the court system to learn where Tim Fahey is being held. Then we go see him. We hear his side of the story."

The Tombs was as massive and threatening as its name suggested, a mammoth, perpetually damp structure poorly built over marshland, fronted with pseudo-Egyptian columns blackened over the years by layers of city soot. Visitors were issued tickets that had to be presented to a keeper before being allowed to leave the building. God help the hapless family member who misplaced or lost his pass.

Josiah Gregory found Tim Fahey within an hour of making the first of several calls to court clerks who owed him favors. His late employer, former US Senator Roscoe Conkling, had insisted on cultivating a network of lower level judicial employees. He claimed that without the grease of their labors the wheels of justice would grind to a dead halt.

"Remanded without bail to the Tombs," Josiah reported. "Subjected to the third degree before he got there, though not by Byrnes himself. Phelan wore the black leather gloves this time, and at least one of my sources said the suspect's hands had to be bandaged. Which means thumbscrews were used."

"I thought torture ended in the Middle Ages," Prudence protested.

"Not in New York City," Geoffrey said. "Nor in the South where I grew up. I saw things done there that no human being should have to endure."

Murderers Row was on the second tier in the Tombs, built like all of the other cells along an iron railed walkway where visitors stood to converse with their incarcerated loved ones. Pass contraband they'd paid keepers to overlook, clasp hands through the bars, raise skirts and lower pants to assuage long denied hungers. On Sundays the catwalks were thronged; today, a Friday, most of the few visitors who had positioned themselves in front of the cells were women and children.

Tim Fahey, asleep or unconscious, lay on a hard wooden bunk. Only after Geoffrey and then Prudence repeatedly called his name did he raise his head. His face had been so badly battered that one eye was swollen closed and the other nearly so. His nose appeared broken, and through the dried blood on his cheeks could be glimpsed deep cuts and flesh swollen purple and black. Dirty gauze swathed both hands. His black wool pants and jacket were ripped and filthy, white collarless shirt spotted brown with blood spatter.

Favoring ribs that were cracked or broken, barely able to stand upright without holding on to the cell wall, Fahey made his halting way to where his visitors stood on the

96

other side of the bars.

"I hoped you'd come, Miss MacKenzie," he said, his voice scarcely audible. "Mr. Hunter." When he moved his lips, the scabs around his mouth cracked open; fresh blood flowed. Prudence reached into her reticule for a clean handkerchief and passed it through the bars. He shook his head, but when she insisted, he pressed the fine scented white linen to his face. It immediately turned red.

"What happened, Tim?" Geoffrey asked.

"They arrested me the day after Nora was buried. Yesterday. Early in the morning."

"Fewer witnesses that way," Geoffrey muttered.

"The detective accused me of murdering her. I told him he was crazy, that I would never have harmed her in any way, but he didn't listen. I was outside when they came. I'd walked up the hillside to where Nora and I used to sit sometimes, looking out over the water and planning our future."

"You were going to buy your own boat," Geoffrey said. It was every fisherman's dream.

"The *Nora*," Prudence murmured.

"I was on my way back to the house, so no one saw them come after me. The detective had brought two uniformed patrolmen with him. I was handcuffed, shoved into a closed carriage, then put aboard a ferry. The next thing I knew I was in what they called an interrogation room and the detective had put on a pair of black leather gloves. He punched me in the face or the belly after every question. He said I was lying, but I wasn't."

"Was it Phelan? Steven Phelan?"

"I found that out later, when one of the policeman called him by name." Fahey raised his bandaged hands. "They used thumbscrews when they decided the beating wasn't enough."

"We'll get a doctor to you," Prudence said. "We won't let them get away with this."

Geoffrey carried a dipper of water from the barrel that stood at the end of the tier of cells. "I can't vouch for how clean it is," he said, passing it through the bars. He exchanged Prudence's small lace-edged handkerchief for his own more substantial one.

Fahey wet Geoffrey's unsoiled linen, then pressed it gingerly to his face. Gradually, inch by inch, he soaked off most of the dried blood. Finally, he held the damp cloth to the eye that had swollen shut. It would be weeks before the cuts healed and the bruises faded, provided he wasn't subjected to the third degree again.

"Can you tell us why the detective thinks you murdered Nora, Tim?" Without having to consult with Geoffrey, Prudence knew that she would have to be the one to ask the painfully personal questions. Only the fact that she was *Nora's Miss Prudence* would persuade Fahey to open up to her. "He must have given you some reason, some explanation."

"It doesn't make sense, Miss Prudence, but the detective kept saying the same thing over and over, as if I knew what he was talking about."

"What was that?"

"He said Nora was seeing someone else on the sly and that when I found out about it I flew into a rage and killed her. He said jealousy does terrible things to a man and that if I'd admit to it, a jury would understand. They're all men on a jury; they wouldn't condemn me because it was really Nora's fault for being unfaithful. He promised to stop the beating as soon as I confessed."

"But you didn't." Geoffrey knew the answer, but he wanted Fahey to say it aloud, to prove to himself that he'd had the strength to withstand the brutality of the third degree. It might help him to bear it when they came after him again.

"No, I didn't. Phelan was telling terrible lies about Nora. I wouldn't give him the satisfaction of breaking me."

"Your hands?"

"I passed out from the pain. They threw water over me and then one of the uniformed patrolmen wrapped them."

"They can't have any evidence because we know you didn't do it." Despite Geoffrey's warning about what the third degree could do to a man, Prudence hadn't imagined that Tim Fahey's injuries would be so bad.

"Is there anything else you remember, Tim? Anything Phelan said that might give us a clue about what he plans to do next?" Geoffrey asked.

"What he said about my Nora shouldn't be repeated, Mr. Hunter. And I swear to you it's not true."

Prudence stepped closer to the bars of the cell. She wanted to reach out a consoling hand, but she thought any touch, however light, would hurt rather than comfort. "Nora and I played together when my mother and I stayed on Staten Island a long time ago," she said softly. "You can tell me anything. I'll only believe the best about Nora."

Fahey hesitated, then dropped his eyes. He would confide in Miss MacKenzie, but he couldn't look at her while he told her the filthy thing Phelan had accused Nora of having done. "He said she was expecting a child, but that it wasn't mine. He said I found out she'd been with another man and that's why I killed her."

Prudence was too stunned to say anything. Her mind flew back to Colonial Park, to the brief sight of Nora's disemboweled body before Detective Phelan drew the burlap wrapping over her again. She shook her head in denial, but Geoffrey wondered if it could be true and how he would be able to prove or disprove the allegation.

"We weren't, we hadn't . . . Nora was a virgin, Miss. I swear by all that's holy that I never touched her in that way. I wouldn't. She was going to be my wife. We loved each other."

"I'm so sorry, Tim," Prudence said. It was all she could manage. The cold had penetrated her bones; the stench of unemptied waste buckets in the horror that was the Tombs made it hard to breathe.

"It doesn't matter what they do to me. I'll never believe what they're saying about Nora. It's all lies." Fahey walked away from them, toward the far wall of his cell and the hard wooden bunk that was the only place he could sit or lie down. He moved slowly, each step taking enormous effort. The pain was intense.

"We'll get you a lawyer," Geoffrey said. "If it comes to it, I can represent you myself."

Fahey was closing them out, drifting into another world. It was as though having allowed himself the release of talking about Nora, he now decided to build a wall around the place inside himself where she still lived. It was the only way he could hold on to her.

"What will happen to him?" Prudence asked as she and Geoffrey followed the small group of visitors being hurried toward the outside world by blue uniformed warders. She clutched her precious pass in her hand.

"That depends on whether or not they decide to bring him to trial and then hang him. If they don't, if his lawyer is good enough and the evidence weak, he'll eventually be released. After that, who can say?"

"He didn't do it, Geoffrey. He didn't kill Nora."

"No. Whatever else he did or didn't do, that crime can't be laid at his door."

"Then you believe him?"

"Fahey is convinced he told us the truth about Nora, but we have to get the real story out of the coroner. If Nora was pregnant, as Phelan claims, there's someone else we have to find before our favorite detective goes looking for him."

"The man who was standing alone at the back of the church during Nora's funeral."

"That's where we start. He had a reason for being there," Geoffrey said. "It will break Tim Fahey's heart if we find out that Phelan was right."

"His heart's already broken."

"Truth can be a terrible companion, Prudence. It can ride you like a demon and give you no rest because you have no defense against it."

"I think I know that better than most people," Prudence said. "Even so, I've learned to prefer the starkest of truths to the most comforting of lies."

That night Tim Fahey was taken to one of the basement cells where sound couldn't penetrate to the floors above. He was systematically beaten into unconsciousness, then thrown into an isolation cell whose only furnishing was a bucket for his bloody wastes.

Fahey's file disappeared. None of the

warders would be able to tell a visitor where he was.

Without paperwork, Tim Fahey no longer existed. At least not legally.

CHAPTER 7

"I've tried every one of my contacts at Bellevue where the autopsy took place," Josiah Gregory said. He set aside Prudence's written account of the visit to the Tombs the previous day, appalled by what a lady of her upbringing had seen and heard. "The report hasn't come across anyone's desk, so it hasn't been filed in the morgue. A copy should have been sent to the Metropolitan Police, but nobody there has logged it in either. It's as though the Nora Kenny postmortem never took place, yet we know it did."

"It has to exist somewhere," Geoffrey said. "The doctor who performed the examination might have kept a copy for himself. He wouldn't be the only coroner who secreted away reports of interesting or baffling cases."

"I'll talk to him," Prudence offered. "He might be more willing to tell what he knows if it's a woman inquiring about another woman."

"Bring up the family connection," Geoffrey suggested.

"Next you'll be telling me to cry discreetly into a black bordered handkerchief."

"If it helps."

"The wounds were made with surgical precision." Dr. Robert Estin unabashedly admired the skill with which Nora's killer had gone about his macabre business. "No extra incisions anywhere. He knew what he was doing."

"When the family came to identify Nora's body, they saw that her throat had been cut and there was a wound to her torso, but your attendant stopped short of uncovering the worst of it."

"You were here at Bellevue with them?"

"Mrs. Kenny worked for my mother for many years. She took care of her during her final illness. Her daughter Nora often came to help out when there were extra chores to be done at my home here in Manhattan as well as the house on Staten Island. The Kennys are family retainers of long standing." Prudence thought she had struck the right combination of laudable concern and discreet reference to a social rank that breathed wealth and power. If Dr. Estin

106

hoped to get out of the Bellevue morgue and into a lucrative private practice, he would need the patronage of patients like her.

"What can I do for you, Miss MacKenzie?"

"Once their grief is blunted by time, Nora's parents are certain to begin asking questions. Autopsy reports are public documents. Painful though it will be, the family may demand to read the details of their daughter's postmortem."

"That's not something I would advise any grieving relative to do." Doctor Estin's collar seemed too tight for his neck. He tugged at the stiffly starched wings beneath his chin and fingered the knot in his black silk cravat. Still in his late twenties, he hadn't yet perfected the art of deflecting unwanted questions and comments.

"Nevertheless."

"And you want to soften the blow."

"Yes. I thought my family doctor would be able to interpret the information in the least painful way." She forced an open, candid smile, gray eyes mutely requesting the young doctor's assistance. It was as close to flirting as she dared go.

"I'd like to help you, Miss MacKenzie, but the Kenny autopsy report has been ordered sealed. I can't say for how long."

"What does that mean, Doctor?"

"The public is not to be allowed access. For the common good."

"Was the report destroyed?"

He looked shocked at the suggestion. "That would be a grave violation of procedure, if not an outright flaunting of the law. The report will be made available at the proper time."

If Doctor Estin had kept a copy for himself, Prudence doubted that any more discreet cajoling would get it out of him. The question she knew she couldn't ask outright was whether he thought Nora had been pregnant. No lady would solicit that kind of information. Since she couldn't risk losing the moral high ground in this strange conversation, Prudence decided to switch tactics.

"If I can't have the report itself," she said, "the next best thing would seem to be as much information as you think I should share with the family."

"That was done at the time of the official identification of the body," he said stiffly.

"I was there," she reminded him softly.

"Of course," he apologized. "Nora Kenny's throat was cut by a single deep stroke of a wide bladed knife. She bled to death within a few minutes."

"The mutilation was done after she'd died?"

"Yes. There is that for her family to be thankful for."

"The mortician who prepared her body for burial is aware of the desecration. Perhaps he's the person to contact."

"He's hardly a medical expert."

"No, of course not. But he could describe to me what he observed. The body had to be washed and embalmed."

Doctor Estin was plainly struggling. He'd done what he'd been told to do, buried the autopsy report and refused to answer any reporter's questions. But now he had the opportunity to curry favor with someone far above him on the social ladder, and if he didn't take advantage of it, some journeyman mortician would reap the reward that should be his. What difference could it possibly make if he told Miss MacKenzie what she wanted to know? And who would ever find out? She wasn't likely to go blabbing to the newspapers. He'd keep back one essential piece of information and take his chances with the rest of it.

He described in clinical terms what had been done to the dead woman, ticking off dispassionately on his fingers the organs that

had been removed, assuring Miss Mac-
Kenzie that her maid had been dead before
the first cut was made below the neck. Aside
from having her throat cut, which he em-
phasized was a rapid and not terribly painful way to go, she wouldn't have felt anything. He had sewed her back up with
smaller than usual stitches when the autopsy
was complete.

What Dr. Estin decided not to tell his
inquisitive visitor about were the signs of
chloasma faciei he'd found on Nora Kenny's
cheeks and forehead, but especially across
her upper lip. Midwives called it the Mask
of Pregnancy, disfiguring brown blotches
that sometimes looked like a ragged mustache painted on the expectant mother's
face. The subject had been only briefly
touched on during his medical studies, but
Estin was positive he was right, even though
in Nora Kenny's case the marks were very
faint. He mentioned it to the detective in
charge of the case, but he hadn't been rash
enough to include it in the written report.
The mortician would have covered the
nearly invisible brown blotches with the
thick cosmetics that often made the dead
look unnaturally alive, but he wouldn't have
mentioned them to the bereaved relatives.

There were many reasons someone's skin

could become discolored. But a young woman? Whose internal organs had been deliberately and meticulously removed?

Speculation wasn't something the police department welcomed. Estin had learned his lesson early and learned it well. He'd shared his opinion with Detective Phelan just to protect himself if another source should come forward and verify the victim's gravid state, but he was careful not to insist on it.

So he never mentioned the Mask of Pregnancy to Miss MacKenzie, who wouldn't be expected to know anything about so indelicate a topic anyway.

"He's hiding something," Prudence reported. "I don't know what, but it's definitely a conjecture he was determined not to share. I didn't get much more out of Dr. Estin than what Detective Phelan told us in Colonial Park. He confirmed that the killer was right-handed. He's positive of that because of the direction and depth of the wound to Nora's neck."

"We all suspected that."

"The other important piece of information is that our murderer has a surgeon's skill with a knife. Dr. Estin was impressed by his expertise. It made me shudder to see him lick his lips in envy."

"He actually licked his lips?"

"Figuratively speaking." Prudence gratefully accepted the cup of strong coffee Josiah handed her. She needed something biting and bitter to match her mood. "Once he started talking, he didn't stop until he'd described every cut. He kept referring to what was done as the *procedure* or the *surgery,* as if Nora were a patient instead of a victim. It made my blood run cold."

"Write it up," Geoffrey said. "Use my office. And while you're doing that, I'm going back to the Tombs to talk to Tim Fahey again."

Prudence was deep in the report she was writing when Josiah knocked on the office door. He closed it behind him as he approached the desk. "It's Agnes Kenny, Miss. She's come to see you and nobody else, she says."

"Agnes?"

"You'll forgive my saying this, Miss Prudence, but she looks terrible. As if she hasn't slept a night since the funeral."

"Show her in, Josiah. And then fix some strong hot tea with plenty of milk and sugar."

"I'll bring it right in, Miss."

112

Prudence swept together the sheets of paper on which she was recording everything Doctor Estin had said. She opened one of Geoffrey's desk drawers at random and jammed the bundle into it before Nora's mother could catch a glimpse of her daughter's name. Then she stood up to greet the woman who had looked after her as tenderly as she had Prudence's mother.

"I didn't know where else to turn," Agnes said.

Prudence seated her on the other side of the desk and poured a cup of Josiah's best Indian blend. It wasn't as strong or black as she knew the Irish liked their tea, but it would have to do. He was right. Agnes Kenny had the look about her of a creature about to collapse. She had aged this past week, become an old woman before her time, lost the brightness of eye and upturned smile of a happy wife and mother.

"Drink some tea, Agnes, and then tell me what's happened."

From her purse Agnes took a small book covered in tooled blue leather. "I found this in Nora's room. Hidden under the mattress." She laid it on the desk and with one finger pushed it toward Prudence. "It's her diary. I never knew she kept one."

"Have you read it?" Prudence asked, picking up the journal that was slightly larger than the palm of her hand.

"All last night. Over and over. I sat up by the kitchen fire so her father wouldn't ask what I was doing." Tears had begun to stream down Agnes Kenny's face. She let them flow unimpeded, as though the weight of them could wash away her sorrow.

"May I?"

Agnes nodded, then sat back in her chair. Exhausted, she lowered the tea cup to her lap and watched as Prudence turned the pages. She'd read what her daughter had written so many times that she'd memorized every sentence. Each word had seared itself into her brain.

"My heart aches whenever I'm with Tim," Prudence read aloud. *"I thought I loved him, but how feeble that emotion was compared to the passion that makes me tremble and cry out every time my heart's true desire holds me in his arms."*

She glanced up. Agnes was whispering the words Prudence had just read aloud.

"I won't read any more unless you want me to," Prudence said.

Nora's mother shook her head despairingly. "You need to know everything, Miss. It doesn't hurt so much now, and you've a beautiful voice. It makes what my Nora wrote sound like poetry."

"I don't know how much longer we can go on like this. Someone is bound to see us eventually. When they do, something terrible will happen to him and my da will make sure I marry Tim. If he'll still have me. Any suspicion of what I've done will be hushed up. How will I bear it?"

"She didn't know what she was doing," Agnes said. "She fell in love and forgot everything else. Duty to family. Her promise to Tim. Everything I taught her. She lied to us. She had to twist the truth to find ways to meet him. No matter where she went, there was some arrangement so they could steal a few moments together. I should have suspected."

"Why is that, Agnes?"

"It got to be that it was Nora, and only Nora, who did all of the household errands. I was glad enough of it because there's always work to be done at home. I'm not much for walking or riding long distances and carrying heavy loads anymore." Agnes's eyes pleaded for forgiveness. She should have kept a tighter rein on her only daughter, shouldn't have let Nora go off so much on her own just to spare a mother's tired feet and sore shoulders.

"You mustn't blame yourself," Prudence

said. "She would have found some way to meet him no matter what obstacles you put in her way."

Agnes nodded resignedly. "I know that, Miss. I remind myself a hundred times a day. I remember what it was like to be young and in love."

"Do you think she cared for him that much?"

"She did. All you have to do is read the rest of what she's written. But please, Miss Prudence, don't judge her."

It was an odd thing to say, Prudence thought. She turned a page, glanced at Agnes again, and continued reading, but silently now. She thought Agnes was best left in her own thoughts; she'd spent the whole of last night getting to know her daughter's secret heart.

"They did love each other," breathed Prudence when she had read the last few entries. At Nora's funeral she had drawn Geoffrey's attention to the olive skinned young man standing at the rear of the church. Asked who he could be, what he was doing there. Now she knew. *He was in love with her.* She heard the answer reverberate in the recesses of her mind and the stillness of her partner's office. *He was in love with her and she with him.*

"We none of us had any idea," Agnes said.

"Do you know who he is?" Prudence asked. "She never mentions his name or describes him in any way that would make it possible to identify him."

"Nora was always loyal to the people she loved. She'd never tell tales on any of her brothers, no matter how much they deserved it. She wasn't taking any chances. We'll never know who he is."

"Agnes, is there any possibility he's from one of the Italian villages on the island?"

"We don't mix with them, Miss," Agnes snapped. "I don't know why you'd think such a thing."

"There was a young man standing at the back of the church at Nora's funeral. He wasn't Irish. He had black hair and olive skin. He looked Mediterranean. Mr. Hunter saw him, too. He agrees with me."

"She wouldn't do that," Agnes said. "She wouldn't do that to herself or her family."

"Would you have tried to separate them?"

"We would have done anything we could to keep them apart. The Kennys are Irish to the core."

"But Irish and Italians are both Catholic," Prudence reasoned.

"You have to feel it here," Agnes said, pointing to her heart. "If you don't understand, I can't explain it to you." Her face closed in stubborn denial. "Whoever he is, he's not Italian."

"I read how she wrote about him," Prudence said.

"He knows something that could exonerate Tim Fahey. If he doesn't come forward with it, he deserves to burn in hell for all eternity." Agnes might someday forgive her daughter's lover for stealing Nora's heart, but she would never absolve him from causing the hanging death of an innocent man she'd long considered another son.

"We can always hope that if there isn't any real evidence against Tim, they'll have to let him go."

"They'll manufacture whatever evidence it takes, Miss Prudence. It's what the police do when they need to get a case off the books. They solve the crime however they can. An Irish girl in the family way and not by the man she's about to marry? It's a recipe for murder; that's how they'll railroad Tim. They'll say he killed her when he found out she'd been playing fast and loose on him. And everyone will believe it."

Prudence stared at Agnes Kenny. *In the family way.* Was it possible Nora's mother and Detective Phelan both suspected the same thing? Had she missed something in

Nora's diary?

"She didn't come right out with it, Miss, but reading between the lines, I'd say she was worried. She'd put on some weight around the waist. Her dresses looked tight to me, but I thought it was nervous eating before the wedding. She wrote about her friend who didn't come to visit; we both know what that means."

"Dear God in heaven." Why hadn't she seen it from the beginning? This had to be the secret Dr. Estin was concealing. There was something about Nora's body that gave away her condition, but only to skilled medical eyes. "Does anyone else know that Nora might have been pregnant?"

"They'll find out. They always do. At the trial, if not before. We can't let Tim be convicted, Miss Prudence. Nora has paid a terrible price for what she did, but it would be a crime and a mortal sin if Tim were hanged for her murder. He didn't do it." Agnes put her cold tea on Hunter's desk, then sat up ramrod straight in her chair. "It's up to you to prove he's innocent, you and Mr. Hunter. Nobody else cares enough or is smart enough. Certainly not the police."

"If we investigate with the information you gave me today, we'll have to find out the

119

name of the man Nora wrote about in her diary. We won't be able to conceal his identity."

"I know what you're getting at, Miss, but I don't see any way out of it. The Kennys will always hold their heads up, no matter what. Promise me . . . promise me you'll find whoever killed my daughter. Promise me you'll prove Tim Fahey is innocent."

"I can only give you my word that I'll do my best, Agnes. Mr. Hunter and I will do all we can." She stood up and walked out from behind Geoffrey's desk.

Agnes got to her feet also, allowing herself to fall into the comfort of Prudence's arms. Only when they heard two male voices on the other side of the door did they break apart.

"He's disappeared, Prudence," Geoffrey announced, rushing into the office. He noticed Agnes, came to an abrupt halt, and held out his hand. "My condolences, Mrs. Kenny. Once again my condolences."

"Agnes has brought some important information to us, Geoffrey."

"Tim Fahey has disappeared." Geoffrey ran a hand through his dark hair, a rare gesture of frustration. "No one at the Tombs knows where he is, who took him away, or what happened to him. There's not even a record he was ever there."

"But we saw him! Yesterday," Prudence exclaimed.

"Nevertheless, he's gone now. We may never see him again."

Agnes Kenny gave a low wail, as desolate and desperate a sound as they had ever heard. She crossed herself, then fell to the floor in a dead faint.

CHAPTER 8

Prudence and Geoffrey were among the first passengers to board the early Staten Island ferry on Sunday morning. Yesterday's good weather had held; the day was clear, crisp, and cold, blessedly free of biting wind and scudding gray clouds. Prudence wore the heaviest outdoor boots she owned, a walking suit that allowed more freedom of movement than most of her costumes, and a small black hat whose veil blurred the features of her face.

"He looked right at me," she explained to Geoffrey, lifting the veil while they talked. "I'm sure he'll recognize me, but for a few moments I'll have the advantage of surprise."

"We don't know how much Nora told him about you." Geoffrey thought that no amount of veiling could disguise her slender height and graceful way of walking. He'd insisted that she carry an ivory handled derringer in her reticule. The umbrella hooked over her arm had a steel tip that could disable a man if applied to the right spot. He'd also taught her how to bring it down hard enough to fracture an arm.

"Unless he asked questions about why she was going to Manhattan, there was no reason for them to talk about the MacKenzie family."

"Your father was a famous judge, Prudence. Everyone on Staten Island knew about the house he built there to save his beloved wife from the city's bad air. And that she died anyway. If the man we're after is an islander, he'll know the story." It always surprised him when Prudence naively assumed that no one was interested in her or her family. There had been a time when the MacKenzie name appeared regularly in the gossip columns.

"I hadn't thought of that, but I suppose it's true."

"I'm just asking you to be careful. I'll stay as near as possible and still be out of sight, but it will take me a few moments to get to you." A knife could open a fatal wound in seconds, a bullet was even faster. "If he seems angry or agitated, step back out of his reach. I'll be watching."

"I don't think I'll have anything to fear

once he knows who I am," Prudence assured him. "If you're right and Nora did tell him about me, she would have spoken as a friend. He cared about her, Geoffrey. You read the diary."

"What I read were the lovesick prattlings of a girl who lost her head when she gave away her heart and body."

"I don't believe either of them killed her, not Tim, and not this secret lover. I think the murderer is somewhere in the city, holed up in his den preparing for his next victim. I know he's a monster, Geoffrey, just like the London Ripper. But unless we find out more about where Nora went last Saturday when she got off the ferry, we may never find him."

"Don't assume anything about anyone, Prudence."

He meant well, but it was annoying to be treated like a schoolgirl who hadn't learned all of her lessons. She'd already made a near fool of herself when'd he'd asked if she planned to visit Windscape on this trip. After the cemetery, perhaps?

"It's closed for the winter," Prudence had mumbled, "and I didn't bring a key."

He'd had the grace not to point out that the Kennys would lend her their key since she was, after all, the rightful owner of the property. And he didn't question why she was avoiding the house where she and Nora had created so many happy childhood memories.

Despite his courtesy she'd wanted to snap out a sharp retort in a voice that dripped venom, but it was not something she was good at. Yet. She contented herself with watching the water and the Lady in the Harbor.

The waves eased her temper and Lady Liberty stiffened her spine.

The cemetery stretched downhill from Saint Brendan's toward the water, as windswept and dotted with Celtic crosses as any to be found in western Ireland. Sea grasses resistant to salt air grew wild along the white pebbled paths; here and there a stunted native holly tree bent against the constant sea breeze. The dark green leaves and bright red berries provided splashes of welcome November color.

Prudence lingered among the crosses and more modest gravestones, but none of the parishioners arriving at the church for Sunday Mass turned aside to join her in paying respects to the dead. The only recent grave was Nora's, unmarked except by the rawness of the mounded earth that hadn't begun to settle yet and the wilting wreaths and bouquets of hothouse flowers that had decorated the altar at the funeral service.

Geoffrey was close by, concealed inside the gravedigger's shack amidst a welter of shovels, picks, sod cutters, woven baskets, and canvas covers to keep the rain out of freshly dug holes. He watched Prudence through gaps between the planks of the poorly constructed door. If necessary, he could be at her side within seconds. Minutes ticked by like hours. The only sounds were the voices raised in song inside Saint Brendan's and the squawk of seagulls. Prudence paced to ward off the chill.

Mass ended, the church doors opened, and as the Irish Catholics of Saint Brendan's streamed out, plumes of cigarette and pipe smoke rose above their heads. Father Devlin shook the men's hands, blessed small children and infants, and exchanged greetings with the women. A few families climbed into horse drawn traps, but most of them walked briskly along the roadside toward homes that were warm and fragrant with banked fires and slow cooking stews. It was too cold a day to linger, despite the bright sun and cloudless sky. When the last parishioner had gone, Father Devlin disappeared into the rectory, though not before shading his eyes with one hand as he looked toward the cemetery.

Prudence had ducked behind a tall plinth as soon as the initial Mass-goers appeared on the church steps. At first she thought the priest had seen her, wondered who she was, and shielded his eyes from the sun to get a better look. Then she realized that his face was turned away from her, angled toward a figure approaching the rearmost stone wall of the cemetery, a shadowy form half hidden in the dense shade of a grove of thickly forested pines. Prudence flattened her body against the angel topped stone column and listened for the sound of approaching footsteps.

She heard the creak of a rusty back gate, then the measured crunch of leather on gravel. The wind carried a scent Prudence could not identify, deeply foreign, redolent of sandalwood and crushed sage. Before she could decide whether to step out of her hiding place to confront whoever had chosen such a seldom-used entrance into the cemetery, Prudence was grabbed from behind and pressed tightly against a man's hard body. He lifted her feet from the ground and spun them both toward the gravedigger's shack where Geoffrey exploded through the door too late to save her.

"Don't come any closer." The stranger's voice was firm, calm, unhurried. His arm tightened around her neck.

Geoffrey dropped his hands to his sides, stood stock still and silent. Waiting. His eyes were locked on her assailant's; neither man moved a muscle.

"My name is Prudence MacKenzie. Nora worked for me, but she was also a good friend when we were children. If you're who I think you may be, you have nothing to fear from me or from Mr. Hunter." It was the only thing Prudence could think of to say. Geoffrey's eyes didn't shift to hers, but she felt a warm current of approbation wash over her. *Well done. Keep talking.*

"I know who you are," the man said. He nodded toward Geoffrey. "If you have a weapon on you, take it out slowly and drop it on the ground."

Geoffrey drew his Army Colt .45 from the holster where it nestled against his ribs, stooped, and laid it carefully in the grass. He'd modified the gun in several ways, the most important being a hair trigger. "A fraction of a second can mean the difference between living or dying," he'd explained to Prudence.

"Now kick it toward me."

"That's not a good idea," Geoffrey said.

"Do it."

"Suppose I empty the chambers and the barrel." Not waiting for an answer, Geoffrey knelt down, spun the cylinder, and ejected six bullets into the palm of his hand. He laid the empty Colt and its now harmless missiles back on the ground. Standing up gradually, he was careful not to make any sudden or threatening movement.

He glanced at Prudence, then turned his attention to the man holding her. "Miss MacKenzie is telling you the truth," he said. "We don't mean you any harm, but we have questions about Nora and what happened to her that only you can answer."

"Please," Prudence said, "I promise I won't scream or try to run." She thought of the derringer nestled in her reticule. "I can't do you any injury," she lied.

She felt the pressure of his arm around her body ease. He let her go and stepped back beyond her reach.

"Did Nora tell you about me?" she asked.

"Often," he answered. "You can pick up the gun and put it back in its holster," he instructed Geoffrey. "Hand the bullets to me."

"Agnes Kenny told us she thought someone had been visiting Nora's grave," Prudence said.

"Every day since it was dug."

"You were at the back of the church during her funeral."

"I had to come. I couldn't have stayed away."

"She wrote about you in her diary," Prudence told him. "But she never mentioned a name and she was careful not to describe you."

"I didn't know she did that, kept a diary," he said. His eyes hardened and a muscle twitched along the line of his jaw. Plainly he didn't like the idea that anyone else had been privy to what should have remained secret. Pride wouldn't allow him to ask Prudence what Nora had written.

"Her mother found the journal. She and I have both read it. So has Mr. Hunter." Prudence decided that nothing but the full truth would get and keep this man's trust. "Nora was afraid that if her family found out, especially her father or her brothers, they would make sure she could never meet you again."

"I'm Sicilian," he said, as if that explained everything.

"Why did you attack me?" asked Prudence, "if you knew who I was?"

"I watched your partner hide in the shed. He was obviously hoping to take someone by surprise. I had to be sure it really was you." He gestured toward the veil covering her face. "Nora showed me a picture."

Prudence raised the veil and deftly pinned it to the crown of her hat. She could feel the weight of the loaded derringer in her reticule, but she thought it was probably useless. Geoffrey had told her that the smaller the pistol the less accurate the shot except at very close range.

"Will you answer some questions for us?" she asked.

"The police have already arrested the man who murdered her. Why do you need to ask questions?"

"Tim Fahey did not kill Nora," Geoffrey said.

"Agnes Kenny has asked us to prove his innocence and find the real killer," Prudence explained. "Surely that tells you something."

"Perhaps only that they're all fools to believe him."

"Why do you say that?"

"Prisons are full of men caught bloody red-handed who go to the gallows denying they're guilty. It means nothing."

"He loved her," Prudence said. "He was beaten within an inch of his life, but he didn't confess. The police used thumbscrews. Nothing they did could make him admit that he'd hurt Nora in any way. Or even that they'd quarreled. And he didn't know about you."

"You speak of him as though he's dead."

"Fahey has disappeared," Geoffrey said. "He was arrested, subjected to the third degree, then made to vanish overnight."

"You'll never see him again if the police don't want him found. The ocean is deep and a body doesn't last long where there are fish to feed on it."

"We have feelers out. Someone saw or heard something. There's always a snitch if there's enough money to buy him."

"Maybe Fahey deserved what he got."

"No, he didn't," Prudence said. "He loved Nora as deeply as you did. Perhaps more." She hoped the comparison would make him angry enough to drop his guard. When she saw his lips tighten and thin to a narrow line, she knew she had succeeded. "They were going to be married after Christmas."

"No. She wouldn't have gone through with it."

"We'll never know." Prudence stepped back from the thunderous look directed her way. She didn't want him furious enough to throw all caution to the winds, just sufficiently roused to want to prove her wrong.

"Nora went into Manhattan to work for you, Miss MacKenzie."

"You can't hold me responsible for what happened to her."

"She had no other reason for being there."

"Are you certain?"

"We met the day before she left. Last Friday. She was looking forward to seeing her friend Colleen again, excited about being off the island for a few days."

"What else?"

"Nothing."

"You must have talked about the wedding. It was only two months away."

"Once. We spoke of it only once. She said she wanted to let Tim Fahey down easily because she'd known him since they were very young. Nora was the kindest person I've ever known. She couldn't bear to hurt anyone. Being in love with me was tearing her apart. She knew what it would do to her family. She made me promise not to bring up the marriage again until after she'd broken the news to Fahey. I didn't like it, but I did as she asked. She said she planned to tell him after she got back from her stay on Fifth Avenue."

"Had she changed during the past few weeks?" Prudence asked. "Did she seem worried or upset about anything?"

133

He thought for a moment, then nodded his head reluctantly. "Something was on her mind. I caught her staring off into the distance with an odd look on her face, as if she were gazing into the future. I teased her about it, but I thought it was nothing more than concern about Fahey. I even wondered if she'd decided to tell her friend Colleen what she intended to do."

"Where were you on Saturday night?" Geoffrey asked.

"I have an alibi, if that's what you're trying to find out."

"You know our names," Prudence said. "Won't you tell us yours?"

"Dominic Pastore." The abrupt shift had caught him off guard, but once he gave up the information, he realized it didn't matter. All they had to do was describe him and anyone on the island would be able to identify him. The Pastore family was well known, well respected, and feared. Dominic was the tallest of his father's five sons and the handsomest, though all were slender, with powerfully muscled shoulders and long legs. What distinguished him from his brothers was the menacing but tightly coiled energy that was also his father's most striking characteristic.

"I was here on Staten Island," Dominic

said. "At a cousin's wedding."

"Nora was killed around midnight," Geoffrey told him.

"The party didn't break up until well after that."

"And I suppose you have witnesses who will testify you were there the entire time?"

"As many as you need."

"Is there anything else you can tell us about Nora?" Prudence asked. She could feel tension crackling between the two men. She hadn't thought of it before, but they were very much alike, these two, though Geoffrey was at least ten years older, more polished and urbane. The younger Dominic would have to grow into the kind of worldliness that only came with age and experience.

"If Fahey didn't kill her, who did?"

"We don't know, Mr. Pastore," Geoffrey said. "The police consider the case closed. We disagree."

"She was killed at midnight, you say?"

"That's the coroner's best estimate."

"What was she doing out alone at that time of night? Why wasn't she safely inside your house, Miss MacKenzie?"

"We think she arrived there, but no one answered the door when she rang the bell. She left a basket on the doorstep, then went somewhere else. We've talked to all of the staff, including Colleen, but no one has any idea where she could have gone." Nothing about this case made sense to Prudence.

"You're sure about Fahey?"

"He didn't do it," Geoffrey said.

"If he did, and if your meddling helps him evade justice, I'll take care of him myself," Pastore said. "It will give me great pleasure."

"Mr. Hunter is an ex-Pinkerton," Prudence said. "They don't *meddle,* Mr. Pastore."

"For the moment I'll choose to believe you. But if I find out differently . . ." Pastore spun on his heel, sending a spray of small white pebbles across the grass. Within moments he had reached the cemetery's back gate.

Before she could weigh the result of what she was about to do and before he could disappear into the shadows of the pine grove, Prudence rushed after him. She waved Geoffrey back, vigorously shaking her head no at him.

Pastore turned when he heard the sound of her running feet on the graveled walk.

"Wait," she called out, "please wait. It's important."

He hesitated, remained where he was, one hand on the gate.

"There's something you should be told," Prudence said, the words tumbling out as she caught her breath. "Nora wouldn't have kept it a secret much longer. You have a right to know."

"Know what, Miss MacKenzie? If you're going to tell me she had decided to go through with the marriage to Fahey, I won't believe you."

"She was pregnant, Mr. Pastore. Nora was going to have your child."

"That's a lie. She would have told me." Disbelief warred with some other emotion deep in his eyes. The muscles of his face contorted, the hand on the gate clenched into a fist.

"I think she was about to do just that. I can't be certain, but it would be logical for her to try to confirm her condition before she said anything. Perhaps that's what was so important that she was in too much of a hurry to wait when she left the basket at the kitchen door."

"You have no proof."

"I do." Prudence took a piece of paper from the pocket of her coat. She had asked Josiah to hire a copyist to make two duplicates of the entries in Nora's diary. One copy remained at the office, the other she brought home. This morning she had taken the most important page with her when she left the house.

She handed it to Dominic. "It's a copy," she said, "so the handwriting isn't Nora's. But the words are hers."

"What do you think, Prudence?" Geoffrey asked.

"He didn't kill her either."

"Is that why you told him she was pregnant?"

"How did you know?"

"By the look on your face and his reaction." Geoffrey took her arm to guide her along the pebbled path to the horse and buggy they had rented at the ferry dock. "I should have stopped you."

"Why?"

"In my book Pastore is still a suspect, and now he knows everything we do. That's never a good idea. We don't have any more leverage over him."

"I thought he had a right to know, Geoffrey. It was his child she was carrying." Prudence stopped, waited until he, too, came to a halt. Faced her. "I think you're wrong," she said as strongly as if he weren't far more experienced than she. As if he weren't the ex-Pinkerton authority in all things criminal. "You may not agree with me, but I'm right.

I know I am. Dominic Pastore did not kill and mutilate Nora."

"Are you saying he's incapable of killing?"

"No. I think he could be a dangerous man. But I believe very strongly that he was as much in love with her as she with him. He wouldn't have hurt her, no matter what she did. Even if she decided to marry Tim Fahey to satisfy her parents and keep a family feud from breaking out on the island. Even then, he wouldn't have harmed her."

"Have you ever heard of the Black Hand, Prudence?"

"I've read about them. Aren't they Italian gangsters who extort money in places like Little Italy?"

"They threaten kidnapping or murder if the victim doesn't pay. And they send a letter signed with the symbol of an upraised hand in black ink. Sometimes there's a stiletto piercing the hand."

"What does that have to do with Dominic Pastore?"

"I think his father may be Vincente Pastore. Did you notice the suit he was wearing? The shoes? All handmade and very expensive. Vincente Pastore didn't have two coins to rub together when he came to this country from Sicily. All he had was a reputation. Now he owns one of Staten Island's highest hilltops. He built a house and a compound the police would love to be able to raid. But he doesn't give them any provocation. I don't know how or when your Nora and Vincente's son came together, but she must have known what she was letting herself in for."

"How do you know this, Geoffrey?"

"It goes back to when I was a Pinkerton. I can't talk about the case or who hired us, but I can tell you that Vincente Pastore is probably one of the most lethal men I've ever investigated."

"You're not saying he killed Nora because of Dominic? Please tell me that's not what you mean."

"He doesn't do his own jobs anymore, but Vincente employs men who kill on his orders. It's a possibility we can't ignore."

"I refuse to believe Dominic would ever consent to something like that."

"He wouldn't have known about it, Prudence."

"Nora's parents had no idea who she was involved with. As far as we can tell, no one else did, either."

"A man like Pastore survives because he always has an ear to the ground. He pays well for information. He knows everything about everyone. He was probably told about his son as soon as an informant realized he and Nora were getting serious about one another."

"Then why didn't he put a stop to it? Order Dominic not to see her anymore."

"I imagine he wanted the boy to sow his wild oats, and perhaps he thought he'd come to his senses once the passion burned itself out. Rebellion is not something he would expect from his son."

"Where do you think Tim Fahey is, Geoffrey? Is he even still alive?"

"You heard Dominic say the ocean is deep."

"Are the police that corrupt?"

"I think they have him stashed in a cell somewhere until they decide what to do with him. The third degree didn't break him. Phelan has to be wondering why."

Her thoughts flew to the handsome young Sicilian who might have escaped his father's past if Nora had lived, if they had managed to put Staten Island behind them and start over in a place where no one knew who they were. She imagined Tim Fahey lying on the floor of a freezing cell, determined not to give in to the men who were torturing him, stubbornly refusing to believe that the girl he loved had betrayed him. One life destroyed, two others ruined beyond redemption.

Oh, Nora, what did you get yourself into? What made you do it?

CHAPTER 9

The ferry back to Manhattan was only slightly more crowded than on the outward run, but the wind had picked up enough to discourage passengers from standing on deck. Prudence and Geoffrey settled onto a padded bench in a corner of the main saloon. After the fresh breezes of Staten Island, the indoor cabin air smelled stale and heavy.

"Geoffrey, you told Dominic we had feelers out," Prudence began.

"I exaggerated. Josiah's contacts are all in the court system and mine are largely left over from my Pinkerton days. This isn't the kind of case where those types of informants will do us much good. Our killer is buried too deep."

"Is it possible he hasn't killed before now?" Prudence asked. "That he isn't known to the police because he doesn't have an arrest record?"

"I think that's more likely than not. Career criminals are caught because they repeat themselves too many times. Their modus operandi becomes a recognizable signature. Any detective worth his salt can list dozens of characteristics he uses to weed through any number of suspects. A burglar who always enters through a rear window at a certain time of night, for instance. A pick-pocket who works the same streets over and over again because they're familiar to him and he feels comfortable there. Until he's caught. Murderers repeat themselves, too."

"I was hoping Dominic would be able to tell us something more than we already know."

"Other than informing him she'd be working on Fifth Avenue, Nora kept him in the dark about where she was going and what she planned to do. Deliberately."

"The pregnancy, Geoffrey. It changed everything for her."

"Either she wanted it confirmed and was afraid to go to a doctor or midwife on Staten Island or someone had given her a name and she'd decided to get rid of it."

"Nora was too Catholic for that."

"Religion doesn't matter when you're desperate."

"You saw Dominic's face. He would have

welcomed a child."

"Now that it's too late."

"What do we do next?"

"Ned Hayes. We pay a visit to Ned Hayes."

There'd been a rumor in the bars frequented by New York City coppers that not only was ex-detective Edwin "Ned" Hayes still alive despite the drugs and the drink, but he was mixed up with Billy McGlory again. He'd been seen going into McGlory's Armory Hall Saloon and Casino on Hester Street — going in then coming out all in one piece and looking very pleased with himself — which could only mean that his odd friendship with one of the city's most notorious criminals was on again. Favors had been exchanged, but no one knew for certain what they entailed.

"Your reputation will be in tatters if word leaks out you were here, Miss Prudence," Ned Hayes said. He raised a crystal glass to his unexpected visitors. Geoffrey sipped the Kentucky bourbon Hayes preferred to all other drinks. Prudence had asked for tea.

"If not this it'll be something else," she said. "I'm beginning to realize how heavy a burden maintaining a good reputation can be."

She was also understanding that just as

Ned Hayes had never fit the Tammany mold, and Geoffrey couldn't be shaped into the perfect Pinkerton, neither could she ever become the type of woman her social class demanded she be. Some moments were pivotal in an individual's life; he or she was never the same afterward.

Injustices had eaten away at Ned Hayes until his only option was to resign from the police department before he was booted out. Geoffrey had never divulged the details of his quarrel with Allan Pinkerton, only that neither man had ever forgiven the other. And a fierce, transforming anger had washed over Prudence at Bellevue when she'd looked down at Nora's body.

Prudence felt more akin now to these two men who considered themselves outsiders than to any woman she could name. Life had opened up a field of choices she had never dreamed could be hers to make. She had already decided that docile spouse of a wealthy and domineering husband would not be one of them.

She wondered what her deceased father would say if she could explain it to him.

"There's one person who can get the kind of information you need," Hayes said.

"That's why we came to you."

"Such a compliment, Geoffrey. It betrays

your Southern roots."

"No one else can get anything from him, Ned. You know that's true."

"McGlory can't be held back if he decides to go off on his own. It's a risky chance to take," Hayes cautioned.

"I don't see that we have any choice." Geoffrey wasn't prepared to compromise.

"Miss Prudence?"

"I told Geoffrey that in my opinion the monster who killed Nora is somewhere in Manhattan. It's not her fiancé or the handsome Sicilian she was about to jilt Fahey for. We have no leads, Ned. This man is a bottom feeder; he thrives on evil we can barely imagine. The only way we'll find him is through the kind of information your friend McGlory gathers to stay in business. He wouldn't be able to keep his saloon open if he didn't know who to bribe or blackmail, if he didn't have his finger on the pulse of everyone and everything that's most corrupt in this city."

"I have to warn you again that McGlory is a law unto himself," Hayes insisted. "It would be a grave mistake to believe I can have any influence over him once he sets his mind to something."

"All we're asking is that he pass along to us anything his network of spies and informers hears that could shed some light on why an Irish maid was brutally murdered and then butchered," Geoffrey said. "Someone had to have seen or heard something. Told someone else as the price of a drink."

"Agreed. You'll never find him on your own without help." Hayes swirled the golden brown liquid around in one of the crystal glasses that had come north in his Southern mother's trousseau. Whiskey tasted better when it was drunk out of heavy lead crystal, so there were only a few of the trousseau glasses left. One by one they'd fallen from his numbed fingers and shattered on the floor beside the chair in which he passed out. For almost a year now, he'd been closer to sobriety than he'd been since the black day when the Tammany Hall bosses ordered him off the force. His crime had been to save Billy McGlory's life and see to it the saloon keeper was nursed back to health. Hayes had slipped now and then, but not all the way down, not as far as he'd once plunged.

The drugs still dulled his appetite and kept him far too slender, but his silvery gold hair was clean, curled, and only lightly touched with strands of gray. The deep blue eyes shone clear of broken blood vessels, and the once blotched drunkard's skin was as smooth and unmarked as a baby's bottom. Ned Hayes had been born looking angelic; there hadn't been a year of his life when women weren't irresistibly drawn to him. Not much about his appearance changed as he grew older. Tyrus kept a close eye on him, as faithful in freedom as he'd once been bound in slavery. But if it hadn't been for the cases thrown his way by Geoffrey Hunter, not even old Tyrus's loving sternness could have saved Ned Hayes from the slow death he'd been chasing ever since the war.

"He'll kill again, Ned," Geoffrey said.

"The only thing that will stop him is his own death," Ned agreed. "From what you've told me, he planned the Kenny girl's murder very carefully and in great detail. He's not a stupid man. Far from it. The fact that no one seems to have seen him carrying the body from wherever he killed her to Colonial Park is the least believable part of the whole tale. Someone saw him. He just hasn't stepped out of the shadows yet."

"But you think Billy McGlory can find out who he is?"

"I'm as sure of that as I am that the sun will rise tomorrow and Tyrus will be chiding me not to drink so much." Hayes smiled and set down his glass. "I know what you're

149

going to ask, Miss Prudence. And no, you can't go to Armory Hall to meet Billy Mc-Glory. It's no place for a lady. The police in this city wink at what goes on as long as they get their graft every week, but that doesn't make what they ignore any less dangerous. I'll call in another favor from Billy, but then we'll have to sit back and wait. Eventually he'll decide he's paid his debt to me in full. When that day comes, even I won't dare go to Armory Hall."

"Why should I care if a girl gets herself pregnant and then killed? It happens every day in this city." Billy McGlory ordered only the best French champagne served on Ned Hayes's infrequent visits. He knew the ex-detective's weakness for stronger drink and the drugs he himself never touched. Part of the debt he owed Hayes for saving his life was not to hurry along his disintegration. Champagne was like expensive water to Ned, and now that Tyrus had succeeded in weaning him off the worst of the narcotics, Billy saw to it that when Hayes did buy, he got only the best, uncut with rat poison or talc. He took his obligations seriously.

"A copycat Ripper would be bad for business," Ned said. He thought Billy looked exceptionally prosperous tonight, clad as always in black, with a blindingly large diamond stickpin lighting up his Irish face. Dark eyes and hair, pale skin that never saw the light of day, a thick, sweeping mustache glistening with brilliantine. McGlory was the king of New York vice, but Ned had never seen him drunk, never known him to be anything but in full control of every one of his senses. His one slip had taught him a hard lesson he never forgot.

"What do you mean?"

"Whoever killed Nora Kenny will kill again. And again. The coppers will eventually have to concede to the newspapers that the murders are connected. And when they do, your business will drop like a granite tombstone. Nobody will believe he'll stop at killing just women. Men who don't think twice about coming to the Armory now will decide to stay home rather than risk dark streets and alleyways. Wives will plead with husbands not to leave them alone, and they won't. You'll lose money, Billy, a lot of money. And you won't begin raking it in again until the Ripper copycat is caught and executed. Or killed outright one of these nights."

"And all you want is information?"

"All we want is the service of the eyes and ears that keep you informed about everything that happens on the streets and in the saloons. The brothels, too," Hayes added. "Somebody saw or heard something. You know there's no such thing as the perfect murder. Never has been. Never will be."

"Where are the coppers in all of this?"

"Byrnes wants the murder off his books. A detective named Phelan has arrested the girl's fiancé, a fisherman from Staten Island called Fahey. He's got him stashed somewhere in the Tombs."

"A fisherman?"

"The girl was gutted, Billy. Phelan figures she cheated on Fahey, who's good with a knife. Means, motivation, opportunity. He thinks he's got an open and shut case."

"But you don't agree."

"I'm here because Miss MacKenzie and Geoffrey Hunter have asked for my help."

"And they knew you'd come to me."

"Who else? Nobody in the city has the kind of setup you do."

"I'll think about it, Ned," McGlory said. Which meant he'd more than likely grant Hayes's request.

"I wouldn't ask you to do any more than that, Billy. Just put the word out. See what happens. Wait for someone who saw something to crawl out of his hole."

Both of them knew it wouldn't take long.

■ ■ ■ ■

"What did you see?" Billy McGlory stood at the end of the long bar in Armory Hall. A circle of respectful silence moved with him wherever he went. If you needed or wanted to talk to McGlory you waited until you were invited to approach. Usually, unless you worked for him or you had something he wanted, the summons didn't come.

Kevin Carney had been taking McGlory's nickel since he was twelve years old. He was a small, wiry man, the product of generations of near starvation in Ireland and the fight for survival in the new world's tenements. His usefulness to McGlory was his ability to glide unnoticed through alleyways and into crowds where his acute hearing and gift for repeating word for word whatever he heard made him an invaluable gatherer of knowledge. Bits and pieces of this and that. Who was doing what. Where a man was hiding. Who was taking down his pants and spilling more than his seed. Carney gathered it all up and brought it to McGlory, who paid him what it was worth and sometimes threw in a little extra.

"I was standing across from Saint Anselm's a couple of weeks ago."

153

"Why? Why were you at Saint Anselm's?" You had to interrupt Carney to get at the nuggets of information or he'd blabber on without pausing for breath until you were ready to clobber him. He heard, remembered, and parroted back everything.

"There's an alleyway there we like."

McGlory didn't have to ask who else had been with him because ever since his first days as an abandoned child on the streets, Kevin Carney had eaten and slept with dogs, as wild as they and just as desperate. People said it was his uncannily developed sense of hearing that made him a valuable member of the pack and protected him. Whatever the truth of the stories told about him, Kevin was never without a dog or two at his heels.

"I heard someone coming out of the church." Kevin always heard before he saw. "He was carrying something over his shoulder. I saw it when he passed under a street light. Something wrapped in burlap that smelled like blood. He was leaving a trail anyone could have followed." A scent trail was what he meant.

"Where did this man carrying the bundle over his shoulder go, Kevin?" You had to be very specific, very literal in your questioning.

"To Colonial Park. Straight to the park. He set the bundle down on the ground, then opened the gate. He used a pick, not a key."

"How do you know that?"

"I could hear it, couldn't I? A piece of metal that he worked back and forth until it made a click and the lock opened. A key doesn't make that sound."

"What did he do when he got the gate open?"

"He picked up the bundle and carried it inside."

"And what did you do?"

"Waited in the bushes. He didn't know me and Blossom were there." Kevin and his dog of the moment.

"What happened after the man came out of the park?"

"We let him go. He still smelled like blood, but not as much as before." Kevin's long nose twitched, as though he were sorting through the smells in the air he breathed. "We went along the path. The scent got stronger the closer we got to her. She was a pretty girl, all curly black hair and deep blue eyes. I closed her eyes. It didn't seem right to leave her staring at nothing like that. There's a streetlight right there where he put her. We could see everything."

"Was she still wrapped up?"

"Tight as you please. In burlap. It would have scratched her skin if she'd still been alive."

"You unrolled it?"

"How else would I know what the man did to her?" Kevin's thin face seemed to lengthen as a deep sadness crept over his features. No matter that he'd lived his entire life in the midst of death, he never ceased grieving. "Her throat was sliced all the way across and very deep. He cut her open from the neck down, and scooped out everything inside. I rolled her up again after we looked. She had beautiful white skin in the moonlight. Like those flowers in Central Park that bloom at night."

"Did he say anything, Kevin? Did you hear him mutter or whisper when he was carrying the body or laying it down?"

"Not a word. Not a sound. And we never saw his face. He had something wrapped around it, a scarf maybe. But we got his scent through the blood. He has a strong scent."

"Why didn't you follow him?"

"We had to keep watch, Mr. McGlory, until somebody could find her." Kevin's dogs didn't eat human flesh, at least not while they were with Kevin. But other night-time scavengers did. "A footman came out of one of the houses as the sun was coming up. Walking a little dog. He had a key to the park. We hid in the bushes until he'd found her. The dog he was walking smelled us, but didn't bark. He knew better."

"And then you left."

"We did. We knew she'd be safe. We waited at the end of the block for a while. We saw the police come, the morgue wagon, newspaper reporters."

"Anyone else?"

"A priest. Mr. Hayes's friend and his lady." McGlory had never mentioned their names, so although Carney knew it was Geoffrey Hunter and Prudence MacKenzie he'd seen, he didn't identify them in any but the most oblique way. McGlory would know who he meant.

"Can you pick up the man's scent again?"

Kevin shook his head regretfully. "Not unless he lays down a new trail, Mr. McGlory. It's easier at night, but it needs to start out fresh." He was almost sure Blossom could sort the man's body scent from the heavy cologne he'd doused himself with and the blood that overlay them both, but he wasn't positive enough to promise anything. If you once gave your word to McGlory, he expected you to keep it.

"One more thing, Kevin. Why didn't you

tell me about this before now? Why did you sit on it for so long?"

Kevin shrugged. He had one weakness he didn't want anyone finding out about because a chink in your armor meant death when you lived rough.

He occasionally didn't know where he was; the spells could last for minutes, hours, even days. The streets around him became shrouded in a thick fog that made movement difficult and memory disappear. He slept a lot when the fog rolled in, and when he woke up it took a while to shake it off. Sometimes it was weeks before he remembered where he'd been or what he'd done during the spell. It was like the blackouts that plagued drinking men, but Kevin never touched alcohol. The drink made his arms and legs thrash uncontrollably and his eyes roll back in his head. Eating helped the spells, but he didn't always have enough money to feed both himself and his dog. The dog came first.

This time it had been two weeks before he remembered that the dream of the man carrying the rug hadn't been a dream at all. He'd come straight to Mr. McGlory as soon as the word went out into the streets that the owner of Armory Hall was interested in the Irish girl's killing. It sounded as though he expected another death. Kevin hoped not. Coppers swung their billy clubs at people like him when they were angry, and nothing made them madder than when people blamed them for not keeping the city safe. As if anyone could.

McGlory handed him a roll of bills. Carney stuffed it into a pants pocket without counting the amount. McGlory never bargained.

"It's going to freeze again tonight," McGlory said. He knew about Kevin's problem, of course. Many of the people living on the street suffered spells where they didn't know who or where they were. The spells got worse and then they died. "You'll sleep inside for a change, Kevin. You and the dog both. You can lay a blanket on the floor of the storeroom. I'll give the order."

"We're all right in the alleyway," Kevin said. Neither he nor his animal felt entirely at ease inside a room with a narrow door between them and safety.

"No more argument," McGlory insisted. He had few soft spots in his character, but he had one for Kevin. As did almost everyone who troubled to get to know him. "You can go back to Saint Anselm's tomorrow or the next day." He thought Kevin looked close to collapsing. He'd probably die before spring, but at least McGlory could help him stay alive for a little while longer. "Keep your ears open when you get there, Kevin. Wait for the man with the rug to come again. It may take a while. I need to know what his name is, where he lives. You'll have to follow him. Stay far enough behind so he doesn't hear your footsteps."

Kevin could follow a deer stepping lightly through the spring grass of Central Park. The sound of a man's feet slapping against pavement was no challenge at all. It was an insult to tell him to be careful; he wouldn't have taken it from anyone but Billy McGlory.

Outside Armory Hall a large red dog of indeterminate but shaggy breed rose to her feet. She followed Kevin Carney inside and down a long, dark hallway to the rear of the building where the kitchens were. Scraps had been laid out on a table for her human and in a bowl on the floor for her. Blossom could smell the bills in her human's pocket and knew they meant food that didn't have to be scavenged.

Tomorrow or the next day, Kevin told her, after they'd eaten and slept, they'd go back to the alleyway. They'd lie in wait. Or maybe they'd hunt.

It didn't matter to the red dog as long as the two of them were together.

CHAPTER 10

Stepping out is what you did when your gentleman caller became a regular, though most of the time Mick McGuire didn't come for Ellen Tierney at the house. It wouldn't do for a policeman to be seen going into the Nolan mansion off Fifth Avenue, even if it was via the areaway steps or the stable yard, and Mick was seldom out of uniform. He liked the military feel of the long, dark blue single breasted frock coat, the domed felt covered helmet, and the shiny eight pointed star badge. He'd paid three hundred dollars for his patrolman's job and was extorting as much as the traffic would bear to acquire the fourteen hundred dollars it cost to buy a promotion to the rank of sergeant.

New York City was a wonderful place for an Irishman to be a copper. With one hand twirling a billy club and the other held out for bribes, a man could stroll his beat and feel like a man. Half the city seemed to be Irish, though it was mostly still the half that lived in the tenements and the luckier ones trying to claw their way up through the ranks of Tammany Hall.

Ellen was a fine girl, a beautiful girl with masses of red gold hair tucked up so tightly under her white maid's cap that not a single wisp escaped when she was working. But Mick had run his huge fingers through the curly strands that glowed in lamplight like a fiery sunset. They twisted and twirled themselves tightly around his policeman's perpetually bruised knuckles. He'd had his way with her more times than either of them could count. She'd nearly cried her beautiful blue eyes out when he'd hammered his way through her virginity, but then he'd wiped away the tears and stroked her into a bliss she'd never dreamed existed. After that she was as eager as he to repeat the experience. The only privacy they had was in the room he rented from a respectable Irish widow who tolerated no nonsense from her boarders and searched their lodgings every day after they'd left for work.

It wasn't so much that Mrs. Ansbro trusted Mick the man as that she allowed herself to be seduced by the beautiful uniform, the shiny star, and the air of authority with which he walked his beat. His presence meant that every neighborhood crook with half a grain of sense avoided her boarding house like the plague. A tenant could forget to lock his door in the morning and return home in the evening to find all of his belongings exactly as he had left them. So when Patrolman McGuire escorted a young lady into Mrs. Ansbro's front parlor as she was setting out on her afternoon errands, she refused to entertain suspicions about her private protector. Which made it dead easy for Mick to guide Ellen up the stairs and into his immaculate room where the sheets were clean, the floor swept, and the chamber pot emptied.

"When we're married," Ellen whispered, not noticing the stiffening of Mick's muscular arm. "When we're married . . ." She sighed with the joy of it, the warmth of belonging to someone, the full belly feeling of security that the sight of his uniform always gave her. They wouldn't be limited to her one afternoon a week off and the hours she stole when the family was out and the housekeeper in a generous mood. They could be together every night, wrapped in each other's arms between supper and dawn, waking every now and then to the delights of carnal knowledge made lawful by the sacrament of matrimony.

Marriage wasn't in Mick McGuire's plan for his future. Not now, and not for years to come. Marriage inevitably meant children, and Mick had handled enough squalling infants who smelled of piss and shit and sour milk to last him a lifetime. He usually remembered to pull out and spill his seed on Ellen's lovely belly. When she protested that the Church would not approve, he assured her that not only did the Church give its blessing to such a sensible precaution, it encouraged it. She was ignorant and naive enough to believe him. *When we're married* froze the blood in his veins and set his mind racing for a way out of the box whose lid he could sense closing down on him.

"I'm being transferred," he told her.

"What does that mean?"

"It means I'll be working in another part of the city. Longer hours, too. But it's a way of getting on, of making my way up the ladder, don't you know."

Ellen tried to grope her way through what Mick was saying. Her heart thudded painfully and she felt a terrible soreness in the depths of her stomach, as though she'd eaten a cream tart that had turned. "But you'll keep your room here at Mrs. Ansbro's, won't you?" she asked.

"For the time being, yes. And maybe I won't have to move at all. We'll just have to see, won't we?"

Which sounded to Ellen a lot more like a warning than a promise.

"I don't know what I'd do without you, Mick," she murmured, running her fingertips across his broad chest and thick mat of black hair.

"Well, you won't have to, will you?" he said, thinking all the while that the sooner he packed his things and got out of Mrs. Ansbro's boarding house the better. He'd leave a letter behind, with just enough of a grain of truth in the lies to make it believable. He had to map out a plan though, before he broke Ellen Tierney's heart; Mick McGuire never did anything without a plan. So he wrapped his arms around her and crooned the tune his mother sang to lull the babies to sleep back in the old country until he felt Ellen's breathing grow slow and deep and even.

He was thinking furiously.

Ellen Tierney knew you couldn't go to Holy Communion in a state of mortal sin without risking hell for all eternity. But tomorrow was the fifth anniversary of her mother's death; she'd promised herself she'd light a candle and receive the Host in memory of the woman who'd wept bitter tears when she lost her youngest daughter to America.

There was no help for it. She'd have to ask Mrs. Flynn for permission to go to Saint Anselm's again tonight after the servants' early supper. She'd hoped she didn't get the same priest as last time. The bright red hair made her too easily remembered and she didn't think she could stand the embarrassment if he recognized her. Father Brennan was the kind of priest who asked questions.

She had another errand she couldn't put off any longer, and there'd be just enough time to get it done, go to confession, and run back to the Nolan mansion without arousing Mrs. Flynn's suspicions. She'd have to time it all carefully, but Ellen was used to juggling several jobs at once. It was one of the things that made her a good housemaid.

The only real shortcoming Ellen had was that she wasn't a fancy seamstress; she'd only ever been able to manage a decent hem or the occasional darn when she set her mind to it, and even then the stitches weren't always straight and even. Her mind tended to wander, and when it did, her needle went off in odd directions, too, which was why she had to make a quick detour on her way to Saint Anselm's. She could hardly breathe, the bodice and waist on her good uniform had gotten that tight, and Mrs. Flynn had a keen eye. All those tucks and darts required to make a smooth fit over the corset. It wasn't the kind of sewing she could manage on her own, but it wouldn't do for anything to be noticed before she was ready to make her grand exit from the Nolan household as a woman about to be married.

She already had a bottom drawer half full of discarded bed linens and table napkins, even a lace curtain worn thin where the sun shone through a window. Mrs. Nolan and Miss Alice were generous with what they didn't want anymore. Mrs. Flynn said it was because they were Irish too, though born in America and into money. Which just proved it could be done, that all of the dreams Ellen had had on the boat coming over could become reality, present situation notwithstanding. She might not ever live in a fine mansion, but Ellen would have her respectable husband, her own house, and a family of fine sons and daughters to show off to the rest of the neighborhood at Sunday Mass every week. And that reminded her. Her back and belly didn't ache, but it was two months now and there was still no bleeding. She needed to count the days again.

"Are you sure there's not something you ought to be telling me, Ellen?" Mrs. Flynn was in a good mood this afternoon. Her household accounts had balanced the first time she totted them up, and she'd managed to keep within the amount Mrs. Nolan allotted her each week.

"Why is that, Mrs. Flynn?"

"The singing. You've been humming and purring away to yourself like Mrs. Nolan's old black cat. I'd swear it was him making that great noise he does when he's having his belly rubbed. Is it to do with Mr. McGuire?"

"You won't be angry?"

"How will I know unless you tell me what it is?"

"He's being transferred to a different and larger precinct. Promoted, I call it. He was keeping the secret until he was sure it would happen. For fear of jinxing it, you know. He hasn't proposed yet, not in a formal kind of way, but if there's more money coming in, I think he will."

"I don't have to ask if you'll accept. I can tell by your face and that awful noise coming out of you. I pity the children who have to listen to the lullabies you'll croak at them."

"I will accept, Mrs. Flynn. I'd be a fool not to."

"So you would, girl. You don't want to stay someone's maid all your days when you could be a policeman's wife."

"You won't say anything to anyone yet?"

"Not until you tell me. For fear of jinxing it." Mrs. Flynn smiled to show she was joking.

"No fear of that. No fear of that at all."

"Is that the way of it then?"

"I'm sure I don't know what you mean, Mrs. Flynn."

"And I'm just as sure you do. Nobody much remembers to count the months after a few years have gone by."

"Mick says he thinks the transfer will happen soon."

"That's all to the good then. You don't want to cut it too close. You don't want them upstairs to find out."

"I'm not even sure myself, to tell the truth."

"The longer you can keep it that way the better, I say. You never know how a man will take that kind of news."

"I know my Mick."

"I hope you do, child. I hope you do."

■ ■ ■ ■

When Ellen asked permission to go to Saint Anselm's for late Saturday afternoon confession, Mrs. Flynn shooed the girl out of the house with a wave of her hand and the admonition to hurry back. It was on the tip of her tongue to warn her to watch out for Mr. Joseph, but at the last minute she decided to say nothing. Mr. Joseph was an odd one, but so was every other member of the Nolan family.

They all thought they kept their secrets to themselves, which just went to prove how new their money was. Old society families knew that nothing could be hidden from household staff. The difference was they didn't try because they didn't care what servants thought.

Miss Alice stayed up until all hours of the night praying her novenas, wanting to become a nun and pestering her father to give his permission when the man was dead set against it. You couldn't look at her thin body and doleful face without feeling sorry for her because you knew she'd never get the only thing she wanted in life.

Mrs. Nolan thought her flirtation with laudanum went unremarked. It didn't. She lost track of the little brown bottles, left them where the maids were bound to come across one as they dusted. Being Irish herself, the housekeeper knew that Lillian Nolan's social ambitions were doomed to failure. It would take more than one generation to forget the family's origins, and nothing could erase the stigma of being Catholic.

Mr. Nolan was cold, so tightly wound you'd swear you could hear him tick. A cruel man. He found fault with everything Mr. Joseph did, mocked Miss Alice's desperate devotions, and had never forgiven his wife Lillian for her uncertain womb. Everyone knew he'd started life as a butcher, wallowing in the blood and guts of the slaughterhouses. There was something about a man whose profession was killing that set your teeth to chattering when he looked at you a certain way. No matter how well he washed, he was still bathed in blood.

Mr. Joseph was the prince of oddness, cocooned inside a flinty shell where no one could reach him. He carried on his father's business, rarely spoke to the sister to whom he had once been close, and scorned the woman who had given birth to him. There were times when his eyes flashed rebellion, but eventually, in the housekeeper's opinion, he would have to give in to the pressure to marry. That would be the saving of him. Domesticity would wear him down. He'd grow a paunch and find a mistress. So far he'd ignored the maids, but Mrs. Flynn was careful to keep them away from him. You never knew when a gentleman would start demanding what he felt was his due.

The young master probably wouldn't recognize Ellen if he saw her at Saint Anselm's. Maids were supposed to be invisible creatures; Mrs. Flynn didn't think Ellen had done anything to attract Mr. Joseph's attention.

"You ask me, that Ellen's going to confession more than she should need to." Sadie Curran, who had cooked for the Nolans since they'd moved onto Fifth Avenue, stood in the kitchen doorway, hands on her ample hips, watching the young maid walk briskly down the street. "I hope she's not in trouble, Moira."

"Mick's a good man," Mrs. Flynn said. "He'll do right by her. Now let's finish our tea before it gets cold."

"Bless me, Father, for I have sinned. It's been two weeks since my last confession."

A young voice. Female. Trembling with either fear or embarrassment. Probably both. Which meant she was about to confess to having committed sins of the flesh. That's the way it was always phrased. *Acts of impurity. Sins of the flesh.* The men tended to use more descriptive words. Not the women. They whispered and sometimes they wept.

"*Miseratur tui omnipotens Deus, et dimissis peccatis tuis, perducat te ad vitam aeternam.* Amen." Father Brennan took care not to slur the Latin syllables, not to rush through the formula, though he was certain the tearful young woman he could glimpse through the cloth covered wooden screen understood not a word of what he was saying. The sound of the Latin was enough to comfort and reassure her. *May almighty God have mercy on you, forgive you your sins, and lead you to life everlasting. Amen.*

"Father, I've committed a sin of the flesh."

"How many times, my child? More than once?"

"Yes, Father. More than once."

"With yourself or with someone else?"

"With a man, Father." She sounded shocked that he would even ask.

"Is either of you married?"

"No, Father."

He caught a flash of white as the penitent wiped her eyes and her nose with a handkerchief. She folded her hands on the ledge beneath the window with its sliding wooden screen and sighed. He knew what she was thinking. The worst was over. She'd gotten the words out and now all she needed was the penance and absolution.

"Say a rosary to Our Blessed Mother, Queen of Virgins, and come to early Mass tomorrow morning to receive Communion. Can you do that?"

"Yes, Father. They're all Catholic at the house, even the family, so there's never any trouble getting to Sunday Mass."

A maid then, probably in one of the mansions along Fifth Avenue. He wondered if she'd been caught in an empty room by the son of the house. She'd have hopes and expectations; they always did, before they were tossed aside. None of them ever learned.

"*Ego te absolvo a peccatis tuis, in nomine Patris, et Filii, et Spiritus Sancti.* Amen." He made the sign of the cross as carefully as he pronounced the words of absolution. Father Brennan was not a priest who hurried through the sacred rituals of his calling.

As he leaned forward to close the sliding wood panel he caught a glimpse of glorious Irish red hair peeping out beneath the scarf the young woman had knotted over her head. She'd whispered her confession to disguise her voice, but everything else about her was familiar.

He knew who she was.

Ellen sensed Joseph Nolan's presence in the church the moment she stepped from the confessional booth and turned toward the main altar. She always knew where he was; it was like the warning buzz of an angry bee just before it sank its stinger into you. Something about him made her uneasy. He smelled of a cologne not unlike the incense that made her dizzy at High Mass when the servers swung their censors too vigorously and clouds of perfumed smoke billowed out into the church.

She'd never dared say it to anyone, but Ellen thought Mr. Joseph looked like one of the warrior angels who had fought against Saint Michael the Archangel and lost. The bad angels were sent down into the depths of hell; they grew horns and tails and tended the fires where souls who died in a state of mortal sin burned for all eternity. That's what he looked like, one of those bad angels who became a devil, the one about to battle Saint Michael in the church's largest stained glass window. Too handsome for his own good, tall and muscular, hair as black as night, eyes as blue as the sky, skin that glowed golden in the summer and was as pale and perfect as new-fallen snow in the winter.

Mr. Joseph had never been accused of being too familiar with the maids, but Ellen didn't trust him nonetheless. He might go to daily Mass and keep a rosary in his trouser pocket, but there was something about him that made her skin quiver and rise up in goose bumps. The whole Nolan family was strange.

What struck her when she first began maiding for them was how little they had to say to one another, how devoid of laughter or tenderness their speech was when they did talk. A master and mistress shouldn't sleep in separate bedrooms, their linens never showing signs of the kind of intimacy it had been impossible to conceal in the tiny cottage where the entire Tierney family shared two rooms.

All of the Nolans left food on their plates at every meal, and sometimes Miss Alice ate nothing at all. She moved meat and vegetables around so it looked as though they'd been tasted, but very little made it to her mouth. Ellen still stole the tastiest morsels before the scullery maid scraped the family's leftovers into the garbage pail.

The Nolans reminded her of the stone statues in her parish church back home, standing in silent judgment on poor petitioners who laid candle stubs and wildflowers at their feet. She'd been afraid of the statues when she was young enough to believe they could step down from their pedestals to chastise her, and she was afraid of Mr. Joseph for much the same reason. He didn't seem wholly human and what he might do next was unpredictable.

She'd be glad to trade her tiny attic room in the big house for whatever Mick could provide for them. The sooner the better, she thought, wondering if today, when she made her confession, she ought to have whispered her suspicion of what might be growing inside her.

Mrs. Flynn had hinted at it, but so far Ellen hadn't been foolish or desperate enough to confide in her. Maids who got themselves in the family way were out the door in the wink of an eye, no matter how motherly the housekeeper seemed to be.

In the way of the world, it was always the woman who got blamed.

CHAPTER 11

Now that she was no longer in a state of mortal sin, Ellen Tierney drank an extra cup of late evening tea and planned out her Sunday. She would go to early morning Mass at Saint Anselm's, light the candle for her mother, receive Communion, and be back before the missus and the young miss rang their bells. Every Sunday the Nolans went up to 50th Street for High Mass at Saint Patrick's Cathedral, the ten-year-old gothic wonder said to rival anything Europe had ever built. The house was quiet while they were out praying with the rest of New York City's socially prominent Catholics.

Once the family dinner had been served and cleared, she'd be free to spend the afternoon in Central Park with Colleen. Mick was on patrol, and maybe it was just as well. Ellen had been neglecting her friend lately. There'd been a time when there were no secrets between them and no thought of hiding anything. Lately though, she'd been reluctant to take Colleen into her confidence. She was in love with Mick and on the verge of starting a new life with him; it might be a breach of trust to share with a girlfriend what she was feeling. Oh, but she yearned to tell Colleen everything, to see her eyes widen and blink with disbelief and shock. There was so much Colleen didn't know that Ellen could describe and relive in the telling. Was it a sin to talk about it? Never mind. She'd say a rosary and hope for the best.

She'd felt guilty suggesting to Colleen that an afternoon in Central Park would do her a world of good, but Mrs. Flynn had encouraged her.

"Sure and hasn't she had a terrible time of it the past two weeks, with that Nora Kenny being murdered the way she was," the housekeeper had said. "Cook heard from the MacKenzie cook that the Kenny girl was supposed to share Colleen's room the night it happened. They'd gotten to be good friends over the last few years. Every time Nora and her mother came from Staten Island, Nora stayed with Colleen. Cook says Mrs. Hearne thought she was a sweet girl. And about to get married. Such a shame."

"You don't think Colleen would feel we were desecrating Nora's memory?"

"You knew her too, didn't you?"

"Not nearly as well as Colleen. Nora came out with us once when she was working at Miss Prudence's and it was our half day."

"The Church tells us not to mourn too long for someone we've lost. Nora is in heaven now, where we all hope to be some day. Colleen has lost one friend; she needs you more than she may realize."

So it had been decided. They'd go out to Central Park together, stroll the pathways, watch the children at play, maybe go as far as the Carousel. Both girls loved the rise and fall of the brightly painted horses and the sound of the music blaring out from the spinning platform. It was shut down on really cold winter days, but it might be open and running tomorrow. They'd take a chance and walk that way.

Ellen finished her last cup of tea for the day and slipped her hand beneath her white apron into the pocket of her black uniform dress.

Her rosary wasn't there.

It was always there, always with her every minute of the day and night, since the moment her mother pressed it into the palm of her hand before she'd left home to catch the boat to America. Frantic, she scrabbled her fingers around the empty pocket, feeling for the beads and the small silver crucifix, searching for a hole through which the rosary might have dropped to the floor. Nothing.

With a murmured excuse, she pushed her chair back from the table and ran up the back staircase to her small attic bedroom. She slept with the rosary curled beneath her pillow, so perhaps it was still there. Maybe she'd been thinking so hard about Mick when she got up this morning that she'd forgotten to put it into her pocket where it belonged. Nothing. The sheet beneath the pillow was cool and flat, and even though she tore the covers from the narrow bed and looked under the mattress and beneath the rag rug she found nothing.

"I've lost my rosary," she announced when she came back downstairs, panic and tears nearly choking her.

Hands fluttered in the sign of the cross; all of the servants in the Nolan household were Catholic. Tired at the end of the day, they were drinking a final cup of tea or hot chocolate in the servants' hall before going up to bed. Their days began hours before the family awoke and didn't end until they were certain the bells wouldn't ring again.

It was nearly eleven o'clock. The younger maids and menservants were nodding in their chairs, their elders postponing the moment they would have to haul their aching bones up four flights of stairs to their attic rooms.

"Did you have it when you got back from going to church this afternoon?" Mrs. Flynn understood Ellen's fears; she too had a rosary given her long ago in Ireland by a mother she'd never seen again after the boat sailed. "Did you have it in your hand when you went to confession?"

"Yes. No. I'm not sure. I think so." Ellen couldn't remember much of what happened in Saint Anselm's after she'd seen Mr. Joseph Nolan there. She thought she recalled the feel of the beads slipping through her fingers as she counted off the Hail Marys of her penance before the main altar.

But had she put the rosary back into her pocket when she finished? All she could remember was seeing Mr. Joseph and feeling his gaze linger on her as she stood up from the altar rail and turned around. She could picture herself making a quick sign of the cross and a sketchy genuflection, but she could not glimpse the rosary beads. Her hand looked empty in her mind's memory. So if the beads weren't in her pocket, she'd definitely dropped them at the altar rail.

"That's all right, then, Ellen. If you dropped them in the church, someone's likely to find them and put them in the Lost and Found basket in the vestibule. They'll be there in the morning when you go to Mass, you'll see." Mrs. Flynn touched the maid's arm lightly as she made her way toward the stairs. "Off to bed with you now. You can say your prayers on your fingers. Our Lady won't mind."

The last one to leave the basement was Mr. Tynan, the butler. He'd locked the doors on the main floor; now he shot the bolt on the kitchen door and checked the catches on the windows. He left one gas light burning low in the hallway at the foot of the stairs, looked around to be sure nothing and no one had been overlooked, then began the long climb to his bed. Half an hour later he was deeply asleep, confident that everyone under his charge would make it safely through the night.

Ellen waited until she could hear the steady bass rumble of snoring from the men's end of the corridor, the higher pitched noises made by the exhausted women in the rooms on either side of her. She'd lain down on her bed fully dressed except for her outdoor boots, which she carried in one hand as she crept stealthily down the four flights of uncarpeted stairs to the basement kitchen and servants' hall. The house was dark and silent. Here and there was the faint flicker of a damped gas light, but Ellen was too determined to be afraid. She knew every room in the Nolan house as well as she knew the lines in the palm of her hand; hadn't she cleaned and dusted and polished those rooms often enough? The bolt on the kitchen door shot open without so much as a squeak. She relocked the area-way door from the outside and put the key in her pocket, tapping it three times for good luck and to make sure it was there for when she came back.

Shawl wrapped tightly around her upper body, she walked quickly down the street toward Saint Anselm's. The large main doors of the church were locked at night, but one of the small side doors was left unsecured. God's House must always welcome the sinner or the saint. If you were Catholic, you knew there'd be a way left open for you to reach the altar. It wouldn't take more than a couple of minutes to dart inside and check the Lost and Found basket. Then she could spend the rest of the night tucked up in her own bed with the precious rosary safe in her hand. For once she wouldn't slide it under the pillow.

She should have put on a coat as well as grabbing the shawl from her hook in the boot room. It was cold tonight, though thank God there wasn't a wind. The sky was black and clear, with stars twinkling in its depths. Perhaps the Star of Bethlehem had risen far off to the east somewhere, ready to lead the Three Kings across deserts to the Christ Child. It was lovely to think about Christmas coming and the Holy Baby. She touched a tentative hand to her belly, wondering if it could be true that an infant was beginning to grow in there. It would be a boy, she thought, with Mick's black hair and blue eyes, to grow up strong and tall like his father. She wanted her rosary. She had prayers to say. A girl needed her mother when she got in the family way; holding the beads in her fingers was like clasping her mother's hand.

When Ellen reached the rectory beside the church, she paused for a moment, looking for lights that would indicate one of the priests was still awake. They were out at all hours, bringing Extreme Unction to the bedsides of the dying, hearing last confessions, and slipping the Holy Sacrament between cracked lips. She'd knelt by many a deathbed in Ireland while the priest intoned the prayers to send a soul home to God. They were good men, most of them, holy men, with only now and then a drunk or a womanizer to disgrace the cloth. Tonight the rectory was as dark as the Nolan mansion had been, the faintest of gas lights glowing deep in a hallway.

She patted the key in her pocket again, three times for luck. Before she could take another step forward she heard a scraping sound behind her. Like the sole of a shoe gliding over the rough concrete of the sidewalk, grating against loose pebbles before it came to a stop. Ellen turned to peer down the street, her eyes skipping from one lamp pole to the next, searching the pools of light for shadows that shouldn't be there. The sidewalk in front of Saint Anselm's church and rectory was always clean swept, no papers drifting along, no cigar butts nestled in the cracks, no piles of horse dung allowed to remain at the curbside. No one was out this late, no one but she alone. And perhaps a cat or two prowling the alleyways.

Shaking out her shawl, Ellen wrapped it around her shoulders again, tighter this time against the cold and the frisson of fear that had set her quivering. Mick told her she'd nothing to worry about in this part of town;

the swells who lived here wouldn't tolerate what humbler New Yorkers had to put up with. Between the Metropolitan Police and the private agencies rich men hired to protect their homes and businesses, it was safer and more profitable for burglars to keep to other neighborhoods. Being assigned to a lower Fifth Avenue beat was every copper's dream. She forced herself to smile; her mother said that if you smiled the devil passed you by.

She heard the scraping sound again as she reached for the iron handle of the door that opened into one of Saint Anselm's side aisles. This time she didn't pause to look; she yanked open the door and slammed it shut behind her, fingers groping to turn the key in the lock. It wasn't there. There was no key, no bolt to slide across to bar entrance to whoever or whatever might be outside. Now the scraping sound settled into the steady rhythm of footsteps someone was no longer bothering to soften. She heard them begin to mount the steps.

Before a hand could reach for the door latch, Ellen whirled and fled across the altar to the sacristy. Surely the door to the room where priestly vestments and gold altar vessels were stored would have a key to secure it against intruders. Not until she saw the empty lock did she realize that she was on the wrong side.

Up the center aisle she ran, too frightened to wonder if she were no longer alone inside Saint Anselm's. She reached the swinging doors leading to the main vestibule. Moments before she pushed her way through them she heard the side door open, felt a cold draft of outside air strike her back. Sobbing now, hiccupping tears and phlegm, she slammed through the thick wooden doors into the vestibule where racks of pamphlets stood against the walls and notices were pinned on every available surface.

She hurled herself against the outside doors, expecting them to open the way they did after Mass when the congregation surged out of the church, but they didn't move. Her shoulders ached as she thudded repeatedly against the iron studded doors. They didn't give an inch.

To one side of the vestibule was the dark opening of the staircase that wound up into the belfry. It was her last chance. As she ran toward it, she saw the pale silver gleam of a crucifix in the bottom of the wicker Lost and Found basket. Her rosary. She stopped for a moment to scoop it into her hand, kissed the crucifix. She felt the first steps of the belfry staircase beneath her feet before something or someone knocked her to her knees. Fingers twined themselves into her glorious red hair; the hand that cupped her skull raised her head above the stone steps.

There wasn't time to gasp out a last prayer before the loud crack, the terrible pain, and the final darkness descended.

CHAPTER 12

The carriage wouldn't be needed until midmorning, but if he was to hear Mass himself this Sunday, Jack Scully, the Nolan coachman, would have to be at Saint Anselm's by six o'clock at the latest. There'd be breakfast to eat afterwards and the horses to curry so they'd look their best on the drive up Fifth Avenue to Saint Patrick's. Mr. Nolan was a fiend about putting on a fine show, though everyone knew he'd started out with a bloody apron over his belly and a butcher knife in his hand. There was no one like a Mick for dressing up fine as a king and putting on airs, Jack thought as he whistled his way down the stairs from his room above the stable. He could say it, being as Irish as Paddy's pig himself, but God help anyone else who tried to put them down. Being good with the fists was necessary to survival in this new world.

The horses heard his footsteps and his

whistling. They stomped their hooves and neighed softly, knowing he'd check their water troughs and hay racks before crossing the yard to his own food and drink. He'd run a firm hand over their withers, touch his forehead to the broad flat spot between their eyes, and whisper something only he and they would understand. Jack Scully was a horseman born and bred; his charges knew he was as much one of them as a two legged beast could be. They loved and trusted him, and he they.

They'd been restless since the first scent of blood wafted through the wooden stable doors in the darkness of the night, but there hadn't been much of it, and as the wet November air weighed it down, they'd settled again. Only now and then did one of the four huge carriage horses shake his head to rid himself of the hint of metallic liquid tugging at his nostrils. They were used to the smell of vermin blood; human blood, though not unknown, was rarer and therefore more worrisome to them.

"All right, lads, we're off to the cathedral this morning, so you'll have to step high and look lively." Scully poured fresh water into the troughs from the large barrel he kept full and clean inside the stable. He scooped hay from the racks, brought it to his nose, and sniffed appreciatively. A sour smell meant there'd be sick animals to treat, but the horses in Jack's charge never had to snuffle their way through damp or rancid feed. Grain and hay were as dry and fragrant in November as they were when freshly harvested from the fields. He petted and stroked, chatted and sang softly to each animal so there'd be no jealousy between them and all four would pull together as one later on.

Start the morning right and the rest of the day will take care of itself, his da used to say as he worked the peat bog that was his livelihood. It was an admonition Jack never forgot, not even when he'd traveled three thousand miles and a world away from where he should have been able to stay . . . if it hadn't been for the famine . . . or for what the English did to his people and his country. Poverty ground you into rags and bone, left you no choice but to learn another way to live or find someplace where you stood a chance of struggling back onto your own two legs again. *Never mind.* Sometimes he thought too much about the past.

He stood for a moment at the stable door, looking and listening, then closed and barred it behind him. He could see lights on in the kitchen windows across the cobbled yard and fancied he could smell strong tea steeping and coffee boiling. Sunday morning meant more than a dish of oatmeal. Rashers of thick bacon and eggs fried so the whites were crisp and the yolks runny. Mounds of potatoes cooked with onions and lumps of sweet butter. Bread fresh from the oven, slathered with jam and honey. He could taste the goodness of it all through the purse of his lips, his mouth watering too much now to whistle.

It was still dark, but the kitchen windows cast light onto the cobblestones that stretched from the rear of the Nolan mansion to the stables. Those windows, lower sash tops level with the pavement, were the only source of daylight in the basement rooms. The house had been electrified, but Mr. Nolan considered one dim bulb hanging from the ceiling more than adequate illumination. He was stingy that way. Gas and oil lamps were good enough if more light were needed, and keeping the glass reservoirs cleaned and filled would take care of any idle time that might come a servant's way. A man didn't become rich by being careless with pennies.

Halfway across the yard someone had forgotten to take in a newly beaten carpet, or perhaps a bundle set out for the ragman had rolled away from the top of the staircase. Jack could just make out the shape of it in the early wintry gloom. He'd pick it up, whatever it was, and not say anything to Mrs. Flynn, saving one of the maids from the housekeeper's scolding she no doubt deserved. It would be his good deed for the day. The younger servants were always tired, still growing but working as hard and as long hours as the adults. He remembered the despair and the fatigue he'd known when he was fourteen. Only being near horses all day had saved him from taking up the drink. You couldn't fall into a stupor when there were animals depending on you.

Strange. The rug or bundle of rags had a shape to it that shouldn't have reminded him of the curves of a woman's waist and hips, shouldn't have tapered down to the slenderness of legs. The sudden November gust skittering across the cobblestones shouldn't have picked up strands of bright hair and waved them in the cold, damp wind.

Holy Mary, Mother of God. It was a girl lying on the ground, a girl who had to be dead or dying from the stillness of her. He ran the last few steps to Ellen Tierney's body and knelt beside it, knowing as soon as one hand touched the cold cheek that life had left her hours ago. While everyone else in the Nolan household slept, she'd gone to her death.

Poor Ellen. She'd been so happy these last few weeks, with her great secret that everyone with a grain of sense could guess, and a future every other maid in the house envied. A policeman's wife. She was supposed to be a policeman's wife, not a body on a mortuary slab.

He crossed himself and gabbled a Hail Mary. It was the best he could do under the circumstances; the priest would give her the last rites. Conditional. In case the soul was lingering. Phrases from catechism classes flashed through his memory as he rose to his feet and sprinted the few yards to the basement stairs and the kitchen door.

Scully's hand was on the doorknob when he stopped dead in his tracks. *Nora Kenny.*

Just a few doors down the street at Miss MacKenzie's. Come from Staten Island as she and her mother had done many a time to help with heavy holiday cleaning. But this time, two weeks ago today, Nora had been found dead in Colonial Park. Five days after that, the man she was supposed to marry had been arrested for her murder.

Kincaid had told him what he knew, which wasn't much, but coachmen were a closely knit fraternity of men sharing a love of horses and a tolerance for being outside in all weathers. He'd said Miss Prudence and her friend Mr. Hunter had gone to Colonial Park to identify the body and that later, after the funeral, he'd overheard them talking about someone getting the third degree. What was the man's name? Irish, of course, because Nora Kenny was Irish. *Fahey.* Tim Fahey, that was it. According to Kincaid, the boyo wasn't guilty. Miss Prudence and Mr. Hunter had promised Nora's mother they'd find the man who'd murdered her daughter.

What else, what else? There'd been only a few lines in the newspapers when the Kenny girl was killed, a few more when Fahey was arrested, but none of the details that usually enlivened a crime story. Which everyone had thought a bit strange at the time, but then forgot about when the killing turned out to be another lovers' quarrel gone bad.

That wasn't all, though. Kincaid had said something else. It was niggling at the edge of Scully's memory. Something about the way the body had been wrapped up. *Wrapped up. Hessian. Burlap. Like a giant cocoon.* He was positive that's what Kincaid had described. And now Ellen.

Scully wasn't mistaken. The material he'd

touched was the kind of rough burlap sacking used to bag the oats, corn, and barley he mixed and fed the horses every day.

The hair on the back of his neck itched furiously. He'd get word to Kincaid as soon as he could, and leave it to the MacKenzie coachman to inform Miss Prudence. Two Irish maids killed just two weeks apart, both of them enveloped in burlap. If there hadn't been anything in the papers describing how Nora Kenny was found, then only the man who'd killed her would know about the burlap wrapping.

Jack Scully didn't like what he was thinking, and he'd never trusted the police. Not in Ireland, and not in America either. He had a feeling Mr. Nolan would be furious if he found out that his coachman had opened his big mouth, but he also knew he was going to find a way to get word up the street to Kincaid.

Now he had to break the news to the butler.

"Mr. Tynan," Jack said as evenly as he could manage. "Will you step outside into the yard with me for a moment? There's something I think you'll need to attend to."

"I'll have to tell the master right away," Tynan said. Like Jack, he'd touched Ellen

Tierney's frigid cheek, then drawn his hand back from the feel of death.

Both men knelt beside the hessian-wrapped corpse; both got quickly to their feet. The maid they'd drunk tea with the evening before was plainly dead; terrible damage had been done to her skull, though the side of her face they could see below the forehead was as lovely as always. The bright red hair she'd had to conceal beneath a starched cap spread stiff and blackened with blood beneath her head, a macabre pillow softening her resting place on the cobblestones. She lay on her side, her body wound tightly in a makeshift shroud, neck hidden, only the head showing. A cord had been tied tightly around the bundle. No telling what lay beneath the loose weave of the hessian cloth; it was not their place to look.

"Stay with her, Jack."

"Will you wake him?"

"I'll have to now, won't I?" Tynan blew on his hands against the early morning cold. Mr. Nolan had a fearsome temper, never more so than when something out of the ordinary disturbed the rigid routine he imposed on his household. "There's no help for it."

Tynan turned and strode across the cobblestones to the house, leaving Jack alone with his discovery. Light from the kitchen streamed out through the opened door then disappeared again.

To the east, Jack could make out a dark grayness slowly turning lighter. It would be dawn soon, a day poor Ellen hadn't lived to see. He didn't dare leave her to fetch himself a coat or a blanket to wrap around his shoulders, so he stomped his feet and beat his arms around his torso. The horses sensed something was not as it should be; he could hear their restless rubbings against the wood sides of their stalls. Mr. Tynan must have forbidden any of the other servants from coming out into the yard; heads bobbed up and down at the windows, but no one climbed the kitchen stairs to keep Jack company. No one dared defy the butler's orders.

Mick McGuire. Mr. Nolan would have to call in the police, but surely it wouldn't be Ellen's beau who came to the house. Hardened though the man must be with what he saw every day walking his beat, he shouldn't have to look down at the body of the girl he planned to marry. Then Scully remembered that beat coppers might find corpses, but it was detectives who investigated how the victims ended up that way. He crossed himself again, murmured another quick prayer. They'd need to send to St. Anselm's for a priest, too. The body had to be washed and blessed, prayed over and buried. There were rituals to being born, rites to dying, neat brackets around the daily business of trying to stay alive. He shied away from the obvious questions. He didn't want to start thinking too hard about who'd killed Ellen, or how or why.

"This way, sir." Tynan led the procession from the house, an oil lamp in his hand to light the slippery cobblestones.

Behind him marched Mr. Nolan and Mr. Joseph, heavy coats over their nightclothes, faces pale and puffed with sleep and shock. It was almost dawn now, the world outlined in gray, dark shapes gradually becoming recognizable.

"You're sure she's dead?" Mr. Joseph's voice rasped in the stillness.

"Of course she's dead. Haven't you seen enough carcasses to know when there's no life left in them?" Mr. Nolan snapped at his son. He didn't bother kneeling to touch Ellen's face. He beckoned to the butler to lower the lamp, then stood where he was, looking down. One slippered foot stretched out to nudge the girl. Dead meat was dead meat, whether human or animal. "What in God's name was she doing outside the house? Didn't she know any better?"

"Shall I send for the police, sir?" Of course he should, but Tynan would do nothing without Mr. Nolan's consent.

"Use the telephone. Tell Cook to get coffee and tea made and served upstairs and down. I'll wake Mrs. Nolan and Miss Alice, but there's not to be a word said to either of them about that." He gestured toward Ellen's blood matted hair and the open, staring eye. "No one except Scully is to be outside until the police arrive." He turned his back on the messy business lying in his stable yard. Tynan hurried to light the way to the house.

Reluctantly, Mr. Joseph followed along after his father, looking back more than once at what had been such a lovely Irish girl, now as lifeless as the butchered cattle hanging from hooks in the family's slaughterhouses.

Ellen lay for more than an hour on the cobblestones before the first Metropolitan Police officers arrived. By that time Jack was nearly as frozen as the corpse, but he didn't dare ignore Mr. Nolan's orders. No one in that household did.

"Terrible thing to find on a Sunday morning," Officer Martin said. He rolled back and forth on his hobnailed boots, hands clasped behind him, long dark blue frock coat shielding him from the wintry cold. He'd take a few notes and stand guard over the body until the detectives arrived, which he thought they'd hurry up and do as soon as someone down at the precinct recognized Francis Patrick Nolan's name.

Fortunately, he'd been on the corner when the boot boy had come tearing out of the Nolan mansion and waved frantically at him. His master had used that new fangled telephone to call the stationhouse, but he'd also sent young Tommy out to find the beat copper. The boy had babbled his message, then sped off back down the street, though when Martin reached the Nolan house, there was no sign of him. Fifteen minutes later Tommy had raced across the cobblestone courtyard, winked and nodded his head at the coachman, then disappeared into the kitchen.

Spreading the news, Martin decided. It was always like that when a body was found — a race to see who could inform the neighborhood first. No harm done.

He turned his attention back to the coachman. "Now when did you say you found her?"

"I was coming across the yard to the

kitchen just after I'd taken care of the horses. I thought at first it was a bundle left out for the rag man." Scully tried to keep his eyes from straying down to what used to be Ellen Tierney.

"Did you see anyone hanging around who shouldn't be?"

"No one. I think she's been dead for a while now."

"Somebody had to roll her up and leave her here."

Scully had been wracking his brain trying to remember if he'd locked the carriage gate into the alley. He couldn't think why he might have forgotten. It was something he did routinely every night, hanging the key just inside the tack room door. No, he was sure the gate had been closed and secured against intruders. So how could Ellen's body have been placed where he'd found it? The girl hadn't wrapped herself up and lain down to die there. Shouldn't there be more blood?

Officer Martin took the heavy glove from his right hand and shoved it into the pocket of his coat. He couldn't write with the thing on, and the detectives would expect him to have done something other than stand around like a clumsy big *amadán*. They'd ask the same questions all over again, but at least he'd have something scrawled across the pages of his notebook.

"I think I hear them," Jack Scully said.

Mr. Tynan and Mr. Nolan led a plain-clothes Metropolitan Police detective across the stable yard, another uniformed officer following behind. Jack thought there would probably be at least one more copper stationed out front of the house for all the neighbors to see and wonder at. The morgue wagon would raise gossip in every household along the street; Tommy had already spread the word to the MacKenzie household. It wouldn't be long before everyone knew what had happened to Ellen.

The master was as impeccably dressed as on every Sunday morning. He wasn't the kind of man to let a servant's murder interfere with what he'd planned for the day.

"Let's look at her now," the detective ordered.

Phelan, he'd said his name was, Steven Phelan. No brogue on his tongue, which meant he'd probably been born in America. "Roll her over, but gently, Officer Martin. Try not to destroy any evidence, if you can."

"Give us a hand, then." Jimmy Martin squatted by Ellen's head, gesturing for the other policeman to take the feet.

The body settled onto its back. Ellen

looked up at them, glazed eyes empty of any expression at all. She was stiffening; soon she'd be as hard as a piece of firewood.

"Let's get her unwrapped," Detective Phelan directed. "She's been beaten on the head. That's as plain as the nose on your face, but that may not be all. We won't wait for the morgue wagon; it may be another hour before they get here."

"Shouldn't we let the priest give her the last sacrament first?" No one had noticed Joseph Nolan's quiet approach. Like his father, he'd dressed for Sunday High Mass at Saint Patrick's. As handsome, neat, and composed as ever, except that his lips trembled as he spoke, and he'd hidden his hands in the pockets of his black frock coat.

"Have you sent for a priest?" Mr. Nolan asked his son.

"I did, Da. Right away. He should be here any minute." It was a measure of Joseph's nerves that he called his father by the familiar Irish diminutive instead of the more formal American word.

"We won't wait," Detective Phelan decided. "There's no telling how long it will take him to get what he needs and be on his way." He took a clasp knife from his pocket and handed it to Officer Martin. "Cut her loose. Let's see why she's wrapped up like that."

It was full morning now, the gray light of dawn lightened into weak November daylight. Scully stepped back, out of notice. No one had told him to go inside, so he'd stay as long as he could. He'd been fond of Ellen, a sweet child who'd saved carrots and apples in her apron pockets and sneaked them out to the stables for the horses. Someone had hit her across the head. That was obvious. He hoped nothing else had been done to her.

Jimmy Martin cut through the rope that was wound around the hessian. Some people called it burlap. Detective Phelan's knife was sharp, the blade honed to a fine razor edge.

"Cut the hessian, too, Martin. All the way from top to bottom."

Ellen Tierney had probably made no more than a gurgling sound as she died. Her throat was slit so deeply it was a wonder her head stayed on at all. She lay naked in her hessian shroud, her clothing folded neatly beneath the body that someone had washed mostly free of blood. A long gash ran from beneath where her breasts had been to where she would have given birth. The skin had closed over emptiness; nothing swelled beneath the surgically neat incision — no heart, no lungs, no womb, stomach, or entrails.

The coroner would confirm what Steven Phelan immediately suspected and knew he would have to report to Chief of Detectives Thomas Byrnes. The similarity between this murder and what had been done to Nora Kenny just two weeks ago was unmistakable. This time he didn't see how they'd manage to keep the details out of the newspapers.

New York City now had its own Ripper.

CHAPTER 13

Alice Nolan's bedroom overlooked the house's cobbled rear courtyard and stables. Long before Jack Scully rose to tend the horses, some noise of clandestine coming or going brought her from her knees to the window, where an innate caution kept her from drawing back the heavy drape and lace curtain. Instead, she slid behind them just far enough to see what lay below in the clear white November moonlight. Nothing at first. She wondered why she'd bothered to interrupt her prayers. Then there was movement alongside the stable where the carriage was driven out through wide wooden gates into the alley. Guarded movement. A shifting of shadows. A blackness gliding through deep grayness. She held her breath.

The man carrying a rolled up rug over his shoulder wore a heavy overcoat and a workman's billed cap. A scarf wound around his neck and covered the lower part of his face. She caught a gleam of reflected moon-light off his eyes, but nothing of his features. How odd that a delivery was being made at this hour; she glanced at the clock on her mantel. It was past three in the morning. She'd nearly managed to keep the all night vigil she'd set herself, not falling asleep a single time, fighting hard not to give in to wandering thoughts.

It helped that she had fitted out one corner of her bedroom as a miniature chapel with a crucifix on the wall and a statue of the Virgin Mary beneath the dying Christ. Best of all, in Alice's opinion, was the Span-ish prie-dieu — dark wood, oiled with hundreds of years of sacred sweat and tears — that had made its way from a Barcelona convent to an antique store in Manhattan and then to her bedroom. She prayed more fervently kneeling at her prie-dieu than anywhere else.

The man deposited the rug on the cobble-stones, then looked around as if to assure himself it lay in precisely the right spot. Almost before she could be certain she had really seen him, he was gone. Alice blinked her eyes, blinked them again. She was weak from fasting, tired by lack of sleep and the effort of staying awake all night to pray, but she wasn't imagining things, wasn't having a vision.

She would never have heard the sound of the gate opening if she had not been deep in interior stillness. The coachman kept all the stable doors as well greased as the oiled and polished bridles and carriage lamps. Jack Scully was his name. Before she'd given up riding as a near occasion of sin, he'd saddled her mare for her and followed behind when she rode the trails of Central Park. Always polite and respectful. With a lovely brogue. She wondered if it would be easier to become a saint if she could live out her life in Ireland. Da was so rich. She'd always called him Da when she was little. Later, when the money came pouring in, he'd insisted that both his children call him Father. *Da* slid off the tongue so easily; *Father* had a harshness about it that had been hard to get used to.

Jack Scully came out of the stable just before dawn broke. She heard his whistle and the light skip of his feet on the stairs from his room over the stalls, then the shifting and neighing of the horses as he poured clean water and tossed feed into their troughs. She watched him start across the yard, saw him stop, bend over the rolled up carpet, cross himself, move at a near run to the kitchen door.

When had the lamps been lit in the base-ment? Light streamed out over the cobble-stones. Alice wondered if she'd dozed off for a bit. When Tynan the butler climbed up the stairs from the kitchen carrying a lamp, she knew there was something unusual about the bundle in the courtyard.

Both men, Scully and Tynan, knelt beside the rolled up rug. Both crossed themselves. *Jesus, Mary, and Joseph.* Someone was dead. That was a body there on the cobble-stones, not a rug at all. And she was the only one in the house who had seen its ar-rival, seen the shape of the man who'd brought it.

Hardly daring to breathe for fear they'd somehow sense her, Alice eased away from the draped window, back into the semidark-ness of her bedroom. She knelt again at the prie-dieu, lowering her face into her hands. Her body began to shake, but there were no tears.

She was too frightened to cry.

"Wake up, Lillian." Francis Nolan laid his heavy butcher's hand on his wife's shoulder, shaking her as hard as he dared.

The damn woman dosed herself with pat-ent medicines every night; she rolled be-neath his grip like a fat drunk. Which she was. No matter what the quacks called their tonics, it was the same as pouring whiskey down your gullet. Eventually you passed out. By this time in the morning she ought to have slept off most of it. She ought to be coming out of its depths. "Wake up, Lillian."

"I haven't overslept, have I, Frank?" Her eyelids felt sticky and hot, her mouth dry and furry. It wasn't like her husband to come into her room uninvited.

"There's trouble downstairs, Lillian. You need to deal with it."

"Me? What kind of trouble?" She struggled to sit up, twisted behind her to pummel the pillows against the high oak headboard of her bed, and reached for the glass on the bedside table.

"No, not that." Francis Nolan swept the glass from his wife's hand. "Plain water," he said, rinsing the sticky traces of opium tincture into the wash basin, pouring clean water from the pitcher beside it. "Here, drink this."

"You don't have to be so brusque, Frank. No matter what's happened, I'll have Tynan sort it out, whatever it is. He's very good at keeping order among the staff."

"One of the damn maids is dead."

She stared at her husband openmouthed, droplets of water dribbling down her chin.

"How can that be, Frank? How can that be?" The first thing she thought of was a clumsy knitting needle abortion because that's how so many of them reacted when they got caught. Fear and panic drove common sense right out of their ignorant heads. "Was it Ellen?" She was walking out with a policeman, *walking out* being a euphemism for God knew what liberties a man could persuade a girl to allow him. *Jesus, Mary and Joseph.* The scandal of it.

"Get up and get dressed, Lillian. See to Alice. The police are here."

"Was it Ellen?"

"Yes, it was Ellen." He crossed himself the way Catholics always do when the name of someone dead is spoken, a gesture that had no meaning at all when Francis Nolan made it. He'd been well taught as a boy; some things stuck no matter how far a man traveled from his roots.

Lillian's hand flew through the air in swift imitation, the cross sketched on forehead, heart, and shoulders, fingers barely touching bare skin and nightgown. She reached out for him when he started to stand up from where he had been sitting on the side of her bed. "How, Frank? Tell me what happened. Alice will ask questions. You know what she's like."

His daughter had been the joy of Francis Nolan's life when she was born, a perfect little female creature who would always love him with every fiber of her being, never really leave him even though she would marry and give him the gift of grandchildren. Over the years she'd grown into his heart's despair until now he could barely stand to look at her. He'd never allow her to be a nun, no matter how hard or how long she pleaded. The Church had tried to steal both his children from him, but he'd not permitted Joseph to become a priest and he wouldn't allow Alice to enter the Visitation community in Brooklyn. What good was it to fight your way to wealth if your damned offspring turned their backs on it?

"We don't know yet what happened. Scully found the body in the yard when he was crossing from the stables to the kitchen. Rolled up in hessian like a rug."

Lillian stared at him uncomprehendingly.

"Burlap, they call it. Coffee beans and tobacco are shipped in sacks made of hessian."

"Sackcloth, Frank. Sackcloth and ashes."

"For God's sake, Lillian."

"Does she have ashes on her forehead?"

"She's been beaten on the head. I didn't look to see if there were smudges." He shook off his wife's grip and stood up. "It's not Ash Wednesday, Lillian. Get up and see to Alice."

"Whatever Ellen did to get herself killed, it can't have anything to do with us. You said she was outside the house when it happened."

"The girl's skull has been bashed in, Lillian. She's had whatever she was carrying inside her cut out, and her body's been dumped in our stable yard like a carcass from the abattoir. I don't know what it means and I don't care. I want the matter dealt with, put away. They can find the man who did it to her or not. It makes no difference to me. She brought it on herself. Girls like that always do."

He watched tears well up in his wife's eyes, followed their tracks down her plump cheeks. Lillian's moods were wide swinging and unpredictable. It would cause more hard feelings later, but Francis picked up the small brown bottle from her bedside table and put it into his pocket. He needed her to be clearheaded. After Mass at Saint Patrick's, after Sunday dinner, he'd give it back to her.

If he hurried the police along, there was no reason why the rest of this Sunday should be different from any other Sunday.

■ ■ ■ ■

Father Brennan knelt beside the dead girl whose glorious red hair was smeared with blood and bits of other things. Not glowing like sunset over water now, her hair had stiffened beneath her, clumped into bundles blackened with old blood. Whether the soul had taken its leave or lingered for a while, as some believed, the ritual was the same. The priest would anoint Ellen's eyes, ears, nostrils, lips, hands, and feet, repeating with the applications of holy oil the rite of forgiveness of sins committed through each of the senses. He looked up at Detective Phelan, waiting for his nod to begin.

"Just the forehead, Father." Steven Phelan had seen the sacrament performed so many times he could probably have done it himself. Maybe even gotten most of the Latin right. In urgent cases, the Church taught that one anointing was enough. Ellen Tierney was no longer an urgent case as far as her life was concerned, but there was a pressing need to get her body into the morgue wagon and out of sight of Sunday morning worshippers on their way to church. Not to mention the crowd of reporters who were bound to descend on the site of the latest horror. Chief of Detectives Thomas Byrnes' edict against answering any questions from the press was still in force. Nothing but the name of the victim. And he meant it.

"*In nomine Patris, et Filii, et Spíritus Sancti. Amen.*" Father Brennan replaced the vial of blessed oil in the satchel he carried with him on visits to the sick and dying, a gift from his parents at his ordination. He could still picture the awe on their faces when he laid his hands on their heads to confer his first priestly blessing. How many blessings had he bestowed since that day? Far too many to count. He looked again at the girl lying on the cobblestones, marveling at the beauty of the undamaged portions of her face, aching for the pain she must have suffered, rejoicing that whatever foulness she had embraced was now washed clean in the embrace of the Divine Saviour. Perhaps you had to be a priest to believe that many people, especially women, were better off dead than alive.

"Will you come inside?" Joseph Nolan asked. "My father has gone in to wake up my mother and sister. I'm sure they'll need your comfort, and the servants as well, of course."

"Had Ellen been working here long?"

They'd offer him a cup of hot coffee and perhaps a decent breakfast. Father Brennan could taste the goodness in his mouth, but he'd have to refuse. He had Mass still to say at St. Anselm's; the fast that began at midnight didn't end until the Eucharist was taken. No exception this morning; he wasn't elderly and he wasn't sick. Illness of the spirit didn't count.

"You'll have to ask my mother or the housekeeper. I don't keep track of servants' comings and goings," Joseph lied. He remembered his first sight of Ellen Tierney and nearly every occasion afterwards, always the mad thumping of his racing heart, the painful swelling he turned away or sat down to conceal.

It wasn't only Ellen. He'd had sinful, throbbingly erotic dreams about every maid who'd ever worked in the house. Young women of his own class didn't affect him that way; their cold correctness and unapproachable distance kept him in check. He never knew what to say to them, but he didn't have to make polite conversation with a servant.

"I only ask because if she's been with the family for a while she'll have a close friend or two among the other servants."

"Mrs. Flynn will answer your questions,

Father." Joseph could sense the impatience of the police detective. As politely as he could, he steered the priest toward the kitchen door. Five minutes with the housekeeper, a quick word and a hasty blessing for the servants, and then upstairs. His father had given explicit instructions.

Francis Nolan didn't have much use for priests, but he never underestimated their importance and influence. Lillian and Alice would weep and pray, only one of them sincerely, but if Joseph knew his father, and he thought he did, the entire family would be in the carriage and on the way to Saint Patrick's right on schedule. Whatever there was to find out about how Ellen had died wouldn't turn up at the Nolan mansion.

Idly, because his mind was flitting from one unsettling thought to another, Joseph remembered overhearing Mrs. Flynn and Cook discussing the girl, their speculations about what was going on between her and her policeman, their conviction that she'd been caught. He wondered where Mick McGuire had been last night and whether Ellen had gotten around to telling him he was going to be a father.

Some men didn't react well to that kind of news.

CHAPTER 14

"There's been another killing just like Nora's, Geoffrey." Prudence held the nickel-plated candlestick telephone in her left hand, the earpiece in her right. "I don't know any more except that the girl whose body has been found worked in the Nolan household at the end of the street. Their coachman sent a boot boy to tell Kincaid what was going on. 'Cut just like Miss Nora Kenny,' is how he put it. Jack Scully, the Nolans' coachman, made the boy repeat the sentence until he was sure he wouldn't forget it. The morgue wagon hasn't arrived yet, but a detective and several uniformed patrolmen are already at the Nolan house."

"Stay out of it, Prudence. Wait for me. I'll hail a hansom cab from the stand in front of the hotel."

"I'm going down there, Geoffrey. I know the Nolan daughter. Alice is her name. She's about three years older than I am, and she was always kind when my governess and I met her in the park. There's an older brother, Joseph, and Mrs. Nolan made a point of calling on my mother when she was ill. The families don't move in the same social circles, but we can at least call ourselves acquaintances. They came to my father's funeral."

"Prudence, don't leave the house until I get there."

She moved one finger rapidly up and down on the bar that summoned an operator. Connections were uncertain at best and often came to an abrupt end with no explanation of what part of the telephone service had failed. She heard Geoffrey calling her name through the staccato clicking, but she didn't answer. She'd made up her mind to pay an early morning call on the Nolans and didn't relish an argument about it. She laid the earpiece down on the desk instead of in its cradle on the candlestick phone.

Geoffrey might figure out what she'd done, but by then it would be too late to stop her.

Prudence nodded politely to the policeman standing at the foot of the Nolan front steps. She seemed to belong there, so he let her pass without attempting to stop or question her. The women toffs were worse than the men; they plain didn't like to be approached by anyone not of their set and made no bones about it. Best to look the other way.

"I'm sorry, Miss MacKenzie," Tynan told her firmly and politely, "but Mrs. Nolan and Miss Alice aren't receiving visitors."

"They'll see me, Tynan," she said, brushing past the butler so quickly he was forced to step back out of her way or risk bodily contact. "I know what's happened, and there's no point pretending it can be kept a secret. The police are here and I'm sure the coroner is on his way."

"Prudence MacKenzie? Is that you?" Alice Nolan descended the main staircase unsteadily, one hand clenching the banister, the other gathering her skirts so they wouldn't trip her up.

"I came as soon as I heard," Prudence said.

"I'm glad you did. My father sent up word that the detective wants to meet with all of the family in the parlor. Will you come with me?"

"I'm not sure I'll be welcome."

"Please, Prudence. I would greatly appreciate it." Alice looked both frightened and uncertain, as though she desperately wanted to say something, but wasn't sure how it would be received.

"You can tell me anything you want, Alice." Prudence led her down the final few steps of the staircase. "I won't say anything to anyone unless you tell me it's all right."

"I saw him," she whispered. Her hand on Prudence's arm shook, and she was as pale as a woman about to faint. "I saw the man carry Ellen's body into the courtyard this morning. Before dawn. I was awake. Praying. And I heard a sound. I looked out my window and I saw him."

"What time was this, Alice?"

"A little past three. I checked the clock on my mantel. I'm sure that's right."

"Then what did you do?"

"Nothing. He didn't see me because I never opened the drape wide and I stepped away from the window as soon as he'd put down what he was carrying."

"You'll have to tell the police."

"No, Prudence, I can't. They'll ask why I wasn't asleep at that hour of the morning, and I'll have to tell them. I can't bear to be mocked for what I do." Alice gulped air and sagged against Prudence, who braced herself to keep the girl upright. "It won't make any difference. I couldn't see anything but a figure carrying what I thought was a delivery, a rug. He laid it on the ground and then he left. I never saw his face or anything else that would make him stand out."

"Are you sure there isn't anything more you could tell them?"

"I know there isn't. They'll have already figured out that someone, a man, had to have carried her into the yard, and I can't add any more to that. Please, Prudence, don't say anything."

"I won't, Alice. I promise. But imagine how embarrassed you'll be if they find out later you deliberately withheld evidence." She tightened her grip on Alice's hand. "It won't be as bad as you think."

"Let's make this quick, Detective," Francis Nolan said. "I've already put through a call to your chief. He agrees with me that the girl was murdered somewhere else and carried here by someone who wants to ruin the Nolan name. I won't let that happen."

Detective Phelan nodded his head in agreement, but he wasn't at all sure that was what Tom Byrnes had really said. He'd have to wait until he got back to the Mulberry Street headquarters of the detective division to find out. In the meantime, he'd tread carefully and question lightly. He had a feeling the chief of detectives would want this case handled the same way the Kenny case had gone, though it might be harder this time if anything leaked to the press. There hadn't been another Ripper story from London, so the New York reporters would leap all over this one if word got out about the way the body had been sliced.

The uniformed policeman who would be making notes of the interview took out his pad and pencil. Detective Phelan seated himself on an elegant brocade armchair. Without invitation.

When Francis Nolan's lips tightened Phelan knew the man was provoked enough to make a mistake if he had anything to hide.

"What can you tell me about Ellen Tierney?" Phelan asked Lillian Nolan, taking in the woman's carefully put together appearance and look of tight control. She wasn't acting like the mistress of a maid who'd been found brutally murdered in the courtyard of the family mansion. He wondered if the husband had told her what to say and how to behave.

"You'll have to ask Mrs. Flynn, the housekeeper, for details about her," Mrs. Nolan said. "The girl did her work adequately or she would have been dismissed."

"How long did she work for you?"

"Obviously not long enough to make any

kind of impression," Francis Nolan interrupted. "I don't understand why the family has to be subjected to your questions, Detective. All the information you need can be obtained from the housekeeper and the butler. My wife does not concern herself with the junior servants. Nor do I."

"I wonder whether young Mr. Nolan can tell us anything." Phelan smiled at the extraordinarily handsome young man leaning casually against the wall beside the fireplace. He was clearly implying that the sons of wealthy families often considered it their right to make free with their mother's maids.

"You asked those same questions outside in the courtyard," Joseph said. "I don't know any more about the girl now than I did then."

Before Phelan could reply, the parlor door opened. A fragile looking young woman stood frozen as her parents, her brother, and two strange men stared at her. "I'm here as you requested, Father," Alice Nolan said.

When she stepped into the parlor, everyone could see that she hadn't come alone. Prudence MacKenzie, as tall and self-assured as Alice was tiny and timid, smiled with every confidence in the world that her presence would be welcome.

Detective Steven Phelan breathed a string of silent curses.

"I'm so glad I thought to come up and offer any assistance my household staff or I might be able to provide," Prudence said, not letting go of Alice's chilly hand. "I met Alice just as I was coming in. It's been a terrible shock for her."

Francis Nolan looked uneasily at the girl he once considered a suitable bride for his son. Joseph had adamantly refused to consider the match because, he said, she was a Protestant. To the socially ambitious head of the Nolan family, religion didn't matter nearly as much as money and an old name. Both of which Prudence MacKenzie had. With the added advantage of being an orphan.

He'd heard rumors about her when her stepmother died. Gossip had it that she was behaving in an unacceptable, even scandalous way. Now here she was sticking her patrician nose into this morning's messy business. He had no idea why she would waste her time on Alice, but Francis didn't look gift horses in the mouth. Prudence was a wealthy young woman sorely in need of a husband to control her. He might be able to salvage something from this debacle.

"It's kind of you to have come, Miss Prudence," Francis said. "I'm sure Alice appreciates your company at this difficult time. As do we all." He looked meaningfully at Joseph, who refused to meet his eyes.

"Detective Phelan." Prudence paid no attention to the puzzled looks from the Nolan family.

"Miss MacKenzie." He was too annoyed to bother being anything but frostily polite.

"Detective Phelan and I met two weeks ago," Prudence said. "In Colonial Park." She stopped then, waiting to see if he would continue the explanation. He didn't. "It was a professional rather than a social encounter."

"I've spoken briefly with your senior staff," Phelan said, attempting to ignore the young woman whose unwavering gaze was unsettling to him and unseemly for her. The visit she and Hunter had made to the Tombs had been reported to him, of course. He'd seen to it that Fahey was moved out of their reach, but here she was again, like a bad penny that kept turning up in your pocket. "I understand the maid in question was walking out."

Mrs. Nolan looked inquiringly at her husband, who nodded his permission for her to speak. "The housekeeper was anticipating having to replace her," she said, conveying unmistakable disapproval of a servant having any sort of private life. "The girl had told her that she planned to marry, which would mean immediate dismissal."

"I believe it was one of your patrolmen, Detective," Joseph Nolan said. "Perhaps he's the one you ought to be questioning."

"We'll speak to him." Phelan didn't like being told how to do his job.

"The girl got herself in trouble and now she's paid for it." Joseph brushed imaginary dust from the mantel as though that would remove the offending maid from their lives.

"I agree with my son," Francis said brusquely, dismissively. "In any case, whether or not she was caught doesn't matter as much as the fact that she'd no business leaving the house at night. Alone. Without permission."

Detective Phelan was liking Francis Nolan less and less. There was a phrase the Irish used among themselves to describe his type. *A Mick on the make.* That's what they called the climbers on the way up who threw off everything that marked them as Irish. They treated their fellow countrymen with the scorn they themselves had had to endure when they first got off the boat. *No Irish Need Apply. No Dogs Allowed.* As soon as he got back to headquarters he'd find out everything Nolan was paying good money to hide. In the meantime, he couldn't afford to forget that the man had been able to get through to the chief of detectives. Via Tammany connections, probably . . . which meant he wasn't someone whose feathers you wanted to ruffle.

"The policeman's name is Mick McGuire," Alice said unexpectedly. When all eyes turned to her, she blushed and ducked her head. "I asked Mrs. Flynn," she mumbled.

"What on earth made you do something like that?" her mother asked angrily. She had a feeling it was considered not quite de rigueur to evince any sort of interest in one's servants and their friends.

Alice's head came up when Prudence pressed her hand encouragingly. "I saw him from my window," she explained. "The policeman. He came out the kitchen door with Ellen on his arm. It was her afternoon off."

"What were you doing looking out your bedroom window?" Mrs. Nolan was incensed. "What if someone had seen you? It's beyond improper for a young lady to be staring out onto the street like some harpy from the tenements."

"My window overlooks the courtyard, not the street," Alice protested.

"Would you have been looking out your window last night, Miss Nolan?" Detective Phelan asked. The mother had taken the interrogation off on an entirely different tack for a moment, but she'd inadvertently given him another line of inquiry. He didn't wait for the daughter to answer. "Did you see Mick McGuire carry the girl's body through the gate?"

Alice stared at him. *How could he know I saw someone? How could he know that?* She felt Prudence's hand tighten around her own again, giving her courage and support. "I don't know who it was," she stammered. "All I saw was the shape of a man carrying a rug. I thought it was a rug."

"What time was that?" Phelan demanded. Sometimes the only way to get information out of witnesses was to hit them hard, badger and thump the truth out of them. "What time?"

"I'm not sure. Past three o'clock, I think. Nearly four?"

"You're telling me that you were looking out your bedroom window at three or four o'clock in the morning and when you saw a man carrying a body across the courtyard you thought it was someone making an early morning delivery of a rug? Is that what you're saying, Miss Nolan?"

"That's enough," Francis Nolan interrupted, cutting Phelan off with an imperious sweep of his hand. "My daughter has told you what she saw. She will not be answering any more questions."

On a nod from his father, Joseph Nolan yanked on the tapestry bellpull hanging beside the fireplace.

"The butler will see you out," Francis Nolan decreed.

"I'll need to ask questions of the staff, Mr. Nolan," Detective Phelan said, taking his time standing up. "I can do it today and be finished or I can come back tomorrow. And perhaps also on Tuesday, if I have to jog their memories."

Prudence thought they looked like two single-minded bulldogs facing off over possession of a square of sidewalk.

"Perhaps today would be better," Lillian Nolan put in. "Then the police wouldn't have to come back at all, Francis." She'd almost called him Frank, but he hated when she used that nickname in front of other people. She didn't want to get his back up, but she didn't want policemen in her house again either.

"Take Detective Phelan downstairs,

Tynan," Mr. Nolan instructed when the butler appeared. "He has questions for the staff." He turned back to Phelan, bound and determined not to allow control over his household to slip from his grasp. "You can start with Scully, and don't take too long about it. I'll expect my coachman to be ready to drive the family to Saint Patrick's on time."

Phelan knew he'd be closeted with Chief Byrnes as soon as he got back to Mulberry Street, so he might as well get statements while he could. He had a feeling the Nolan family would become unavailable after this morning, and that Byrnes would be directing this case from afar. He needed to find out what the staff thought of Patrolman Mick McGuire and whether any other young stallion had come calling for the dead girl.

He looked back over his shoulder as the butler led the way out of the parlor. Miss MacKenzie had ensconced herself as comfortably as though she were one of the family. He hated knowing she would probably end up learning far more about the Nolans and their dead maid than he would. And that she'd pass the information on to the ex-Pinkerton partner who had been asking too many questions down at the Tombs.

Byrnes had reprimanded Phelan for the damage done during Fahey's second third-degree interrogation, but not too severely because the chief had been known to rough up a man so badly his own mother couldn't recognize him. Phelan had carted Fahey off to the prison infirmary, signed him in, then promptly misplaced all of his paperwork. He ought to be healed up by now, at least enough to be put back into a regular cell as soon as his charge sheets miraculously re-appeared. They could have him tried, sent up the river or hanged in a couple of weeks. That should get the toff and his girlfriend off his back.

If Mick McGuire turned out to be dirty, as nearly every cop on the force was, includ-ing the chief, he'd go the same way. Not without proof, of course, but that was always easy to come by. McGuire had a reputation for using his fists too often and too hard as he kept order on his beat. The press would make mincemeat of him, and he was probably guilty. Who better than a copper to fake a copycat killing?

"Detective?" came the soft voice with the edge of steel in it.

He turned around, hat in hand.

"I just want to say how much Mr. Hunter and I value your work."

Which meant they knew he was behind Fahey's disappearance and they weren't planning on getting off his back anytime soon.

CHAPTER 15

"The victims have to have characteristics in common," Geoffrey Hunter said. "You can't have two nearly identical murders without something to link them together. It's not logical." He was pacing from one end of Prudence's library to the other, stopping occasionally to slide a book from a shelf, glance at its title page or the first few paragraphs of text before returning it to its place.

"I've made a list of what we know about Ellen Tierney," Prudence announced, swiveling her head to follow Geoffrey's progress back and forth across the carpet. "I'll do the same for Nora."

"Start with age and nationality. Ellen was nineteen years old, so was Nora. Both Irish."

"Nora was born in this country," contributed Prudence. "As was her father. It was her mother, Agnes, who came from Ireland."

"Both Catholic."

"Yes, but so are most of the Irish who've emigrated."

"The ones from the northern counties are Protestant. Many of them ended up in the southern states. The North Carolina mountains are full of their descendants."

"Don't get off track, Geoffrey," Prudence scolded. She loved that his mind leaped nimbly from one topic to another, but she was determined to keep everything organized. "Back to the lists. Similarities in age, nationality, and religion duly noted. Next?"

"Ellen's hair was red, Nora's black."

"But both had blue eyes."

"Height? Size?"

"Ellen was taller than Colleen. I remember seeing them together on one of their half days. Nora was much shorter, hardly bigger than a child."

"So our murderer doesn't confine himself to one type of female." Geoffrey absent-mindedly laid a book he hadn't opened on a table instead of returning it to its shelf.

"Not if you're talking about looks."

"What else?"

"Mrs. Nolan said her housekeeper informed her that Ellen thought she would be married to a policeman by the new year. Nora's wedding was set for then, also. I was planning to attend. I'd even decided on a wedding gift."

"Both girls were brides-to-be."

Prudence doodled a tiny cradle and a question mark in the margin of the two-columned list she was making. When she looked up Geoffrey's eyes were riveted to what she had designed. "I think it's best to speak frankly," she said. "Not beat about the bush or cloak certain topics in euphemistic circumlocutions."

"We know that Nora was pregnant. Was Ellen also carrying a child?" Geoffrey didn't think he had ever been that blunt with a woman.

Prudence blushed, but only slightly. "Joseph Nolan said something surprisingly improper when I was there, given that ladies were present in the parlor when he made the comment. He said the girl had gotten herself in trouble and paid for it. His father agreed with him."

"Did you get the impression he was speaking from personal knowledge?"

"He's difficult to read, Geoffrey. He sounded condemnatory, but not the slightest bit guilty himself. More to the point, both the Nolan men seemed to be making an effort to blame Mick McGuire for the murder. Joseph Nolan told the detective he should be questioning McGuire instead of wasting his time and bothering the family. Francis Nolan isn't the gentleman he pretends to be. Perhaps that's why I don't remember my father ever speaking of him despite the fact the Nolans are near neighbors."

"I don't imagine this autopsy report will be made public, any more than Nora's was," Geoffrey speculated. "If Byrnes has his way, the papers won't print any of the details."

"Ned Hayes leaked a story to the *New York Herald* once before. He could do it again."

"To Russell Coughlin, you mean?"

"Why not? Coughlin has credibility with his editor and he'll go to any length to beat out the competition."

"Let's wait," Geoffrey said. "Coughlin may pick this up on his own. In the meantime, would Colleen know? About Ellen, I mean."

"She might. I suppose it's possible Ellen confided in her. The one person I don't think Ellen would have said anything to was Mick McGuire. Not yet. Especially if she wasn't sure. He might have reacted badly. She wouldn't have wanted to take the chance if it was a false alarm."

"Whoever our killer is, he's taken precautions to be sure no one would know whether either of his victims was expecting a child."

"I hate to think about that, Geoffrey. It brings up horrible images. Sometimes when I was very little I'd be sent to the kitchen when the doctor came to visit my mother. I can remember Cook's strong fingers tearing the innards out of the chicken she was going to roast that night. I had nightmares."

"What else did Ellen and Nora have in common?" Geoffrey asked. He watched as Prudence brought herself back into the present. She was strong, he thought, and getting stronger every day.

"Ellen was a maid. Nora helped her mother take care of a family of six men — her father and the five brothers. Ellen's universe centered around the Nolan household here on Fifth Avenue. Nora was a world away on Staten Island and rarely came into the city as far as I know. But those are differences."

"There's always the possibility the two killings were unrelated, except for being performed by the same monster."

"I don't understand." Prudence looked up from studying her lists.

"What I mean is that it may be a waste of effort to look for similarities between the victims. Each of them might have been an entirely random choice."

"You don't really believe that."

"No, I don't, but I thought I'd see what you thought of the idea." Geoffrey smiled. He liked that Prudence questioned and challenged everything he said.

"I don't know much about people who kill, other than what I read in the newspaper about the Ripper," Prudence said slowly, thinking aloud as she put together an argument that would be both accurate and convincing. "What allowed them to identify his victims in the first place were the similarities. All of the women were prostitutes, all worked the Whitechapel area, all were slashed and mutilated, the only difference being the degree of destruction. The police seem to feel that was more a function of time than anything else. In other words, the London Ripper fled when he thought he was about to be interrupted or discovered."

"I'm following you."

"Our murderer has had all the time he could want. He's been able to kill and mutilate and then wrap the bodies up as neatly as you please before taking them where he intended them to be found."

"Agreed," Geoffrey said.

"That wouldn't happen if they were random killings, if he struck when opportunity presented itself. He planned Nora's death.

Ellen's also. He thought through what he was going to do and how he would dispose of the bodies. Nothing was left to chance. That's the most important similarity. Ellen and Nora both encountered him in a place and at a time of his choosing."

"Place first. Wherever it is, they felt safe," Geoffrey decided. He had to get inside the killer's mind, had to think like a man who planned to take advantage of the innocence and gullibility of inexperienced girls.

"Staten Island and Fifth Avenue. Nora wouldn't have been familiar with all of the streets around Fifth Avenue and I can't think of any reason why Ellen would have visited Staten Island."

"I remember your saying that Colleen and Ellen went out together on some of their half days. Was Nora ever here working for you when she might have spent time with them? Could they have made an afternoon of showing Nora the places they liked to visit? We already know she had no difficulty getting here from the ferry dock."

"I can ask Mrs. Morgan to check the household diary," Prudence offered. "She would have noted the dates and hours Nora worked. And if we need to go back to when Mrs. Barstow was housekeeper, we have those records, too." Prudence got up from her desk, crossed to the fireplace, and tugged on the bellpull.

"Do you ever think of Mrs. Barstow when you ring for the new housekeeper? Or of Jackson before Cameron appears?"

"I do, Geoffrey, though not nearly as much now as I used to. For the longest time, I had nightmares about her body in the stables, as if I were somehow responsible for her murder. She never did anything more serious than spy on me for Victoria. It was always Victoria who slipped the additional laudanum into my food or drink. She didn't trust anyone else in the house not to feel some loyalty to me. Except Jackson. I sometimes think Mrs. Barstow was as much my stepmother's victim as I was. She didn't deserve what Jackson did to her."

"He was still alive when Danny Dennis and Kincaid took him to Bellevue, but he didn't last long enough to receive any kind of treatment," Geoffrey said, remembering. "Kincaid told me later that Danny refused to identify him. He said that in Ireland they believe a dead man buried without a name is the devil's plaything and that he wanted to be sure the bastard ended up where he belonged, in an unmarked grave in Potter's Field on Hart Island."

"Sometimes I wonder if I'll ever be able

to forget any of what happened because of the Great Blizzard."

"You will," Geoffrey promised. He could have told her that he doubted he'd ever put behind him the far worse nightmares he'd lived through as a Pinkerton, but he hoped life would be kinder to Prudence than it had been to him. He wanted her to have hope, to believe in herself. And in him.

There was so much about Judge Mac-Kenzie's daughter that was unlike other young women of her age and class. Somehow she had escaped the sameness of the lovely, accomplished society belles whose mothers and governesses molded and shaped them into carbon copies of one another. Well mannered, well dressed, well coiffed. Good dancers, skilled conversationalists, practiced flirts. Bound by the limitations of good taste and marketable virginity.

Prudence was both brave and vulnerable, an intriguing combination that aroused Geoffrey's admiration and his desire to protect. Her mind had been trained by one of the best jurists in the state; she probed for answers, weighed evidence and arguments, and was never entirely satisfied with results that would have gratified anyone less demanding. She challenged her partner's intelligence, something no other woman had ever done. She surprised him, confronted him, treated him with the careless affection she might bestow on a brother, and occasionally looked at him in a way that made him wonder if she could possibly have guessed what was happening to him. What was beginning to grow between the two of them.

When she spoke of the Great Blizzard, he drew back, instinctively sensing that the wounds she carried had not healed. Then she would seem to have forgotten the losses and the pain enough so that he dared to move ever so slightly closer. It was an odd sort of minuet they were dancing, he thought, likely to break any moment into the breathless sweep of a waltz. He imagined holding Prudence in his arms — her lovely face in profile; tall, slender body moving in obedience to his direction; the fragrance of her hair; the scent of perfume on her skin; the sway of hips; the oneness of two people dancing in concert.

"Geoffrey?"

"Sorry. I was woolgathering." From the amused look on her face, he knew she thought it a most un-Pinkerton thing to be caught doing.

The butler who answered Prudence's summons had been in her family's service since before she was born. Summarily dismissed by Judge MacKenzie's scheming widow, he had reluctantly and only briefly left the household, returning immediately after Victoria MacKenzie's fatal brush with the laudanum she had used to control her late husband's daughter. Never again would he allow anything or anyone to harm the child he loved as if she were his own.

"Would you ask Mrs. Morgan to come up, please, Cameron? She'll need to bring the household diary with her. I want to check the dates when Nora Kenny worked here. And especially whether she might have spent a half day with Colleen and Ellen Tierney."

"I know she did. I remember how much they looked forward to it. It would have taken a month of half days to do and see everything they planned. I don't recall the date, though. Shall I send Colleen up with Mrs. Morgan? She'll remember where they went."

"Yes, please do. And come back up yourself, Cameron. Mr. Hunter and I are putting together a list of things that Ellen Tierney and Nora had in common. We need every scrap of information anyone can provide."

"I'll have Cook prepare an early tea." He exited the room as quietly as he had entered.

"You're very fortunate in your servants, Prudence."

"My father said that if you treat a man or woman with respect and have a care for their dignity, there's no reason why you shouldn't be able to spend a lifetime together. He provided handsomely for Mrs. Dailey, my mother's housekeeper. The same for Cameron. He doesn't need to earn his livelihood anymore, but he won't consider leaving until he's trained someone he approves of to take his place. And please don't ask me when that's likely to happen."

Colleen had a wan look about her, as though she had very recently gotten up from a sickbed. First Nora, now Ellen. It was all she could do to close her eyes at night for fear she would be next. She hadn't confided her dreadful apprehension to anyone; it was as if giving it voice would also grant permission for it to happen. She went about her duties in a sleep deprived daze, breaking down into tears whenever she was alone. She didn't want to contemplate what had happened to her two friends, but she couldn't stop thinking about it.

"I've brought the household calendar,

Miss MacKenzie," Mrs. Morgan said.

"What we're looking for are recent dates when Nora Kenny came here to work." Prudence glanced at Geoffrey, then at Colleen. "Once we know what they are, I'd like Colleen to tell us whatever she can remember about where in the city they might have gone together, especially if Ellen went with them."

"Nora was here in September, at the end of October, then again two Saturdays ago." As soon as Cameron had told her what Miss Prudence wanted, Mrs. Morgan had searched for Nora's name in the household records and marked the places where it appeared.

"Colleen, do you know if Ellen ever went to visit Nora on Staten Island?" Geoffrey was prepared to explain why he had asked the question, but Colleen anticipated him.

"She never did, sir. She would have told me if she had. Ellen was so wrapped up in Mick McGuire that she was sparing very little of her free time for her girlfriends. If you're thinking to find a place where they both could have gotten someone's attention, it won't be on Staten Island. That I can promise you."

"What did Nora do at the end of October? Why did you send for her, Mrs. Morgan?"

"It was the two-headed girl, Miss." Colleen's cheeks reddened.

"What two-headed girl?"

"The Two-Headed Nightingale. Miss Millie-Christine. She was the featured attraction at Mr. Dorris's variety theatre and museum on Eighth Avenue. Each head speaks a different language, German and French, if I remember right. And then the heads sing in harmony. Nora came on the Monday. That would be the twenty-ninth. I had the afternoon off, and so did Ellen, but Mick was on duty, so we three went together. It was the strangest thing I've ever seen. And the crowds were terrible. I read in the paper the next day that five thousand people went to see Miss Millie-Christine that Monday."

"Nora wasn't paid for that day, Miss Prudence." Mrs. Morgan's right forefinger secured the page with the relevant entry. "But the following day, October thirtieth, she polished silver and darned sheets. Then on Wednesday, October thirty-first, I sent both Colleen and Nora to Saint Anselm's to help get the church ready for All Saints Day."

"Was Ellen Tierney at Saint Anselm's?" Prudence tried to keep a rising excitement from her voice.

"Yes, Miss, she was. Mr. Nolan always sends some of his household before an important feast day. That day Mrs. Flynn could only spare Ellen, so she asked if I could lend her Colleen. It happened I could, seeing that Nora had done the silver the day before."

"What did the three of you do at Saint Anselm's, Colleen? Can you remember?"

"Mainly we dusted and polished the pews. Jerry Brophy, he's the sacristan, he kept us busy. According to him, there's always work to be done."

"Can you remember who else you saw or spoke to at Saint Anselm's that day? Take your time. This is important, Colleen." Geoffrey leaned forward in his seat, eyes fixed on Prudence's maid.

"Father Mahoney, the pastor. He and Father Kearns, his assistant, were both there. Mostly they were talking to the organist and the choir director about the music to be played and sung at High Mass the next day. I remember hearing the organ now and then as they decided. Father Brennan was hearing confession even though it wasn't a Saturday. The Ladies Sodality came in with flowers and then two of the nuns from the school brought in altar linens. Mr. Nolan came with a special bottle

251

of wine. He said it wouldn't do on the Feast of All Saints to put cheap wine in the chalice. I heard him say it as clear as anything."

"Which Mister Nolan, Colleen?"

She closed her eyes as she pictured the wide central aisle of Saint Anselm's. The figures standing there. "Both, Mr. Hunter. They came together, Mr. Joseph and Mr. Francis both. I remember thinking how much alike they looked. Anyone could tell they were father and son. Mr. Joseph carried the bottle of wine, but it was Mr. Francis who said that about not wanting to have cheap wine in the chalice on All Saints Day."

"Where were Ellen and Nora when the Nolans came in?"

"Ellen was in the confessional booth, but she came out and went up to the altar to say her penance. She kept her head down and pulled her scarf up over her head so they wouldn't recognize her. I'm not sure why exactly, but I know she didn't like Mr. Joseph. She said he was odd and she tried to keep out of his way, but she never explained."

"And Nora, where was she?"

Colleen screwed up her face as she tried to remember, but it was no use. She couldn't picture Nora anywhere in Saint

Anselm's while the Nolans were there. "I think she may have gone with the Sodality ladies to put water in the flower vases. Jerry Brophy was giving orders right and left. He gets panicky sometimes when Father Mahoney gives him too much to do. He's a good man with the simple things, but he's easily confused."

"How long did the Nolans stay?"

"Not long, Miss Prudence. Not more than five or ten minutes. Mr. Francis Nolan is always in a hurry, always going somewhere. He took Mr. Joseph with him when he left."

"Is there anything else you can tell us about Ellen? Or about Nora?"

"Ellen and I were planning to spend this afternoon together in Central Park. Mick McGuire was supposed to be on patrol." Colleen's face collapsed as the tears began to flow. Mrs. Morgan put an arm around her shoulders and led her toward the door. Cameron watched them go.

"I'll speak to her, Miss Prudence. She'll need time to settle, but she's a good girl and she's desperate to help find the person who killed her friends. A dollop of whiskey in her tea will help; she'll forget she's talking until there's nothing more to tell." Cameron beckoned German Clara into the library. Mrs. Hearne had sent the maid up with an opulently laden tea tray for Miss Prudence and her guest.

"Thank you, Cameron."

The only sound after he left was the crackle of flames in the fireplace.

"I think we know what the common place was," Geoffrey finally said. He held Prudence's chair as she got up and walked toward the table where German Clara had laid out their tea.

"It has to be Saint Anselm's," Prudence agreed. "It has to be."

"You can put six names on your list of suspects."

"Francis Nolan, Joseph Nolan, and the sacristan Jerry Brophy."

"Don't forget the priests. Father Mahoney, Father Kearns, and Father Brennan."

"I cannot imagine that a priest would commit such heinous crimes."

"No one is exempt, Prudence. I've known criminals with the faces of angels and the manners of society gentlemen. The worst thing you can do is eliminate a suspect because he seems to be above suspicion. It hamstrings you from the beginning."

"Is that something you learned when you were a Pinkerton?"

"I've always known it. You forget I'm a

Southerner. We grew up on our plantations surrounded by hatred, nourished by distrust, drunk on our own importance, and blind to whatever threatened the make believe world we'd created. No one was innocent where I was born and bred, Prudence. It was a dark place; I was glad to leave it."

"We have to go to Saint Anselm's, Geoffrey. We need to talk to the priests."

CHAPTER 16

"Have you ever questioned a priest about a murder?" Prudence asked.

"I don't think I've ever interrogated a priest about anything," Geoffrey said.

"Not even when you were a Pinkerton?"

"Not even then."

"It's bound to be awkward. Just calling them Father all the time will feel odd."

"If you'd rather not go . . ."

"Half my household staff is Irish and Catholic. Yet I've never set foot inside Saint Anselm's or spoken to a single one of the priests there. How very blind of me." Prudence spoke the last words softly, as if she were alone.

"I doubt anyone in your social circle would find that the slightest bit odd. Servants don't inhabit the same world as their employers." Geoffrey held out his hand to help her from the carriage to the sidewalk in front of Saint Anselm's rectory.

A housekeeper answered the door and ushered them into an empty parlor warmed by a recently kindled fire. A large crucifix hung on one wall, a portrait of Pope Leo XIII over the fireplace. New York's controversial Archbishop Michael Corrigan stared from a place of honor on the wall opposite the crucifix. Brightly painted statues stood in the corners, each with either a lit votive candle or a small vase of flowers on its pedestal. The air was heavy with the smell of burning firewood, wilting flowers, and melting candle wax.

"I'm Father Gerard Mahoney, pastor of Saint Anselm's." The man introducing himself to Geoffrey was nearly as wide as he was tall, with a florid complexion and tufts of white hair floating around his ears. The top of his bald head shone as brightly as the recently waxed and buffed parlor floor. He wore a clerical collar and a cassock with a row of tiny buttons marching down the front. Black trouser legs and a pair of shiny black indoor shoes peeped out from beneath the cassock's hem. Father Mahoney's ringless hands were as white and soft as a woman's.

Taking the seat closest to the fire, he waved his visitors to two uncomfortable-looking horsehair upholstered armchairs.

So far, the pastor had avoided looking directly at Prudence, as if, being a woman, she were of little importance. Or perhaps just invisible.

"How may I help you today?" he asked Geoffrey, blue eyes bright with curiosity.

"Miss MacKenzie and I are making inquiries, Father, and we have reason to believe that you might be of assistance." Geoffrey handed him their business card. He wondered if Mahoney would continue refusing to look at Prudence now that she had been named and introduced.

"We're not here on church business per se, Father," Prudence said, compelling his attention. She hadn't liked him from the moment he walked into the room and pointedly ignored her.

"A member of your parish was murdered on Saturday night." Geoffrey clipped his words so they sounded like the staccato knocks of a fist against a door.

The priest crossed himself, but his face remained expressionless.

"Ellen Tierney," Geoffrey said.

"She worked for the Nolan family," Prudence contributed. "Francis and Lillian Nolan. Their son Joseph. Daughter Alice. I understand the family members are very generous benefactors of Saint Anselm's." It was the wildest of guesses, but she had to take the chance. Every church had its core of wealthy men and socially competitive wives who saw to it their place of worship was worthy of them; churchgoing was as much a part of society's fabric as having the right ancestors and a large bank account.

"May she rest in peace." Father Mahoney was a cautious man. He knew about Ellen Tierney's death, of course, because Father Brennan had described the early morning call in painstaking detail, but what he needed to find out was on whose authority these two expensively dressed strangers were asking questions about her. You didn't advance in Archbishop Corrigan's conservative Catholic world unless you knew when to keep your mouth shut and your head down. Saint Anselm's was a comfortable ministry, not the finest in the city, but far from being the worst. The merest breath of scandal could cause a transfer to one of the tenement parishes.

"Detective Phelan may have spoken to you about Ellen." *Look at me,* Prudence commanded, and he did, as if unable to resist the silent pressure of this confident young woman. "Mr. Hunter and I have been asked to investigate her death." She raised a hand to ward off the question the priest seemed about to ask. "We are not at liberty to reveal the name of the individual whose interests we represent. Mr. Hunter is a lawyer with an office on Wall Street."

There. She'd dropped what amounted to a social bomb, leaving Father Mahoney to draw the inevitable conclusion that Mr. Francis Nolan had hired expensive investigative counsel from the bastion of New York's business community to look into the affair of his maid's murder. The priest would have to ask himself why. The lack of an answer should unsteady him just enough to provide more information than he intended to give.

"Ellen was in Saint Anselm's on Saturday evening for confession." Geoffrey took a notebook out of the breast pocket of his well tailored suit. It was a leather-bound version of the grubby pads on which the Metropolitan detectives made their notes and reporters scribbled their stories. Just seeing a pencil move across paper intimidated witnesses. They wouldn't later on be able to deny what they'd said because the words written down were preserved forever.

"I wasn't hearing confessions Saturday. You'll have to talk to Father Kearns and Father Brennan." The silence lengthened until Father Mahoney felt himself forced to fill it. "Father Kearns is my assistant pastor. Father Brennan arrived at Saint Anselm's a few months ago." More silence. "He did give the last rites to the Nolan girl who was killed. The Nolan maid, I mean. I remember now that he was the priest on duty when the call came in."

"Her name was Ellen Tierney," Prudence said softly.

"Yes, of course. Ellen Tierney."

"Where was Father Brennan before he came to Saint Anselm's?"

Father Mahoney seemed relieved to be able to look away from Prudence to answer Geoffrey's question. "England," he said. "London, to be precise."

"Isn't that unusual?"

"The Church is universal." Score a point for Father Mahoney. He didn't particularly like the new priest assigned to what he thought of as *his* parish, but the urge to defend the man was as natural as the necessity to protect Holy Mother Church from criticism or scandal.

"What can you tell us about Ellen Tierney?"

"The police have already asked about her. Detective Phelan was here this morning."

"And what did you answer, Father?" Prudence kept her voice low, insistent, urgent.

261

If Father Mahoney were uneasy around independent women, he would be thrown off balance by one who pushed and prodded, refused to allow him to retreat behind the safety of his clerical collar.

"I don't understand why I should repeat that information to you." There was the faintest hint of belligerence in his voice. This man rebelled against following any woman's orders.

"I think it's in the best interests of your parish that you do, Father. If, that is, you wish to continue to enjoy the generosity of one of your most munificent laypeople."

"You should ask someone in the Nolan household, someone who worked with Ellen."

"We're asking you." Prudence suspected he wouldn't have recognized Ellen Tierney in church or on the street, and was embarrassed to admit it. "Perhaps Father Kearns and Father Brennan might join us?" she suggested.

She watched Father Mahoney tug on the bellpull that summoned the housekeeper, listened as he gave her instructions, and sat quietly while they waited for the other priests to join them. Silence could be as unnerving as the most pointed of questions.

By the time the parlor door opened to

admit the junior priests of Saint Anselm's, Father Mahoney's round red face was streaked with trails of nervous sweat. He pulled a large white handkerchief from the pocket of his cassock and wiped his forehead and cheeks.

"They're asking about Ellen Tierney," he explained after brief introductions had been made. "Mr. Nolan doesn't seem to think the Metropolitan Police are up to the job of finding out who killed his maid."

"We didn't say that, Father," corrected Prudence in the same steady tone of voice that had already unnerved the priest. "We never revealed the name of our client. We most especially did not mention Mr. Francis Nolan in that context, either in so many words or by inference." Which convinced the three priests that it had indeed been the head of the Nolan family who had set these interlopers on the trail of whoever had deprived him of the services of a trained servant.

"Of course. I didn't mean to imply that you had."

"Ellen was a lovely girl," Father Kearns said, coming to the rescue of the man he worked for. "She was walking out with the policeman Mick McGuire." He knew that she had been doing much more than walking out, but that was privileged information protected by the sacred seal of the confessional. A priest was supposed to be willing to die rather than reveal what had been told him in the confidence of the Sacrament of Penance.

"What else can you tell us about her?" Geoffrey took over the questioning. "How often did she attend Mass? Did she work on any of the church committees or join any of the organizations the parish sponsors?"

"Ellen had very little free time. She was a junior servant, remember. A housekeeper or a butler might have spare hours in the week, but not a maid. She had her half days off, but not much more than that. Lately she'd probably have spent them with Mick McGuire."

"Was there talk of marriage?"

"It may have been too soon, Mr. Hunter." Father Kearns knew it was actually a bit late.

"So she didn't volunteer with any other ladies to polish the church pews or iron the surplices worn by the altar boys?"

"Not to my knowledge. She might have done it occasionally, but not on a regular basis. Ellen usually attended the early Mass on Sunday."

"What about confession? Did she come to

that? Saturday afternoons, as I understand."

"I wouldn't know, Mr. Hunter. What passes between a penitent and his confessor is secret and sealed. Names are not required."

"I didn't ask what she might have said in confession. Only if she came to Saint Anselm's on Saturday afternoons when confessions were being heard."

"Again, Mr. Hunter, I wouldn't know."

"Wouldn't know or refuse to tell?"

"Believe whichever you choose. I have nothing more to say on the subject."

Geoffrey turned to Father Brennan, the priest recently arrived from London. "What can you tell us about Ellen Tierney?" he asked.

"Nothing, I'm afraid." Father Brennan spoke with a faint Irish brogue, as though his years in England hadn't quite succeeded in uprooting him from the country of his birth. "I was called to the Nolan house to administer the Last Sacrament. It was all very pro forma. I may have seen the girl while she was still alive, but I can't be certain. I've not yet managed to meet all of the parishioners. If put to the test, I'm not sure I could remember the names of the ones I have been introduced to." He smiled wryly, as if both amused and dismayed at his apparent failure.

Quite handsome men, Prudence decided, her eyes on the two younger priests. She'd written off Father Mahoney as any kind of viable suspect or witness, but she was curious about what the women of the parish thought of Fathers Kearns and Brennan. Catholic priests did not marry, and were presumably celibate; she wondered how many of them actually kept to the letter and spirit of their vows.

"There's another young woman we need to ask you about," Geoffrey continued. "She may have been at Saint Anselm's two weeks ago, also on a Saturday afternoon. Also for confession. Her name is Nora Kenny."

"I don't recognize the name," Father Kearns said. "Is she a member of the parish?"

"May I know why you're inquiring about her?" Father Mahoney asked. As pastor, he was the individual ultimately responsible for the spiritual welfare of the men, women, and children nominally under his care. It didn't hurt to remind these strangers and his two assistants who was in charge.

"She's dead. Her body was mutilated in the same way Ellen Tierney's was." Geoffrey watched closely as comprehension slowly came to the clean shaven priestly faces.

"Desecrated." The way Father Kearns pronounced the word left no doubt in anyone's mind that he now realized the murder itself may have been only one of the sins committed against the dead girl.

"I don't understand why you've come to Saint Anselm's with these questions." The pastor's face was nearly as white as his hair, then his cheeks flushed with anger. "Where was this other girl killed?"

"Nora Kenny," Prudence reminded him in that same soft but insistent voice. She kept her face impassive when he glared at her.

"Her body was found in Colonial Park on the Sunday morning after she was murdered." Geoffrey looked intently at Father Brennan, but the priest didn't volunteer the information that he had administered the church's Last Sacrament to this murder victim also. "We don't know where she was killed."

"The police never asked us about her," blustered Father Mahoney. "I would have been informed if Saint Anselm's was involved in any way." He glanced at his assistants for confirmation. "Father Kearns? Father Brennan?"

Kearns answered for both of them. "You're right, Father. There can't be any

267

connection between this Kenny girl and Saint Anselm's. Especially if she wasn't a parishioner."

"Except that Nora Kenny and Ellen Tierney knew one another. It's possible that both of them came here for confession. To one of the three of you." Geoffrey leaned into the silence his accusation produced, studying each priest's reaction. "Let's go back to Nora Kenny. That would have been two Saturdays ago. November tenth."

The seconds stretched on, the tension tight and unbroken.

"As it happens, I remember that I was the only one hearing confessions that Saturday," Father Brennan finally said. "Father Mahoney was ill and Father Kearns had been called away to a deathbed."

"What time did confessions begin?" Geoffrey asked.

"At three-thirty. We start early in winter so as to finish before dark."

"You must have gone into the church before three-thirty."

"About fifteen minutes earlier."

"Were there people already waiting?"

"Yes."

"Describe them for us, Father."

"I'm not sure I can. I didn't look closely

at anyone. Sometimes it embarrasses people."

"Explain that."

"We try to maintain anonymity in the confessional. The idea that it's a nameless penitent speaking to God's representative on earth. The distance makes it easier for a sinner to confess. It's not always true, but usually."

"So you came into the church and walked up the side aisle and into a confessional booth without recognizing anyone kneeling in the pews?"

"I would say that's accurate. I wasn't trying to identify anyone."

"Nora Kenny was a very small girl with black hair and blue eyes. She was born in America so she wouldn't have had an Irish brogue."

"I don't remember anyone like that."

"Are you sure?"

"If you're asking me because you want to know what she said in confession, I couldn't tell you anyway. I'm sure you've heard of the Seal of the Confessional?"

"So she was there."

"I didn't see anyone in the church who answers to the description you just gave me."

"You prayed over her corpse as she was

being carried out of Colonial Park, Father." Geoffrey watched for a reaction, but Father Brennan disappointed him. No uncontrollable facial tic or rapid blinking of the eyes. No flush of fear or anger. "Does that help your memory?"

"I wasn't told her name," Brennan said smoothly. "I don't think the men carrying the stretcher knew it." He sighed. "It doesn't really matter, though. The prayers are said conditionally over the dead, just in case the soul might be lingering. It's not necessary to know a name for the sacrament to be efficacious. But it is sadder."

"I won't have you badgering one of my priests," Father Mahoney interrupted.

"Only a few more questions, Father," Geoffrey soothed.

"We understand that young Mr. Nolan had at one time expressed a desire to be a priest himself," Prudence said.

"I believe he did." Father Kearns's smile faded. He'd been at Saint Anselm's long enough for Father Mahoney to have told him Joseph Nolan's story. It was one of those parish tales that everyone knew and relished because the ending was still in doubt. If there was nothing else to gossip about, there was always Francis Nolan's two strange adult children and their missed vocations to the religious life. "The Nolans are a good Catholic family," he said.

Father Mahoney got to his feet. Immediately, Fathers Kearns and Brennan joined him. "We've answered as many of your questions as I feel we need to. We'll remember these two poor girls in our prayers, but that's all we can do."

It went against the grain to tell parish secrets to outsiders, and there were things about young Joseph Nolan that didn't bear too close examination. Lately he'd seemed odder than usual, as if he were teetering on the brink of some catastrophic decision that would have dire consequences. He had the look about him of a drinker who's been on the wagon contemplating the glass of whiskey that will tip him back into inebriation. Father Mahoney weighed the good of the parish against his private doubts about Joseph Nolan's stability, and opted to damp down even the hint of scandal.

"And I wouldn't have talked to you at all if one of the poor dead girls hadn't been a part of the Nolan household."

Where Joseph Nolan saw her every day, Geoffrey thought.

Father Brennan held the parlor door open as the pastor and Father Kearns passed through.

When the housekeeper appeared to show them out, Prudence and Geoffrey left without another word being spoken.

"That was one of the oddest conversations I've ever had," Prudence said as she and Geoffrey climbed into the carriage that would take them back to Fifth Avenue. She glanced across the street as something bright caught her eye. "I think there's a dog and a redheaded man over there in the alley. They look like they've made a hut for themselves out of cardboard."

"There are people like that all over the city," Geoffrey told her. "In the winter the police stations open up their basements for them. At least it gets them out of the cold."

"Did you get the impression the pastor was hiding something?"

"Mahoney went out of his way not to link any of the Nolans to Ellen Tierney's murder, but I thought Father Kearns was on the point of letting us know that the younger Nolan is worth keeping an eye on."

"I want to talk to Colleen again when we get home," Prudence said. "I'm not sure I asked the right questions. I keep thinking something is about to make sense to me, then whatever it is slips through my fingers."

"We know that Ellen Tierney went to

Saint Anselm's regularly. We have Colleen's verification of that. And we're sure that Nora Kenny was there at least once before the day she was killed."

"She had time after the ferry docked to stop by Saint Anselm's on her way to Fifth Avenue, yet Father Brennan claims he didn't see her. Why, when she left the hens at the kitchen door, didn't she stay to knock until someone opened it? Or go around to the stables. As a last resort, she could have rung the front doorbell. Cameron might have scolded her, but at least she would have been safe. That's the great mystery, Geoffrey. That's what we have to find out. The only thing that makes sense is that she was in such a hurry to get somewhere, somewhere she was expected to be at a certain time, that she didn't think she could spare the extra few minutes to attract someone's attention."

"Just as important, she must have felt safe about where she was going or who she was supposed to meet. Safe enough so it didn't occur to her that someone should be informed of her whereabouts. Could she have been meeting a female friend? A cousin? She might have written to this person to set up a time and place to meet."

"Wishful thinking, Geoffrey. She spent her

whole life on Staten Island. She didn't know anyone in the city but us."

"Then the only other thing I can suggest is that she had an appointment with someone who was either going to confirm that she was pregnant or perform an abortion."

"I'll grant you a visit to a midwife but not to an abortionist. Nora had to know that many pregnancies end in miscarriages. I think that's why she hadn't told Dominic what she suspected. Despite the danger of being found out, she had decided to wait. There's something else. We know that Ellen went to confession at Saint Anselm's. Suppose Nora did, also. Not for the convenience of stopping in as she was passing the church, but because she didn't want to confess to her parish priest on Staten Island."

"What difference would that make?" Geoffrey asked.

"It might take her back there later than was safe. Suppose the lines were long. We already know that only Father Brennan was hearing confessions that Saturday. What if she gave up, got tired of waiting, went to the house with her hens, then changed her mind at the last minute and raced back to Saint Anselm's to catch the priest before the church closed for the evening? What if someone saw her alone on the street? What if that's how she was caught and killed? Off her guard because she was hurrying back to the church, or even nearly there? Could that be the link? Proximity to Saint Anselm's?"

"Our murderer lives or works nearby?" In his mind's eye, Geoffrey was picturing the streets around Saint Anselm's.

"Why not? He's killed two young women, two servants. He has to lie in wait for them somewhere, has to have chosen a spot where he's sure potential victims will pass by. The girls would be careful near the mouths of alleyways, might even cross the street to avoid them. But no one thinks anything bad can happen within the precincts of a church. So why wouldn't that feeling of safety extend to the street in front of the church? After all, you're only a few steps from sanctuary. I think that's our link, Geoffrey, but I'm not sure we could convince anyone else of it."

"Perhaps not Detective Phelan, but why not Ned Hayes?"

"He won't be blinded by reverence for religion."

"We need an unbiased, neutral eye."

"It's not just any church. It's Saint Anselm's. It has to be," Prudence decided.

The lace curtain in the rectory parlor window twitched as the carriage drove off.

For a long time the man standing behind it stared out into the empty street.

Chapter 17

Joseph Nolan had wanted to be a priest from the day he made his First Holy Communion. Instead, he became a butcher.

When he was ten years old his father, Francis Patrick Nolan, handed him a tin lunch pail and a sharp butcher knife. Then he took his son to one of the family owned slaughterhouses in lower Manhattan where Joseph stood on a wooden box and used the long, wide blade of his knife to slit the bellies of freshly skinned steers hanging upside down from hooks in front of him. He learned to evade the gush of entrails, schooled himself not to gag at the stench of blood and excrement, became quick, deft, and skilled at the job of evisceration. Francis occasionally nodded his approval; he believed that to tell his son he was proud of him would weaken the boy.

Francis Nolan was a rich man. He never told anyone how he'd managed it, but in

1861 he secured an Army Commissary Department contract as victualler to the Union troops. With the profits that poured into his pockets, he climbed into what the *New York Times* called the shoddy aristocracy, that crowd of brand new millionaires who made their fortunes from the conflict that tore the country apart.

Substandard uniforms. Poorly stitched shoes. Hardtack alive with worms and weevils. Rifles that misfired. Medical supplies that never reached field hospitals. Bacon so green or salty it was inedible. Rancid pork, dried beef a soldier could crack a tooth on. Desiccated vegetable cakes that turned into stinky green mush when dissolved in water. Whatever the Commissary Department needed was farmed out to hordes of suppliers eager to pay as many bribes as it took to buy themselves the lucrative contracts.

As the post-war years passed, the millionaires of the shoddy aristocracy gradually slipped into the ranks of the cultural and business elite of New York City. They married dowerless daughters of old families and turned respectable. Learned how to dress and partner a lady in the dance, how to manage their silverware and curtail their drinking. Kept their mouths shut, listened and learned. Not too long after the *Times* first bestowed the title on them, few cared who might or might not be shoddy. New York City was built and run on money. Society, for all its pretensions, couldn't exist without the substantial fortunes and profligate spending of its new members.

Joseph Nolan wasn't allowed to lay down his knife until he had learned the lessons his father set out for him. Francis was shrewd and demanding; not until his son mastered every skill of a workstation was he moved to another. Only when Joseph could step effortlessly into any man's place in all of the lines that stretched from killing floor to packaging was he permitted to remove his bloodstained apron and rubber boots.

The Nolans became respectable. To see father and son leave their Fifth Avenue mansion in the morning was to imagine them on their way to a bank, a law office, a gentleman's club, or the stock exchange. The most important advancement Francis made to his new way of life was to open offices well beyond the stink of the several slaughterhouses he now owned. He directed the Nolan empire from a wood paneled retreat that would have satisfied a Vanderbilt. Nolan meat was served in the finest New York restaurants and homes, yet the

Nolan name was never associated with commerce. Empire Quality Meats and Purveyors. The company name had a ring to it and was entirely anonymous.

The family was wealthy beyond even Francis's early dreams, but everyone who knew them agreed that the Nolans weren't happy. Not a single member of the family was content with who he was or what he possessed. Francis could never be rich enough, Lillian would always crave the social position from which being Irish and Catholic excluded her, and young Alice feared the touch of a man and yearned for the cool, safe chastity of a nun.

When people gossiped about the Nolans they speculated most often and most freely about Joseph, the handsome son who hadn't married. There were some who said he never would, that he was one of those sad cases known as missed priests, men who did not answer their heart's call to the priesthood. Misfits in a secular society. They were often gentle, frightened souls who seemed baffled by life's choices. Women felt sorry for them and yearned to comfort them.

But in Joseph Nolan's case, denial had sharpened and embittered him so that everything about him had an edge to it. Marriageable young ladies who were initially attracted by his good looks and affluent prospects soon avoided him; he made them uneasy, though it wasn't anything overtly objectionable he said or did. It was more who he was, the essence of the man. Something about him set off alarm bells, a reaction that would have amused his father, who considered him an unambitious weakling.

Francis was deeply disappointed in his only son and didn't trouble to hide his dissatisfaction whenever it was just the family together. In front of outsiders, the Nolans didn't break ranks. They were Irish enough to know that their only hope of making it through life was to stick together.

Kevin Carney and Blossom kept watch in the narrow alley across from Saint Anselm's, the man and dog huddled close for warmth inside a makeshift cocoon of torn newspapers, blankets, and rags. The dog's name hadn't originally been Blossom, but she looked so dejected and smelled so much worse than Kevin himself that he decided she needed cheering up. Sitting on her rear haunches and leaning against her human, she was bigger than the man, her thick fur as mottled red and matted as the hair on his head. Kevin had never grown a beard.

No one knew why.

They seldom spoke as they observed the church, only an occasional muffled growl or clicking of teeth breaking the silence, but they were in agreement. The man they had seen coming out of Saint Anselm's two weeks ago with the fragrant rolled up body on his shoulder had not put in another appearance while they were there. They took turns sleeping during the daylight hours, and Kevin left Blossom on duty when they grew hungry or thirsty. Not that he was a more skillful scavenger, but he did have Billy McGlory's money in his pocket, which made for better feeding than what could be pawed out of a garbage bin.

It wasn't often that Billy McGlory made a mistake, but when he insisted that Kevin and Blossom bed down in his storeroom on Saturday night, he'd made one that was to have grave consequences. Whoever killed Nora Kenny had struck again, but this time the burlap cocoon had been laid inside the stable yard of a private home. If they'd been in their alleyway, Carney and his dog might have seen the rug man again, would have followed and stayed with him. Instead, comfortably full of steak and potatoes, they'd been lying on a pallet of blankets snoring away the midnight hours in the back room of the Armory.

Kevin felt sorry for the Irish girl who'd been killed on Saturday night, but he knew there wasn't a thing in the world he could have done to prevent it. He was a realist. People died. Other people killed. He hoped Mr. McGlory would explain to them what was going on; the newspaper stories that appeared in the Monday morning editions were confusing and contradictory. One paper proclaimed in huge headlines that a Ripper was at work in the city; another printed only a few inches about an Irish maid killed by an unknown assailant.

They saw Miss MacKenzie and Mr. Hunter arrive at the Saint Anselm rectory on Monday afternoon and ducked down out of sight behind their cardboard barricade when they left.

"She may have seen us," Kevin told Blossom, "but I don't think it matters."

They grew twitchy as night fell and then another whole day passed. Newsboys shouted a headline about a copper who'd been arrested for killing his girlfriend. Both of them Irish.

It wasn't a good idea to bed down in the same place too many times in succession, but Kevin reminded Blossom that they were working for Mr. McGlory, which meant they had no choice in the matter. Both of them shuddered and moaned as they took turns dozing.

He didn't know what dreams disturbed the dog's sleep, but Kevin himself only ever had one nightmare. He sat on the floor of a small room that smelled of sickness where a woman lay on a stained mattress, a blue faced baby cradled in her arm. The woman didn't speak, the baby didn't cry. Time passed and the stink got worse. When he left the room, he passed a copper lumbering up the tenement stairs. He stepped out into the street and never went back.

They had just finished a cone of newspaper filled with fried potatoes and bacon from the vendor on the corner when they heard footsteps. Kevin heard them before Blossom, but she confirmed the approach of their prey with a quick whine. Not even bacon interfered with the dog's extraordinary nose. They slunk back into the smelly darkness of the alleyway, aware that while the man probably couldn't find them by scent, he most certainly would be able to see them unless they hid. A streetlamp stood at the mouth of the alley, its light pooling on the sidewalk, casting fingers of illumination into the darkness. It was still dusk, Tuesday evening; the man hadn't waited for full darkness to fall.

At first, it didn't seem the man would go into the church. He walked past it, not even turning his head to say a quick prayer or nod hello to the power who dwelled within. He must be in a terrible hurry to forget something like that. Kevin made a rapid sign of the cross in silent apology and Blossom snuffled politely. They might not be rich, but they knew their manners.

The man turned back and walked quickly up the steps, opened Saint Anselm's huge central door, and disappeared inside. He was back out again before they could decide whether to creep out of their hiding place. He carried a small black bag in one hand, the kind of satchel doctors often used to transport their medicines and instruments. He was in a hurry, didn't spare even a few seconds to look around him. They let him go.

Joseph Nolan was a full block ahead of them before Kevin and Blossom crept out from their alleyway. It didn't matter if they occasionally lost sight of him; the scent trail he was laying down was strong, even in the midst of all of the other smells through which he was moving. He didn't smell of blood; Kevin decided he must have washed it off with strong soap and then doused himself with a leathery smelling men's cologne to hide what he might have missed. No matter. Each human gave off a distinctive odor that no soap or perfume in the world could entirely obliterate. A good nose would always find it.

Blossom agreed. Nose to the pavement, she rarely so much as twitched a nostril at any other trail though she did stop once to relieve herself of some of the potatoes and bacon.

When Nolan hailed a hansom cab, Kevin and Blossom trotted along behind the vehicle, having told the horse pulling it not to give them away. The streets were congested with traffic, slowing vehicles to a frustratingly sluggish crawl. Kevin and his dog used the frequent stops to rest and look around them.

Twenty minutes after he'd climbed into the hansom cab, Joseph Nolan descended in front of a house that looked no different from every other brownstone on the street except that its parlor windows were so heavily curtained that not a speck of inside light shone through. A curious person could stand right in front of Madame Jolene's establishment, hearing and seeing nothing out of the ordinary. Even when visitors climbed the steps, rang the bell, and were admitted, the outer door opened into one of two small vestibules illuminated by the weakest of gas lights. You might catch a glimpse of a pert maid wearing a black uniform complete with frilly white apron and cap, but nothing more interesting than that.

Kevin and Blossom made their way around the end of the block to the service alley behind the house, where Kevin knocked softly on the kitchen door, a measured tattoo that beat out a code not shared with clients. The woman who welcomed him with open arms was taller than he by a full two heads, and it would have taken three or four Kevins to match her weight.

"Are you delivering something for himself?" she asked, rubbing vigorously on Blossom's flea-bitten ears. Himself being Billy McGlory, whose name it was sometimes best not to mention aloud.

"Not tonight, Miss Brenda." If Mr. McGlory chose to tell Big Brenda what it was about, that was his task to do. Until he received further instructions, Kevin would say as little as possible. "There's some information as is needed about one of the gentlemen."

"Is there now? You'd better come in and

sit yourself down at the table. I'll send word up to herself that you're here."

Herself was a madam whose house was bankrolled by McGlory, protected by the Metropolitan Police, and patronized by a stellar roster of political and financial bigwigs. Jolene had started her new life in America as a Gaelic speaking immigrant whose thick accent in English had been almost impenetrable when she got off the boat. She soon discovered that the accent meant she could claim any nationality she chose, and that deciding to be French brought a higher price for what she was selling on her back. Or any other position a client wanted. She'd been at it for more than twenty years now; there were times when she imagined she actually *was* French. Nobody cared enough to challenge her.

"What is it, Kevin? Brenda says you're here for information." Madame Jolene dressed in black silk, her low cut bodice and bustled skirts heavily beaded with black crystals and shiny jet that reflected candle and gas light in hundreds of tiny explosions. Perfumed, rouged, and powdered, coal black hair swept atop her head and liberally sprinkled with more of the black crystals and jet beads, Jolene was frighteningly beautiful, a fairytale witch come to life. She no longer drank alcohol or indulged in laudanum, seldom gambled on anything less sure than herself, and had a reputation among her girls for being fair and occasionally generous — if you worked hard. Met your quota. Satisfied your clients. Didn't get pregnant. Like McGlory, she had a weak spot for Kevin Carney. Few people knew why. No one dared ask.

"His name is Joseph Nolan. Himself wants the complete story on him."

"The complete story, is it? That may take some time. He's just gone up with Sally Lynn. Paid for two hours. If he has any secrets, Sally Lynn will know what they are, but you'll have to wait until he's through."

"I can do that."

"Brenda will see that you get something to eat. The dog, too." Kevin looked so much like Jolene's youngest brother, long dead of poverty and the cholera, that every time she saw him she had to fight back tears. It didn't do to remember too often what you'd left behind. "The cot in the shed's made up, if you want it. You can take a pot of charcoal out with you." She always made the offer and he always turned it down.

"Two hours you say?"

"He seldom stays longer than that. But he never stays less, either."

"I wonder what he does for two hours." In Kevin's experience, ten minutes was ample time to milk the wiener.

One of Madame Jolene's rules was that unless a client turned violent, a girl couldn't pick and choose who she'd go with, *go with* being the euphemism for whatever the client requested and could pay for. Not that Sally Lynn had anything against dressing up and playacting, but what Mr. Nolan wanted gave her the shivers. The same thing every time. Never any variety. And if she tried to introduce something new, he'd turn cold and mean eyed until she fell back into the regular routine. He was the most baffling client she'd ever had, but at least he wasn't dangerous. Mind numbingly repetitive, but safe. And he tipped well, which, since Madame allowed a girl to keep half of what a client thought was a little something extra just for her, made Joseph Nolan bearable.

He liked to give directions, as if she didn't know how it started or what came next.

"Everything," he instructed, "take off everything."

He flicked a small cat-o'-nine-tails up and down, never striking her with it, never allowing it to come close enough to hit her accidentally. He seemed to be satisfied with the sound and the sight of the whip swishing through the air. She had to pretend to be afraid, which she did, mewling like a lost kitten, batting her eyes rapidly, fumbling at the belt to the Chinese robe she wore.

When Nolan had first brought the costume he wanted her to wear she'd almost laughed. Caught herself just in time, warned off by the look on his face — as though he were trapped in a trance or a vision, head tilted upward, eyes half rolled back in their sockets, mouth open but soundless. He held the soft black serge and the starched white linen on his outstretched hands until she was ready, until she had washed every inch of her body with the special odorless soap he had brought. When she was cleansed and dry he slipped the black gown over her head, sighing in contentment as the graceful folds covered her from neck to feet. He looped a white rope around her waist, tying three knots in each of the two pieces hanging down along the line of her skirt. Finally, he slid the starched white linen wimple over her head, tugging until only her face peered out of its folds. He pinned a white veil to the starched headband of the wimple, then stepped back to admire his novice nun.

If that had been all, Sally Lynn would have

hiked her skirts up and gotten on with it. Some clients never removed a single garment during the whole experience; they were usually the ones who paid for thirty minutes and finished with time left over. But with Joseph Nolan, the costuming was just the beginning. There were prayers to say, which she had to repeat word for word after him because she had only the vaguest idea what the Latin meant. She folded her hands in the traditional prayer position, genuflected, stood up, took a few steps, genuflected again. She bent from the waist, resting her hands on her knees, then knelt with arms outstretched and head bowed. He watched, correcting her posture, the angle at which she held her head, the smoothness with which she dropped to one knee and got up again. Always the same actions performed in the identical sequence, always the incomprehensible Latin phrases.

The first time Joseph Nolan had put on a priest's collar and cassock Sally Lynn was stunned. He looked so authentic, as if he'd just stepped down from the altar.

"Father?" she'd exclaimed.

He'd blessed her, and when they were finished gave her the largest tip she had ever received.

The part Sally Lynn really disliked was

when he knelt, bared his back to her, and crossed both arms against his chest. She knew what it meant, and that it wouldn't do any good to refuse. Madame Jolene would blame her if he took his fat purse elsewhere. Rules were rules, and it wasn't Sally Lynn who was beaten until rivulets of blood bubbled up through broken skin.

Nolan wept as she laid on the lash, but wouldn't allow her to lessen the pain by letting up on the strokes. The few times she tried, he grew frighteningly angry; it was the closest he came to turning the whip on her. He wanted to suffer. He insisted that she beat him with the full strength of her arm. She turned her attention inward, raising and lowering the cat-o'-nine-tails mechanically. Eventually she was only vaguely aware of what she was doing.

"The first time he came he used a different name, but he doesn't bother with that anymore. It's Joseph Nolan, all right." There were clients waiting in the parlors, but Madame Jolene had instructed Sally Lynn to answer Kevin's questions. She hadn't been able to bring herself to invite Carney and his dog into her private office, so Big Brenda had cleared off a space at the end of the long kitchen worktable, setting down a pot of the heavy stewed tea that kept the Irish working class going when there wasn't enough food to fill their bellies . . . which there seldom, if ever, was.

Tuesday was one of two weekly baking days at the brothel, the same as in a well-run private home. So there was white bread and butter, slices of rich yellow cake smeared with dollops of currant jelly, and twisted pieces of unsweetened dough into which sharp cheddar cheese had been mixed. For every two bites Kevin Carney took, Blossom received at least one.

"We pretended we didn't know who he was, as we do for all of our gentlemen clients who prefer to be called by an alias, but I make it a point not to do business with anyone whose identity I can't discover." Madame Jolene crunched down on one of the cheese straws. It would have tasted even more delicious with a nice glass of sherry, she thought regretfully, but she'd vowed herself off spirits after a disastrous night she'd rather not remember, and she wasn't a woman to go back on her promises. "Tell Kevin what he needs to know, Sally Lynn."

And so she did, unselfconsciously providing details that soon had Big Brenda's shoulders jerking with suppressed laughter. The cook had left them alone at the table, but she didn't miss a word Sally Lynn said as she mixed puddings and chopped soup vegetables for the next day's lunch. Working hours were topsy-turvy, as the whores were at their busiest when respectable women slept. Since Big Brenda herself had once entertained clients, though she had unfortunately and rather quickly grown too tall and too broad for the job, she was neither shocked nor surprised by what she heard.

There were men who liked girls to dress up like their mothers or the upstairs chamber maid, others who could only achieve release when teased along with pinafores. One death obsessed client had paid handsomely to have a coffin stored in a spare closet; he eventually bought out his girl's contract and set her up in her own house, presumably decorated as an undertaker's establishment. Over the years Big Brenda had heard just about everything, but nothing had tickled her funny bone quite as much as the thought of Joseph Nolan dressing Sally Lynn up as a nun.

"You can forget you were ever asked about him," Kevin instructed when Sally Lynn had dredged up every bit of information she could remember about her best paying client. He slid a five-dollar Liberty gold piece across the table, but it got no farther than

Madame Jolene's fingers. Sally Lynn shrugged her shoulders; she knew she'd eventually get her half if there was enough left over after her tab had been paid for the month.

"Back to work," Madame Jolene instructed.

Sally Lynn took another gulp of the strong, sugary tea that would have to see her through until closing time. Nobody wanted a drunken whore in a well run house, neither clients nor madam, so whatever a girl drank in the parlors was liberally watered down. She wondered what Big Brenda was fixing for the meal she served at the end of the night. You slept better on a full stomach. No one knew that better than a girl who'd cried until morning because the hunger pains kept waking her up. Sometimes, toward the end of an evening, food was all she could think of. Clients thought the anticipatory smile was for them; it wasn't.

One more mouthful of tea and she was off.

"I'll give the floor a good sweep and a mopping," Big Brenda said as she closed and locked the door behind Kevin and his dog. Their smell lingered in the kitchen, despite the aromas coming from the oven and the pots steaming on the cookstove.

Madame Jolene drew in a deep breath.
Unwashed human and unwashed dog.
Urine soaked alleyways and rotting garbage.
The sharp tang of the newsprint they
wrapped themselves in to keep out the cold.
Kevin wouldn't last much longer. Neither
would Blossom. Life on the streets was
always short and usually violent. She
thought of the little brother who had died
so long ago, and who would have looked
just like Kevin Carney if he'd lived to
become a man. Probably better that he
didn't, given the years of suffering life would
have brought him.

Madame Jolene rubbed at the ink stain on
her right forefinger. She'd tot up her accounts again tonight. Once upon a time she
had dreamed of getting rich enough to sell
out, but that had never been a realistic
aspiration. The best she could hope for was
a fat cushion to keep her safe, coins enough
in her purse to continue paying off the
police and to pay back, with interest, what
Billy McGlory had advanced her, what he
now demanded as a silent partner. You
could depend on Billy, but only if you
played the game his way. It was how she ran
the house, and why they understood one
another so well.

Flipping the gold Liberty five-dollar piece in the air and catching it on the fly, Madame Jolene went back to work.

Chapter 18

Mick McGuire understood what he was in for as soon as he was arrested. The way they did it told him everything he needed to know. He wasn't quietly ushered out of his precinct through a rear door and taken down to Mulberry Street for a private talk with the detective in charge of the case. Not on your life. They came to his boarding house the Tuesday morning after Ellen was killed, when he was supposed to be off shift and after he'd been up all night drinking whiskey to drown his sorrows. The timing wasn't accidental; they'd planned it that way.

Hands cuffed behind his back, uniform coat hanging wrinkled and unbuttoned from his shoulders, unshaven face mottled and drawn, Mick McGuire stumbled down Mrs. Ansbro's immaculate front steps while a crowd of street urchins booed him on and reporters waved their notebooks in the air.

Just in case anyone could be in doubt, the coppers hanging on to his arms volunteered his name more than a few times and confirmed that yes, he was being arrested for the brutal murder of Ellen Tierney, his erstwhile girlfriend. Her that was found in Mr. Francis Nolan's stable yard Sunday morning, and a terrible thing done to her they weren't at liberty to discuss until Captain Byrnes decided to release the details.

Mick had ridden in a Black Maria before, of course, but never as a prisoner in cuffs and leg irons to keep him from toppling between the two rows of wooden benches. The same coppers who would have drunk a beer or two or three with him at the end of a working day stared at him with frank disgust. A really bad cop made all of them look worse than they were and gave the reformers more ammunition. What the hell was the matter with him? He didn't have to kill the girl, did he? And then cut her up like that? There wasn't a shred of sympathy or understanding for Mick McGuire. The chief of detectives had ordered it to be that way.

McGuire was too important an arrest to trust to someone who might be tempted to go easy on him. With Steven Phelan to lend a hand from time to time, Byrnes himself put on the black gloves, lit a cigar that would envelop the suspect's head in fumes, and set to work.

"Why did you kill her, McGuire?"

"I didn't, sir. I swear to God I didn't."

Byrnes gave him no time to catch his breath and choke back the vomit a punch to his midsection had spewed out. He hammered him like a boxer softening up his opponent before landing the hit that would knock him out. Mick's head snapped from side to side, the bones in his neck cracking with every twist. His ribs caved in under a fusillade of precisely timed blows not quite heavy enough to break them in half and puncture his lungs. Pain was the goal of the third degree, pain and confession. The Metropolitan Police had perfected their favorite method of interrogation; they seldom killed a prisoner outright because more often than not they got the cooperation they were after.

McGuire had seen and participated in too many third degrees not to know how they were run. He knew exactly what was coming to him. Whether it would prompt him to confess to a crime he hadn't committed before his face got battered beyond repair and his jaw broken was a moot point. He was determined to keep on protesting his innocence, given the fact that a rope waited for him if he admitted guilt. The first time he passed out, Byrnes motioned to Steven Phelan to throw a bucket of vinegar water on the prisoner. Ostensibly it was to clean out his wounds, but in reality the stinging burn of the raw vinegar sometimes broke a man faster than fists.

McGuire shook his head like a bear getting ready for the dogs, but he couldn't stand; they'd tied him to a splintery wooden chair.

"We can make it go easy or hard on you. You know that. So now tell me. Why did you kill Ellen Tierney? Was it because she was pregnant? Is that why you did it?"

McGuire stared down at the wet floor, at his polished boots soaking in the vinegar water. He'd had his suspicions when she started talking about marriage all the time, but he hadn't been sure. He should have moved faster, should have gotten himself out of Mrs. Ansbro's comfortable room before the murder happened. The boarding house was too close to where the body had been found. Dumped. He tried to think, tried to come up with an alibi for the time when she was being killed, but he didn't have one.

He'd worked Sunday, but only half a shift. They'd sent a couple of men out to take him to the mortuary where he'd stared at the body and couldn't believe it was really her. All that glorious red hair lying stiff with blood around her head, the crimson and black necklace under her chin. That's what coppers called a slit throat, *a necklace*, especially if it was a woman wearing it. Nobody was accusing him of anything then. That happened later, when Byrnes had had a chance to think about it and pick out his suspect. By that time, McGuire knew it was all over for him. It was too late. His only hope was not to crack under the third degree, to hold on and pray that another killing while he was behind bars would eventually set him free.

He knew how prisoners broke under the third degree, spilling out one at a time the facts that condemned them. The important thing was never to say anything, not to respond to any of the questions, to ignore the goading designed to make a guilty man explode. Once you started talking, you didn't stop. And while he knew he wasn't guilty, Mick also knew that many an innocent man had been railroaded straight to the gallows. He wouldn't be a scapegoat for anyone, he decided, clenching his teeth and sending his mind somewhere else. They could beat him all they wanted, he wouldn't crack. He'd never beg them to stop, never trade the lies they wanted to hear for an end to pain.

There was something else, too. As a copper, if they succeeded in locking him up, he wouldn't last long enough to learn the prison ropes. He'd get a knife in the ribs or his head held down in a toilet, neither of them an easy way to go. He could survive the cells in the Tombs where prisoners were locked up while they waited for trial, but he'd never make it through the kind of sentence given to murderers who didn't hang.

The rhythmic pounding went on until the two detectives were too tired to continue and their fists in the black gloves hurt too much to strike another blow. McGuire was bloody and only semiconscious, but in his own way he'd beaten them. Except for the single sentence denying any guilt in the killing of Ellen Tierney, he never said a word.

"They took me to the prison infirmary," Tim Fahey told Prudence and Geoffrey. "According to my medical chart, I fell down the stairs while trying to get away. An attendant handcuffed me to the bed." He pressed a hand to his bruised and bound ribs as he leaned against the bars of his cell for support. "How did you find me?"

"Josiah." Prudence smiled at their secretary's persistence. "He never stopped demanding to be shown a copy of your transfer documents and I think he called in nearly every favor he was owed."

"Will you thank him for me? A lot of people arrested the way I was get permanently lost in the Tombs."

"There's been another murder, Tim," Geoffrey said. "Another Irish maid. She spent time with both Nora and Colleen Riordan. In fact, she worked just a few houses down the street from Miss MacKenzie's. Her name was Ellen Tierney. Did you know her?"

Fahey made the sign of the cross and murmured a quick prayer. "I know the name because Nora mentioned her, but she never came to Staten Island to visit. Was she . . . ?"

"Just like Nora. It has to be the same man. The press didn't print any of the details of Nora's killing because they weren't given them. Byrnes ordered the autopsy suppressed. The only way this man could have duplicated what was done to Nora is if he was the one who murdered her."

"They'll have to release me," Fahey said. "If I was in here, how could I have killed again? There's no way they can pin this one on me." In his mind he was nearly a free man.

"It won't be that simple." Geoffrey handed a copy of that afternoon's *Tribune* through the bars. It was folded open to the story of Mick McGuire's arrest. "Someone dug up or the department deliberately leaked McGuire's past disciplinary actions. He has a nasty reputation for being too vigorous about enforcing shakedowns. He wasn't satisfied with the bag coming into his precinct, he had to add to it on his own, and sometimes he ran into victims who weren't inclined to make an extra payment just to finance his promotion to sergeant. There's no history of him cutting anybody up, but he's sent more than one storeowner to the hospital."

"Nobody has had the nerve to bring charges against him," Prudence said, "but everyone knew what was going on."

"He isn't a slasher?" Fahey said desperately.

"No, but they're pinning Ellen's murder on him just the same. Phelan gives the identical reasons he did when they arrested you. According to him, McGuire found out that Ellen was cheating on him, got mad drunk, and cut her up."

"We know it doesn't make sense," Prudence added. "Two identical killings ascribed to two different men? All it's going to take is one really smart reporter with good sources. Once the questions start flying, Byrnes will have to drop the charges."

"Byrnes is a law unto himself," Geoffrey reminded her.

"What happens next?" Fahey asked. "Do I go to trial?"

"I'm working on trying to get you out on bail," Geoffrey told him. "The best thing you can do is nothing at all. Don't answer any questions, don't do anything to draw attention to yourself. Rest and sleep as much as you can. You need to heal, Tim."

"What will happen to him, Geoffrey?" Prudence asked as they handed their visitors' cards to the guard at the main entrance to the Tombs. The cold, overcast day matched her mood, but the hansom cab into which they climbed had a basket of hot bricks on the floor. Danny Dennis had a long history of taking care of Miss MacKenzie and Mr. Hunter. He left the trap door in the roof of the cab open by a couple of inches so he could better hear their conversation.

"They're setting him up," Geoffrey said.

"What do you mean?"

"It's in writing that he injured himself by falling down a staircase while trying to escape. It's also in his record that he was taken care of in the infirmary and returned to a regular cell pretty much on the mend. The next time Tim Fahey attempts an escape he won't survive it. They may not use the stairs excuse again, but it will be something just as effective. Only more lethal."

"What about McGuire?"

"They can always claim that since he was a copper, he knew the details of the Nora Kenny case. They'll accuse him of faking a copycat killing when he murdered Ellen." Geoffrey thumped twice on the roof of the hansom. "Danny, I'd like to go by Ned Hayes's place before we go back to the office."

"Is it time for him to call on his reporter friend from the *Tribune*?" Prudence asked.

"Maybe. But it's past time for him to have heard something from McGlory. Word from the streets gets back to him faster than over a telephone line. Ned warned us that Billy might take the bit between his teeth and run with it if he's got a personal interest in catching up to our New York Ripper. We need to know if that's what's happening. Fahey and McGuire are too close to the rope for my liking. It wouldn't take much to put it around their necks."

"Time is running out."

"For both of them."

The cobblestones where Ellen Tierney's body was found had been repeatedly scrubbed and thoroughly rinsed; there was nothing left to mark the spot where she had lain. Yet Alice was irresistibly drawn to where she could reimagine the scene, checking for details she might have missed, straining her ears to imagine a sound she hadn't detected. She made herself faint and dizzy with the intensity of her concentration until she had to sit down in the chair she'd drawn close to the window and lean her head into the enveloping folds of the drapes.

She was positive she'd witnessed poor Ellen's murderer bringing his victim home. Strange to think of it that way, *bringing her home,* but those were the words that leaped into her mind. Her father had interrupted Detective Phelan's interrogation and then used his influence with Tammany Hall to make sure the Metropolitan Police stayed away from his daughter and every other member of his family.

The few questions the detective had managed to ask both frightened and unnerved her. Alice didn't think she could bear it if she had to explain what her vigil was for . . . so that someone in heaven, God or Our Lady or one of the saints, would change Francis Nolan's mind so he'd allow his daughter to become a nun at the Visitation Monastery in Brooklyn. It sounded odd even to her.

If she so much as hinted at what sometimes went on in the private lives of the Nolans, her father would see to it that she suffered. She didn't know exactly what he would do to her, but from past experience she knew it would be unpleasant. No amount of apologizing or pleading would soften the punishment. In Francis Nolan's world, you were made to pay for what you did.

Something had upset Joseph at dinner, though Alice had no idea what it could be. No one had mentioned Ellen's name or even obliquely referred to what had so disturbed the household on Sunday. As often happened, the meal was taken in a silence broken only by the scrape of silver against china and the faint noises of polite eating and drinking.

Maybe Da *had* said something; Alice knew

her mind had been wandering. Joseph suddenly stood up, muttered a vague excuse to his mother, threw his linen napkin on the table, and stormed out of the dining room. They heard his footsteps race up to his second floor bedroom, then down again. Then the thud of the front door. After that there had been an oppressive stillness that weighed down each of the remaining courses.

Alice couldn't remember what she'd managed to eat; everything she put in her mouth tasted like uncooked flour.

"The other girl's name was Nora Kenny, Miss Alice. I never met her, but our Ellen knew her through Miss MacKenzie's maid Colleen. The three of them were of an age, you see, and when Nora came over from Staten Island and they had a few free hours, they'd spend them together." Mrs. Flynn wasn't sure she'd been clear enough in her explanation. "Nora's mother had worked for the MacKenzies for years, out there on Staten Island, so whenever extra help was needed, either she or Nora or both of them would come into the city."

"I understand. Thank you, Mrs. Flynn." Alice had drifted downstairs to the housekeeper's room after discovering that her mother had gone early to bed and her father withdrawn into the smoking room where no one was ever permitted to disturb him. No matter the illness or indisposition that made her keep to her room or take to her bed, even if it was nothing more serious than loneliness, Mrs. Flynn always saw to it that Miss Alice was well cared for and cosseted. There were times when Alice fervently wished Moira Flynn and Lillian Nolan could have changed places.

Tonight Alice wanted to talk to someone about Ellen Tierney.

"It's terrible, what's happened to those two girls," Mrs. Flynn said, pouring tea. "Drink this up, Miss Alice. I've put honey in it for your throat." She spread butter on thin slices of toasted soda bread. "Soda bread sits easy in the stomach. Just take a bite or two. You'll start feeling better."

"I was so surprised, so shocked."

"Of course you were. So were we all downstairs. Mr. Tynan has told the rest of our girls they're not to be out alone, no matter the time of day or where they might be going. And when they do go out, they're to stop by me first and then again the minute they get back."

"Oh, no, Mrs. Flynn."

"Yes, Miss Alice. You know how coachmen are, the worst gossips in the world. Well, Jack Scully has been talking to Miss MacKenzie's Kincaid. He says our Ellen was cut up like their Nora. Mr. Tynan thinks it's just a matter of time before one of the newspaper reporters discovers that and writes a story about an American Ripper. Wouldn't that be something now?"

"Was Ellen . . . were either of them . . . ?" Alice couldn't think of the right words to ask the question.

"Interfered with? If they were, no one's saying anything about it. They arrested Mick McGuire, which is no great surprise to anyone. He's a handsome boyo, but with a temper on him like nothing I've ever seen. You don't know the fist is coming at you until it lands. If he's that bad sober, there's no telling what he'll do when he's taken a few."

"It's too awful to think about."

"Upstairs and off to bed with you, Miss Alice. I'll take you up myself. There's no sense worrying yourself into a spell. You've too soft and tender a heart. I've always said that, right from the time you were a tiny little girl."

Mrs. Flynn helped Alice out of the chair that seemed to be holding her prisoner, clucking sympathetically all the while. She'd been surprised when her employer's daughter appeared in her parlor doorway, and she wasn't certain it was her place to tell her what Scully had reported about the Nora Kenny murder being so like Ellen's, but if she didn't, then who would? Worse than Miss Alice knowing what happened would be her stewing and fretting over what she didn't know but could only imagine. Not that Mrs. Flynn revealed everything Jack Scully had told her. There was such a thing as reticence and discretion.

Especially with someone as delicate as Miss Alice.

The door to Joseph's bedroom had been left ajar. Not by more than a finger's width, but enough to tantalize. Alice hadn't been inside her brother's private quarters since the last time they'd played the game. Years ago. She couldn't remember how many.

"I'm all right, Mrs. Flynn. Really I am. I can put myself to bed. Perhaps if I could have another cup of tea, I'd manage to fall asleep." Alice stood in the middle of the second floor hallway, positioning herself so the housekeeper's back was to the cracked bedroom door. Every member of the household knew that Mr. Joseph's room was sacrosanct; the door was always closed and locked. Even the maid who cleaned and changed the linen had to do so under his watchful eye.

"I'll have Cook brew up one of her tisanes, the one with chamomile flowers in it. That should help you drift off." Mrs. Flynn started back down the stairs. "I'll put an extra teaspoon of honey in it, Miss. Your voice sounds scratchy."

Alice took a few steps toward her bedroom in case Mrs. Flynn turned around. As soon as the housekeeper was out of sight, she changed direction. She took a deep breath to steady herself, then slipped into Joseph's room and closed the door behind her. Snicked the latch in place in case someone should be passing by and try the knob. She hadn't much time, no more than five or ten minutes; Mrs. Flynn would hurry Cook along and either send or carry up the tisane herself.

Joseph always kept his room meticulously neat; even as a child he'd returned each toy or book to the place he'd chosen for it. Nothing and no one was permitted to interfere with whatever his system was. The very few times a maid moved an object as she dusted there'd been temper tantrums and a tight lipped anger that lasted for days.

He'd kept the props for their play locked

away somewhere; he'd never told Alice where he hid them. Whenever he summoned her, the habit and cassock were already laid out on his bed. Later, as the play grew more intricate, more frightening, he'd taken what he called God's tools out of a leather sack that looked as though it had been stored somewhere dusty. She remembered running her hand over it once, surprised at what clung to her fingers and palm.

Nothing would be in his bedside tables or armoire, but she took a quick look just in case. No leather sack or ball of material stuffed under the bed or behind the books stacked neatly in glass fronted cabinets along one wall. Nothing out of place, nothing to indicate that he might have played the game by himself. Recently perhaps. He'd been furiously angry when a weeping Alice told him she would no longer put on a nun's habit and follow his orders, even though the cassock and collar he was still wearing so intimidated her that until that last day she hadn't dared defy him.

"You'll come back when I tell you to," Joseph had snarled at her, the small whip with the hooks on the end of its nine leather tails clutched in his twitching right hand.

"I won't," Alice had cried. "You can't make me. I'll tell. I'll tell and then Da will send you away. Or something worse." She couldn't imagine what that might be, but it didn't matter.

Saliva dripped from the sides of Joseph's mouth. He was like a dog on a hot afternoon, worked up with running too hard in the heat and about to collapse.

Alice never did go back. Nothing her brother promised or threatened could convince her to set foot in his room again, or to trail miserably behind him into the dim recesses of the attic.

She played her own game of nun after that, but in her game there weren't any whips and nobody ever made Alice take her clothes off.

CHAPTER 19

Billy McGlory seldom left the safe confines of Armory Hall nowadays, but something stirred in him when Kevin Carney's eyes shone with excitement and his voice danced up and down the scale as he described tracking Joseph Nolan through the streets of New York to Madame Jolene's establishment. Once upon a time McGlory had known every crack in every sidewalk of the streets he too had called home. He'd found a place for himself in the Irish gangs that were as dangerous to belong to as they were comforting, like a family that rallied around you when you needed it but cut your throat if you ratted on any of its members. Which was a large part of what had made him what he was today. There were times when someone like Carney could make him wish for a minute that he was much younger, still living a life that teetered close to violent death with every breath he took.

Edwin Hayes always reminded him of those days because Ned had saved him from the death Billy undoubtedly deserved. Hayes had pulled him out of the street where he'd taken a knife wound to the gut, the kind of cutting almost no one survived. Then he'd secreted him with a healer whose skin and accent told McGlory she was New Orleans born and bred, a conjure woman in whose tiny, overheated rooms he'd been nursed and dosed and voodooed back into life.

He remembered lying in a narrow bed for weeks, rag and corn husk dolls dangling over his body from strings tied around nails driven into the ceiling. The flickering light of dozens of candles confusing his vision, the smell of incense and bitter herbs prickling his nostrils, the ever present sound of Mama Oshia chanting and tinkling her bells. Mumbling. Talking to her gods and goddesses as if they were next door neighbors who'd dropped in for chicory coffee and conversation.

Hayes had been fired from the Metropolitan Police for spiriting McGlory away and into hiding. Then had come the fast downward slide that McGlory hadn't thought anything but the grave could stop. He'd seen to it that the drugs Ned ingested were free of the rat poison often used to cut them, but he hadn't interfered much more than that. Something or someone else had snatched the ex-detective back from the abyss, so Billy hadn't been able to pay off his debt. And the thing about Billy McGlory that everybody knew was that he always paid his debts.

He'd known about the Kenny killing before Ned Hayes came to warn him that rumors of a Ripper would be bad for business. And incidentally ask for the fruits of his network of informants. Even before Ned finished laying out his argument McGlory had known he was right. He'd sent out the word and within days Kevin and his dog had shown up. There were two dead girls now and two highly unlikely accused murderers in the Tombs. It was only a matter of time before another carved up body appeared and the story the police were so intent on concealing broke wide open.

McGlory thought he knew what Byrnes was doing, but he doubted even the experienced and jaded ex-detective Ned Hayes had figured it out. In his own way New York's chief of detectives was as diabolical a strategist as the criminals he pursued. The way McGlory saw it, Byrnes would keep Tim Fahey and Mick McGuire in the Tombs indefinitely. He'd tied them individually to the murders of the two women, so their eventual executions should satisfy the ordinary citizen's need for justice. In the meantime, Byrnes had his best undercover men fanned out around the neighborhoods where the bodies had been found. If a couple of them hadn't made the mistake of trying to pump some of McGlory's informants, he might never have known they were there. They'd been trained personally by Byrnes, which made them the best in the city. The chief liked to boast that he'd match his detectives against Pinkertons or Scotland Yard any day and come out the winner. And maybe he would.

When Ellen and Nora's killer struck again, he'd be trapped and disposed of just as ruthlessly as he'd dealt with his victims. Whoever he was would disappear without a ripple, as forever gone as the body he would have been caught laying out. No Ripper for the newspapers to accuse Byrnes of allowing to terrorize the city, no comparison between what was happening on the streets of Whitechapel and a copycat's introduction to New York City. Byrnes would be more powerful than ever, his reputation unbesmirched by the specter of failure. It was a supremely crafty way to handle the situation, McGlory decided. He couldn't let him get away with it. Not if he had any intention of paying off the debt he owed Ned Hayes. Which of course he did. It was the one principle he clung to, the steel rod in his backbone.

He had information for Ned, and at first he thought he'd summon him to Armory Hall. But it wouldn't do for Hayes to be spotted there too often by Byrnes's undercover men. The next best thing would be to send a messenger, but Billy liked to play his cards close to the chest. The absolute worst way to handle the situation was for Mc-Glory to corner Ned in the Hunter and MacKenzie offices. So that was what he decided to do. The area around Wall Street was Byrnes's infamous Dead Zone, off limits to any mug with a record. He figured all the chief of detectives' extra officers would be elsewhere. He actually couldn't have asked for a better setup if he'd designed it himself.

And just for the hell of it, he'd take Kevin and his dog with him.

Josiah Gregory settled back into his desk chair and breathed a sigh of contentment. The last of Martin Parish's workmen had left after days of continuous banging and sawing, plastering and painting. A cleaning crew was hard at work in the offices now connected to Hunter and MacKenzie's original suite by a perfectly plumbed door that looked as if it had always been there. That was the test of whether or not something had been done right. Whatever you changed needed to look as though it had been part of the plan from the beginning. The furniture would be set in place before Josiah left for the day; he'd paid a hefty tip to make sure it happened.

Instead of the three or four days he'd suggested to Miss Prudence, it had taken two full weeks to create the office and conference room she wanted. The building's owner had stalled and then refused to bargain over the rent of the adjacent empty office suite, and at first Josiah had refused to consider the outrageous price he was asking. He held out for a week, until Mr. Hunter told him to close the deal and get on with it. By that time Martin Parish had picked up another job, so it had cost even more to persuade the contractor to change his schedule. Mr. Hunter hadn't flinched when his secretary laid the bill on his desk, hadn't even blinked twice. It wasn't the first time Josiah speculated on the difference between the rich and everyone else.

■ ■ ■ ■

The man who stood over him had materialized out of nowhere. Josiah was sure he
hadn't dozed off for more than a couple of
minutes, but he didn't hear the cleaners
anymore, and the light shining through the
windows was coming in at an angle as
though the November afternoon were well
advanced.

"May I help you?" Josiah squinted, but
the man had positioned himself so the
window lit him from behind. His features
were hard to make out.

"Tell Ned Hayes I want to see him."

"May I ask who's calling?" Never say the
person being sought is not in the office.
That wasn't the way to get information.

"Just tell him Billy needs to talk to him.
He'll know."

*Billy? What would a man named Billy be do-
ing calling on Edwin Hayes? And why here?
Hayes certainly wasn't a member of the firm.*
Knowledge hit Josiah with the force of a
hammer blow. There were thousands of men
named Billy in New York City, but only one
Billy McGlory. Only one saloon keeper who
was so much more than that.

"He's not here. Sir." All Josiah could think

of was getting McGlory out of the office, down the corridor, out of the building, and back to Armory Hall where he belonged. Josiah read the papers every day as avidly as any other New Yorker titillated by the mayhem waged in streets far away from where civilized people lived. He knew as much about Armory Hall's proprietor as the police. And it made him distinctly uncomfortable.

An odor of well rotted garbage suddenly hit Josiah's delicate nose, followed within seconds by the sight of a small man and a large dog. When they crowded through the doorway to stand by his desk, the stench made his eyes water. Billy McGlory didn't seem to notice that the atmosphere had changed.

"They're on their way up, sir. They were in Dennis's cab, just like I said they'd be."

"I don't like waiting, Kevin." What McGlory meant was he was used to other people waiting for him, used to making the kind of entrance that left no one in doubt about who was in charge. Kevin's miscalculation had Billy standing by a flunky's desk like somebody who wasn't anybody. It put a sour taste in his mouth. "What's in there?" he demanded, pointing toward a closed door.

"That's Mr. Hunter's office, sir. He's not here either."

Before Josiah could stop him, if he'd dared, McGlory wrenched the door open, stood for a moment assessing the size and emptiness of the room, then moved with long, confident steps across the Turkish carpet and behind Geoffrey Hunter's massive carved walnut desk. He sat down as though he belonged there, motioning Kevin and the dog to join him.

Footsteps sounded on the stairs.

"I see we have a visitor." Ned Hayes smiled past the shocked and dumbfounded Josiah to where McGlory waited.

By this time Geoffrey had reached his office door. He paused for a moment, then stepped into the room as nonchalantly as though criminals, street people, and smelly dogs were everyday visitors. He had met Billy McGlory once before, but it had been on the saloon keeper's turf, upstairs in Armory Hall in the retreat that was a luxurious counterpoint to the flashy tawdriness where the drinking and swiving public bought their entertainment. Every Pinkerton trained nerve alert and tingling, he knew that whatever had drawn the Irishman from his lair was vitally important.

"Mr. McGlory," he said, extending his

right hand. "Welcome. We weren't expecting you."

"I don't make a habit of advertising my whereabouts, Mr. Hunter. It makes for a longer life." McGlory stood and walked around his host's desk, courteously vacating Geoffrey's chair.

So this lady standing in the doorway was Victoria MacKenzie's stepdaughter, the one whose fortune the only woman ever to get the better of Billy had tried to steal. She had the look about her of a young woman who knew who she was and where she was going. Not unlike Victoria herself, though McGlory doubted Miss Prudence would stoop to blackmail to achieve her ends.

He bowed elegantly. "Miss MacKenzie, it's a rare pleasure to make the acquaintance of a lady like yourself," he said, tamping down the Irish cadence of his speech just enough to keep it from grating on aristocratic ears. "My name is Billy McGlory. I had the honor of meeting your father once, a number of years ago."

"Mr. McGlory." Knowing what she did about him, Prudence wasn't sure what else to say.

Blossom ambled over to the female human whose fingers reached out automatically to scratch her itchy ears.

Kevin Carney stared mouth agape and as if turned to stone, then reached out to pull Blossom back. The fine lady smelled like the Central Park flower gardens in a warm spring. She smiled at him without shuddering and shook her head no, digging her fingers into the dog's thick red fur. An ecstatic Blossom leaned against her skirts.

When he didn't know what else to do, Josiah Gregory made coffee.

He carried a heavily laden tray into Mr. Hunter's office, ceremoniously serving his employers and their visitors, including the odd little man whose aroma penetrated to every corner of the office and would no doubt imbed itself permanently into the Turkish carpet he was sitting on. The secretary poured cream into an extra saucer for the equally pungent dog.

"Josiah will stay to take notes," Geoffrey announced in a voice that brooked no contradiction.

"No names," McGlory stipulated.

"We'll call you a consultant," Prudence said. She felt slightly dizzy from the odors swirling around her and the heat of the huge dog who had come back to lean against her leg after loudly licking clean the saucer of cream. *The essence of good manners is not to notice anything out of the ordinary about anyone you meet.* She wondered if her father the Judge had ever been forced to share a very small room with the likes of Kevin and the dog so inappropriately named Blossom.

"Tell them about following Joseph Nolan to Madame Jolene's," McGlory said, cutting into Prudence's short reverie.

"From the beginning, Mr. McGlory?"

"I'll let you know when you can leave out something, Kevin."

"All right then, sir." Kevin took a deep breath and began. "Blossom and I were in an alleyway across from Saint Anselm's a while back," he said. "We'd built ourselves a nice little shelter of newspapers and cardboard boxes to keep the cold and the wind off."

Josiah wrote fast and furiously, only pausing now and then to shake out his aching fingers or use a small, sharp penknife on the tip of his pencil. He looked around the room once, but didn't dare smile at what he saw. The three detectives were following Kevin's torturous narrative with rapt expressions on their faces. Mr. McGlory had gotten up to stare out one of the windows, and the massive red dog had gone to sleep. By the time Kevin got to the information Sally Lynn Fannon had given him, it was all

Josiah could do to concentrate on good note taking instead of picturing the nun and the priest in the prostitute's bedroom.

"That's enough, Kevin," McGlory interrupted when the little man embarked on a block by block description of what he had seen as he and Blossom trotted from the house of ill repute to Armory Hall. "You can stop now and drink up your coffee."

"I had no idea," Prudence said. "I was at the Nolan house right after they found Ellen Tierney's body and I saw Joseph in the parlor there. The whole family was being questioned by Detective Phelan."

"I'm sorry you had to hear all of that, Miss Prudence." Even after years as a New York City detective, Ned Hayes still had a Southern gentleman's exaggerated courtesy for the frail sensibilities of ladies. It didn't matter that Prudence was breaking every mold as quickly and as completely as she could; he still thought of her as an exotic flower best displayed in a crystal vase.

"There's something else," McGlory said. "Get yourself together, Kevin. We're leaving in a few minutes. We've been here too long as it is." McGlory turned back to the window, glanced down at the pedestrians on the sidewalks below and the snarl of horse drawn vehicles that made getting anywhere in this city a nightmare. He was pretty sure he'd given anyone following him the slip, and he had two bodyguards standing in the lobby just in case, but he was still trespassing on territory Byrnes had declared off limits for the likes of him. He had to be on his way. "Someone else came to see me besides Ned."

"He wants to be notified when we've found Nora Kenny's killer," Geoffrey said. He stood up and began the pacing that signaled his mind was working so rapidly he had to move his body to keep up with it. "A young Sicilian gentleman from Staten Island."

"No names," McGlory cautioned. "The Irish and the Italians don't get along in this city, but we've staked out our territories and as long as nobody steps out of line there's a kind of truce between us. Except for the hotheads, that's the way we like it. Business is good, the reformers haven't got anything new to scream about, and the coppers take their money and leave us alone. People understand a husband killing his wife or two drunks fighting until one of them goes down, but they get uneasy when they think the gangs are getting ready to declare war again."

"So it's in your best interest to supply the

information you've been asked for." Ned Hayes thought it made perfect sense and wondered why he hadn't realized this would happen.

"I was expecting something," Geoffrey said. "I knew he wouldn't let it go, but I didn't know which direction he'd go off in."

"Keep an eye out. He's got someone on you round the clock, and if that doesn't work, I'll have to send him a name. But that will be the end of it."

"In more ways than one," Ned confirmed.

"Byrnes won't know what's going on until it's all over. His coppers will find a body with enough evidence to prove the point, and then it's back to business as usual."

"It's retribution for Nora's death," Prudence contributed. "He can't let it go or allow it to be carried out by anyone else."

"Honor," Ned agreed. "I don't pretend to understand their code, but if your Sicilian friend considers himself a man of honor, he'll live by it."

"That man is carrying a knife in one of his boots," Kevin said. He'd gotten to his feet and wandered over to the window McGlory had been looking out of. "And he's got a gun. You can see the bulge under his arm when he turns around." He pointed to a figure seemingly indistinguishable from anyone else on the crowded sidewalk below.

Blossom barked. She'd seen him, too. Yesterday, and then again trailing behind them today. He'd kept too far behind for her to pick up a strong scent, but a brief whiff was enough to imprint him in her brain. She liked the smell of summer sage and pine needles he used to enhance his human signature. She hoped she wouldn't have to kill him.

Jerry Brophy wasn't sure how he felt about celebrating Thanksgiving tomorrow instead of the feast of the martyred Bishop Saturninus of Toulouse. Some people thought Thanksgiving too Puritan and too secular a holiday to be marked with Catholic prayers and a special sermon, but after Cardinal Gibbons ordered the observance in Baltimore, other clerics had followed his lead. The priest could wear either red or green vestments to say Mass, which Jerry thought a nice compromise since red represented the blood of martyrs.

It was part of Brophy's daily routine to identify the feast day and the liturgy; the sacristan nun from the school checked that he'd laid everything out correctly, but Jerry almost never made a mistake. He worked from a list of things he had to do in the order they needed to be done. That way there were fewer of those terrifying moments of paralysis when he couldn't remember who or where he was, and what he was supposed to do.

He'd never been to a proper doctor about his condition, but he knew well enough what it was. *Fits.* He wasn't the only one in his family to have them. There was a long, fancy word for the malady, but he never used it, not even in his own mind. He liked *fits* better. It felt like what he experienced when the circles of light started dancing in front of him and then the blackness descended and he fell. He had been free of the problem for several months now, but made out his list every night just the same because a list made all the difference. Even when the words on the paper blurred into sparkling haloes he could picture the list in his mind and concentrate all of his energy on the skittering words until they settled down and made sense.

Jerry liked to arrive at Saint Anselm's at five o'clock. AM. Precisely. He had his own keys to the small side doors and the massive Gothic arched main doors, which he never opened until thirty minutes before six o'clock Mass. He liked to spend the first half hour of his working day locked inside

Saint Anselm's by himself, safe from interruption, alone in the vast empty space with no one to yell at him or criticize when all he was doing was trying his best.

He ran white gloved hands over the altar rail, rubbing at the dull spots until they gleamed. Sometimes the parishioners who knelt to receive Communion smudged what he'd buffed to a high gloss. He learned the trick with the cotton gloves from a housemaid who'd seen him worrying the wood with a cloth. So much easier if you didn't have to grip a bit of rag in your fingers. He lifted the kneeler pads to bang out the marks made in the cushioned leather by heavy knees. Jerry liked everything about his altar rail to be pristine.

A tiny smear of blood appeared on one of his white gloves. Women were always doing that, bleeding and leaving signs of their uncleanness behind wherever they went. A sudden gush of bitter gall surged into his mouth. He swallowed convulsively until the last drop of corrosive fluid had been forced back down into his stomach.

The sight of the blood thrust him into a past he had tried hard to obliterate, never to think of consciously. Father Mahoney had long ago given him absolution; his sins were not as great as those of his wife, but

Jerry never felt really clean. He always wondered whether some of the blood had seeped into the skin beneath his fingernails. He looked for incriminating circles of crusty residue, wondering how long it would take them to disintegrate and disappear.

Once before, a couple of weeks ago, he'd had the disturbing feeling that someone else had been in his church during the hours Father Mahoney said it should be closed. Close a church? That didn't seem right, but if he didn't lock the big arched doors the alms box would be emptied of its coins, the Lost and Found pillaged, and the sacred gold on the altars stolen. It had happened. Not at Saint Anselm's, but at other churches. Now they were all locking their doors at night. Beggars who used to sleep in the pews had to go elsewhere. Jerry felt sorry for them, but what could he do?

He stared at the tiny smudge of blood on his clean white cotton polishing glove. He must have soiled it when he picked up the cushion from the kneeler. Just a drop. As if a needle or a pin had pricked a seamstress's finger. He looked down at the cushion, ran the glove over its surface. Nothing more. Just the one drop. He wondered what that meant.

In Jerry's experience there was never just

one drop of blood. The girls and women his wife and her mother aborted often gushed blood, and sometimes shoving cotton batting or towels up inside them didn't stem the flow. When that happened they bled until they died. It wasn't the fault of Jerry's wife; she'd aborted dozens, maybe hundreds of unwanted complications without a problem. She always made that clear before she started working. Always told the patient and whoever brought her that there was risk involved in what they were about to do. Hardly anyone backed out. Almost every one of the girls laid down on the table and gritted her teeth.

Jerry would take the mother, boyfriend, or girlfriend who accompanied the patient out into the parlor where he collected the money and talked to them through the worst of the moaning. No screaming. The women chewed down on a piece of soft wood and clutched the sides of the table with desperate hands, but they didn't scream. Bridget made it clear. One scream and you were off the table and out the door, aborted or not.

Jerry's job was to clean up when it was over. Usually there wasn't much mess, but sometimes there was blood everywhere. On the table. On the floor. Soaked into towels and rags that had to be steeped in cold water and salt, then dipped into vinegar to loosen the stains. Jerry scrubbed the floor on his hands and knees, fumes of vinegar or ammonia stinging his nose and his eyes, eating into the skin of his hands until it was rough and red. His wife drank a cup of tea and pointed out spots he'd missed. Sometimes her mother was there, but usually she tended to her own business behind the shop she and her son ran.

Both women were dead now. Jerry's wife died of a summer fever that burned the life out of her in three days. Father Mahoney gave Bridget conditional absolution and prayed for the souls of all the babies she'd killed, though you could tell he'd rather have consigned her to the flames of hell. He heard Jerry's confession, too, and didn't fire him from his job at Saint Anselm's. Nobody could clean and polish like Jerry. Nobody kept at it until what had been stained and dirty was as fresh and sparkling as new. Jerry liked to clean more than anything else he had to do to stay alive.

Bridget's mother tended to her during the worst of the fever, then went home, laid down in her bed, and burned up just like her daughter. The son sent word to his brother-in-law when she breathed her last.

Jerry helped clean the bedroom where the dead woman lay and then the storeroom where she had emptied her clients of their unwanted burdens.

Girls in trouble who didn't know Bridget was dead continued to come by the apartment with tears in their eyes and a few hard earned coins clutched in desperate hands. Who else could they turn to? Couldn't he help them out? Everyone knew he'd assisted his wife many a time. Surely he knew what to do, didn't he? He directed them to Neil, his brother-in-law.

Jerry took the blood-soiled glove off his hand, worrying the spot that shouldn't be there, rubbing and wrinkling the glove until he'd made it worse. By the time he put it to soak in cold salted water, he'd need to add vinegar or ammonia. What he'd found two weeks ago had also been blood, but not bright red and liquid as this drop had been, and not at the foot of the altar.

It had been a dark smudge in a far corner of the vestibule that he'd first thought was a bit of greasy dirt. But it hadn't come up the way dirt did. It had stuck stubbornly to the grout in between the marble slabs of the floor, grout Jerry had painstakingly scoured with a small brush. He knew it was blood because he remembered what old blood looked like when he'd cleaned his mother-in-law's apartment. He'd washed down every inch of that space, then gone home to scrub his own apartment again. And again. He was still cleaning it, though his wife and her mother were no longer bloodying it up.

Women were always bleeding, always leaving their dirty blood around for people to step in or get on their clothing. He didn't know why they were like that, so dirty. Only that they were.

Chapter 20

Madame Jolene's whores slept until early afternoon most days. Weekday nights were nearly as busy as Saturday night when clients could be counted on to be both numerous and raucous. Not that Madame Jolene permitted displays of drunken enthusiasm that would warrant the intervention of her bouncer or the well bribed police; it was just the way men were.

The house was quiet during the morning hours. Except for the two maids moving through the downstairs parlors cleaning up the remains of last night and setting things to right for the evening to come, hardly anyone else was awake. Bawds who didn't get their beauty sleep very quickly began to look their ages. And then some. Their profession wasn't kind either to bodies or to souls; it showed on the wrinkled, raddled faces of the few old timers who hadn't yet been reduced to haunting street corners or tenement cribs. Madame Jolene's house was a safe place to be if you had to earn your living on your back, but it wasn't a sinecure. Any girl who neglected her basic health or appearance was out the door before she could beg for a second chance. Business was business, the madam cautioned each new hire. Just getting by wasn't good enough.

Sally Lynn Fannon had been one of Madame Jolene's favorites since she began working at the brothel nearly three years ago, a skinny, hungry virgin willing to sell that precious commodity as soon as she could. Anything to stave off the slow starvation that had already melted any hint of plumply voluptuous flesh from her bony frame. Jolene took her in, instructed her in the ways of whoredom and the house, fed her until her hair shone and her skin lay smoothly over pinchable flesh. Then she put her out for bid. Discreetly, of course. The winner paid a considerable price for Sally Lynn's innocence, rendered up on command without a whimper or demur. That obstacle lucratively out of the way, the newly initiated whore settled into the life with commendable industry and success.

Except that it was all a lie.

Sally Lynn remembered every step along the path of her near destruction.

The first time had been a quick groping in an upper hallway, skirts bunched up around her waist, a finger and then something considerably bigger thrusting inside her, an explosion of wet heat, and a stifled moan. She never made a sound, never said a word. She knew what would happen if she refused him — abrupt dismissal without a reference. As close to a death sentence as you could get without the actual rope around your neck. He was gone the next day, back to Harvard, leaving behind nothing of himself and the encounter except sore and bleeding female parts.

Four weeks later Sally Lynn lay atop Bridget Brophy's kitchen table, holding herself as still as she could while the abortionist inserted a long, slender knitting needle into what had begun to grow inside her.

Fortunately for her patient, Bridget was sober that day, her hand steady, and the knitting needle freshly washed in carbolic after its previous use. Jerry had been on one of his cleaning binges; not even his wife's tools, usually concealed in a dirty towel shoved beneath a loose board in the kitchen floor, had escaped his bucket of boiling water and bar of lye soap.

Bridget fixed a pot of hot tea when the

procedure was over and the table scrubbed clean again. Sally Lynn was her only client that day and she was feeling generous.

The day before, while Jerry was polishing Saint Anselm's, she'd added a few more coins to the stash she kept hidden from her husband. One by one she'd dropped what she thought he wouldn't miss down into the hollow uprights of their metal bed frame, alternating bits of rag with the silver so the money wouldn't rattle when he pulled the bed out to clean under and behind it. The endless scrubbing drove her wild; she was leaving as soon as she had enough squirreled away to set up somewhere on her own. She hated being dependent on what Jerry earned working at Saint Anselm's, but there didn't seem to be much of a choice. Rent had to be paid, food and drink bought. Bridget had an unquenchable thirst for whiskey when she could afford it, beer in buckets when she was down to Jerry's last penny.

"You're small," she said. "That could be worth something if you want it to be."

"What does that mean?" Sally Lynn asked. It didn't hurt as much as she'd been afraid it would, and there wasn't much bleeding. She'd stood up to use the chamber pot after her first cup of tea, and a lump had plopped out. Mrs. Brophy had been inordinately pleased with Sally Lynn and with her own expertise.

"You're lucky is what it means. The next time a man asks if you're a virgin, say yes and hold out for as much as you can get."

"Won't he know? They say a man always knows."

"It doesn't exactly grow back, but a girl as narrow as you are, if she's only done it a few times and then doesn't do it for a while, gets tight again. Sometimes there's a bit that wasn't torn the first time. That's why I say you're lucky. A good whorehouse has clients who pay well for the young ones."

"I'm not a whore, Mrs. Brophy."

"Yes, you are. You just weren't paid for it and it looks like you're not going to get caught at it. You're a smart girl, Sally Lynn. I can tell because you got yourself to me in time. The dumb ones keep hoping it will go away by itself. They wait too long, and then they get desperate. They try to get rid of it themselves after someone like me turns them down. Those are the ones who die, poor little tramps."

"How long will I bleed?" The conversation was making Sally Lynn more uncomfortable than what Bridget Brophy had done to her.

"Four or five days. Like a regular cycle." Bridget set her tea cup down and leaned across the table. She curled her fingers around one of Sally Lynn's hands and held on tight. She was about to give advice she was pretty sure the girl wouldn't want to hear.

"Just make sure you get yourself out of that house before the young master comes back."

In her desperation, Sally Lynn had revealed more than she intended.

"He's the only one who can swear to what happened. Other than you and me. And Jerry." Bridget glanced at the motionless form of her husband leaning against the stove with his bucket of carbolic and dirty rags at his feet. He never left her alone with a client afterwards in case something bad happened. Even more than his wife, Jerry didn't like to take too many chances.

"That boy will be at you again or he'll get you dismissed if you don't accommodate him." Bridget dug her fingers into Sally Lynn's wrist so the girl had to pay attention.

"The missus won't give me a reference if I leave sudden like. She'll suspect something is up with me."

"I do business at one of the best houses in

the city," Mrs. Brophy said proudly. "I know someone who works there; she got me in with the madam for old times' sake. You'll have to wait a while, a month or two maybe, but by then you'll be as good as new. You'll be able to fool anyone who examines you. Take my word for it."

"I'm not a whore, Mrs. Brophy," Sally Lynn repeated.

But she was. One of Bridget's predictions came true sooner than Sally Lynn anticipated. The young master came home from Harvard unexpectedly; she was out the door without a reference the morning after his arrival. A month and a half later, starving but intact again, she went back to the Brophy apartment.

Bridget escorted Sally Lynn to Madame Jolene's rear door.

When Big Brenda appeared in the kitchen to put on the day's first pot of coffee, Sally Lynn was dressed to go out. She was hungry, but for what she had in mind, hunger would be a good thing. She'd put on a couple of inches around the waist in the past month or so, and the other thing hadn't happened either, so she was starting to worry that she might be caught again. It was early enough to get it taken care of;

maybe she'd combine a quick consultation with her other errand. It was a shame that Bridget Brophy had died of a fever, but Bridget's mother had been the one to teach her everything she knew and she'd seen to Sally Lynn once before when she'd tried to earn a little extra and gotten careless. She hoped she was still doing business.

She'd stop by Saint Anselm's afterwards. Sally Lynn hadn't been to Mass very often during her days as a professional harlot, but she'd always felt soothed and calmed by the mystery of what a church promised. She remembered and cherished that consolation from a childhood that hadn't lasted nearly long enough. Youth ended at the age of thirteen, when she put on a kitchen skivvy's plain gray dress and apron and plunged her arms into a sink full of greasy water and burnt pots. The hot water and the bending over nearly killed her at first. Her hands and arms were always red and chapped, and her back felt like it would snap in two when she straightened up. But Sally Lynn was tough; she'd survived.

By the time she was seventeen she'd worked her way out of the kitchen and into the upstairs hallways and bedrooms of the house. Which was where the young master had found her.

"Going out then?" Big Brenda asked. She was trying to decide between making corn griddle cakes or sticky buns. "Does the madam know?"

"I wasn't about to wake her up to ask permission." Sally Lynn started to reach for a piece of the ham Big Brenda was slicing, then remembered where she was going and why. "She won't mind as long as I'm back before the first client arrives."

"See to it that you are," Brenda admonished her. She was only the cook in this establishment, but she liked to pretend otherwise. She'd had ambitions to own a house of her own, to dress in black silk and manage a stable of girls like Madame Jolene. But that dream had evaporated when reality chained her to a stove. Cook she was and cook she always would be.

"Can I pick up anything for you on my way back?" Sally Lynn never minded doing an errand for someone else. She was good-natured that way.

"I don't think so, love. But it's kind of you to ask." Brenda touched the whore's cheek affectionately with a hammy forefinger. "There now. Run along, and if Madame says anything I'll speak up for you."

Sally Lynn sat alone in the quiet of Saint

Anselm's for nearly half an hour before anyone else intruded. In the dim church, she felt peaceful and loved, surrounded by banks of flickering candles, welcomed by the red eye of the sanctuary lamp. She could never explain satisfactorily to herself or to anyone else why she liked sitting in empty churches; it was just something she'd done ever since she could remember.

Voices whispered to her in the silence, warm, friendly reminders of people she had lost, some she had never known in this life but grew to be on familiar terms with because of the tenderness in their tones. They never reproached her for what she did, and she never felt the need to explain or excuse herself. It was like reliving those few wonderful floating moments just before she drifted into sleep after a hard night. She was as light as air, and just as transparent.

She recognized the priest who came into the church through the sacristy, genuflecting before the altar, then standing there with head bowed for a few moments. His name, she recalled, was Father Brennan, too handsome a man to be a priest, with a lovely English accent that held hints of a melodic Irish brogue. The women of the parish loved him, though every now and then someone would wish aloud that he'd learn to be a bit faster in the confessional. This was America, after all. Time was money.

Sally Lynn never went to confession because she didn't think she had anything to confess. She and her voices had long ago made peace with the only way she could earn a decent living. There wasn't any anger or malice in what she did. She usually didn't mind the poking and prodding, and the clients were sometimes absurdly grateful for a smile and a well meant lie. She always told each of them how wonderful he was; even the most chary businessman believed her.

Lately though, ever since Mr. Nolan had begun bringing the nun's habit, the priest's cassock, and the whip, she'd suffered bouts of uncertainty. What she did wasn't the problem. It was how she was dressed while she was doing it that bothered her conscience. She wasn't a real nun, and she never intended any disrespect toward the Brides of Christ, but there she was, standing barefoot in her brothel bedroom dressed for all the world as if she'd taken the vows of a Benedictine or a Sister of Charity. She wasn't sure which religious order the habit Mr. Nolan handed her was meant to signify; she had a strong feeling it would be better not to ask.

It had been almost three weeks ago that

she'd seen Mr. Nolan talking with Father Brennan, just there, in the main aisle before the altar. Then Father Brennan had disappeared into his confessional booth and Mr. Nolan had gone to kneel beneath one of the stations of the cross. Sally Lynn had sat as still as a rabbit caught out in the open who believes itself invisible if it doesn't move. Mr. Nolan never so much as glanced toward the dark corner near the rear of the church, which was her favorite spot. He'd never once asked her to call him by his first name the way many of her other clients did, so she never thought of him as anyone but Mr. Nolan.

She hadn't come to Saint Anselm's last week; she'd been too tired and too sore to venture out into the windswept November streets. The voices waited patiently for her. Whenever she chose to come, they cushioned her aches with their concern for as long as she stayed. And it didn't matter what church she went into; they were always there, as if they knew where she'd be before she did.

Several times she'd taken an omnibus up to Saint Patrick's, the immense gothic cathedral that never failed to awe and diminish everyone who entered it. She wondered if she had time today to get up to

50th Street, decided she didn't, and sank back into the pew she'd almost left. Saint Anselm's wasn't magnificent like Saint Patrick's, but it was a comforting, homey church, its smells of furniture polish, melting candle wax, and the steaming outdoor garments of parishioners as familiar as the strong perfumes and even stronger body odors of the brothel.

There he was again, Mr. Nolan himself, looking every inch the respectable gentleman he was. No clerical collar, no cassock, no whip in hand. Standing talking to Father Brennan. Smiling, one upraised arm swinging downward as he made an important point. The priest nodded his head in agreement.

Father Brennan beckoned toward the sacristy, then gestured that someone inside should come out. Jerry Brophy, polishing rag in hand, dressed in the long dark blue cotton coat he wore to clean. Sally Lynn made herself as small as she could, knowing if he caught a glimpse of her face, he would recognize her and remember what he'd witnessed on his wife's kitchen table. She sent a question out to her voices. *What are they doing here all at once, these three men I know too much about ever to be comfortable in their presence?*

To Sally Lynn's knowledge, Father Brennan was guilty neither of abortion nor twisted fornication, but she recognized him as a type she knew well, a man who was never more than an inch or a breath away from evil. He might be an anointed priest of God, but something about him told her he was one of those odd ones who thrived on thoughts of blood and butchery, yet didn't cross the line from contemplation to action. Until they did.

She couldn't identify what in Father Brennan's looks or demeanor told her who and what he was, but she trusted her instincts. She stayed out of his way whenever she came to Saint Anselm's and only nodded brief hellos when he smiled at her.

Sally Lynn knew she would have to leave soon or she'd be late getting back to Madame Jolene's. Her other errand had taken longer than she'd anticipated, but it wasn't something she could skip. Tomorrow was Thanksgiving. Shops all over the city were closed. She'd known that if she were to get what she'd promised a client she would obtain for his pleasure, it had to be today. She'd decided there would be time if she hurried, and hurry she had because Madame Jolene's rules were simple but strict. Every girl had to be dressed and perfumed and in place ready to work before the first client crossed the threshold. The only exception was the few days a month a girl couldn't work, although there were clients who preferred it that way. Thankfully not many.

She slid toward the end of the pew in which she was sitting. The package wrapped in brown butcher paper made a loud crackling sound. Mr. Nolan whipped his head around. She froze, bending her head so that all he would be able to make out in the dimness was the top of her hat. There was a shuffle of feet, the sound of a question being asked, an answer given. Still she waited.

She heard the main doors open in the vestibule just behind her, a slow creak as someone eased them shut. Footsteps, a cough, a muffled sneeze. The doors opening and closing several times. Drafts of cold air swirling around her ankles. She looked up once, in time to see Father Brennan walk toward the sacristy. He turned around before entering the small room where vestments and sacred vessels were stored. Their eyes met as he raised one hand to bestow a blessing, then he disappeared. Sally Lynn shuddered.

"What are you doing here?" a voice hissed. A hand came down on her shoulder. She twisted around to shake herself free. Jerry Brophy's enraged face was inches from her own. "You don't belong here. Get out. Get out, I tell you."

He held on to her shoulder so tightly she was afraid he'd rip the sleeve out of her coat. The hissing never stopped, even when he yanked her to her feet and propelled her into the vestibule like a naughty child. She didn't try to wrench herself free. She might have dropped her package. It wouldn't have done any good, anyway. Brophy was far stronger than he looked. Sally Lynn was used to being roughly handled; the safest thing to do was ride it out. The mauling and shoving were usually over faster that way. Her shoes clattered on the floor as her feet repeatedly lost their footing.

"Don't come back," Brophy growled when he finally let her loose.

They were outside in the darkening November afternoon, the gas street lamps just beginning to flicker. She teetered on the topmost tier of stone steps, half afraid he would push her all the way down them to the sidewalk.

"You don't belong here. Don't come back," he snarled.

More frightened than she'd ever been with a client, Sally Lynn inched her way along the metal railing that only the old and the infirm used. Step by step she made her way down to the street. By the time she caught her breath and found the strength to stop sobbing, Jerry Brophy was no longer watching her.

In his place before the great gothic arched doors of Saint Anselm's stood Joseph Nolan.

He wasn't smiling.

CHAPTER 21

The best Kevin Carney could calculate when it was all over, Blossom woke him up sometime between midnight and dawn the Sunday after Thanksgiving. The dog's rough tongue licked at his face until the skin became tender to the touch and wet with drool. She was whining at him, nipping his ears and the tip of his nose, making little huffing sounds deep in her throat as though he were a puppy needing encouragement or a reprimand.

He was hot, hot all over. It felt like he'd rolled too close to one of the barrels street people filled with whatever trash would burn enough for them to warm their hands over. He reached for the buttons on his coat, but Blossom used her sharp teeth to keep his fingers from fumbling them through the buttonholes.

What was happening? What was the matter with the dog? What was she trying to tell him?

Kevin's throat burned when he tried to argue with Blossom; the only sound he could make was a whimper of pain. He put one finger to his mouth, then held it out toward the streetlamp. Nothing dark on the end of it, so he wasn't bleeding. No taste of iron on his lips. But, Jesus, Mary, and Joseph, he was hot.

He tore the cap from his head, feeling a rush of cold air through the greasy mat of his hair. Blossom barked and crouched down on her two forelegs, grabbed the grubby sailor's knitted cap with her teeth and shook it violently from side to side. When Kevin didn't seem to understand, she repeated the hat shaking, then held it out to him in a muzzle gone soft with entreaty. He put the cap back on his head. Blossom smiled at him. Her human was sometimes slow, but he got the point eventually.

Saint Anselm's loomed across the street, a dark bulk of brick and stone growing out of the pavement like a rectangular mountain. The streetlight cast shadows across its steps and into the recessed doors. There was no sign or lingering airborne scent of a passing human.

Kevin had no idea how long he'd slept.

He remembered creeping back into the alleyway after a hasty trip to the corner to spend a few of Mr. McGlory's coins for more of the fried potatoes and bacon he and Blossom loved. He'd used the greasy newspaper the food was wrapped in to oil the cracked skin on his hands, then pulled his mittens over them. Bits of newspaper were lying at his feet, ripped to tiny nesting shreds by Blossom's sharp teeth. Neither of them ever let anything go to waste. He thought he was thinking clearly, but then he couldn't remember why he and Blossom were in this alleyway across from the church. Were they waiting for someone? The street was empty. There was no one standing in front of Saint Anselm's.

The coughing saved him. Shook Kevin's brain loose from whatever had gripped it, and made him realize there wasn't a barrel of burning trash in the alleyway; the heat he felt was coming from deep within himself. He was sick. He hoped it wasn't the pneumonia, but he knew it started just like this, with coughing that wrenched your insides into knotted ropes of pain and a fever that burned out all your strength and made you sob like a baby. Once it settled in the lungs, the pneumonia killed you slowly and painfully. He'd seen plenty of people die from it. Every winter the bodies piled up in doorways or on park benches like cordwood someone had forgotten to take inside for the stove or the fireplace.

He had to get up. He had to move, had to get to a place where someone would pour a strengthening broth into him and sponge the heat from his forehead.

Blossom danced on her four nimble legs, pulling her human along by his coat, pausing when he stopped to cough, tightening the muscles in her back when he needed to lean on her. She was a big dog, bigger than any one of her ancestors, the happy accident of a long line of matings between males and females who singled each other out with a sure instinct for survival of their young. She knew where Kevin needed to go, knew where there would be help generously given with no questions asked. She'd been there many times; so had her human. They always ate well and a shed out back had been set aside just for them, though they rarely used it. Her human was stubborn and proud, traits she didn't think boded well for the breed.

Madame Jolene's brothel was as still and silent in the final hours before dawn as Saint Anselm's had been. One client lay slumbering upstairs in Spanish Lola's room, a privilege for which he paid dearly. He was too young to have much experience with whores, so he fancied himself deeply in love; it never occurred to him that Spanish Lola didn't reciprocate his passion. Or that she was a good ten years older than she pretended to be. John Landers's father was a banker, his uncles were bankers, his older brothers were bankers, and one day he too would be a banker. In the meantime, he was learning lessons other than those taught in vaults and oak paneled offices.

Kevin nearly wept with relief when he realized that Blossom had led him through the streets to the only place in the city where someone might give a fig for his welfare. Big Brenda the cook had told him the story of Madame Jolene's youngest brother, how he'd died, and why the madam was tenderhearted toward Kevin. *You look so much like the lad, the way he would have grown up, you might as well be his ghost come back to life. I've seen a picture of him dressed for his First Communion. It's you, all right, Kevin. Mark my words.*

It was all he could do to stand upright and reach for the railing of the back steps. He lifted one foot, placed it on the first step, and nearly collapsed from the effort. Blossom bounded to his side, steadying him with the heavy pressure of her huge body. When he seemed to have balanced himself, she leaped down to the ground, circling, snuffling, running off a few steps, then back again, nose to the frozen earth, ears pricked at attention, her plume of a tail first rigid, then wagging frantically.

If someone had put a bucket of coals in the shed, they'd long ago burned themselves into ash. Kevin needed to get inside the house, inside where the kitchen fire was banked at night but never allowed to go out.

Three more steps to go. He could just distinguish their outlines in the moonlight. This backyard of Madame Jolene's house wasn't well lit. Deliberately so. A few clients always preferred to exit more discreetly than through the front door. Left foot. Right foot. Kevin hauled himself closer to the kitchen door. He could almost reach out and touch it, but he didn't dare let go of the railing. Not yet. If he fell he knew he would never be able to get up. Blossom might lie down beside him and with her warmth, try to keep him from freezing, but it wouldn't be enough. The fever would burn him and the icy November night air would chill him until they met somewhere in the center of his body and killed him.

One more step. Kevin glanced quickly behind him, looking for Blossom. She was still doing her strange dance, sniffing the ground, circling frantically, rushing off in one direction, then another, coming back to snuffle and circle over and over again. There was a scent she could follow only so far and no farther. Someone or something laid down a trail then vanished; her talented nose couldn't find it again. And it was driving her crazy. The sight of her and the nearness of the kitchen door made him happy. They'd made it. Whatever was bedeviling Blossom, they'd made it. They were safe.

"Come here, girl," Kevin ordered, then he lunged for the kitchen door. He expected it to support his weight, thought to find a locked doorknob beneath his fingers. But the door swung inward at his first touch and he fell into the kitchen, landing sprawled on the floor, the rag rug on which Blossom usually curled herself bunched beneath his head and chest. He slipped into unconsciousness.

Blossom couldn't nudge the door shut behind her master. His legs were in the way, and they were too heavy for her to move. She whined and pawed at him, nipped the only ear she could reach, barked once, twice, again. Nothing. He didn't move, didn't even groan. She knew something was very wrong with him. She could smell it on his breath and in the vapor that hung above his skin. Her human's scent, but sharp and pungent. His skin was hot; she couldn't cool him down with her tongue. A terrible rattling noise filled the kitchen when he breathed. The dog knew what that meant. She'd heard it many times before.

Blossom put her nose to the wood floor, casting about for a particular scent. The dark woman whose face turned soft and loving when she looked at Kevin or the woman who trailed her fingers along Blossom's always itchy ears. Either would help him. But someone had washed this floor, washed away all the good scent trails. Except. There. One tantalizing trace of something. Just a whiff of a smell, but enough to tell her that someone had walked across this floor after it had been washed, walked straight across the room then back again to the door that was still open, down the stairs, and into the yard. It was the same scent trail she'd picked up outside, then lost again. Over and over. Picked up. Lost. Picked up. Lost. Something else, too. The suggestion of something familiar. What was it? Who was it?

Kevin breathed in harsh, gasping gulps of air. Blossom made up her mind. She would follow the human scents into the deepest part of the house, where she had never been. Where one human had come from, there were bound to be others, and perhaps one of them would be the woman with the caressing fingers.

Nose to the floorboards, Blossom left Kevin in the kitchen and made her way through a dining room and three parlors to the foot of a wide staircase. These floors had not been scrubbed clean. The only other place she'd smelled odors this strong all mingled together was inside Billy Mc-Glory's saloon. The visit had been fascinating but brief. Kevin had explained that her size and delicious fragrance were off-putting to some humans. She understood. She didn't always like the way humans smelled either.

Up the stairs Blossom went, the scent trail she was following getting fainter and fainter as another odor overlaid it. This new smell never meant anything good; humans didn't spill their own blood willingly. She hoped it wasn't the lady with the soft fingers whose blood scent now filled her nostrils. She could hear Kevin gasping below her and she knew instinctively that he hadn't much time left.

Time had run out for the lady whose personal aroma Blossom now recognized, distorted by the blood, but no longer unknown. This was the lady who had come to the church the day before the humans greedily stuffed themselves with food for what they called Thanksgiving, though Blossom wasn't sure what they were thankful for. The lady had been alone and melancholy. She lived in this house and often sat in the kitchen with them when Kevin came to visit. Once she'd put her plate on the floor for the dog to lick clean. An angry man had pushed and shoved her out of Saint Anselm's and down the stone steps. Blossom had smelled her fear leap across the street into the alley where she and Kevin crouched, watching.

Nails scratching on the wooden floor, Blossom hurried down the second floor hallway to the last door on the right. The scent of human blood grew overpowering, though not a drop of the red liquid had flowed under the doorframe. She sat on her haunches and stretched her neck out to grab hold of the doorknob with her teeth. It was a trick her human had taught her, but this time it failed.

Blossom did the only other thing she knew would bring humans running; she put back her head and howled. Howled and howled. Loud enough to wake the dead. Loud enough to bring Madame Jolene storming from her private suite into the second floor hallway.

"What the hell is going on out here?" the madam demanded, no trace of her famous French accent softening the words. Whores from bedrooms on the second and third floors crowded around her. "What is that dog doing here? Someone shut it up and haul it downstairs."

John Landers, clad only in his unbuttoned trousers, reached for the enormous, foul smelling animal whose shrill howl was enough to shatter eardrums. Blossom didn't budge. She seemed to slide away inside her skin, so that he stood with a fistful of loose dog determined not to be dragged anywhere. Behind him, Spanish Lola rolled her expressive black eyes and clutched her feathered robe around her pendulous breasts.

Blossom lunged for the door, pulling the young, broad shouldered John Landers with her. At the last minute, she dug all four feet into the floor and stopped. Dead on a dime. Landers let go of the handful of fur and skin he was clutching as he stumbled over the huge dog and crashed against the door of Sally Lynn's room.

Dozens of candles still flickered within, though many others had burned themselves out. The walls and the floor had been painted a bright, garish red, and sworls of red decorated the tall mirror in which clients liked to watch themselves at play. On the floor lay a cocoon the size of a human being, whatever was inside wrapped many times in gauzy white fabric. The bed curtains. The bed curtains from Sally Lynn's four poster workplace had been taken down, smoothed and coiled over and under and around something that lay on the floor. Something with masses of curly black hair spread fanlike beneath her head.

Someone screamed.

"Dear God in Heaven, Jolene, you got yourself a real mess here." Ned Hayes was never so Southern as when he was waked up early in the morning and dragged off to a scene of murder and mayhem.

"No need to take the Lord's name in vain," chided Tyrus Hayes. He'd taken care of Mr. Ned through slavery days and into freedom, and he knew his former master shouldn't be alone when he started wading through blood again. Blood made the liquor flow and the white powder disappear. Neither one of which hungers Mr. Ned was strong enough to control on his own. Tyrus was eighty-one years old, twenty-three years out of slavery, but all that history didn't matter a bit to him. His world began and ended with the man who'd been laid in his arms as a baby.

"He's yours now to look after, Tyrus," the mistress had said. Once in a while she'd inquire after her son, but not often enough for it to count.

"She's just like what was done to the other two," Ned said quietly, folding back the layers of filmy bed curtains that hid the horror of Sally Lynn's throat and belly. "Almost exactly like the others."

"Now how can you know that, Mr. Ned? You never did see them for yourself."

"Mr. Hunter described them to me, Tyrus."

"Then how come Miz Jolene called you to come when she got the police and a Pinkerton man? It don't make sense to me." Tyrus began picking up and folding the pieces of clothing that lay around the room.

"Tyrus, I need you to do three things for me," Ned instructed, knowing Tyrus would neaten and straighten and clean until there wasn't a clue left. "Go to the Fifth Avenue Hotel and wake up Mr. Geoffrey Hunter. Tell him what's happened here and that I need him as fast as he can make it. Then go to this address and pound on the door until Mr. Russell Coughlin answers it. He's a newspaper reporter. Tell him Ned Hayes is sitting on the story of a lifetime at Madame Jolene's Gentlemen's Retreat. He knows where it is. When you get back here, help Miss Brenda tend to Mr. Carney."

"I can do that, Mr. Ned. I can do that." Mr. Geoffrey Hunter was second only to Mr. Ned in Tyrus's estimation. With him on the scene, Tyrus wouldn't need to worry so much about what the sight and smell of all that blood was doing to his master. Mr. Geoffrey had a way about him that calmed his friend and focused him on something other than the liquor and the drugs. Tyrus didn't know much about newspaper people, but he had to trust Mr. Ned's instincts.

The Fifth Avenue Hotel was only a few minutes away. The sooner he got there and back, the sooner he'd be able to help Miss Brenda because there was nothing in the world Tyrus liked better than caring for sick folk. He'd pulled Edwin Hayes out of death's clutches more times than either he or Death could count. That street fellow needed a boiling hot bath to steam out the pneumonia or catarrh or whatever chest devil was ailing him. It wouldn't hurt to take off a few layers of dirt in the bargain. Tyrus didn't believe in coddling his patients. It only made them linger in their illnesses longer than they needed to. Best be on his way.

"Why did you send for me, Jolene?" Ned asked when they were alone.

The madam had shut Sally Lynn's door behind the departing ex-slave, shushing the horrified whores whispering in the hallway, waving them back off to their beds with hands that left no room for argument.

"I couldn't very well send for himself," she said. "He doesn't like it when there's trouble not of his making."

"You mean you were afraid you'd get the blame for this. Billy McGlory might shut you down if he thought you couldn't handle your clients and your girls. Shut the house down for a while, deal with its madam in a way that neither one of us cares to contemplate, then open it up again under new management. That's why you didn't send for him to come get rid of the body so nobody would know what happened to it. No body, no crime."

"I couldn't, Ned. One of my clients spent

the night. That young banker family idiot who thinks he's in love with Spanish Lola. He's the one who broke the door down. He saw everything. He knows it was a murder, and he's the kind who believes you have to call the police when someone gets killed. I'd never be able to count on his silence if I tried to keep it quiet. He'll blabber it all out the first chance he gets."

"All right. So you play it legit. That should make for a nice change."

"That's not the kind of house I run. You know it from the old days, Detective." It wouldn't hurt to flatter the man kneeling beside the corpse that used to be Sally Lynn.

"Have you sent for the police?"

"George has gone down to the precinct. My bouncer," she explained. "He doesn't have a police record."

"You're not on the telephone?"

"I am. But not the house. The operators listen in to every call they put through. Some people forget that, but I don't."

"McGlory needs to know, Jolene. He won't take it well if one of his informants has to tell him."

"I'm scared, Ned. I've been in houses before where a girl got beaten up real bad or messed with herself to get rid of something and bled to death. I've seen a lot, but

I've never seen anything like this." Jolene tried and failed to stifle a sob that came from somewhere deep inside, where the human heart was supposed to be. Madams couldn't afford sentimentality; successfully running a business like theirs meant they grew hard scabs over all the soft spots. Sally Lynn had been a good whore, taking what came her way without complaint, getting on with servicing the clients whose hungers kept food on the table and a roof over their heads. This shouldn't have happened to her. She didn't deserve it. "I really am scared, Ned."

"J'ai très peur," he said absentmindedly, wondering if the stroke that had slit Sally Lynn's throat had come from the left or the right. If he unwound the bed curtain from her neck again, Jolene was liable to faint. He'd wait.

"What does that mean?"

"It's French for *I'm really afraid.*"

"I knew that." But of course she hadn't.

CHAPTER 22

"The police say to lock the door to her room and not let anybody in," reported George Bright. Unlike most of the bouncers who worked in brothels, George never mistreated a girl or demanded favors. Madame Jolene frowned on the practice of breaking in a new whore by violence and intimidation, and wouldn't allow it in her establishment. She'd hired George because he was exceptionally even-tempered, extraordinarily muscled, and indifferent to the sexual attractions of women.

"How long?" she asked. Sally Lynn's body needed to be out of the house before the evening's clients began arriving.

George shrugged his massive shoulders. "It didn't look to me like they were in a hurry."

"Did you tell them it was a mutilation?"

"I said she'd been killed and cut up real bad."

"Are you worried about your johns being scared off?" Ned Hayes came up the stairs from the kitchen floor, a coffee cup in one hand and a honeyed popover in the other.

Behind him trailed a tall, dark man a whore might be tempted to accommodate without the usual charge, just for the welcome change of it. A younger man followed, rumpled, wrinkled, and moving as though he hadn't had enough sleep to absorb the whiskey he'd drunk the night before.

Jolene recognized the type. She wasn't sure she approved of Ned bringing a newspaper reporter into her house. "I do run a business."

"I know you do. Better than most. And you're good to your girls. That counts for a lot, Jolene. The police won't be out to give you a hard time." Ned smiled to reassure her. "I want you to meet the best ex-Pinkerton in New York City. You couldn't have anyone better on your side than Geoffrey Hunter."

Madame Jolene raised one eyebrow in silent query.

"Hunter and I have been working together. Sally Lynn isn't this killer's first victim," Ned explained. "And unless we catch him, she won't be his last." He turned to the shabby younger man who'd pulled a narrow notebook and chewed pencil stub from his pocket. "This is Russell Coughlin. He's a reporter for the *Tribune.* We need him if we're going to force Chief of Detectives Byrnes to admit what's really happening in his city."

"Go get yourself some breakfast, George," Jolene ordered, turning to the bouncer. "I'm sure you did the best you could." She watched him skip down the staircase like a boxer working his legs. Docile and dumb. Ideal husband material for someone. Too bad it wouldn't be a woman. "We need a few minutes of privacy before the police arrive." She unlocked the door to the room where Sally Lynn lay stiffening. "Nobody will look for us in here."

It smelled like a butcher's shop where someone had used the wrong kind of soap to scrub down the counters. Heavily perfumed instead of laced with lye or carbolic. The blood smell tended to settle near the floor while the perfume floated toward the ceiling. No one had blown out the candles; a few continued to burn in overheated air and widening pools of wax. Sally Lynn lay on the floor in her filmy cocoon.

Geoffrey Hunter stood over the body, eyes taking in the blood spattered walls, the pool of red beneath the murdered woman's neck and head. He was like Jacob Riis's camera on a tripod, snapping photographs to preserve what the eye saw and the mind might forget. "There are differences," he said. "Significant differences."

"That's why I sent Tyrus in such an all-fired hurry to get you here before the police could mess up the scene," Ned Hayes agreed.

"He's either escalating or he exploded in a fit of anger he couldn't control. The other killings were ritualistic acts; this one was personal."

Russell Coughlin circled the room, his pencil scribbling furiously over the pages of his notebook. He'd go straight to the *Tribune* offices to write the string of stories this murder deserved. Graphic, shocking, accusatory. If his editor had the guts to let him do it, he'd point a finger of blame directly at Chief of Detectives Byrnes. Demand on behalf of his readers to know why two innocent men had been subjected to the third degree and left to languish in the gloom and damp of the Tombs. Ned Hayes had filled him in on condition of remaining deep background. He didn't want his name in the papers again. He'd had enough of that kind of notoriety.

Coughlin had agreed; he'd do anything a

source wanted as long as the facts checked out and the story flowed.

"There's a lot no one knows about Sally Lynn and one of her clients, Detective," Madame Jolene said, edging closer to Ned Hayes.

Hunter stepped back away from the corpse. He would watch and listen, interrupt only when necessary. Coughlin did the same. Both men remained within earshot, both understood the importance of what was about to be revealed. Madame Jolene clearly had something on her mind she wanted Ned Hayes to hear. She'd called him Detective, so whatever lay between them went back to his days with the Metropolitan Police. Despite his being a former copper, she seemed to trust him.

But she had no confidence in a newspaperman. "You've got enough to write your story, Coughlin. It's time for you to go. You don't want the coppers to catch you here."

"I might have some questions," he protested.

"I don't want to have to call George to escort you out. It's not a pleasant experience."

Coughlin understood his role in the drama being enacted in front of him. He'd been privy to the secrets of New York's underbelly long enough to know when to pull back. He flashed an appreciative grin at Madame Jolene then made himself scarce. She hadn't told him not to interview the whores. He figured he had a good fifteen or twenty minutes before the coppers arrived. He needed to be out the door as they came in.

"Did Joseph Nolan come to see Sally Lynn?" Ned Hayes nodded toward Sally Lynn's body as the door closed behind Russell Coughlin.

"He was one of her regulars," Madame Jolene answered.

"And she came to you with a complaint." It wasn't a question because Ned could read people's faces as easily as he did a newspaper.

"Sally Lynn wasn't a whiner. She was a good girl. Worked hard and gave her clients fair value for their money. Nobody ever had a word to say against her."

"Something was bothering her. You wouldn't have that look in your eyes unless something was going bad."

"He brought her a costume to dress up in. Wore one himself, too."

"All the time?" Ned asked.

"Lately, yes. She told me it didn't start out that way . . . the dressing up and the rest of it."

"Don't drag it out, Jolene. It doesn't make it easier."

"Sally Lynn didn't mind it too much at first. She said she kind of liked what she saw in the mirror."

"What was that?"

"A nun. A barefoot nun," Jolene said.

Hunter had listened attentively while Ned questioned Madame Jolene. Now his eyes fixed themselves on the body wrapped in its filmy bed curtains. He was imagining Sally Lynn dressed as a nun, slipping that likeness into the mental images he'd carried out of Saint Anselm's rectory. The three priests in their cassocks, narrow white collars encircling their throats. It was a suspicion he wouldn't share with Coughlin, though he understood why Hayes had decided to let the reporter in on the investigation. There was always, in every case, a delicate moment when confidentiality warred with the need to force an action. He had known the scale to tip both ways.

"Makes a change from the upstairs maid or a lollipop girl," Ned commented. He knew Geoffrey wanted him to keep Madame Jolene talking.

"I told her it wasn't all that unusual. I've seen it before. They cry and beg forgiveness and then get on with it."

"What was different this time?" Ned pressed.

"It got so he didn't want anything else," Madame Jolene explained. "He'd bring the nun's habit with him in a small satchel, then take it away again. After a while, he added a priest's collar and cassock. So they'd both be dressed up. He'd chant prayers in Latin, bless Sally Lynn like she was receiving a sacrament, sing hymns."

"What else? That's not all, Jolene. You know better than to try to hide anything from me. It never worked in the old days and it won't work now."

Hunter turned his attention back to Madame Jolene. Ned was as skilled as any interrogator he'd ever worked with at bringing a witness around to what was important.

"He used a whip. A small cat-o'-nine-tails with wicked little hooks on the ends of the tails."

"I thought you didn't allow that kind of thing in your house," Ned remarked.

"I don't, when it's one of the girls who might get hurt. But this was him. *Mr. Nolan.* He'd beat on his own back until he couldn't lift the whip anymore, then he'd make Sally Lynn do it. He wouldn't let her stop until there was blood." Madame Jolene's lips tightened in a grimace of distaste.

"Did anyone else see it happen?" Hunter asked. Selling time at a peephole was only one of the clandestine ways a house made extra money.

Madame Jolene shook her head. "My clients know they don't have to worry about that."

"When did she come to you?" Hayes continued. The question Hunter had asked was an important one, but Ned had already known the answer.

"Just this week, Detective. Not more than a few days ago. I told her not to worry, to go along with what he wanted and I'd have a word with him first chance I got."

"What did he say?"

"I never got to talk to him."

"Somebody killed her," Ned insisted.

"Whoever it was sneaked into this house after we'd all gone to bed. I always check on my girls last thing at night. They're sound sleepers, George and Big Brenda, too. I've never had trouble like this before. Never."

"You didn't hear anything? Didn't wake up in the night and not know why?"

"Nothing until that dog started howling. That woke all of us up. Whoever came in the house was long gone. Brenda said the kitchen door was open, but that was because

Kevin's legs were blocking the doorway."

"Does she remember locking it?" Ned asked.

"She's conscientious. I've never known her to forget."

"We need to look at Sally Lynn before the police get here." Hunter said.

Ned nodded agreement. "Are you sure you want to stay for this, Jolene?"

She stared at him, comprehension slowly draining the color from her face. But she stood her ground, fists clenched at her sides. Sally Lynn was still one of her girls; she'd face whatever was necessary to make sure the dead woman was done right by. And if Ned Hayes meant what she thought he did, she wouldn't faint or otherwise disgrace herself, no matter how bad it was.

"Check the door. Make sure it's locked. We don't want someone walking in on us," Hunter said.

Madame Jolene rattled the doorknob, then returned to stand beside the two men. "Can you lift her onto the bed, Detective? I can't bear looking at her lying there on the floor. It's so hard."

"She doesn't feel it, Jolene," Ned said reassuringly. "But I don't see any harm in putting her where she belongs." He knew this murderer had left nothing of himself behind.

Together Hunter and Hayes placed the dead woman on the bed where she had earned her living. Wherever the first blow had been struck, whether it rendered her unconscious or killed her outright, there was enough blood smeared on the walls and on the floorboards to disguise where the gutting had taken place. The entire room had served as her abattoir.

"Let me," Jolene said softly. Her long fingers with their buffed and polished nails were deft, swift, and as gentle as if the girl were still alive. She'd closed her eyes earlier when Ned had done a brief examination of Sally Lynn's remains before he'd sent for Mr. Hunter. Now she gasped once when the girl's poor throat was revealed, then ground her teeth together until the pain of it shot through her cheeks to the top of her head. Tears formed and dropped from her eyes, but she didn't pause for a moment. She knew that if she stopped, she might not be able to start again.

Sally Lynn's body had been young and beautifully formed; she hadn't been in the life long enough for the hours of abuse she suffered each night to have marked her. Now she lay exposed and sliced open like a rag doll readied for new stuffing. She'd been washed and wiped dry after the cutting had been done, perfume from her dressing table poured liberally over the slashed skin. She stared back at the woman who had ruled her life in this house, unseeing blue eyes filmed over and beginning to sink in their sockets. Jolene coaxed the lids down, but they would not stay. Sally Lynn's body could not be persuaded to close the windows to her soul.

"Don't," Jolene said when Ned Hayes reached out to touch the folds of skin collapsing down, across, and into the empty abdomen.

"I have to find out what's been taken," he explained. "What's been left. I wouldn't do it if it weren't important. There have been two others, but so far the police have kept that quiet. If there's a connection, if the same person killed all three, he won't stop. He'll kill again and again. Until he's caught."

"You don't have to look," Hunter said gently. Madame Jolene had held up well so far, much better than he had expected. He admired courage wherever he encountered it.

"Yes. I do. I have to witness for her. I have to take the place of the mother who should be weeping over her."

As gently as possible, with the reverence

that would made the examination easier for Jolene to bear, Ned lifted aside the skin that was already puckering along the cut edges. He folded each long piece back, then probed the cavity as quickly and thoroughly as he could. He slid a forefinger into the gaping slit of the throat, satisfying himself that the thrust had been a backhanded stroke from left to right, made with such force that the bones of the spine had been partially severed.

"You'll need this for your hands," Jolene said, holding out a woman's handkerchief edged with lace. She'd moistened it in the washbasin that sat atop a small dresser. The water had turned the white linen pink.

"We'll wrap her back up again," Ned instructed, "as like to the way we found her as we can."

Jolene did not protest when the two men laid Sally Lynn back on the hard floor where her killer had positioned her, where the police would find her when they finally arrived.

They stood together at the door, looking back into the room, not saying a word. For Ned Hayes, the hardest part about being a copper had always been seeing the wreckage of a human being in the aftermath of violent death. He'd never forgotten a single one of them; they haunted his dreams.

Geoffrey Hunter's features were set and grim. His face betrayed nothing of what he was thinking or feeling.

Jolene yearned for a life where death came as a blessing when a peaceful old age welcomed it.

Billy McGlory came and went like a dawn shadow no one is quite sure of having seen. Big Brenda handed him a cup of coffee, but never said his name aloud.

She and Tyrus had carried Kevin Carney into the sick room just off the kitchen where whores who were too ill to work could be nursed back to health within calling distance of the woman who fed them nourishing soups and washed the fever sweat from their bodies. They called it the infirmary, though it only held one bed, a small table, and a single chair. Big Brenda had nailed a crucifix above the bed, like she'd seen done in the clinics and hospitals run by the Sisters of Charity. Whether anyone prayed in the brothel infirmary didn't matter; it was the presence of the cross that counted.

McGlory sat in the chair beside Kevin's bed. He set the coffee cup on the bedside table, then took one of Carney's hands in his own. Blossom perched on her haunches watching his every move. She snuffled when he touched her human, but sensing no harm meant, allowed it to happen.

"Kevin. Kevin, lad. Wake up and tell me what you saw."

Nothing. The man who lived on the streets and spied for the owner of Armory Hall lay as still as the dead whore upstairs. Clean, too. Big Brenda and Tyrus had washed him as thoroughly as she did her kitchen floor, which had only been possible because Kevin was unconscious and couldn't fight her off. She'd trimmed his hair, working as fast as she did when there was dough to roll out. Carney was as neat as a pin, the sheets pulled tightly across his chest and tucked under the mattress on either side of him for good measure. He was breathing better. Big Brenda had poured a concoction of whiskey, lemon juice, laudanum, and crushed rosemary down his throat. It was kill or cure, and more often than not, her remedies cured.

"Will he live, Missus?" McGlory knew a man dead to the world when he saw one. It would be a while yet before Kevin came out from under the influence of what he'd been given.

"I've seen worse, though he was in a

mortal bad way when I started working on him."

He handed her a five-dollar gold piece.

"What's that for?" She wasn't as terrified of McGlory now as when she'd looked up from tending to her patient and realized who she was smiling at.

"I'll send someone around to find out how he's doing." By which he let her know that she'd have to earn the gold coin with her ears and her tongue. He wouldn't have taken it back if she'd dared return it. When McGlory hired you, you stayed hired.

Then he was gone . . . long before the police arrived to see what new trouble Madame Jolene would pay them to get her out of.

Blossom, bathed and defleaed by Tyrus Hayes, smelling as sweet as her name suggested, continued her watch.

The first thing he had to do was notify Chief of Detectives Tom Byrnes that his worst nightmare was coming true. Detective Steven Phelan knew from his initial examination of Sally Lynn's body that there was no more point trying to conceal what was happening in the city. Either the Whitechapel killer had crossed the Atlantic or an imitator had taken up a knife in his stead.

Two weeks had separated the Kenny and Tierney killings. Sally Lynn died a short seven days after Ellen. And this time the newspapers would print the truth of the murder scene, every lurid detail. He'd seen Russell Coughlin slipping past a handful of whores gathered in the hallway outside the dead girl's room. It was too late to stop him.

The thought of it chilled Phelan to his bones, though the room where the whore had lived and worked was stiflingly hot. He blew out the candles that still burned and opened a window to let in some breathable air. The smell of a murder scene often stayed with you as long as the sight of what had been done. He didn't know a copper anywhere who didn't suffer from nightmares. That was one of the reasons they all drank as much as they did.

The coroner from Bellevue had taken less than ten minutes to make his initial determination.

"It won't be official until I've done an autopsy and written it up," Dr. Robert Estin told Phelan, wiping his hands with a mixture of water and carbolic. There was a new idea going around in some medical circles that invisible bugs could contaminate a wound and jump from one person to another. He'd decided to take precautions.

"Your killer has removed the organs I'd like to have a look at, but I don't believe either one of us needs them to understand what happened here. He slit her throat, then gutted her. Plain and simple. The killing itself probably happened fast; the girl might not even have had time to realize what was going on. We can certainly hope so. One thing, Phelan. This is the third girl I've seen in the last three weeks with the same kind of cutting done on her."

"If Byrnes were to ask, would you be able to tell him that all three dead girls had been killed by the same man?"

"I've got notes that didn't make their way into the official autopsy reports. In case I need to jog my memory. Or I decide to write a book someday. When you find whoever killed this girl, you'll have your answer."

"Yes or no?"

"Between us and off the record? Yes." The coroner finished wiping and drying his hands. He held them up to his nose and shuddered. "I wish I knew for sure whether this does any good. I'm going to smell like carbolic for the rest of the day." He put the damp towel back in the leather bag that held his tools. "Byrnes is probably the best we've ever had, but he's likely to go off half cocked if he has to admit there's a Ripper working in New York City. When he releases the autopsy reports, the newspapers will have a field day accusing him of arresting and trying to frame a fisherman from Staten Island and one of his own coppers to cover it up. My guess is the papers will jump the gun. It's the Sunday after Thanksgiving, Detective Phelan. A slow news day." Estin smelled his carbolic hands again. "I've seen what his third degree can look like; it's not something I'd wish on any man. It gets results, but I've got my doubts about the reliability of what you beat out of a suspect." He waited for Phelan to tell him whether either of the men had confessed to a crime it was now obvious he hadn't committed, but the detective just asked another question.

"What else can you tell me?"

"He's right-handed. But you already knew that. What I don't understand is why he left this one in the same place he killed her. The other two weren't murdered where we found them. That's your big mystery, Detective. What happened to make our Ripper change his pattern?"

"Don't call him that. Not yet."

"He needs some kind of a name. You don't want to wait for the newspapers to give him one."

Steven Phelan sighed and ran a hand

through his thick hair. He could feel gray strands popping up through the black like creases on an old man's face. This case would age him.

"Take her away," he told the attendants from the morgue wagon. "We're done here." There wasn't any more he could learn right now from the body that had once been the pride of Sally Lynn's working life.

The four-poster bed was heavy and ornate; the curtains must have floated from it like mist over a river. Clothes hung neatly in the armoire, perfumes and cosmetics sat in neat rows on a silver tray, the brush that still contained strands of her hair was otherwise clean. Sally Lynn had tried to live as neatly as if she had a lady's maid to straighten up after her.

It always happened to the ones who didn't deserve it.

CHAPTER 23

Saving the Metropolitan Police Department from renewed attacks by the city's reform-minded clerics depended on how quickly the chief of detectives could present his side of the story Russell Coughlin was writing for the next edition of the *Tribune.*

"Is that it?" he demanded of Steven Phelan. They were sitting outside the brothel in a hansom cab whose leather curtains had been rolled down and secured against prying eyes. Phelan had used Madame Jolene's fiercely guarded telephone to inform Byrnes of what he'd found, but Byrnes had cut him off before he could give any details over the wire. The hansom cab belonged to the police department and the driver only ever had one customer.

"It's the same man," Phelan said confidently. "I saw all three of the bodies. There's no doubt in my mind, even though this last time he left the girl where he murdered her."

"It's a break in his pattern. I don't like it."

"Everything else was the same, right down to wrapping the body up when he'd finished with it."

"What does the coroner say?"

"We may have a problem there. Estin kept private notes, information he didn't include in the autopsy reports."

"Buy the notes. Pay him a reasonable amount but make sure he knows that there can't be a copy anywhere. Explain to him that if he talks to a reporter on his own he'll wish he hadn't."

The whole time he'd waited for Byrnes to arrive Phelan had worried over what he was obliged to reveal next, but there was no way the chief wouldn't eventually find out. "Ned Hayes was on the scene when I got here. So was Geoffrey Hunter."

"What about Judge MacKenzie's daughter?"

"No sign of her."

"That's one small thing to be grateful for."

"I'd bet my last dollar Hayes was the one who leaked the story to Coughlin."

"Who leaked it to Hayes?"

"That was Madame Jolene. She's usually got a calmer head on her, but I think she toyed with the idea of not calling in the police at all. Getting rid of the body, cleaning up, and then opening for business tonight as if nothing had happened. My guess is that Hayes disabused her of the notion that she could get away with it."

"I have calls out to all the papers that I'm giving a statement in half an hour, so I've got to get back to Mulberry Street. You stay here to close the scene and find out whatever Hayes and Hunter know. Flatter them if you have to. Suggest cooperation. We need to get this solved before our killer has a chance to strike again." Byrnes was fully aware of the impossibility of what he was asking, but he hadn't made his reputation by hanging back and doing things the way they'd always been done. He'd keep his fingers crossed that the London Ripper would claim another victim. And soon. That would at least put paid to the notion that he'd decided to grace New York City with his presence. A homegrown copycat wouldn't generate nearly as much bad publicity. New Yorkers might be perverse enough to take some kind of twisted pride in their own killer's audacity. You could never predict how people in this city would react to anything.

He ran over in his mind exactly what he would say to the reporters. *A prostitute has been killed and from the evidence of what was done to her body, it has been determined that the man who took her life may also be guilty of the deaths of Nora Kenny and Ellen Tierney.* Questions. Questions. Questions. All of which he intended to answer to keep the press in line. Then he'd volunteer the information that until this new theory could be proved beyond a shadow of a doubt, the suspects currently in custody would remain in the Tombs. For the sake of guaranteeing public safety. Until Sally Lynn Fannon's assailant had been caught and had confessed. Only then, and only if the evidence warranted it, would Fahey and McGuire be released.

Byrnes leaned back in the cab and closed his eyes. It helped to picture what he planned to do before he actually did it. He thought of himself as an actor preparing for a role, readying himself to step out on stage.

It had to go just right or everything he'd built would be in jeopardy.

"He's the key to what happened last night." Looking down at the sleeping form and listening with cocked ear to the stertorous breathing, Detective Phelan stood at the foot of the bed where Kevin Carney lay. "The cook says he's better, but it sounds painful to me." He motioned to the chair that was canted just far enough from the side of the bed to indicate that someone had recently been sitting there. Someone who'd left in a hurry. "Who do you think was here?"

Geoffrey Hunter shook his head, as if he had no idea or it wasn't important. "Take your pick. Most likely the cook. She's done a good job with him. Carney probably owes his life to her."

"Her name is Brenda Mulligan," Phelan said, consulting his notebook. "She told me she washed the dog, too."

Blossom thumped her tail vigorously against the floor. Except for worry about her human, she was feeling better than she had in a long time. Less itchy.

The two men stared at Kevin as if wishing him to wake up and begin talking would make it so. But it didn't. Kevin Carney, tucked away in a bed for the first time in years, slept deeply and dreamlessly. The noisy breathing that concerned Detective Phelan was phlegm loosening itself in his lungs. Big Brenda could have told him that, had he asked her. Kevin didn't have the pneumonia, just a chesty catarrh. He was on the mend and she fully intended to keep him that way.

They left the door open a crack in case a

miracle happened and Carney woke up. Big Brenda had coffee waiting for them, a basket of hot popovers on the kitchen table, a slab of butter and a honeycomb sitting in white china dishes beside it.

Ned Hayes was eating his third popover, now and then dipping it into a brew that looked deadly dark and thick. "Tyrus told her how I like it," he explained. "New Orleans style. I don't expect you Yankees will take to it."

"No one in his right mind would do that to decent coffee," Big Brenda declared. She'd welcomed Tyrus's help with Kevin and Blossom, but only reluctantly allowed him to tinker with one of her smaller coffee pots. The result was an affront to the nose and the eye. Smelled like burnt weeds and looked like dirty pond scum.

She'd found new clothes for Kevin from the piles of garments left behind by satisfied and forgetful clients, but the ex-slave had gathered up the rags Kevin had been wearing and dumped them into the wash pot in an open sided shed behind the house. She could see out the window that he'd got a fire going and was stirring the clothes with a wooden paddle taller than he was. The man could work. She'd give him that.

"I'm going to need to feed the girls," she

said briskly, putting hands on pillowy hips and following the trajectory of popovers from basket to mouths. People who ate her cooking knew to show their appreciation. "This is a working establishment."

"We won't be long." Detective Phelan stirred milk and sugar into his coffee. "We'll get out of your way faster if you could leave us alone for a while, Miss Brenda. And shut the door nice and tight behind you," he added as she turned on her heels and huffed a bit for show.

He'd not said a word about meeting with Chief Byrnes in the hansom cab, but he had a feeling the two men sitting opposite him hadn't missed a thing. They'd settled in around the table as if they were comparing notes back at Mulberry Street, fellow coppers picking each other's brains. If that was the way they wanted to play it, Phelan could adapt. He hadn't forgotten a word of Byrnes's instructions.

"We have a Ripper." Phelan drank off half his coffee.

"Imported or homegrown?" Geoffrey asked.

"The last Ripper killing in Whitechapel was November ninth. There hasn't been another one since," Phelan reminded them.

"Nora Kenny was murdered the night of

November tenth." Ned Hayes kept a policeman's notebook in his head. He seldom forgot anything.

"Which means the London Ripper wouldn't have had time to get to New York City." Geoffrey had mentally calculated dates and distances.

"And if we're all of the opinion that our three victims were killed by one man, that pretty much confirms that it's a copycat."

"The mutilations are the same, so we can say with reasonable certainty that we're looking for one man. Agreed?" Phelan looked from Hayes to Hunter. Both men nodded their heads. Phelan pushed the basket of popovers in Hunter's direction.

"Is there evidence to confirm that the Whitechapel killer hasn't left London?" Geoffrey thought with a lawyer's bent as well as a Pinkerton's training.

"No evidence either way."

"That could be a problem when your chief of detectives issues his statement to reporters," Geoffrey said.

"What makes you think he'll meet with the press?" Phelan asked.

"It stands to reason, doesn't it?" Ned wasn't inclined to mince words about the police department that had treated him so badly. "He made a disparaging comment about Scotland Yard and the London Ripper when he should have kept his mouth shut, so there isn't a reporter in New York City who won't jump on him now. No police force in the world could catch that kind of killer in thirty-six hours. Not Scotland Yard and not the New York Metropolitan Police. Unless he manages to win them over to his side, the papers will have a field day when he has to eat his words. They'll make him sound like a pompous fool."

"He's counting on readers being more interested in details of the crimes than in a vendetta against him."

"Politicians always think they can hide from the press." Ned Hayes laughed quietly and blew on the scalding liquid he'd poured from the small pot at his elbow. "Reporters dig out every bit of dirt you fancy you've concealed. I know that from my own experience."

"Our copycat's mutilations haven't been exactly like the London Ripper's," Geoffrey prodded.

"Two slashes across the throat in Whitechapel, one here in New York," Hayes agreed. "The crime scenes left a bloody mess there, while here the bodies are neatened up and then carried away from wherever the cutting was done. Except for Sally

Lynn. She was left in place, where she was killed."

"The American papers reprinted some of the photos and the descriptions of how the London Ripper cut and what organs he took away with him," Phelan contributed. "Maybe that's all our copycat cared to imitate."

"I wonder why he left her in her own room. It's different from Ellen and Nora. I don't like an unpredictable killer," Geoffrey mused. "It makes me nervous when a pattern is broken."

"The time of the killings hasn't changed. All three done on a Saturday night or early Sunday morning."

"Was Sally Lynn Catholic?" Geoffrey asked.

Phelan and Ned stared at him as if they hadn't understood the question.

"Was she Catholic?" he repeated.

Ned stood up so suddenly he knocked over the chair he'd been sitting in. Blossom nudged open the door to Kevin's sickroom and stood in the doorway with ears laid back and fur ruffled along her spine. She kept her growl low for fear of waking up her human, but she was clearly ready to protect him against whatever new threat lurked in the kitchen.

"It's all right, girl," Geoffrey said. "It's all right. Ned's just gone to get the answer to a question, and he was a little impatient about it."

"She was Catholic," Ned reported from the doorway leading to the parlors. "Big Brenda said she was as Catholic and as Irish as Paddy's pig."

"With a name like Sally Lynn?" Phelan paged through his notebook. "Sally Lynn Fannon, according to Madame Jolene."

"I think you can be certain that at least Sally Lynn isn't the name she was born with."

"Geoffrey, why did you ask if she was Catholic?" Ned eased himself back into his chair and reached for another popover.

"I've been looking for a pattern that would link this new killing to the others. Why a sporting lady after two housemaids?" Geoffrey shrugged. "All three victims were female, Catholic, and Irish. Those are the only commonalities I trust."

"I understand slitting their throats," Phelan said. "We see that all the time. It's a favorite way of getting rid of someone. Quick, effective, silent. If the victim is taken by surprise it doesn't require any extraordinary strength or skill." He paused. "The hard part is what he's done to the rest of their bodies. A woman shouldn't be cut open like that. It goes against nature."

"Three Sundays. Three young Catholic women. What else does that suggest?" There was a gleam in Geoffrey's eyes that told his comrades he expected to hear the right answer from them. "Think," he urged.

Steven Phelan, who had been born and raised Catholic, and whose mother steadfastly believed that her policeman son went to Mass every Sunday, tried to dredge up answers from the depths of his altar boy past. No use. He could still recite the Latin prayers and knew when to ring the bells, but not much of what he'd learned in catechism class had stuck.

It was Ned who whispered the right words. "It's a church building. That's the location they have in common. They've all been in the same church recently. Whoever killed them saw them in that church, and something about them set him off. But they had to come to him to trigger the impulse to destroy. That's it, isn't it, Geoff?"

"I believe so. I don't think the killer picked them at random from the street."

"He couldn't kill in the church, though," Phelan said. "There would be blood everywhere. How would he clean it up? We always hear about it if some drunk tries to drink the holy water or piss in a collection basket. A church is the safest place anybody in this city can be."

"That's the point. Look at the girls we're talking about. Ellen Tierney — from what we've been told, a maid in a strict household — and a copper's girlfriend. There's lots of places she wouldn't go, but she'd never hesitate about a church. Neither would Nora Kenny. Even if it wasn't her own parish church, she'd still feel at home there. And safe."

"Whores don't go to church on Sundays," Phelan commented. "They're usually sleeping off Saturday night."

"I haven't worked out the details yet," Geoffrey said, making honey circles on the table with his fingertip. "It's a gut feeling I have about this. Allan Pinkerton was a demon about some things, but he always said a detective's best friend was the feeling he got in the pit of his stomach. I've got one now."

"The only thing a girl would feel safer about than being in a church alone would be being in a church with a priest." Ned spoke so quietly his voice was almost a whisper. "I don't want to think too hard about that."

"Prudence and I have already talked to

the priests at Saint Anselm's. We came away with nothing concrete, nothing to suggest that one of them isn't what he seems to be." Geoffrey frowned. "I'll look over her notes again. We might have missed something."

In his tiny room, Kevin raised a finger to keep Blossom from whining with joy at the sight of her human using his ferocious hearing again. It meant they'd be off trotting along the streets soon.

Inside was comfortable, but outside meant freedom.

Prudence and Josiah Gregory waited in the carriage until the morgue wagon swung into Bellevue's rear entrance, Josiah fidgeting with the fingers of his black leather gloves. He'd acted on impulse when he learned that Ned Hayes had sent Tyrus to bring Mr. Hunter to the scene of another killing.

As far as Josiah knew, neither Mr. Hunter nor Mr. Hayes had thought to inform Miss Prudence, but Josiah had worked too many years for the late Roscoe Conkling not to fear the wrath of someone left out of something important, supposedly for her own good. By the time he used the new telephone to tell Miss MacKenzie that a third girl had fallen victim to whatever the police had decided to call New York City's latest horror, he'd known the body would be on its way to Bellevue. Without a moment's hesitation Miss Prudence told him that's where she would be going, also. He'd had no choice but to offer to accompany her. Now all Josiah had to fear was Mr. Hunter's displeasure . . . which, compared to what he imagined would have been Miss Prudence's wrath, wasn't worth worrying about. He resolved to sit still and stop tearing at his gloves.

"We'll give them time to unload and put her on a table," Prudence said. "Did you get her name, Josiah?"

"Sally Lynn Fannon, Miss."

"Refresh my memory." Prudence remembered perfectly well what he'd already told her, but she needed time to prepare herself for another visit to the bodies of the Bellevue Morgue. Accompanying the Kenny family when they'd come to identify Nora had been one of the hardest things she had ever done. She hadn't forgotten either the sights or the smells.

"Mr. Hayes was at an unsavory establishment," Josiah began. Even to his own ears that sounded inappropriately culinary. "The victim in question was a young woman of dubious reputation who plied her trade in a house of ill repute." There. He thought he'd done it rather nicely. He'd managed to replace the cruder words used by the police with two of the euphemisms to be found in any respectable newspaper article.

"Say what you mean, Josiah. She was a prostitute working in a brothel."

His ears flamed red. He nodded his head miserably.

"Shall we go?" Prudence opened the carriage door as the now empty morgue wagon reappeared on the street, lumbering along to pick up another body somewhere. No hurry. The dead had all the time in the world. "Are you coming, Josiah?"

He'd tried to think of a way not to, but he hadn't been able to come up with an excuse that wasn't transparently cowardly.

"Yes, Miss."

The smell in the Bellevue morgue always made first time visitors gag. Buckets stood in the corners for the weak stomached. An eye watering stench of carbolic, formaldehyde, and decay hung like a miasma in the air. Cold. Damp. Acrid. As though no windows were ever opened . . . which they weren't. There was a viewing room to one side of the larger space where bodies were stored before being autopsied or released for burial, but it already held its full complement of remains. Relatives were expected momentarily. They had appointments.

Prudence approached the attendant as though he weren't standing in front of the door trying to block their way. "The young woman in question arrived a few moments ago," she informed him, stilling his protests with several folded bills slipped into an outstretched hand.

He led them to a far corner where Sally Lynn's rolling table had been wedged in between two larger and riper bodies. "Not too long," he said, leaving them to keep watch outside this vault that was off-limits to visitors.

"She's beautiful," Prudence said.

At first glance Sally Lynn had the look of a proper young lady who'd fallen asleep over her knitting. Dreaming perhaps. Until you realized her eyelids weren't quite closed and that something reddish black around her neck was trying to peep out from beneath the sheet that had fallen away from her face.

"I'm going to pull the sheet down," she murmured into the silence, "before that attendant decides to come back and send us on our way. Take notes, Josiah. This may be the only chance we have."

"Yes, Miss."

Prudence tugged gently at the stained

sheet covering Sally Lynn's body. Whatever she had been wearing had been removed so that she was as naked leaving life as she had been coming into it.

The first thing they saw was the throat. Josiah's notebook and pencil clattered to the floor, but Prudence continued the downward movement of the sheet until the entire torso lay revealed. Neither of them had ever been this close to the kind of destruction a violently wielded knife could wreak on a human body.

"The newspapers reprinted the photographs taken of the Whitechapel victims," Prudence said. "They were horrible to look at, but nothing like this."

Sally Lynn's skin had turned the color of ice on a frozen lake — dirty white with a tinge of blue to it. The gash from which her life's blood had spurted was long and deep, an ugly pair of ragged lips stretched tight into an obscene smile. A small block of wood had been placed beneath the dead woman's head to tilt it forward. With a wound as deep and vicious as this one, there was a danger that the weight of the skull would detach it from the few threads of muscle and sinew holding it on.

Josiah Gregory retrieved his pencil and stenographer's notebook and began to sketch frantically, his pale face set in determined lines. Somehow he would create a visual record of the dead Sally Lynn Fannon while at the same time preserving a transcription of whatever comments Miss Prudence made. Roscoe Conkling had declared more than once that Josiah was worth two ordinary secretaries; he'd prove the truth of that statement today.

As she studied Sally Lynn's exposed body, Prudence remembered reading in Geoffrey's medical book about Caesarean sections, when a possibly still living child was cut out of the belly of its dead or dying mother. Slit open the abdomen, pull out the infant, close up the mother, and wash the body for burial. She had thought at the time that only a man desperate for a male heir would demand that such a procedure be performed on his wife.

Sally Lynn had been cut from breastbone to pubic bone, scooped out like a melon, then cleansed, the incised skin folded neatly over emptiness. There was only one reason Prudence could think of to perform such an operation; the womb and its contents had to be removed. They were an affront to the killer. They ate away at the core of who he imagined himself to be. They violated all he held sacred. They catapulted him into madness.

"Could she have been with child?" Prudence asked.

"My understanding is that ladies of her profession who get caught rid themselves of the encumbrance. It's bad for business." Josiah's writing hand trembled as he realized what he'd said.

"What do you suppose he does with the organs he removes? He has to hide them somewhere."

"He may burn them, Miss Prudence. To get rid of any evidence."

"I've seen enough, Josiah. I don't know what to make of it yet, but I won't forget this. Are you finished with the drawings?" When he nodded and closed the cover of his notebook, Prudence drew the sheet up over Sally Lynn's body and face.

"Are you all right, Miss Prudence?" He took a deep breath to steady himself.

"I should have been on the scene, informed at the same time Ned Hayes sent word to Geoffrey. I don't think I'll forgive Ned right away for excluding me. Or Geoffrey. Either we are partners or we are not." Prudence glanced one more time at Sally Lynn's remains, then turned on her heel to march resolutely out of this city of the dead.

"He probably thought to spare you," Josiah said.

"Florence Nightingale proved in the Crimea that women could stand as much suffering and horror as men. Her nurses saw far worse than we did today. That was thirty years ago. We don't seem to have made much progress."

Josiah knew what she meant, but it wasn't a topic on which he wanted to express an opinion.

As they climbed into her carriage, Prudence turned for one last look at Bellevue, site of so much of the city's suffering. "I know she was only a whore. But I think it's a terrible thing to waste a life. Any life."

Chapter 24

By the time Kevin and Blossom reached Armory Hall, some of the lingering scent of Brenda's perfumed soap had faded, but Carney's new clothes and the dog's shampooed fur made them almost unrecognizable to Billy McGlory's bouncer. He was smart enough to make no comments and ask no questions.

"I'm sorry, Mr. McGlory," Kevin apologized. He'd never before been invited into the saloon keeper's private office. The sight and feel and smell of all that leather and sweet cigar smoke was making him dizzy. "I'd have been here sooner, but I had a little problem on the way."

"Big Brenda said you were flirting with pneumonia."

"Catarrh. I was a chesty child, always coughing and spitting up and running fevers hotter than tea water. It'll carry me off some day, but for now the fever's gone and I'm right as rain again."

"I see Brenda did well by you."

"By the both of us," Kevin corrected. Talk about him and you had to talk about Blossom, also. They were inseparable; she got her feelings hurt if anyone forgot her.

"Tell me what you learned. What made you go to Madame Jolene's Saturday night?"

"Closer to Sunday morning it was."

"Start at the beginning, Kevin."

"Blossom and I were keeping watch the way you told us, across the street from Saint Anselm's in the alleyway there. I'd built us a shelter out of cardboard boxes and newspapers. People throw their newspapers away without hardly reading them at all. It's a terrible waste is what it is."

"You and Blossom were watching Saint Anselm's."

"Always one or the other of us with eyes and nose and ears fixed on it. When I went up to buy food, Blossom stayed on guard."

The dog thumped her tail at the sound of her name. An aroma of gardenia shampoo wafted up from the floor where she lay.

"We had the fried potatoes and bacon again. We like to eat what we're used to, you know, and the potatoes and bacon we get from the vendor on the corner there where Saint Anselm's is are crispy and hot.

He puts a fancy twist on a piece of news-paper and in go the potatoes and strips of bacon. You can have vinegar and salt on your potatoes, if you want. Usually I sprinkle a little of both on mine, but Blossom has hers plain. She's not big on salt."

"So after you brought your food back and after you ate it . . ."

"Well, that's when we saw Miss Sally Lynn."

"Tell me about that, Kevin. Where did you see her and what was she doing?"

"She was stumbling down the steps of the church. Grabbing for the rail with one hand and carrying a package." Had he answered the question? He wasn't sure. Best to tell everything. Mr. McGlory had a way of cutting him off if it was too much. "She came out from inside the church. Jerry Brophy was pulling her along by the arm. Rough-like."

Blossom obligingly sat up so her human could demonstrate how the man who liked to clean had grabbed Sally Lynn. "He shook her, too, and he was hissing at her like a snake. 'Don't come back. You don't belong here. Get out.' He said that over and over again. In between the hissing and the sput-tering. You could tell she was upset, but she didn't argue with him. Didn't say a word.

We've seen Miss Sally Lynn at Saint Anselm's before, and up at Saint Patrick's, too. Now that's a grand church. Cathedral is what you call it when it's that big and fancy."

"Finish telling me about Miss Sally Lynn, Kevin."

Kevin blinked his eyes rapidly to pull his mind back to where it had been before he got distracted by the cathedral. What a fine place it was. Blossom nipped the loose skin on the back of one of his hands. She was good about guessing when he needed a little extra help concentrating. "So she came down the steps reaching for the iron railing and nearly dropping her package, and a couple of times she tripped, but she didn't fall." Kevin's hands imitated feet walking down stairs. "Then when she got to the bottom she looked back and what she saw frightened her."

"How do you know she was frightened?"

Kevin was embarrassed for Mr. McGlory's ignorance. "We could smell it, the fear. It was faint at first, then it got very strong very fast."

"Tell me what she was looking at."

"Not a what, sir. A *who*."

"Did you recognize him, Kevin?"

"By his smell and by his face. Both. It was

the man who pays money to play with Miss Sally Lynn. Blossom doesn't like him, so neither do I."

"What was he doing at the top of the steps?"

"Just looking. He came out of the church when Jerry went back in, but he didn't walk down the steps. He stood there with his back to the door and stared at Miss Sally Lynn. He wasn't smiling when he looked at her, and he didn't say hello or good-bye. He just stared."

"Did he go to Madame Jolene's?"

Now Blossom nudged her cold nose into the palm of Kevin's hand to give him courage and remind him that she loved him. He wouldn't dare lie to Mr. McGlory, but the truth about his falling asleep on duty would be shaming. Humans didn't like to be shamed. Neither did Blossom, so she understood Kevin's hurt.

"That's when the catarrh came on me. I'd been fighting the cough for a while, but then I couldn't see or hear anything, and it felt like walking through a crackling fire that was burning me up." Kevin ducked his head and tickled Blossom's nose to let her know he appreciated her loyalty. "I fell asleep, Mr. McGlory, right there in the cardboard shelter and the newspapers. When I woke up the fever was bad. Nobody was around and it was close to morning. Blossom led me along the streets until we got to Miss Jolene's. I knew she'd take care of me."

"Big Brenda said she found you sprawled in the kitchen."

"The door was open, Mr. McGlory. I meant to turn the knob but it opened when I fell against it and the next thing I knew I was on the floor, lying on top of Blossom's rug. She was following a scent trail out in the yard, whining and turning in circles, but she kept losing it. That's odd, you know. Blossom never loses a scent trail once she's picked it up."

"What's the next thing you remember, Kevin?"

"Waking up in that little room off the kitchen. All clean and warm and not burning hot anymore. They were sitting around the kitchen table, Mr. Hunter and Detective Phelan and the one who used to be a detective but isn't now. Mr. Hayes. They were talking about Miss Sally Lynn. I listened to them and so did Blossom."

Billy looked down at Blossom, who smiled back at him. "What did you smell out there in Jolene's backyard?" he asked her. "Who was it who managed to get away from you?"

She cocked her head to one side and

turned down an ear, trusting her human to interpret for her.

"She doesn't know, sir. It was a familiar scent or she wouldn't have deviled it the way she did. But then I fell, see, and she had to get help for me."

"Tell me what you heard in the kitchen, Kevin. Can you remember?"

Of course he could. Word for word, inflection for inflection, he repeated the conversation exactly as if it had been written down. Blossom barked to imitate the sound Mr. Hayes's chair made when he overturned it.

"I want you to go back to Miss Jolene's house, Kevin. I don't care what excuse you have to think up for why you left, as long as you don't tell anyone where you went or why. Or who you talked to. Do you understand?"

"Yes, Mr. McGlory."

"I'm assigning you and Blossom to protect the house and the women who work there."

"That's Mr. Bright's job, sir. He won't like that we're taking it away from him."

"You're not. You're helping out, that's all. And Kevin, what you hear and knowing who comes to the house is as important as what you do."

"Do we have to sleep inside?"

"Two more nights. Then you can stay in

the shed."

"Miss Big Brenda always puts a pot of coals out there in case we come by."

"She's a good woman. They all are in that house."

"Will they still be there?" Prudence asked as the carriage rolled away from Bellevue.

"I don't imagine Detective Phelan will leave until he and his policemen have gathered up the last bit of evidence they can find. Mr. Hunter will insist on staying, and Mr. Hayes will probably not want to go either." Josiah fussed with his stenographer's notebook, making sure none of the pages had doubled over or become wrinkled, inserting his pencil stub into the leather loop that held it in place along the notebook's spine.

"I want to see her room before they clean it up," Prudence declared. She tapped on the roof of the carriage to signal Kincaid to whip up the horses.

"The police won't clean it up, Miss. They never do. That'll be left for the maids. Blood everywhere, I'd say. If that's where the girl was killed."

"Sally Lynn Fannon," Prudence reminded him. *The dead shouldn't become anonymous.*

"If Madame Jolene wants to use the room

for entertaining clients tonight, she'll have the maids and Big Brenda the cook in there with mops and pails and brushes before the last policeman closes the door behind him."

"Surely she wouldn't, Josiah?"

"She would, Miss. Madame Jolene says she's running a business and anyone who thinks any differently is a fool."

"How do you know so much about her?"

"Mr. Conkling handled a case there once. Very small case. Settled out of court and no one the wiser. No names in the papers." Josiah's ears and cheeks throbbed red; he was mortified to have to reveal that secret to such a genteel lady.

"What else can you tell me about Madame Jolene?" Prudence asked.

"She's not French, though she tells everyone she is. Mr. Conkling tried to talk to her in French once; she stared at him and refused to answer. Then she said she'd made a sacred vow never to speak her native language again when she emigrated. Mr. Conkling said her French accent was unlike any he'd heard when he traveled to Paris. He liked her, though, so he pretended to believe whatever she chose to tell him. About being French anyway."

"How many women work for her in that house?"

"She has ten girls, Miss."

"Josiah, have you ever availed yourself of the services offered in a brothel?" Prudence smiled as he turned bright red and began to cough. "Never mind, just tell me whether you've ever been inside one of these places. I need to know what to expect."

"I had occasion to visit Madame Jolene's establishment in the course of the case that was settled out of court."

"Why?"

"Why?"

"Why did you and, I presume, Mr. Conkling, go to a house of ill repute?"

"The complaint involved a certain degree of physical discomfort that might or might not have been mistakenly delivered." It was the best he could do under the circumstances. "Mr. Conkling had to see the location of the alleged mishap. I accompanied him to take notes and make sketches."

"As you did for me today."

"Yes, Miss."

"What did the girl's room look like? I presume that's where you went."

"Yes, Miss."

"The room, Josiah."

"Small. Most of the space taken up by a large bed." He didn't dare look up from the notebook to which he was clinging as if to a life raft. "Rather fanciful decoration. Strong smell of perfume. An armoire for clothes, a washstand with basin and pitcher. The customary receptacle under the bed. Except for the brightness of the colors of the bedclothes and drapes, a very ordinary room. There was some art on the walls, but I didn't study it." Just remembering the subject matter of the crude paintings he'd glanced at made his palms sweat.

Prudence appeared to be conjuring up the scene Josiah had described. Her delicately arched eyebrows puckered as she roamed mentally around the workplace of a soiled dove, the euphemism commonly used to refer to women who sold their bodies. *Ridiculous nomenclature,* she thought. Too romantic by far for what she now understood to be the reality of their lives. The stench of cheap perfume that Josiah recalled was no doubt liberally sprayed around the room to cover more unpleasant smells.

"What do you make of all this, Josiah?" she asked. "These three murders."

"I'm not sure, Miss." Mr. Conkling had never asked his secretary's opinion about any of the cases he handled, nor about any of the debates or bills on which he worked during his congressional career. Josiah had kept his thoughts to himself for so long that he hesitated before answering the question. "I think it must have happened so quickly that they felt very little fear or pain. The killing part, I mean. And that was a mercy, given what came afterward."

"We haven't focused on that, on the actual moment of their deaths. The cutting and the desecration of the bodies are so horrific they draw the mind away from the simple act of killing. Yet it must have been very swiftly done. No one has reported hearing any sounds of flight or a struggle. No screaming. No cries for help."

"Could they have been drugged first?" Josiah thought of the laudanum that had nearly taken Miss Prudence's life.

"No. There wasn't any smell of ether or chloroform about the bodies. Nothing else would act as quickly. Laudanum has to be ingested." She smiled reassuringly at Josiah. One thing she had determined upon was not avoiding the mention of the addictive narcotic whose casual use would always be a danger to her.

"Knocked unconscious then?"

"Ellen perhaps. But not even the coroner mentioned finding damage to the back of Nora's head. That's where someone would most likely be hit if the intention was to knock her out. And the motive wasn't violation." Prudence sat quietly for a moment, then rephrased what she had just said. "Rape. The motive wasn't rape. I need to start calling things by what they are. If the motive for attacking Nora, Ellen, and Sally Lynn wasn't rape, and nothing was stolen from them, why were they killed?"

"The Tierney and Kenny girls wouldn't have had more than a few small coins on them. We won't know if anything was taken from Sally Lynn's room until we talk to Mr. Hunter or Mr. Hayes," Josiah said.

"Apparently neither of those gentlemen believed I ought to be invited to the site of the killing to see it for myself. If you hadn't used the telephone to call me, I'd be drinking my morning coffee in blissful ignorance. If I haven't thanked you before, I do now, Josiah."

"We're almost there, Miss." Josiah folded the coach rug he'd lain across his knees and legs.

"Stop, stop now!" Prudence pounded on the roof of the carriage with the steel tipped umbrella Geoffrey had convinced her to take with her wherever she went. "That's Danny Dennis's hansom cab. See it? Just turning the corner, coming down the street toward us."

Josiah peered out the carriage's left side

window. "Who's in it?"

"Joseph Nolan, that's who. I'd recognize that cab and especially that horse anywhere."

"What's Nolan doing in Danny's hansom cab?" Josiah was thoroughly befuddled.

"It was Mr. Hunter's idea. He said Nolan wouldn't take the family carriage to a brothel. He couldn't trust the coachman to keep quiet about where he went. So Geoffrey decided to hire Danny to keep an eye on the Nolan house and be the closest available hansom whenever Nolan decided to hail one. Danny's been shadowing him ever since. Certainly earning his coin."

"It can't continue for much longer, Miss. Mr. Washington, the horse that pulls Danny's hansom cab, is too distinctive. Those teeth, for one. Nolan is bound to wonder why the same cab keeps turning up."

"I'm sure you're right. That's the ugliest horse I've ever seen. Unforgettable. After today, Geoffrey will have to find someone else. Danny must have dozens of driver friends who'll jump at steady money."

From where the carriage had stopped at the far end of the street, they watched as Danny Dennis negotiated a sharp turn before he reached the knot of curious onlookers standing in front of Madame

Jolene's establishment. Policemen in their distinctive dark blue frock coats and tall hats guarded the front door and the two police wagons parked outside. It was obvious that a serious crime had been committed inside the brownstone that looked exactly like all of its neighbors. The New York Metropolitan Police didn't respond in force to anything less than murder.

Mr. Washington turned effortlessly in the cobbled street that was barely wide enough to allow two vehicles to pass each other without touching. The curtains had been drawn tight across the front of the cab. No doubt it was Joseph Nolan inside. He hadn't expected to meet the police.

"If he doesn't know she's dead, it means he's innocent of Sally Lynn's murder," Prudence said, watching the cab as it drove back in the direction from which it had come. "Or if he did kill her, then he didn't think the body would be found this early and he was coming back to remove something he left at the scene. Something that could identify him. Kincaid can take us as far as the corner. We'll find a cab there and follow Nolan. He may recognize this carriage."

"That's too dangerous, Miss."

"I don't see that we have a choice, Josiah.

There's no one else who can do it but us."

"I wish you'd reconsider, Miss."

Prudence wrenched open the carriage door. "Out," she commanded. "Out. Go tell Mr. Hunter and Mr. Hayes where I've gone. If they hurry, they may be able to catch up. I won't get out of the cab unless I have to. I just want to know where Nolan is going." *And why he panicked when he saw the police wagons.*

"No, Miss, I'm coming with you." Josiah scribbled a message in his stenographer's notebook, then ripped out the page and folded it into quarters. "Wait for me," he called up to Kincaid as he tumbled out of the carriage and ran up the steps to Madame Jolene's front door. He thrust the note at a policeman who automatically moved to stop him from entering the brothel, followed it with a handful of banknotes, and shouted desperate directions. "See that Mr. Geoffrey Hunter gets this right away. He's inside with Detective Phelan. It's a matter of life and death." He shoved the stenographer's notebook into the policeman's reluctant hand. "Take this, too. Tell him to read my notes and he'll understand everything."

That business about it being a matter of life and death sounded ridiculous, he thought as he bounded down the steps and into the carriage again. *Like something out of a penny dreadful.* But he hadn't been able to come up with anything else that conveyed a sense of urgency. And really, it didn't matter what the copper thought as long as he delivered the letter and the notebook to Mr. Hunter.

Josiah had never done anything this rash before, but he knew Miss Prudence was determined. She wouldn't be dissuaded no matter how foolhardy he tried to convince her she was being. His heart pounded, blood roared in his ears, and he thought it highly likely he'd pass out any minute, but he wasn't about to let her ride into danger alone.

And she was right about one thing. They had to keep Danny's cab in sight.

CHAPTER 25

The policeman on duty at Madame Jolene's front door was used to frantic pleadings from the public. Most of the time he paid little attention. Officer Jenkins shoved the money into his pocket before one of the coppers pacing up and down the sidewalk saw the wad and demanded his share. He debated throwing the note away, but it was freezing cold outside on the stoop and he was perishing for a cup of hot coffee. Every time he cracked open the door to peer inside he caught a whiff of something baking and heard voices coming from the kitchen. That's the way it always was. If you walked a beat, you could expect chilblains on your toes, arthritis in your fingers, and chapped, raw skin all over your face. Winter wasn't a patrolman's favorite season.

He didn't see the point of making such a fuss about another whore getting killed; it was the kind of thing that happened every day. But he'd known something was up when the leather curtain of a hansom cab was pulled back and he caught a glimpse of Chief of Detectives Byrnes himself sitting inside. Ten minutes later Phelan got out and the cab rolled off toward Mulberry Street. The body was gone, but Phelan was still inside the house, and nobody had bothered to explain why he was spending so much time with an ex-Pinkerton and a former detective with ties to at least one of the saloon keepers the reformers were after.

Maybe it was a good idea to see that the note got delivered after all. And someone might offer him a cup of coffee. At least he hoped so.

Kevin and Blossom heard voices in the kitchen long before they climbed the steps to eavesdrop on what was being said. Blossom was for going inside to lie down in front of the fireplace on the braided rag rug that had her smell on it, but Kevin shook his head no. He'd sneaked out of the sick room without a word to anyone, and he had a feeling Miss Brenda might still be mad about that. Women liked it when you told them where you were going and why. He'd rather not have to argue with her if he needed to leave again. He signaled to Blossom to sit and lean her body against the wood door for a touch of the warmth seeping through from inside. They could hear just as well from out there as they could if they were sitting at the table, but out there no one would tell them to go away. Mr. Mc-Glory was always happiest when Kevin had secrets to tell him.

"I don't know what possessed the man." Geoffrey Hunter was as close to shouting as he ever got. He seldom allowed his temper to erupt; the violence of it frightened even him. "He should have realized what the consequences would be."

"He writes that she was very angry." Ned paged through the stenographer's notebook, pausing at the sketch of Sally Lynn's body, skimming Josiah's descriptive prose. At least he hadn't written his notes in abbreviations that no one but the person who wrote them could read.

"*She* was angry?"

"He quotes Miss Prudence at the morgue saying that she didn't think you'd ever had any intention of allowing her to see the murder scene."

"She's right. I didn't."

"That's your first mistake, Geoff." Ned Hayes turned another page. "Prudence saw Nora's body in Colonial Park. You didn't hide anything from her then. So it made it worse to exclude her from this scene."

"The woman was murdered in a bordello, Ned."

"She was a whore."

"My point exactly," Hunter snapped.

"You can't shield her," Hayes said quietly. "She doesn't want to be treated like a child. Prudence MacKenzie is educating herself to the world her father gave her a glimpse of through the law. She won't appreciate it if you slam the door on her."

"She's following Joseph Nolan," Geoffrey said. "The man dresses up like a priest and lacerates his back with a whip. If it comes to a confrontation, I don't think Josiah is any match for him."

"Kincaid won't let anything happen to either of them. If he senses they might be getting into trouble he'll have those bays whipped up and off at a gallop. Judge Mac-Kenzie didn't have anything but the best horseflesh in his stable and Kincaid is a master at the reins."

Patrolman Jenkins stepped forward from the corner where he'd taken his cup of hot coffee to drink as close to the fireplace as he could get. "Begging your pardon, sir, but the man who gave me the notebook didn't stay in the coach for long."

"What do you mean?" Phelan asked.

"I watched it as far as the corner. Two people got out, the little man and a taller woman. They hailed a hansom cab and the carriage turned in the other direction and went down Fifth Avenue. But they weren't in it."

"Jesus, Mary, and Joseph." Detective Phelan pushed open the swinging door into the parlor area, nearly knocking Big Brenda off her feet. "Send that sergeant of mine in here," he ordered. "Where's he gone to?"

"He's directing the lads who're taking out the last of the soiled linen. You told them to remove anything that had Sally Lynn's blood on it."

"Get him," he repeated. "The lads can finish on their own."

"Can we open this evening? Madame Jolene has been asking, and I've had to tell her I don't know."

"You can open. I don't know why you'd want to, but once we finish here, you can open. Tell her I said so. Tell her I'll return if I have to, if anybody's held out on us." Phelan turned to go back into the kitchen. Too late to hope Prudence MacKenzie wasn't swallowed up in busy city traffic. There were hundreds of nearly identical hansom cabs in New York City. If anything happened to her, it would be a scandal the city wouldn't soon forget. Chief Byrnes would have his badge.

"I paid Danny Dennis to keep Nolan in his sights," Hunter was saying. "He's a good man, Dennis. If Nolan isn't using his own carriage, he's being driven by Danny. And Danny will catch on to being followed soon enough."

"But he won't know who's following him. He won't have the inkling of an idea that it's Miss Prudence. Not to mention Josiah," Ned reasoned. "If Nolan realizes what's happening, he'll tell Danny to lose whoever it is, and Danny will do it. He's the best driver in the city."

"They'll be all right then." Geoffrey tried to sound more reassured than he felt. "Danny will twitch them loose like a dog shakes off water. Once Prudence's driver loses sight of Danny's cab he won't be able to find it again. And Nolan will never know who was after him. He won't even be sure anyone really was. So she'll be safe. Despite herself, she'll be safe."

And the next time he saw Josiah he'd give him a piece of his mind the secretary wouldn't soon forget.

"Danny is turning into Central Park," Prudence said.

"The road he's taking goes past the sheep meadow and the Carousel," Josiah told her. "I can't imagine Nolan stopping to admire the sheep, and the Carousel is closed when the weather is bad. It doesn't make sense."

"In a strange way it does. If he has something in that cab with him that he's desperate to hide, he has to dispose of it before the police connect him to Sally Lynn and decide to question him. I don't think he knows yet where he's going or what he'll do. He's counting on the inspiration of the moment, and in the meantime, as long as he's in Danny's cab and the police don't know where he is, he's safe. If it's the nun's habit and the cassock he's trying to get rid of, he can toss them anywhere in the park and feel confident they won't be traced back to him."

"He can't know Sally Lynn is dead," Josiah argued. "Unless he's the one who killed her."

"Maybe not when he first ordered the cab to turn around. But all it would take would be a question shouted out to someone on that street."

What's going on?

Dead whore over to Madame Jolene's place.

Who?

The one with the black curls, Sally Lynn she called herself.

"It's Sunday. He can't hide out at his office, and he probably doesn't dare return to the house on Fifth Avenue. Maybe the park was the only place he could think of to go." Prudence banged on the ceiling hatch near the rear of the cab until it slid open. "We'll let you know when we want to get out," she instructed the driver. "Stay far enough back so the cab in front of us can't be sure we're following."

"He already knows. That's Danny Dennis up there, Miss. Nobody can put one over on him."

"If Danny knows, then Nolan probably does as well," Josiah reasoned.

"Looks like Danny is stopping at the Carousel, Miss," the driver said. "Least-ways, he's pulling over and slowing down."

"We're getting out," Prudence decided. "Stop, driver, stop right here." Dennis's cab disappeared from sight around a bend in the road. "Get down, Josiah. It's not far. We'll walk the rest of the way. He won't see us coming." She handed the driver a tip large enough to make his jaw drop. "Whip up your horse and pass by that other cab without stopping. You've got to be going fast enough so nobody can tell whether

440

you're carrying any passengers. Understand?"

"I do, Miss."

"If anyone tries to stop you, keep on going if you can. If you can't, and somebody wants to know where your passengers got out, you tell them it was at the entrance to the park. A lady and gentleman. That's all. Nothing more."

"Nobody'll get a word different out of me."

They watched the cab careen down the roadway. Following instructions and buoyed by the biggest tip he'd ever gotten, the driver was making good speed. He'd whip by the Carousel so fast he'd be gone before anyone realized he was there.

"I should have gotten his name," Prudence said. "I don't know what I was thinking of. We'll never be able to find him now."

"Does it matter?"

"It would have been nice to hear from his own lips what he saw when he passed the Carousel. Whether Danny or Nolan looked up as he raced by them."

"Danny will know who he is," Josiah said. "He can identify every cabbie in the city. They all recognize each other's horses and vehicles. According to Danny, the horses are as distinctive as children. Or so he claims."

"He would."

"Stay off the road, Miss. There's less chance Nolan will hear us."

"He may not even get out of the cab. In fact, I'd be surprised if he did."

"I'm not following your logic."

"Consider. He's vulnerable to blackmail. So this morning he begs off going to Saint Patrick's with the rest of the Nolan family because he has to think through what he's going to do about Sally Lynn. He has to have sensed that she's close to telling Madame Jolene what he makes her do. Maybe she's already talked to the madam. Or he's the one who killed her and he wants to know if the body's been found. Whichever it is, he's on his way back to the brothel, he comes around the corner, sees the police everywhere, and orders his driver to turn around. Now where does he go? He needs time to think through what he's seen and plan what to do next."

"Whether he's worried about blackmail or he's a murderer, Nolan has to be close to panicking right now. He doesn't know what the police have learned, but he's got enough common sense to feel threatened. He de- cides to have Danny pull off the road at the

442

Carousel, and then he'll sit in the cab until he's figured out what he has to do to keep himself safe. You're right. He won't get out." Josiah slid across an icy patch. "It's too cold."

But when they reached the Carousel, Joseph Nolan was standing on the revolving platform, one arm draped around the neck of a fawn-colored stallion with a bright red saddle and bridle sadly in need of repainting. Danny Dennis and Mr. Washington were nowhere in sight.

"Wait." Prudence pulled at Josiah's arm until he was close beside her, hidden behind the trunk of an ancient ash tree.

"I thought you said he wouldn't get out of the cab," the secretary whispered.

"The road's too narrow here, so he's sent Danny on ahead to find a wider spot and turn the cab around. He doesn't want any witnesses to whatever he's planning to do."

"Now what?"

"We wait."

"Look, Miss, he's carrying something," Josiah said. "It looks like a leather briefcase. Half the businessmen in New York walk around with them. That's got to be what Kevin described as a satchel."

"He's going to get rid of it, Josiah. He's just looking for a place to hide it until he

443

can come back without anyone seeing him."

The freezing temperature hadn't been so bad when they were walking, but now Prudence began to shiver. She wasn't shod for icy pathways and she wasn't dressed for anything colder than the interior of a carriage warmed by pots of charcoal. She should have told the hansom cab driver to wait outside the park for thirty minutes, then return for them. She'd given him a large enough tip. Maybe he'd come back on his own.

"I hope he hurries up. I don't want to crouch here in this forest all day."

"You're not crouching and it's hardly a forest," Prudence chided. "Watch him now. He's moving. He's going somewhere."

Joseph Nolan was weaving his way around the Carousel, stopping now and then to get his bearings. When he finally stepped off, he seemed to disappear, as if he'd fallen into a hole.

"He's gone down into the tunnel where the horse turns the mechanism," Prudence breathed. "My father told me about it when he brought me here. He thought it would amuse me, but I cried. There's a horse and a mule down below the Carousel, hitched to a metal pole that he pulls around and around in a circle all day long. In the darkness. So that children up above can pretend to be riding real horses and shriek and laugh in the sunlight. It has to be horrid down there."

"Like workhouses or the prisons where they make the inmates march on tread-mills." Josiah had visited some of Roscoe Conkling's less fortunate clients in their places of incarceration.

"It's empty when the Carousel is closed during the winter. A perfect hiding place."

"Wouldn't they lock the entrance to the tunnel?"

"I suspect a man like Joseph Nolan would have figured out a way around that. Detective Phelan told us the gate to Colonial Park where Nora was found had been picked."

Prudence led the way from one tree to another, Josiah behind her. Every step took them closer to the clearing in which the Carousel stood in deserted winter splendor.

"That's far enough," Josiah hissed. Miss Prudence scared him almost as much as Mr. Conkling had.

"He's coming out again."

Joseph Nolan, leather briefcase hanging from one hand, was standing in front of the Carousel when Danny Dennis swung his cab over to the side of the road and halted Mr. Washington. He looked around before

445

getting in, as if to be certain that no one lurked nearby, as if something had caught his attention and he needed to know what it was.

Mr. Washington stomped his feet and shook his great white head, steam pluming out his nostrils. Danny Dennis said something to his fare, Nolan answered back. Minutes later they were gone, the clop of Mr. Washington's hooves and the noise of the wheels scraping along the frozen roadway fading into the distance.

"He left something behind," Prudence said, stepping out from among the trees. "I'm sure of it."

"The briefcase was lighter. He carried it differently," agreed Josiah. "I don't suppose you'll want to leave until we find out what it was."

"We'll wait a few more minutes. Just to be certain he doesn't decide to come back."

"He won't, Miss. It's too cold."

"You also said he wouldn't get out of the cab, Josiah."

"Did I?"

"You did. But to be fair, so did I."

It was the second time that afternoon Josiah would regret listening to Miss Prudence.

CHAPTER 26

"Do you remember where Nolan was standing when he disappeared?" Josiah laid one gloved hand on the arched neck of a dappled wooden steed whose immovable front legs pawed the winter air. He threaded his way in and out among rearing animals and small sleighs.

"I remember riding this Carousel when I was a child," Prudence said, lost for a moment in nostalgia. "That horse over there was my favorite — the white pony with the blue saddle and reins. I always thought he was neighing at me. His teeth are all chipped now, poor thing."

"Our driver said they'll be freshened up for spring. That's one of the reasons the ride closes down for a while. I have a bad feeling about this place, Miss. We need to hurry up."

"Here, Josiah," called Prudence. She had worked her way to the rearmost section of the shelter under which the Carousel stood. A jumble of equipment and bits and pieces of this and that had been piled against a back wall, presumably to be refurbished when the weather permitted.

A few feet away, off to the side, yawned a ramp leading downward into the earth. This was where the horse and the mule that powered the Carousel entered, where they were yoked to the mechanism that drove the circular platform on which the wooden horses above them galloped in frozen splendor. Round and round, day after day, stopping and starting again to the sound of the operator's boot knocking against the wooden flooring right above their heads.

"I can't see a thing," Josiah said, peering down the ramp into what looked like a very large earth walled cellar. He paused to allow his eyes to adjust to the darkness after the bright glare of ice and patches of snow in the park.

"Nolan had to have had a lamp," Prudence reasoned. "And he would have left it here so he could come back to retrieve what he hid."

"How long?"

"I think that depends on what it is. If it's something he doesn't want to destroy, then he only needs to hide it for as long as it could link him to one of the murdered girls."

"Certainly to Sally Lynn."

"Geoffrey says the vast majority of killings in New York City are never solved."

"I doubt there's much effort when the victim lives outside the law."

"Or if she's a servant," Prudence said, thinking of Ellen Tierney and Nora Kenny.

"Here. I almost tripped on it," Josiah said, triumphantly holding up a small lantern by its curved carrying handle. "It looks like a carriage lamp. He must have taken it from Danny's cab. The glass chimney is still warm." He rummaged around in his coat pocket until he found a tiny box of safety matches.

Josiah had only recently begun to experiment with the cigarettes marketed in square paper packets, artfully decorated with green leafed lilies and swirls of gold curlicues. He'd never liked the cigars most men smoked, but he found these flavored and perfumed tobacco products both relaxing and delicious.

Will he never cease surprising me? Prudence thought as she lit the kerosene lantern. Holding it out in front of her, she slowly descended the ramp that was barely wide enough to allow a horse or a mule access to the round track beaten into the ground by hundreds of thousands of hoof-beats. For anyone who loved horses, it didn't bear thinking about.

"It's worse than I thought it would be," Prudence said, lowering the lantern whose sputtering light was bright enough to be blinding when held too close to the face. "That must be where the Carousel's operator sits." She pointed up toward a rectangle of wooden ceiling between whose rough planks beams of daylight slanted into the cellar. It was like being in an abandoned mine, earthen walls reinforced with crudely planed wooden supports, dampness oozing into the glacial air to become icicles. Lumps of dried horse dung lay frozen to the ground.

"Where would he hide something?" Josiah asked. He turned in a slow circle, examining earthen walls, roof, and floor. "I'm looking for a hole dug out somewhere and then quickly filled in. Any kind of disturbance that seems different from the dirt around it."

Prudence took the hissing lantern into dark corners while Josiah circled closer to the horse track, peering through the gray winter light that penetrated the operator's platform. First one then the other reached out toward a promising spot, only to pull back, disappointed. Dampness sometimes made the earth look disturbed when it was only cold and wet.

"I was so certain he'd left something behind," Josiah said. "So certain the briefcase seemed lighter when he came out."

"We can't give up yet, Josiah."

Prudence walked toward a pile of wooden slat boxes stacked haphazardly beneath the operator's platform. At first glance, they looked as if they'd lain there untouched since the Carousel was closed down for the worst of the winter weather. But there were scuff marks on the ground around them, and the clear imprint of a lantern base in the loosened dirt.

"Here." Prudence handed the lantern to Josiah. "This is where he hid his prize, whatever it is. He wasn't down here long enough to do any better than take advantage of what was already here. We forgot about the element of time."

"Open the top one."

"It's empty. I can see through the slats." Prudence picked up the box and set it on the ground. "They're not heavy," she said, picking up another crate. "This is what we're looking for."

The top of the crate opened easily. Inside lay a bundle of dark clothing looped around with a white cord that had three knots tied at each end. Prudence could feel her hands trembling as she fumbled with the rope. Finally, the clumsily secured cord was unloosed and the bundle fell apart.

"A nun's habit," Josiah breathed.

Prudence held the garment against her body, the starched wimple and novice's veil stark white in the dim light coming through the plank ceiling. "There's a rosary here, too," she said. "It's so big I think it's meant to be worn hanging from the waist."

"What's the other piece?"

Prudence set aside the nun's habit, then shook out the heavy black cloth. A starched white collar fluttered to the ground, a small cat-o'-nine-tails falling atop it. "It's a priest's cassock," she said, stunned by what they had found. "That's a whip, Josiah."

He stooped to pick it and the collar up from the damp ground. "There are nasty little hooks attached to the leather thongs." He bent his head to look more closely. "I think there's dried blood on them, Miss Prudence."

"Did he kill her, Josiah? Is this evidence of his guilt that he's trying to hide?"

"How stupid. He should have burned all of it when he had the chance."

So intent were they on examining what

Joseph Nolan had hidden that neither Prudence nor Josiah heard the scrape of footsteps against ice.

"That would be a desecration," a man's voice boomed against the earthen walls. "These garments have been blessed. They can't be burned like ordinary clothing."

Joseph Nolan blocked the only exit from the horse round. One hand held a blade that shone brightly in the reflected light of the lamp, the other rubbed at his clean shaven chin. "She made a very beautiful nun," he said longingly. He swayed, as if in a dream, then straightened, shaking his head to clear it. "Is she really gone?"

"Don't you know, Mr. Nolan?" Prudence tried to match the quiet, even tones of the man who might have killed and mutilated three women.

"I forget things sometimes. It makes Da very angry." Nolan swung the finely honed butcher blade with the ease of long practice. It was the preferred knife on the evisceration line, where carcasses dangled from ceiling hooks and men stepped up to slit them open with one strong downward motion.

"Why did you kill Sally Lynn?" Josiah was terrified, but he stepped in front of Miss Prudence, clutching the priest's collar and cat-o'-nine-tails in one trembling hand, the lantern in the other.

"Why? Why did I kill her?" Nolan took a step forward, coming deeper into the darkness of the tunnel. He shook his head from side to side as if seeking an answer to the question.

The lantern Josiah held sputtered and spit as its fuel began to burn low.

"May I fold these?" Prudence asked. She gestured to the habit and the cassock she had dropped. They lay crumpled one atop the other on the ground. "They'll be ruined otherwise."

Without waiting for an answer, but feeling Nolan's eyes on her, she picked up the nun's habit, adjusting the sleeves neatly across the front of the garment. She laid it reverently atop one of the crates, then folded the wimple and veil. Out of the corner of her eye she saw Josiah tighten his grip on the lantern, almost imperceptibly moving first one foot and then the other until he was standing squarely facing Joseph Nolan.

Josiah's arm arced back then swung forward with all the strength he could put into it. He let go of the lantern at the last possible moment, then grabbed Prudence by the arm.

"Run!" he shouted.

The lantern flew through the air toward Nolan, who seemed mesmerized by its trajectory. By reflex action he raised the butcher knife, catching the lantern flat on, deflecting its fall so that it crashed to the ground. The glass shattered and a pool of fuel ignited, the flames dancing toward but not reaching their target. Prudence and Josiah were cut off. Nolan still blocked their escape, aided by the river of flame that should have consumed him. It was already burning itself out. There had been barely enough fuel to create a distraction.

Holding on to one another, Prudence and Josiah backed toward the mechanism to which the horse and the mule were hitched when the Carousel was in operation. Two metal arms stretched out from the central pole around which the patient animals circled all day long. They clung to the farthest bar; it was the only barrier between them and death.

Joseph Nolan stared at the lantern fuel soaking into the earth, flames leaping and falling as they burned themselves out. It was as if the fire held him spellbound.

"I grabbed the rosary," Prudence whispered, never taking her eyes from the man in whose home she had drunk tea only a few days before.

"Danny Dennis will come looking for us. He's bound to," Josiah said. He held the cat-o'-nine-tails behind him, wondering whether he could flick the knife out of Nolan's hand before it cut him to ribbons.

"Danny has no idea we're down here."

"I wasn't sure," Nolan said conversationally. The flames had subsided, freeing him from their allure. He moved closer through the gloom. "I glimpsed something, but I couldn't tell who or what it was." He shrugged his shoulders, the butcher knife held lightly in his hand. "I've always been the cautious type. That's why I came back. I'm sorry you decided to follow me, Miss Prudence. I never intended it to end this way for you."

"Nothing has to end, Joseph. May I call you Joseph?"

"My sister used to call me Joe when we were little. Then Da decided Joe was too common. She had to use my full name and we couldn't address him as anything but Father. He's desperate to forget what he came from."

"What about you, Joe? Do you want to forget who you are?" Prudence tried to remember the sound of Alice Nolan's voice, mimicked it as best she could.

"I've always known who and what I am."

Nolan's right hand began to swing slowly back and forth, his fingers loosening then tightening their grip on the butcher knife. It was the way the men on the evisceration line kept their muscles from cramping during the long hours of disemboweling sheep and cattle.

The last of the fuel from the smashed lantern burned itself out. A single flame flickered, faded, licked upward one final time, died.

Like us, Prudence thought. *We're desperate to keep him talking, but we're running out of things to say. He's getting nervous, impatient. When he moves, we won't be able to stop him.*

"Mr. Nolan," Josiah cajoled. "We'll give you back your things. You can take them away with you. No one will ever know. Just lay the knife down so you can carry them."

It almost worked.

Joseph Nolan stretched the arm holding the butcher knife toward the stack of crates where the nun's habit lay neatly folded. But then he glanced down, saw the cassock still lying crumpled in the dirt and gave a small choking gasp. The priest he had always wanted to be lay scorned and soiled at his feet. "Pick it up," he said.

When neither Prudence nor Josiah moved

from behind the push bar, he raised his voice and yelled. "Pick it up, I tell you!" The hand grasping the knife swung back and forth rhythmically, as though he were using a scythe to cut down weeds. The whir of the blade cutting through the cold air was deafening. Without the lantern's glow, the steel reflected silver fragments of the daylight shining through the planks of the operator's platform above them.

Prudence and Josiah could not take their eyes from the foot-long knife that seemed to be exploding in the darkness like fireworks detonating across a night sky.

Danny Dennis had stopped his cab just shy of the park entrance to let his fare out again. No explanation, not much of a tip either. Joseph Nolan shifted the briefcase he carried to his left hand when he reached into a pocket to pull out some change. Something different there, something about the way the leather satchel moved. Danny could have sworn it was lighter and much less full than it had been when Nolan got out at the Carousel. Odd. Everything about the man Mr. Hunter had paid him to follow was odd.

He waited, getting down from his perch to adjust Mr. Washington's bit and harness, check the reins, lift up his hooves to knock out clods of frozen dung and dirt from the horse's shoes. When he wanted to, Danny could move as slowly and methodically as a man twice his age. Head down, shoulders hunched, he faded into the life of the street, just another winter coated figure among many. Nolan watched him for a few minutes, then decided he was no threat. He walked back into the park.

Danny stayed where he was, putting a feedbag on Mr. Washington's nose to let passersby know he wasn't for hire. He'd wait a while, then meander back into the park himself. Nolan couldn't make it out the other side in under twenty minutes at a brisk walk. As cold as it was today, he didn't think he'd wander the paths, many of which hadn't been shoveled clear of ice. Nolan's behavior puzzled him, and whatever was a puzzle eventually turned into a worry. He'd had Danny wait for him out of sight while he did whatever he did at the Carousel. Met someone? Been stood up by a woman who'd promised to join him there? Hansom cabs were every cheating spouse's favorite vehicle, anonymous and safe. They never thought about the driver sitting just above their heads.

But Nolan isn't married. So why the secrecy? He'd given the brothel's address without a trace of diffidence; he plainly didn't concern himself that his driver would know what was behind the brownstone's unremarkable front door. Then he'd changed his mind. Almost at the same moment that Danny registered the presence of police in the street had come a tattoo of thumps from inside the hansom, followed by the noise of the trapdoor sliding open.

"Turn around," Nolan had ordered. "Turn around."

Danny always boasted that Mr. Washington could reverse direction on a dime, and he proved the truth of it then. They were heading back the way they'd come before the coppers got a good look at them. There'd been a carriage at the far end of the street, though. He only got a brief glimpse, but Danny was certain it was Miss MacKenzie's vehicle, with James Kincaid driving. He'd been about to tip his whip in recognition of the other driver, then thought better of it. Nolan had to be kept in the dark about his connection to the firm of Hunter and MacKenzie, Investigative Law. He'd have to count on Kincaid's sharp eyes noting Mr. Washington's quick turnaround. Deciding it was worth mentioning to Miss MacKenzie or Mr. Hunter.

Danny saw nothing out of the ordinary as

he drove past the Carousel again. Not a trace of Nolan standing about or striding off across the park. The man must be walking faster than he'd thought he would. He decided to drive to the other side of the park, out that entrance and along Central Park West. Up and back a few blocks. If he didn't spot Nolan by that time, he'd turn around and come back to the Carousel. Perhaps give Mr. Washington a rest and investigate on his own.

Nolan had left one of the carriage lanterns somewhere. Danny had seen him take it from its hook before he climbed onto the Carousel. He hadn't brought it back, and Danny had pretended not to notice. Where had the man gone that he needed a lantern to light his way? Reason enough to give the Carousel the once over. If he remembered correctly, there was a pit beneath the wooden horses where a real horse labored in darkness to drive the platform.

Maybe he wouldn't leave the park after all. Maybe he'd just turn the cab around and go back to the Carousel right now.

CHAPTER 27

Kevin Carney and Blossom had picked up a few street odors since the last time they'd been at Armory Hall, but Billy McGlory's bouncer didn't hesitate to let them in. The word was out. As strange a pair as they made, the skinny little Irish street beggar and his enormous dog had been ushered into McGlory's private office where they'd stayed closeted with him for nearly an hour. Until Billy changed his mind about them, best to treat the duo as near royalty or next of kin. The bouncer could have sworn the dog smiled at him as she trotted past.

"It was him all right. I heard the patrolman telling the detectives all about it. Miss MacKenzie and Mr. Josiah set off after the one who came to visit Miss Sally Lynn, but Danny Dennis won't know who they are because they sent their carriage home and hailed a hansom cab."

Blossom thumped her tail on the Turkish

carpet. She thought her human had summed up the situation nicely. She couldn't understand why the other human seemed confused. Puzzled.

"You were supposed to stay at Madame Jolene's, Kevin. I didn't tell you to come here."

"I thought you'd want to know what I found out."

"Start at the beginning. Where were you and Blossom when you picked up this information?"

"On the kitchen steps. Outside."

"What were you doing out there?"

"We'd just come into the backyard, see, and we heard voices from inside. We thought they'd stop talking if they saw us, so we made sure they didn't."

"What were they saying?"

"Miss MacKenzie and Mr. Josiah went to Bellevue to visit Miss Sally Lynn in the morgue."

McGlory nodded his head encouragingly. Blossom nudged Kevin. It meant he was supposed to continue talking, telling the story.

Ten minutes later he'd finished. Blossom didn't think he'd left out any of the important details, but with Kevin you could never be sure. When he rambled, which he did if no one interrupted often enough to keep him on track, it was difficult to follow the trail he was laying down. Sometimes even Blossom dozed off, though she always kept her eyes politely open.

"What will happen if they catch up with him, Kevin?"

"Maybe the same as was done to Miss Sally Lynn?" He looked at Blossom, who cocked her head, folded down an ear, and barked. Just once, and not very loudly. It was her *sad but true* bark. "Blossom thinks he'll kill them, Mr. McGlory."

"Have you ever known her to be wrong?"

Kevin didn't like to criticize Blossom's ability to predict human behavior, but once in a while she *was* wrong. He waited for her to admit it, but she sat silent and unmovable. "She won't change her mind, sir."

"Then we'd best do something about the situation." McGlory stood up, smoothed down his vest, caressed the diamond stickpin on his black silk cravat, and opened the office door. He spoke a few quiet orders to the two men waiting outside, then came back in and sat down again. "Now, Kevin, how do you propose we go about locating Miss MacKenzie and Mr. Josiah? I'm sending word out onto the streets, but we need more than that."

"We follow the cab, sir. Danny Dennis's cab. He'll lead us to them."

"The trail's gone cold. You said yourself the hansom disappeared around the corner when Nolan spotted the police. There's not a chance in hell of finding it now."

Blossom barked again, stood up, batted her long feather of a tail against her human's leg, and smiled at Billy McGlory. Flirted, actually. Like a showgirl boasting about how well she can dance.

"She follows Mr. Washington's scent trail. Every horse smells different from every other one. Animals know that. We get a blanket from the stable where he has his stall, Blossom learns the scent, and we go back to the corner where Mr. Danny turned the cab around."

"Can she really follow a horse's trail through the streets of New York? After dozens of other cabs and horses have trodden over it?"

Blossom rolled up the skin along her muzzle where humans would have had lips.

Billy McGlory sent a man on the run to get the blanket. "Double quick," he told him.

It would be a shame if Miss MacKenzie were to be sliced up after all she'd been through.

Sometimes Alice Nolan had to make up sins to confess. You couldn't kneel in the quiet darkness of the booth with nothing on your soul for the priest to absolve. She had a list of venial offenses that she varied week after week, reeling them off with the assurance of a practiced sinner. As long as she included the sin of lying, she had nothing to worry about.

The problem was the penances she was given.

Say three Hail Marys, three Our Fathers, and three Glory Bes.

No rosary, Father?

No rosary. Now make a good Act of Contrition.

Alice yearned for a real penance, a punishment that would take days or weeks to accomplish. She yearned to be told to fast, to kneel for hours before the crucifix, to flagellate herself the way so many of the saints had done. But it never happened. Week after week it was the trio of Hail Marys, Our Fathers, and Glory Bes. She added extra prayers and skipped meals, but it never felt right. The penance had to come from the priest. It couldn't be something she made up. It had to be genuine.

She thought confessing to fornication might be what she needed.

Joseph fornicated. She knew he did from the dark bags under his eyes when he wouldn't look at her across the breakfast table.

She knew he was also indulging in impure acts with himself. Once, very late at night, she'd crept to his bedroom door and listened. He'd had to wait until their mother and father were snoring in their beds, and then he'd put a rolled up blanket against the doorsill. She'd stretched out on the hall floor and poked hard enough with one of her carved wooden hair sticks to dislodge the roll an inch or so.

She'd heard him. Grunting and panting and gulping and then the harsh, guttural sound he couldn't completely stifle. She thought he must do it very often, maybe every night. He looked old for his age, old and worn out. Terrible things happened to people who abused themselves. Sometimes they went crazy, like in the stories Mr. Poe had written, which she wasn't supposed to read, but did.

If she confessed to impure acts, the priest would have to give her the kind of penance she wanted. She didn't think he would ask for details, but if he did, she could hide her face in her hands and pretend to cry. He'd know she was deeply sorry for her sins, but that wouldn't stop him from decreeing a harsher penance than three Hail Marys, three Our Fathers, and three Glory Bes.

There was a real sin she could confess, except that she was too ashamed to admit to the way it had ended and she'd done everything she could to forget it had ever happened.

When they were children, and even after they should have known better, she had dressed up as a nun and Joseph had put on a priest's cassock. They played for hours and hours, never tiring of the game despite its limitations, repeating word for word the scenes they contrived and duplicated over and over again.

He was the parish priest, she the sister teaching in the parish school. Sometimes he was the confessor, she the penitent. Or he recited Holy Mass, and she was his server. She could be the Mother Superior of a convent where teaching nuns lived, a nursing sister in a hospital ward, a missionary dying of cholera or yellow fever.

Then the pretending changed. Joseph changed. He became fierce and angry because she could never do exactly as he directed. It made her gag.

When Joseph was in his early twenties and Alice had just turned seventeen, he ordered her to lower the nun's habit below her waist and kneel before him again. She refused. She threatened to tell their parents if he bothered her with the game any more. And she meant it. He raised the whip to strike, but she stared at him with the cold authority of his father's eyes. The cat-o'-nine-tails froze in midair. Neither of them ever spoke of that moment. It was as though none of it had ever happened. Except that Alice still burned with shame when the memory of what he had forced her to do crept past her defenses. She had just about convinced herself that it couldn't be a mortal sin because she hadn't consented of her own free will. Or had she? She'd worked so hard at blocking it out that it was hard to remember.

Alice concentrated on the sin she was planning to confess. The worst thing a woman could do was have a child out of wedlock. They called it *getting caught* because there was no way out except a quick marriage, the street, or risking death at the dirty hands of a baby killer. So maybe what she would do is tell the priest that she *thought* she was caught and was desperate enough to consider doing away with it . . .

the child. He'd be horrified, furious with her, disgusted, angry enough to give her the stiffest possible penance so she'd change her mind. He'd want her to come back to confession again the following week. And the week after that.

Alice sighed with relief. She'd found the single perfect way to get what she wanted.

And no real danger to it.

Prudence wondered if she had ever really *seen* Joseph Nolan, looked past his expensive clothing and immaculately groomed hair. Short hair, lightly pomaded and combed flat against his head. Piercing eyes that looked out at you from under brows that were too heavy for his narrow face. He held his head high on a long neck, arched slightly back as though surprised by something you'd said. She thought he must be close to thirty, though the dry, dark skin below his eyes belonged to a much older man. Suffering was said to mark a person's face. If so, Joseph had suffered, was still in the grip of whatever agony possessed his mind and his soul.

I must be very tired, she thought, *or losing my mind. There's a man with a butcher knife in his hand swaying back and forth just steps away from me and I'm wondering how he got those circles under his eyes. I'm sorry for his pain and his suffering.*

Joseph Nolan decided there was time for one final scene before he had to go. Miss Prudence could act the part of the young nun, Josiah Gregory the older priest. The novice would make her first vows to the consecrated life of a Bride of Christ, the priest would hold both her hands in his while she pronounced the sacred words, and then he would give her the document to sign with her name in religion. What should that name be? A catalogue of female saints ran through his mind, but the only one that seemed appropriate was Agnes, patron saint of virgins.

"You look like an Agnes," he said to Prudence. "She was only twelve or thirteen when she was martyred, but she was beautiful, wealthy, noble, and chaste. It's a good thing Charles Linwood died during the blizzard. If he'd lived, you couldn't be Agnes because you wouldn't be a virgin. You'd be a wife."

It made perfect sense. He picked up the nun's habit and held it out toward Prudence. When she made no move to take it, he folded it across the push bar. The wimple and veil followed. He draped the cassock and the Roman collar beside the habit.

471

"You'll be the priest," he told Josiah. He brandished the butcher knife, then lowered it when the terrified little man nodded his head vigorously.

"I'm going to count to ten," Nolan explained. "When I reach ten you will be ready." He slid a thumb along the blade of the butcher knife, raising a thin line of blood that he sucked dry. "The knife is very sharp. I can make it so you won't suffer, or the blade can slip and slide instead of slicing deeply. The Chinese call it the death by a thousand cuts."

Their only hope was to get close enough to him to use the heavy wooden rosary that hung from the waist to the hem of a nun's habit, and the knotted white cord symbolizing the three vows of poverty, chastity, and obedience. Or the hooked cat-o'-nine-tails. It had to be in those few moments when he was counting to ten, when he was distracted by the rustling of habit and cassock being pulled into place. There was no plan, no discussion, just the quick meeting of eyes. Prudence and Josiah. Two minds coming together as one, two determined spirits gambling their lives on the element of surprise and the superhuman strength that sometimes came to victims in the face of attack.

Prudence dropped the nun's robe over her head and wrapped the white cord around her waist, pretending to tie it but winding it tightly around her fist. The moment Joseph looked away or turned his back to lead them toward the spot he had chosen for his final playlet, she would leap on his back and sling the cord down across his arms and chest tight enough to cause him to drop the butcher knife. Josiah would dive for his legs and wind the heavy rosary around them as many times as he could manage before he fell. And hope it didn't break. They had to tie off the cord and the rosary before he realized what was happening to him, truss him up like a roast for the oven. No time to think it through, no time to do anything but look one last time into each other's eyes.

If they did not succeed in overpowering him, Joseph Nolan would kill them.

Mr. Washington had a lovely, distinctive scent that warmed Blossom's nose delightfully. The cold didn't usually bother her, but she welcomed the flare of his heat dancing through her nostrils, up her long snout, and into her brain. Danny and his horse weren't traveling very fast, but Blossom was single-minded and paid no attention to interesting distractions. It was Mr. Washington she was tracking and no other.

Billy McGlory had handed Kevin a leash, which he stuffed into a pocket before Blossom could see it and be insulted. He'd explained as clearly as he could that he and Blossom worked best when no one else was along to get in their way, but he wasn't paid any attention. McGlory ordered the carriage he kept in a stable around the corner from Armory Hall. The two men who had been outside his office when Kevin first arrived returned, accompanied by three others. Kevin thought one of the newcomers must be important because Mr. McGlory stood up to greet him and the stranger was wearing a black wool coat and hat that only toffs and bosses could afford. The man was young, so perhaps he was mistaken. No names were volunteered and no one shook hands. Kevin nodded his head and Blossom put her paw down and her nose to the pavement.

When Blossom turned into Central Park, then stood to one side of the roadway sniffing the air and dashing back and forth as if she'd lost the scent, McGlory's two bodyguards jumped out of the carriage following along behind them. Within seconds the men protecting the stranger in the black coat joined them in the roadway.

"Stand still," Kevin shouted at them. "You'll confuse the trail." He watched Blossom as she trotted forward, then backwards as she crossed Fifth Avenue, weaving her way skillfully through the traffic, and then recrossed the street to come back into the park again.

"What's going on?" McGlory asked, leaning out his carriage window.

"Danny's cab went into the park, then came out and crossed Fifth Avenue. It looks as though he halted it there for a while before driving back in again."

Blossom barked to tell Kevin he was right, then started off, faster now as she was more sure of the scent and there were fewer competing smells to have to sniff through. Kevin trotted along close behind her, pacing his stride to hers, breathing in short puffs of air that sounded like small bellows working up a newly lit fire.

The bodyguards climbed back into their carriage. Two other McGlory men in a hansom cab ordered their driver to block the entrance to the park. Money changed hands and weapons were shown. The hansom cab came to a halt squarely across the roadway. And there it sat.

They had nearly reached the Carousel when Blossom suddenly halted, her haunches planted firmly on the grassy verge of the narrow road, her head pointed upwards.

Kevin knelt down in front of her. "What is it, girl? What's wrong?" He signaled to McGlory's driver to stop the carriage, shaking his head vigorously as doors opened. "No, not yet," he called. "Something has changed, but I don't know what it is. Wait there."

Blossom wanted to tell him that she'd run into two other scents she wanted to follow, but she wasn't sure Kevin would understand. Once he made up his mind about something, it was hard to change it, and right now he was determined to find Mr. Washington. Blossom thought Mr. Washington could take care of himself, but she wasn't so sure about the two people who had stood for a while hidden in the trees before moving out onto the grass again.

One scent was stronger than the other; the human female's leather paw coverings were thin. Lingering above the main scents were two distinct ribbons of something that wasn't quite fear, but close enough to make the hairs on Blossom's back bristle. The woman who had scratched her ears and the man who had given her a saucer of cream had been chasing after the man in Danny

Dennis's cab, the cab Mr. Washington pulled. She remembered the story she'd listened to when Kevin made her sit outside on the kitchen steps instead of crawling indoors to sprawl in front of the fire. Miss MacKenzie and Mr. Josiah. She thought again about what a huge horse Mr. Washington was, how big and powerful his hooves. The boot prints whose outlines she could sniff out were small, and the man was much older than the woman.

Follow me, Blossom barked, then she leaped out from under Kevin's comforting hand. Running as fast as she could, the scent trail growing stronger with every bound, she raced toward the brightly painted Carousel and its circle of elaborately carved steeds.

McGlory's driver whipped up his horses, then reined them in sharply as soon as they reached the Carousel. The bodyguards were out and on the ground before the second carriage stopped rocking. The driver tossed a pistol down to his boss, then turned his attention to calming his agitated team.

Onto the platform Blossom ran, through the forest of wooden legs, off to the side, disappearing before Kevin and the others could reach her.

McGlory, who hadn't done his own work

in years, was only a few paces behind Kevin and Dominic Pastore when they heard the screaming.

CHAPTER 28

Blossom hurtled down the horse ramp under the Carousel, nails clicking on its icy surface. Joseph Nolan turned, butcher knife raised to strike.

The dog leaped onto his chest, forcing Nolan's head backwards, sinking her fangs into his neck. She smelled madness on him, the crazed, confused anger that sometimes destroyed animals in the heat of summer. Humans called it rabies. There was madness of the body and madness of the mind; the man whose soul she was freeing had lost all power of reason. He was scarcely human anymore.

If Nolan could have sliced open the dog, he would have, but in the instant that Blossom hurled herself through the air, Prudence hauled with all her weight on the arm brandishing the knife. Joseph felt a warm rush of blood against the cold flesh of his neck and knew that the animal whose weight had flung him to the ground had found and severed the artery that would bleed him out in the time it took to say an Act of Contrition.

Blossom stopped slashing when the blood gushed against her muzzle. It was over for this human, though he still had a few minutes of life left in him. She didn't like blood on her fur; it was hard to lick off once it stiffened and matted the fine hairs under her coarse outer coat. She kept her paws on the human's chest because prey could surprise you, but she pulled back from the spurting that reminded her of the fountains in the park. Except that water was clear and refreshing to drink, and blood was not.

The screams echoing off the walls of the underground horse track ebbed into silence. It had been the surprise and fury of Blossom's attack that had forced desperate cries for help from Prudence and Josiah's throats. The dog ignored them, though the high pitched shrieks hurt her sensitive ears and she might have tried to bark them away if she hadn't had a muzzle full of flesh.

The man and woman lay on the damp ground where their desperate assault had landed them. Joseph Nolan's blood saturated the nun's habit and the front of Prudence's dress. Josiah, tangled up in the cassock and the rosary he hadn't had a chance to use, was as muddied as a street urchin. But they were alive. Alive and no longer alone with a madman.

The enormous dog whose shaggy red fur smelled equally of wet horse dung and strongly scented soap nosed insistently at one of Prudence's hands, nudging the fingers up from the ground and onto her head where they began scratching gently, reflexively. Dogs knew that when a human scratched their heads, it wasn't only the animal who benefited. Even when Blossom's ears weren't particularly itchy, she encouraged Kevin to rub them. It calmed him down and brought a smile to his face.

Josiah looked long and carefully at Joseph Nolan before he shrugged off the cassock and began unwinding himself from the rosary. Nolan was bleeding to death before his eyes. Josiah watched as the man's pupils dulled and his breath ceased to flutter across the pool of blood. He recognized the strange little person who whispered something into the dog's ear and then winked at her. Such unlikely saviors.

"Get them out of here." The man's back was to the ramp entrance, so his face was obscured, but Josiah recognized the voice.

"How did you know?" he asked.

"Blossom," McGlory answered. "She followed the scent of Danny Dennis's horse from where he turned around the hansom cab when he saw the police. Don't ask me how she did it, but she did."

"And we'll all say a prayer to Saint Jude for that impossible miracle," came another familiar voice.

"Mr. Dennis! We didn't think you'd seen us." Prudence dropped the bloody nun's habit onto the ground.

"I didn't. But you have a fine voice for yelling, Miss MacKenzie. Mr. Washington wouldn't leave the park. He flat refused. So I turned around and came back. That's when I saw Mr. McGlory's carriage and heard the screeching." He was out of breath from running, but he brandished the whip he carried in one hand and raised the club he held in the other.

Billy McGlory nodded toward Prudence and Josiah. "It's best if they're not seen in my rig, Dennis. Can you take them back to Miss MacKenzie's house?" The bodyguards faded into the deep blackness along the walls.

"I can, sir, of course. Will we be needing a doctor?"

"Not for him," Prudence said. She stepped over one of Joseph Nolan's outstretched legs and shook some of the mud off her skirts. "And not for me, either. Josiah?"

"I'm unhurt, Miss." He bent to gingerly stroke the smelly dog who had saved their lives. "What did you say her name was?"

"Blossom," blurted out Kevin, his hands running over his best friend's head, legs, and flanks. "Is she cut, Miss?"

"I don't think so." Prudence touched her nose to Blossom's. A quick lick was her reward.

"All right, Kevin," McGlory said. "Get Blossom away from here, too."

"I'll take care of them all, sir," Danny Dennis volunteered.

"Send me word, but don't come yourself."

Danny wrapped blankets around Prudence and Josiah, tucking them into the hansom cab like precious, breakable cargo. Kevin squeezed himself in as best he could, and when Danny handed him a blanket, he hid inside its folds.

Real ladies made him nervous; whenever they saw him on the street they pursed their lips and wrinkled their noses. Once in a while one of them tossed him a small coin and laughed when he scrambled for it. He wished he could be in one of his cardboard boxes right now, snuggled under a nice pile of newspapers with Blossom stretched out beside him. He liked to sleep with his head nestled on her fore shoulder, though sometimes when he woke up he found he'd curled right up against the length of her, his hands gripping the thick fur as though he would fall if he let go.

"All right now, girl," Danny said. "Up you go. You'll ride outside with me."

Mr. Washington turned his head to greet Blossom. So this was the dog who'd tracked him through the city streets and into the park. Intelligent and determined. He rolled his lip back in a friendly fashion to show her his teeth.

"What do you want us to do with the body, Mr. McGlory?" One of the bodyguards stepped out of the shadows and into the striped daylight coming down into the horse ring from the operator's perch above. He lit the small carriage lantern McGlory's driver had brought into the pit.

McGlory turned to the slender stranger in the black coat. "You've a claim on him that I intend to honor."

"He's dead now. That's all that's required."

"Is that enough?" McGlory nudged the knife with one immaculately shod foot. "Do what you want."

Dominic Pastore shook his head. "Nolan owed Nora his life and he's paid the debt. He very nearly had the whole of his throat ripped out while he was still conscious. It's over."

"Then we'll leave him for the police to deal with." McGlory held the carriage lamp above his head and nodded to his bodyguards. "Take a last look around. Make sure there's nothing that could link him to Miss MacKenzie. Or to ourselves. One of you tell the first beat copper you run into that you saw a dog come running out of the Carousel with blood dripping from its mouth. Tell him you think someone's been attacked. Give him this."

Billy held out one of the five dollar gold Eagle coins he was never without. No awkward questions would be asked.

"It's him, all right," Detective Phelan said. "It's Joseph Nolan."

"His throat's been gnawed and the blood vessels punctured." Ned had seen worse during his days as a New York Metropolitan Police detective, but not by much.

"He didn't die easily." Geoffrey Hunter picked up the butcher knife that lay within a finger's reach of one of Nolan's hands. "It

485

doesn't look as though he had time to defend himself. The knife's clean."

"A dog? Or a pack of dogs?" Hayes asked.

"One dog was seen running out of the Carousel area with a bloody muzzle. That's all we know. The policeman didn't get the name of the man who gave him the information."

"Paid off?"

Phelan shrugged. "Probably."

"At least we can be certain Prudence and Josiah didn't see this," Geoffrey said. "Danny must have spotted their cab following him and shaken them off."

Ned Hayes held up the nun's habit with its now filthy white linen wimple and white novice's veil. "This is what he had Sally Lynn wear." He bent to retrieve the knotted cord, the rosary, and the priest's Roman collar and cassock. "There can't be any doubt."

"Do we let the reporters in?" The copper who asked the question stared at the bloody corpse then shook his head. If he'd been the first to discover the body, he'd have found a way to make it pay.

"Might as well," Phelan answered.

Chief of Detectives Tom Byrnes would want as much good publicity out of this as they could get. A third woman was dead, but so was the man who'd killed her. And the others. There was a tidiness about what had happened to Joseph Nolan that would appeal to the readers of New York's daily newspapers.

A killer who cut his victims open needed to die at least as badly. The reporters would emphasize the coroner's conclusion that Nolan had sliced his victims *after* they were dead while he himself had had his throat ripped open while he was still alive. The symmetry was good. Someone would point out that it hadn't been the police who'd caught him, but one of the animals wandering the city streets, living off whatever it could scrounge or kill. By that time the reading public would be so relieved they wouldn't care. Once Fahey and McGuire were released and their innocence confirmed, the story would be as dead and buried as Joseph Nolan.

"I'll go back to Madame Jolene's place," Geoffrey said. "Tie up the loose ends."

As far as the Metropolitan Police was concerned, there weren't any loose ends. Tammany would use its influence to bury whatever needed to be concealed. Phelan wanted to wrap up this case as quickly as he could. If there were still some unanswered questions he could live with that. As long as there weren't any more slit-throat murders. One of the reporters had coined that phrase after Ellen Tierney's death, *slit-throat murder,* and it had caught the popular imagination.

"Go ahead. There won't be any of my men there and I've released the crime scene. Big Brenda will be pushing the maids to get all of the rooms ready so the house can open on time tonight."

"Sally Lynn's?"

"I didn't see any point keeping it locked up. The coroner examined the body on site and we bagged up anything that could be used as evidence. There's nothing more to find."

"I'll tell Madame Jolene that one of her best clients won't be coming back. It'll settle down the rest of the girls to know he's dead. No more threat. No danger."

"There's danger every time they take a john inside a room and close the door behind them. The whores know it, I know it, and you know it." Phelan didn't like having to deal with what was routinely done to ladies of the night. Chokings, beatings, disfiguring knife wounds. Prostitutes were among the most vulnerable of the city's inhabitants; their lives were usually short and brutal. Nobody defended them, not even the pimps and madams who lived off their earnings.

"I'll come with you, Geoff," Ned Hayes offered. He handed over the bloodied bundle of clothing whose symbolism had so obsessed the dead man. The heavy wooden rosary snagged on the buttons of his coat.

"Keep it as a souvenir," Phelan laughed. "We've got enough to prove Nolan did it. Killed Sally Lynn and two other women as well. I don't think Captain Byrnes will want to hold that rosary up at a press conference and have to explain how it was used. I doubt you'll read anything at all in the papers about the kind of dress up games Nolan liked to play. Archbishop Corrigan would be all over Byrnes in a minute. The Church runs a lot of this city from behind the scenes. Don't let anyone tell you different."

"What loose ends were you talking about?" Ned asked quietly as he and Hunter walked up the ramp into cold, bright sunlight. He tried shoving the rosary into one of his coat pockets, but it wouldn't fit.

"I don't know. I may have to figure them out on the way."

Ned stopped to coil the rosary and wrap his scarf around it. "Does it strike you that the solution to this case suddenly became too convenient, too neat?"

"Much too neat. Coincidental, too. I don't trust coincidences and I don't like easy answers."

CHAPTER 29

It would be said later that his son's death forever changed Francis Patrick Nolan, but that wasn't true. The boy had always been a disappointment to his father, so it wasn't Joseph's loss that ate away at him. It was knowledge of the secret life his son had led.

The story appeared in all of New York City's daily papers. Newsboys shouted the grislier bits on every street corner. "Avenger dog rips Slit-Throat Killer."

Joseph Nolan's body lay in the Bellevue morgue viewing room for crowds to come and gawk at until his enraged parents paid Warneke and Sons Mortuary Services an exorbitant sum to haul it away at night when there would be no witnesses to document where the corpse had been taken. Hastily but well embalmed, Joseph was buried in the churchyard of an obscure parish miles outside the city. No stone marked the grave, then or ever.

Christmas was approaching. New Yorkers forgot about the Slit-Throat Killer as soon as they crumpled up their newspapers and used them to light their kitchen fires. All but the father. Detective Phelan had told him the truth about Joseph's odd predilections at Madame Jolene's, while at the same time assuring him that the police department had decided to sit on the details. The humiliation of siring a son who pranced around in a priest's cassock and paid a whore to dress up like a nun burned at Francis Nolan until the only thing left was a hard nugget of stubbornly unquenchable anger.

He stopped talking to his wife and daughter. Meals were taken in a silence broken only by the clatter of silverware against a plate. Lillian retreated into the laudanum haze she'd flirted with for years. Alice made quiet preparations to enter the Visitation convent in Brooklyn. She'd mentioned it once, and once only, the day of Joseph's burial, before her da erected his wall of silence.

"Go," he'd said bitterly. "Go wherever the hell you want. I'll not stand in your way."

When she asked for the money she needed for the dowry the Visitation order required, he'd scribbled a note to his banker and handed it to her. Alice took out the funds that same day, afraid he'd change his mind. But he didn't. He was through with ungrateful children and finished with a wife who'd birthed two such useless pieces of human wreckage. Lillian had been fertile, but too weak to carry to term all of the children he'd gotten on her.

The only things left in Francis Nolan's life that gave him satisfaction were the slaughterhouses that reeked of beef on the hoof and the fleet of horse drawn wagons carrying his cuts of meat to all of the city's best restaurants. He wasn't as rich yet as the men who gambled fortunes on Wall Street, but he would be. Someday.

Everybody ate meat.

"I'm so sorry you're not well, Prudence," Alice said. "I wouldn't have disturbed you had I known, but you were so kind to me when Ellen was murdered and the police were asking those awful questions that I wanted to tell you myself before it became common knowledge."

"What is that, Alice?" Prudence's badly bruised ribs were tightly taped and Doctor Worthington had wound thick gauze bandages around both her wrists. The medicine he would have prescribed for any other patient was poison to her, so she was reduced to the time honored remedy of hot tea with lemon, honey, and a teaspoon of brandy. No amount of cajoling or scolding had persuaded Prudence to tell him how she had sustained the massive bruising that made movement painful.

She'd had to confide in Geoffrey, of course, and Josiah had provided details aplenty. He was less contused than she, but sporting the first black eye he'd ever suffered. He'd bought himself a dramatic pirate's patch to conceal the discoloration.

"I'm mending very quickly," Prudence assured Alice. She shifted her weight on the sofa, a grimace she tried to conceal giving the lie to her claim of swift healing.

"You must have taken a terrible fall," Alice commiserated.

"I did. But there's no permanent damage, so let's not talk about me any more. What is the wonderful news you've come to tell me?"

"Only that my father has finally given in to my request. I'm to enter the Visitation Convent after Christmas, Prudence. Mother Superior said I would be most welcome to test my vocation among the sisters. Isn't that marvelous?"

It was probably the last thing Prudence

would describe in that way, but she wasn't Catholic and had only the vaguest notion of what nuns did with their lives after they shut themselves up behind stone walls. The bright smile on Alice's sweet face and the tears of happiness in her eyes spoke volumes.

"We shall all miss you," Prudence said, "but I wish you great joy. I hope you find what you're looking for."

"Oh, I will. I know I will. When I'm allowed visitors I'd like it if you came to see me." Alice's eyes fell to her lap. "No doubt you've heard about Joseph," she murmured.

"Perhaps it's best not to speak of him," Prudence suggested. "It can only bring you sorrow."

"I pray for him." Alice almost confided that she had thought of a way to get extra penances that she could apply to what was bound to be Joseph's long term in purgatory, but she knew Prudence wouldn't understand. Would probably think her as addled in the head as her poor brother. Alice was convinced that Joseph had whispered an Act of Contrition in his last moments, saving him from the eternal fires of Hell. She was planning to put her plan into action in a few days . . . the next time she went to confession.

"I know you're terribly tired, Prudence," she said, getting up to leave. "I'll come back soon, I promise. Is there anything I can bring you? A book perhaps?"

"That's very kind, Alice, but I have everything I need."

"Well, then. I'll be on my way." Alice very carefully and gently deposited a kiss on Prudence's cheek before she left.

When the parlor door closed behind her visitor, Prudence struggled to her feet and walked gingerly back and forth from the fireplace to the windows overlooking Fifth Avenue, counting her steps as she went. Yesterday she had managed a hundred, today her goal was an additional fifty.

She'd taken Geoffrey's fury as best she could, too exhausted then to fight back. It was probably just as well she didn't; Prudence had never seen him so angry. By the time she had put together a good argument in her defense — after all, if it hadn't been for her following him, they might never have caught Joseph Nolan — she decided against using it. She'd seen the pallor of her partner's skin and recognized the effect of fear. Her father had looked like that when her mother's consumption began to threaten her life. Geoffrey was at war with a circumstance that might have taken her life, might have taken her from him. She knew it as certainly as she knew it would be a very long time before either of them brought up the subject again.

Josiah had just stood there, swathed like Prudence in Dr. Worthington's dressings, his eye purpling and swelling. He'd caught the rough side of Geoffrey's tongue also, for allowing Miss Prudence to do something so foolhardy. It would never, never happen again, Geoffrey promised them. And Josiah hadn't argued with him either.

He, too, understood the fear that drove the rage.

Josiah had thought they were a good match for each other the first time he'd watched them together. He still thought so. And he wondered how long it would take them to discover it.

Not until the Saturday following Sally Lynn's murder did Madame Jolene allow Geoffrey Hunter and Ned Hayes more than the most cursory of visits to the brothel.

"Unless you're here as clients, you can take yourselves off," she'd told them when they brought the news of Joseph Nolan's death. "I've got a business to run."

"Don't you want to know how he died, Jolene?" asked Ned Hayes.

"I hope it was at least half as bad as he deserved."

"He had his throat ripped out by a dog."

"What kind of dog?"

"Nobody knows."

"Come back in a week or so, when things have settled down," Jolene had said, easing the door closed as George the bouncer moved into position beside her. "We're expecting an overflow crowd tonight. I've already got more advance requests for Sally Lynn's room than the girls can accommodate. I guess murder is better for men than the ginkgo they sell down in Chinatown."

"They're all exhausted and sleeping late." Big Brenda poured fresh coffee and took a pan of hot cross buns from the oven. "I know how you like your sweets, Detective," she said, setting out plates and forks. She sat down at the kitchen table, a woman as large as her name suggested. "I don't know when I've seen the parlors so full. Upstairs, too. Madame Jolene got real strict about appointment times. Usually, if we're not busy, the girls hang around the parlor playing cards and chatting up the regulars in between clients, but not the last few days. If I heard Madame say once that she was running a business here, I heard her say it a hundred times."

"We're really interested in just one client." Geoffrey Hunter took his coffee black, but he bit into one of the hot cross buns with all of the gusto Big Brenda could want. "Delicious," he said, wiping the sugary frosting from his lips and fingertips.

"We need to know everything you can tell us about Joseph Nolan." Ned Hayes reached for his second bun.

"He's dead, Detective."

"I know he's dead, Miss Brenda. I saw his body."

"Then what's the point?"

"Loose ends. We're clearing up the loose ends."

"I'd have thought you'd let the police do that."

"They're busy. This close to Christmas people start drinking to celebrate, and before you know it they're trying to kill each other. Nothing has changed in that respect since I was on the force."

"What do you want to know?"

Geoffrey Hunter took out his notebook. He didn't really need it, but seeing their words written down made witnesses remember more than they thought they could. The written word was always more serious than the spoken word. "I'm going to give you two dates, Miss Brenda. You tell me whatever you can about what you saw or heard happening here in this house on those days."

"That's all?"

"Saturday night and into Sunday morning, November tenth and eleventh." He wrote on a fresh page in the notebook, ripped it out and handed it to her. "Now here's another one. Saturday night and into Sunday morning again, but this time it's two weeks later, November twenty-fourth and twenty-fifth. That was just before Thanksgiving." A second page followed the first. "Take your time, and if you need to jot something down to jog your memory, go right ahead." He gave Big Brenda the pencil he'd been writing with and took another out of his jacket pocket.

"I don't want to get anybody in trouble." Brenda twirled the sharpened end of the pencil in her mouth, getting it good and wet for the laborious task of writing.

"We mainly want to know if there's anything you can tell us about Joseph Nolan on those dates," Ned Hayes put in.

"I remember November tenth and eleventh because of reading about the Ripper's latest killing in the paper. The girls were all nervous and Sally Lynn started fretting and worrying about Mr. Nolan coming to see her that night, Saturday night . . . because of what he always had her do. Dressing up like a nun and using the whip on him. I guess we can talk about it now he's dead."

"Go on," Ned encouraged her.

"Madame Jolene calmed her down the way she always does, but it was harder than usual that day because she'd promised to talk to Mr. Nolan, but she hadn't done it yet. Sally Lynn wanted to go to Saint Anselm's that afternoon, but it was cold and she was complaining about being sore. Madame Jolene convinced her to stay home and drink a hot toddy."

"You're sure it was Saint Anselm's?"

"No, I'm not sure, Detective. It could have been Saint Patrick's because she liked to go there, too, but I'm thinking it was Saint Anselm's that day."

"Then what happened?"

"Mr. Nolan came at around nine o'clock, like he always did. You could have set your pocket watch by that man. What was different about that night, and why I remember it, was he paid to buy Sally Lynn's time for the whole night. That's expensive. He'd only done it a couple of times before. Sally Lynn didn't much like the idea, but there wasn't anything she could do about it. Clients make that kind of arrangement with Madame, and she doesn't allow for any arguing."

"Go on." Hunter's voice betrayed suppressed excitement. Ned Hayes hadn't taken another bite out of his hot cross bun since Big Brenda mentioned Saint Anselm's.

"He spent the night, just like he paid for, and there wasn't any trouble. Sally Lynn came down to the kitchen to take him up a tray the next morning. Coffee, eggs, and toast. I put a dish of marmalade I make from Seville oranges on the tray."

"What time did he leave?"

"Earlier than most gentlemen who buy a girl for the night. About eight o'clock. Sally Lynn said he had to be at Saint Patrick's before the rest of his family got there. She was angry about something, and it wasn't like her to get riled up over nothing. I think she was trying to get up the courage to talk to Madame Jolene about him again, but I don't believe she ever did. I'd have heard."

"Are you sure he was here all night on November tenth?"

"He paid for it."

"Are you positive?"

"Mr. Hunter, if you don't believe me, you just go ask Madame if you can take a look at her ledger. She writes down every client's name and who he sees and what he pays for. When he comes and how long he stays. I've seen her mumbling and muttering over her accounts, as she calls them, and I know she never leaves anything or anybody out. You just ask her for the ledger. I doubt she'll let you see it, but there's no harm trying."

Madame Jolene wouldn't hand over her ledger, but she did open it to the page that listed the house's clients and receipts for November 10, 1888, running her finger down the entries until she found what she was looking for.

"May we see that entry?" Ned Hayes requested.

Jolene shrugged her shoulders, but complied. "There," she said, pointing to a notation midway down the page. "Joseph Nolan arrives at nine in the evening, pays for a night with Sally Lynn, and leaves the next morning, November eleventh."

"Were there any other overnight clients that Saturday?" Before she could refuse to answer his question, Ned reached out and covered one of her hands with his own. "I know you don't give out clients' names, Jolene, but this is a murder I'm not sure we've solved yet. I wouldn't ask if I didn't have to. And it may be that whatever you tell me doesn't have to go any further." He kept his hand on hers as she struggled to make up her mind. "You can trust me," he promised.

"Only the banker's boy, John Landers." The finger skipped to another name. "Here he is. Spanish Lola. All night. Not the first time, either." She tapped her polished fingernail on the page. "Here he is again last week, the night of December first into the next morning. He's the one who fell against Sally Lynn's door and burst it open. We wouldn't have found her until the afternoon if he hadn't tripped over the damn dog. We got him out of here before the police came. He hasn't been back."

"Can you show us November twenty-fourth? That's another Saturday." Hunter's face settled into the mask all the best Pinkerton operatives learned to wear when a case began to jell. *Wait,* Allan had always counseled. *Wait until you're sure.*

This time Madame Jolene relinquished the precious ledger, handing it to Ned Hayes before she leaned back against the small rolltop desk whose key she always wore in a hidden pocket sewn into her corset. "He didn't do them all, did he?" she asked, though it wasn't really a question. "Nolan was here the night the first girl was killed, so it had to have been someone else. He was with Sally Lynn two weeks later, too, though not for the whole night. That was a quick one. He was gone by eleven."

"Don't show this to anyone else," Ned Hayes said. "Not yet."

Madame Jolene took the ledger from him, reached behind her for the pot of black ink that stood beside a gold pen holder. Before they could stop her, she'd spilled enough ink on the November tenth page to blot out most of the entries. The proof that Joseph Nolan was almost certainly innocent of Nora Kenny's murder was gone forever.

"I divided her clothes up among the rest of the girls. There's nothing unusual about that. We do it whenever someone leaves or there's a problem with paying what's owed." Madame Jolene was getting impatient. She had a sense of what Ned Hayes and Geoffrey Hunter were trying to prove, but they'd already taken up too much of her time and she didn't see how looking through Sally Lynn's wardrobe would help. Unfortunately, she knew Ned well enough from the old days to be sure he wouldn't give up until she caved in and gave him what he wanted.

"How many girls got her clothes?" Ned asked.

"Four of them are the same size. Sweet Linda, Dotty, Marguerite, and Zelda. The rest took turns picking from Sally Lynn's perfumes and jewelry and handkerchiefs, things like that. Nobody was greedy, Detective. Everyone liked Sally Lynn. It was more wanting a keepsake than anything else."

"We'll talk to the girls who got the clothing," Geoffrey said. "Then we'll work our way through the rest of them."

"What exactly are you looking for?"

"I don't think we know, Jolene," Ned confessed. "But we'll recognize it when we see it. If we do."

"You can go sit at Big Brenda's kitchen table. I'll send them in to you one by one."

"Tell them each to bring everything they have that belonged to Sally Lynn. No matter what it is. They're not to leave anything out."

Ned Hayes's hearing wasn't acute enough to register what Madame Jolene whispered under her breath. It was just as well.

Dotty was a well-built blonde with a broad, sincere-looking smile and a vacuous look in her beautiful blue eyes. She took a few moments to arrange a pile of nightgowns and stockings on the scrubbed wood of the table. "No one else wanted these," she explained. "They're a little worn, but I

506

like that. The silk feels soft on my skin." She ran a plump white hand over the top-most gown, sighing with pleasure as the silk rippled beneath her fingers. "We only ever had cotton where I grew up. Real cheap cotton with stickers in it that scratched something fierce."

"Where are you from, Dotty?" Geoffrey asked softly. He thought her accent told the whole story, but he wanted to be sure.

"Alabama."

"Sharecroppers?"

Dotty shrugged her shoulders. "That's why I left."

"Did Sally Lynn ever tell you whether she bought all these gowns herself or if someone gave them to her?" Ned asked. He'd recognized the accent, too, but he'd heard too many stories like Dotty's.

"She never said anything to me about them. Sally Lynn could be closemouthed when she wanted to."

"Is there anything you can remember that she might have said about any of her clients?" Geoffrey looked at each gown's label, shook it out, held it up, refolded it.

"Madame Jolene has a rule about that. We don't talk about them unless we want to find ourselves out in the street. Nobody is stupid enough to fancy that."

It was the same with Sweet Linda and Zelda, piles of clothing that told them nothing. Sally Lynn was friendly with everyone who worked in the house, but she confided in no one.

"You'd be surprised," Sweet Linda said, "how many whores don't ever tell the truth about themselves. When you get a curious client, and especially if he's a big tipper, you just make up whatever you think he wants to hear. It's a lot easier that way, and it gives you something to think about while he's getting on with it."

"I'm beginning to think this is a waste of time, Geoff," Ned said. They were alone for a few minutes, waiting for the last of the four girls who had been given Sally Lynn's clothing. Big Brenda had left the coffee pot on the stove for them and he poured himself another cup. It didn't taste anything like the Louisiana coffee Tyrus brewed, but at least it was keeping him awake.

"I only picked out a couple of things," Marguerite declared as soon as she came into the kitchen. She deposited a black and white bundle on the table. "Well, three actually, though they all go together." She unfolded a black, high necked, long sleeved dress, a white apron edged with lace, and a small, frilly cap that was obviously meant to be pinned atop a bun of piled up curls. "It's new. She bought it for a client, but I don't think she ever wore it."

"Do you know the name of the client?" Geoffrey asked. Something about the maid's costume was making the hairs on the back of his neck tingle.

"We never talk about clients," Marguerite said. "Madame Jolene has a rule about that, and she's real strict about enforcing it."

"What makes you think this maid's outfit is new?" Ned was running his fingers into the skirt pockets, but finding nothing.

"Sally Lynn did tell me she'd gotten it the day before Thanksgiving. She was afraid she'd ripped or dirtied the apron because she said someone pushed her down some steps and the paper it was wrapped in broke open. I was going to help her with the sewing, if she needed it, but when we looked, everything was all right. There weren't any tears."

"Do you remember if she said where she was when she got pushed?"

"She went there all the time."

"Where is that?"

"Saint Anselm's."

"And did she tell you where she bought the uniform?"

"I didn't ask her, but there's only one

shop around here that sells domestic service uniforms and does the alterations right on the premises. She had to have it let out around the waist."

"Do you know the name of the shop?"

Marguerite stood up and gathered together the three pieces of the maid's uniform they'd been examining. "I can't tell you any more than I already have." Her face flushed red and her fingers were trembling.

"She knows the name and location of the shop, but she won't tell us." Ned stared at Marguerite's retreating back. When she'd reached for the uniform, he'd put his hand on top of it, and she'd backed away, leaving it behind as she spun on her heel and walked quickly out.

"She may have availed herself of the special services performed in the back room," contributed Big Brenda, bringing a basket of root vegetables into the kitchen from the winter larder. "I heard enough to know that you frightened her. She won't answer any more questions."

"What is it, Miss Brenda?" Geoffrey asked.

"Girls in this profession always need the help of a certain kind of woman, no matter how careful they are. I can't think of a one who hasn't got caught sooner or later."

"Are you saying the uniform shop is a

front for an abortionist?"

"No, it's a genuine business right enough," Big Brenda said. "A mother and son run it, but I heard rumors that the mother passed on not too long ago. She was the one who took care of the girls who came to her. She had a daughter who did the same, but I don't know where the daughter lives. Or even what her married name is. It's a dangerous profession for everyone involved. If there's ever even a hint the coppers might be getting ready to pay a visit, they shut down or move."

Ned handed Big Brenda his notebook and a pencil.

"Madame Jolene isn't going to like this," she muttered, but she wrote a name and an address. "Take the uniform with you. See those two letters stitched into the seam of the skirt? That's their mark."

Big Brenda wasn't foolish enough to mislead Ned Hayes with phony information, but she thought it was a shame to set him and Mr. Hunter on the trail of someone who really only ever helped girls who got caught and had no other alternative.

Helped or killed them. The poor creatures were willing to take the risk, so where was the crime in that?

CHAPTER 30

Alice Nolan's confession did not go as she had planned. Five decades of the rosary and the Stations of the Cross. That was it. She was too embarrassed to argue and too upset to be coherent. She'd done the best she could to make the priest believe she was contemplating the heinous crime of ending the life growing in her womb, but he hadn't taken her seriously. He'd cut her off in mid-sentence, scolded her severely, and made her begin again. She hadn't confessed properly, he told her. She hadn't waited for the prayers that began the ritual, and then what she'd told him was a pack of lies. That invalidated the sacrament.

When she'd calmed down, they started over, and this time she made no mention of the fruits of fornication. The penance was for the great lie she had made up and her abuse of the sacrament; it wasn't a fitting way to behave in church.

"Think of Our Saviour's suffering as you make the Stations," the priest said. "Place yourself beside His Blessed Mother at the foot of the cross. Make a firm resolution to sin no more." He raised his hand in the ritual blessing. "Now make a good Act of Contrition."

Just before the priest slid back the wood panel separating him from the penitent, he leaned closer to the screen that wasn't fine meshed enough to conceal a sinner's identity.

"Are you all right, Alice?" Father Brennan asked solicitously.

Too startled to hear herself called by name to be able to answer, Alice merely nodded.

"Don't forget to make your Stations."

Jerry Brophy gathered up the half dozen altar boy cassocks and surplices that needed mending or alterations. Every two weeks he put together a bundle for his brother-in-law to pick up when he delivered the previous order. The nuns who taught in the parish school saw to the priestly vestments. Made of pure silk and embroidered by skilled, dedicated fingers, they were not to be trusted to a lay person. But Neil always did a good job, and Bridget had insisted that her brother get the work instead of someone else. She'd always said that family could be counted on when nobody else could be trusted.

Father Brennan had stayed late today, but he was always slower than any other priest in the confessional. Jerry poked his head out of the sacristy. There came Brennan, skirts swishing along the red carpet that ran up the altar steps and pooling around him as he genuflected before the Host. Jerry approved of this Anglo-Irish priest. He was severe and short tempered enough to be worthy of his vocation and just on the ragged edge of going over into the kind of ecstatic and painful religious fervor you read about in *The Lives of the Saints*.

Jerry caught a glimpse of Alice Nolan huddled in one of the pews. Now what on earth did that timid little nothing of a girl have to confess?

"All ready then?" Father Brennan asked him, pointing to the neatly wrapped bundle on one of the chairs.

"Neil will be here in a few minutes, Father. He's a very precise kind of person, never late."

Father Brennan stepped back out onto the altar, just far enough to be able to look into the nave. He shook his head despairingly, then came back into the sacristy.

"Is it poor Alice Nolan, Father? She doted on her brother. What a terrible thing to have happen."

"Father Mahoney has signed her papers to the Visitation and written a letter attesting to the sincerity of her intention, but I've got my doubts."

"She acts more like a nun than some of the nuns over at the school."

"She'll have to stop pretending she's someone she's not if she's going to make it at the Visitation."

"What do you mean, Father?"

"Now she's saying she's pregnant when you and I both know it's impossible," Father Brennan burst out. He was furious at Alice for trying to put one over on him and it wasn't like he was revealing a sin told him under the sacred seal of the confessional. The girl had blurted it out before he'd made the sign of the cross to start the formal confession and then she'd continued babbling something about abortion until he finally told her to stop, catch her breath, and start again. "That wasn't a confession, Alice," he'd said. "It was a silly story you made up and I won't dignify it by pretending to believe a word you said."

The girl had told a lie, not a real sin, though he couldn't for the life of him figure out why. He wondered if she'd snapped, the way women did sometimes when they couldn't bear to face reality. He laid it all at Joseph Nolan's door, and though he quickly said a prayer for the repose of that wicked soul, he couldn't help but hope he was roasting away on the hottest griddle in Hell.

"It's a joke she's playing on you, Father."

"If she tries something like that at the Visitation, they'll send her home in a strait-jacket, and then where will she be?" Father Brennan stormed off to the rectory, furious at himself for mentioning Alice Nolan at all to Jerry Brophy. He'd skated close to violating the sacred seal, but he was certain he hadn't actually done it. He examined the circumstances again as he remembered them, decided he was blameless, and determined to put the whole incident out of his mind.

He had to watch his step in the underground passage that led to the rectory from the basement of the church where the crypt was. He was the only one of the three priests who used it regularly. Since he'd been brought up in Ireland, the damp and the darkness didn't bother him. It was preferable to having to raise a hand in blessing to the red-haired man and his monster of a dog who seemed to have taken up permanent residence in the alleyway across the street.

"What did you tell them, Davey?"

"Just that the uniform they brought in was definitely from this shop, but they figured that out themselves from the initials on it. I don't know why they bothered asking. They even knew who bought it."

"Who was that?"

"The girl up at Madame Jolene's who got herself killed last Saturday night. Sally Lynn Fannon."

"What else did they want to know?"

"They asked about your mother, may she rest in peace."

Neil Slattery waited patiently. He knew there was more, and he suspected Davey had been warned not to reveal too much to his employer. The boy wasn't bright, but he did well enough for an hour or two when Slattery had to make a delivery or pickup. He laid the twenty-five cent piece he'd promised Davey on the counter, then placed another one beside it. "Can you remember anything else, Davey?"

"They wanted to know if two other girls had bought uniforms here."

"What were their names?"

"I had the man print them out so I could

look them up in the book," Davey said confidently. He wasn't very good at reading but with a little bit of time and effort he could match words that looked alike. "Here it is." He drew a scrap of brown wrapping paper out of his pocket. "Alterations. They came back for alterations. That's what I told them. But I didn't let them see the book themselves. You told me that was private."

Nora Kenny. Ellen Tierney.

Slattery held the piece of brown paper out over the chimney of the gas lamp sitting on the counter. When it caught fire he let it burn until there was nothing left but ash. "What did they look like? Can you describe them?"

"One was very big and dark, the other had light hair and blue eyes," Davey said proudly. Remembering and describing was a game he often played with his mother. "They didn't talk like we do. At first I had a hard time understanding, but after a while I got used to it."

"Did they say they were coming back?"

"I forgot what you told me, Mr. Slattery, so I said you wouldn't be here any more today."

"Did you tell them where I'd gone?"

"Saint Anselm's. That was right, wasn't it, Mr. Slattery? I told them you always went to Saturday afternoon confession at Saint Anselm's."

"Take your money now, Davey, and go on home to your mother. She'll be expecting you. And forget about the men who were asking questions. They had no business bothering you like that."

"Do you want me back tomorrow, Mr. Slattery?"

"Tomorrow's Sunday. The store is closed. I'll send a note around when I need you again."

Neil Slattery turned the sign in the door to CLOSED. He folded Davey's black apron and put it in a drawer beneath the counter, turned off the gas lamp, and looked around to be sure everything was as it should be. Dozens of domestic uniforms hung from racks on two of the shop walls, flat, ghostly shapes waiting to have life breathed into them. The sewing machine where his mother, and now he did alterations sat in a small alcove along the back wall behind the counter. He could work and watch the shop's street door at the same time. Boxes containing stiffened maids' caps, aprons, black stockings, and removable cuffs filled floor to ceiling shelves to the left of the door that led into the back storage rooms and the staircase to the apartment above the shop.

One of those back rooms had been his mother's private preserve when he was young. Then his sister had been trained there to assist. When she left them to get married, Neil had taken her place, though sometimes clients objected. His mother never argued, but when she handed back the coins they'd put in her hand, they changed their minds and let him do what had to be done. He was good at it, faster than his mother and nearly as skilled.

One day he picked up a carving knife and discovered that the heft of the sharp, heavy blade felt more natural in his hand than anything he'd held before.

Everything changed.

Alice was the last parishioner in the church when she started her Stations, but she liked being alone to pray. No one was around to peer curiously at her blotchy, tear-stained face; she wasn't one of those girls who wept prettily.

It might be full dark by the time she knelt before the last Station, but no one at home would notice she wasn't there. Joseph was dead, her mother had climbed into a laudanum bottle, and her da had as good as disowned her. She thought the housekeeper, Mrs. Flynn, might remember to send up a tea tray, but they were all still so shaken downstairs by Ellen's murder and Joseph's horrible death that she might not. Jack Scully would stay with his horses once he'd put them up after driving Da home, and Tynan the butler looked aged beyond his years. She was so often invisible in her own house that Alice knew she wouldn't be missed.

The First Station. *Jesus is condemned to death.* She stood in the aisle looking at the painted wooden plaque hanging on the wall. The artist had pictured Christ standing with head to one side, the Crown of Thorns on his brow, hands tied before him, a Roman soldier leading him from the crowd presumably gathered for the pronouncement of sentence. Alice had picked up a prayer book from the vestibule, and now she knelt in one of the pews to read the meditation and recite the prayers for this first step in what was called the *Via Crucis* in Latin. Alice wondered if many of the prayers she would say in the Visitation convent would be in Latin. *Concentrate, concentrate. Don't let yourself get distracted.*

Jesus carries the cross. Jesus falls the first time. Jesus meets his sorrowful Mother. Each station had its painting, the wooden plaque surmounted by a cross. Explanation of the scene, meditation, prayers. The repetition created a rhythm that was hypnotic in the silence. A faint trace of incense tickled her nose, her eyes strained to see in the dimness. The church was chilly, but she'd worn a warm winter coat and put on thick gloves before leaving the house.

Alice was so tired. She'd kept another vigil last night, worrying over what she would say in the confessional, then disgraced herself by weeping. More than anything she wanted to lie down and fall asleep. After the Stations, she had to say a rosary. She decided to say the Joyful Mysteries in honor of the Virgin.

Just a few minutes. She'd pray better if she could close her eyes for just a few minutes. She'd kneel at every station, say all the prayers slowly and fervently, not skip a single word of the meditations. Not let her attention wander during the rosary. Her head full of promises, Alice sat back in the pew where she had been kneeling, brought her feet up, curled them under the broad skirt of her coat, lay down until her head rested on her arms, and fell asleep.

Alice thought she was alone in the church. But she wasn't.

"If we've reasoned this out correctly, he'll choose another girl today," Geoffrey Hunter said.

"And if we're not in the right place, she'll be dead by morning," Ned Hayes commented.

"We're not wrong, Ned. We've thought this through too carefully."

They were hidden as far back in the alleyway opposite Saint Anselm's as they could get and still be able to see the front of the church and the sidewalk on either side of the main steps. Closer to the mouth of the alley Kevin Carney and Blossom melted into the brick wall, sheltered by an odd structure of cardboard boxes and newspapers that looked like a pile of windswept debris. Their job was to hear and scent out the killer's approach before he came into view. They'd been there since early afternoon.

The expected stream of parishioners climbing the stairs to go to Saturday afternoon confession did not materialize. Too close to Christmas, they decided. Too many things to do, shops to visit, homes to clean and decorate.

Being Protestant, they didn't realize that December eighth was the Feast of the Immaculate Conception, a holy day of obligation in the Catholic Church when the faithful were required to hear Mass and encouraged to receive communion. The parish calendar had changed to accommodate the feast; long lines had waited outside the confessionals yesterday. Today there was only a token hour of confession for anyone still in need. Perhaps two dozen people, mostly women, straggled into Saint Anselm's late that afternoon. One by one they came out again. Nobody stayed inside the church longer than fifteen or twenty minutes.

Each time someone approached or left the church, the watchers froze in place, but nothing happened. People came and went in apparent unconcern and perfect safety.

There was no wind today, but the pavement beneath their feet was as cold as a block of ice, and even the thickest gloves gave little protection to fingers that had to stay still. Noses ran, eyes streamed, cheeks and foreheads reddened. Heavy clouds obscured the pale winter sun; by late afternoon everything had a gray cast to it.

A woman carrying a market basket appeared at the corner, bent over with the weight of what she was carrying. Blossom sat up, tilted her head, lifted her muzzle, and flicked her ears forward.

"What is it, girl?" Kevin whispered. He stared at the figure for a moment, then sat on his haunches, grinning. He glanced back at Mr. Hunter and Mr. Hayes. They, too, were following the woman's progress down the street, but so far they didn't seem to realize who she was.

Prudence had sent Colleen out to a second-hand clothing store with instructions to buy an assortment of well-worn skirts and shirtwaists. "Boots, a shawl, and as face concealing an old hat as you can find," she'd instructed her maid. She was heartily sick of sitting on the sofa concentrating on healing her bruises and struggling through Louisa May Alcott's *Jo's Boys*. Her father had given her the novel two years ago, when it was first published. She hadn't been able to get interested in it then, and she still dozed off every third page or so. Dr. Worthington would have approved.

The woman carrying the heavy market basket reached the steps in front of Saint Anselm's then suddenly darted across the narrow street and into the mouth of the alleyway. She unwound a moth-eaten gray knitted scarf from around her neck and chin, smiling broadly at the success of her deception. "I've brought hot coffee and sandwiches," she said. "I thought by this time you'd be desperate for them."

Geoffrey took the basket from her and placed it on the ground. "You shouldn't be out, Prudence," he said.

"I'm perfectly fine, Geoffrey. It's been a week." She pushed up one sleeve of the overly large shirtwaist she was wearing. "Look, no bandages. I can flex my wrists again." She demonstrated.

Blossom crawled on her belly until her nose rested against the wicker basket. Was that beef and bread she smelled?

They both looked down at the dog happily ensconced near her next meal. Blossom the Peacemaker.

Prudence busied herself pouring cups of heavily sugared milky coffee and unwrapping sandwiches. She'd instructed Cook to include the biggest soup bone in the kitchen for Blossom, who picked it up in her enormous jaws and nibbled delicately at the gobbets of beef clinging to it.

"How much longer do you plan to stay?" Prudence asked. She could feel the cold already, though she'd only been in the alley a few minutes.

"Until something happens," Geoffrey answered grimly. "Every one of the murders has been done on a Saturday night, the body found the next morning. And there was always a link to Saint Anselm's. Nora, Ellen, Sally Lynn. We think each of them came to this church on the day she was stalked and slaughtered. The killer repeats himself by choice, circumstance, or compulsion. Perhaps all three."

"I did what you asked, Ned," Prudence said. "Josiah found copies of the newspapers for the dates when your reporter friend remembered a story that resembled our murders. It made a change from reading Louisa May Alcott."

"What did you learn?"

"Not as much as we'd hoped. But enough so that we might get Detective Phelan interested. If he'll cooperate."

"How many?"

"Seven over the past six months, not including Nora, Ellen, and Sally Lynn. All of the women were very young, either working as maids when they were killed or with a past history of domestic service."

"Which would give them a potential link to the uniform shop." Ned poured a healthy dollop of bourbon into his coffee and offered the flask around. Kevin was the only one who refused.

"They were all knifed, but the mutilation and wrapping the bodies in hessian is a new development. Josiah thinks there had to have been some sort of crisis that caused the change. He has a theory."

Ned poured more bourbon into his cup.

"He thinks that instead of a cocoon, we should think of the wrappings as swaddling."

"Isn't that what's done to newborns to keep their limbs straight?" Geoffrey asked.

Prudence nodded. "I asked Doctor Worthington about it when he came to unwrap my ribs. He said it has a calming effect, especially for babies with colic. The impression I got was that since they couldn't move, they screamed themselves to sleep more quickly."

"What does that have to do with our killer?"

"I don't know. And neither does Josiah. The only other thing we could come up with was a straitjacket, but that only covers the upper part of the body. We've run out of ideas."

"Look." Ned Hayes stepped forward then back into the shadows. "Is that who I think it is?"

"Alice Nolan." Prudence recognized her

immediately. "Stand still. She's so absorbed in herself she may not even look in this direction."

"What's she doing here?" Ned swallowed the last of the bourbon and tossed his empty cup into the wicker basket.

"They're Catholic. Saint Anselm's is their parish church," Hunter reminded him.

"Ellen Tierney worked in the Nolan household. And came to Saint Anselm's for confession the day she was murdered." Prudence waited until Alice disappeared into the church, then hastily rewrapped what remained of the sandwich she had been eating. Blossom surrendered her bone without argument.

"We haven't been able to confirm that. The housekeeper says she did, but the priest on duty claims not to have seen her." Ever the Pinkerton, Geoffrey refused to jump to unproven conclusions.

"I don't like coincidences, Geoff," Ned said.

"Neither do I."

"Shall I go in after her?" Prudence volunteered.

"Not you. And not right away. Give her twenty minutes. That's what we're clocking everyone else at. Fifteen or twenty minutes. If Alice isn't out by then, Kevin goes in."

Geoffrey snapped open the lid of his gold pocket watch, stared at the face as if he'd never seen it before, then closed it again, slipping the heavy timepiece back into a vest pocket.

Kevin and Blossom glanced at the two men and the tall, slender woman standing deep in the shadows, then edged their way closer to the mouth of the alleyway. Blossom raised her head to sniff the currents of air that were human height; Kevin's shoulders rose to his earlobes and he bent forward like a stork over a pond of fish. They didn't have to be told that something might be up; they knew it instinctively.

The minutes ticked by slowly, unhurried by the frequency with which Geoffrey consulted his watch.

A tall priest wearing a biretta and a caped cassock came down the street and mounted the church steps. Red piping ran along the edges of the cape; the buttons were covered in red silk. A scarf protected the lower half of his face from the stinging cold.

"The red means he's a monsignor, one step down from a bishop," Ned explained. "We had to know things like that when I was on the force."

"A monsignor at Saint Anselm's?"

"Where did he come from? It wasn't the

rectory." Prudence had been watching in that direction.

"I don't like coincidences and I don't like anything that's out of the ordinary. Alice Nolan is still in there and nobody has come out for the last fifteen minutes or so. She may be alone." Geoffrey snapped his watch shut and put it back into his vest pocket.

"Except for the monsignor," Prudence reminded him. "Alice has been in there for half an hour, Geoffrey. The monsignor arrived fifteen minutes ago."

Hunter and Hayes looked at each other, then moved quickly down the alleyway, sweeping up Kevin and Blossom as they passed them at a run and made for the steps into the church.

"Alice Nolan isn't somebody's maid, and she's certainly not a lady of easy virtue," panted Ned Hayes.

Blossom was whining, standing on her hind legs with front paws scrabbling on the wooden door. She wouldn't bark unless her human told her she could, but she was plainly agitated.

"The door's locked." Geoffrey tried each of the handles on the three pairs of doors. "All locked," he reported.

Kevin disappeared around the side of the building, reappeared seconds later. "Side doors, too."

On his knees before the main door, Geoffrey inserted a burglar's pick into the lock, making minute adjustments as he worked the cylinders. He was practiced and fast at lock picking, but not quick enough to stop Hayes from tapping his foot impatiently and Blossom from whining in short, frantic bursts.

"Got it!"

They burst through the door and into the vestibule, Blossom barking because Kevin had finally told her she could. Hayes pulled a Remington revolver from a holster worn strapped under one arm. An Army Colt .45 suddenly materialized in Hunter's right hand, and Prudence fished her derringer from the bottom of her reticule. Kevin armed himself with a folding knife from his boot, a present from Billy McGlory that Billy would have been surprised to know he'd given.

The church was empty.

The first thing Alice was aware of when she woke up was a funny smell, bitter and sweet at the same time, sharp and pungent. She tried to wipe it from her nose and her eyes, but only succeeded in rubbing it deeper into her skin.

She'd fallen asleep, curled up like a child, her head pillowed on her arms. Then nothing. Velvety blackness. The sensation of floating. Not even the suggestion of a dream. What was it she was supposed to be doing before fatigue overcame her? Praying, yes, that was it. Making the Stations of the Cross. The little prayer booklet was still in her coat pocket along with her rosary. She could feel the slender bulk of one and the bumpiness of the other against her hip.

She rolled herself over to keep the rosary beads from digging into her skin. Opened her eyes. Tried to sit up. Her head ached, and every muscle in her body felt made of jelly. The harder she pushed against the floor, the less progress she seemed to make. *Pushed against the floor?* Beneath her bare hands she could feel the coldness of stone. She was no longer lying on the insulating warmth of a wood pew; she was in a small stone vault whose ceiling arched above her head into blackness.

She smelled something burning. Panic gave her strength. She crawled toward a pillar, forced her hands and shoulders to drag her upwards until she was resting her back against it.

There. There it was. The source of the burning smell.

A single candle flamed and flickered in a bank of red glass votive lights. When it went out, she'd be in darkness. But awake. Awake and knowing that something terrible was hidden in those shadows, an unnamable horror coming for her with eyes that could see where she could not.

She had to have light. *Mary, Mother of God, help me,* she prayed.

Angel of God, my guardian dear, to whom God's love commits me here, ever this day be at my side, to light and guard, to rule and guide. Amen. It was the first prayer she'd learned as a child, before religion had become so confusing. She'd imagined her guardian angel floating just above and behind her, protective wings outspread, a loving smile on its beautiful face. Or perhaps that was the picture on the first holy card she'd been given. She couldn't remember, but it didn't matter now. She babbled the prayer over and over as she inched her way up the stone pillar, her back and legs strengthening, holding her up, her resolution growing firmer with each successful movement. *To light and guard, to rule and guide.*

Light was what she needed. By the time she reached the slanted iron stand with its banks of votive candles she was walking normally. The stabbing pain in her head had eased, and the sickening smell on the skin around her nose and mouth had evaporated. Alice lit five more candles with one of the long tapers from the holder next to the coin box attached to the front of the stand. She needed to conserve those candles until she could find more. She remembered that the sacristan often stored boxes of votive candles under the stands that displayed them. Yes, there they were, pushed back nearly out of sight. Dozens and dozens of them. She chirped a birdlike laugh and heard it echo off the stone walls.

I'm in the crypt, she decided, and immediately felt comforted. The rich dead of the parish lay all around her in marble tombs surmounted by carved figures of cherubs and small animals. The crypt had been one of her favorite hideaways when her mother brought her to Saint Anselm's as a child. Lillian had been a member of the Altar Society, arranging flowers and laying out linens for Mass. She had been a gentle mother then, fond and indulgent. She'd smiled when Alice skipped away from her side and down the stairs into the crypt. There was only one way in and out of the underground vault.

Lillian knew her child would be perfectly

safe down there.

"She has to be here somewhere. We saw her go in." Ned Hayes stood in the middle of Saint Anselm's central aisle, his Remington revolver cocked and ready.

"The monsignor, too. He never came out, either." Hunter climbed the altar steps, tried the locked door of the sacristy.

Kevin and Blossom walked slowly down one of the side aisles, stopping at each pew. "She'll smell like a nun," Kevin told Blossom. "No perfume. Maybe talcum powder. Plain soap and water." Pew after pew and scent after scent they searched, dismissing woman after woman. Blossom wondered why human females splashed cologne on themselves; it didn't smell like anything good to eat and it made her want to sneeze.

It was Prudence who found the glove, crumpled on the floor under a pew opposite the Fourth Station of the Cross, *Jesus Meets His Sorrowful Mother.* She waved it triumphantly overhead, and when Blossom bounded across the church, held it to her nose.

"How can we be sure it's hers?" Ned put the safety on his gun and holstered it.

"Her initials are stitched inside the cuff. A.N. Alice Nolan." Prudence turned the bottom of the glove inside out.

"Kevin, can you tell Blossom to find Miss Nolan's trail?"

"She knows. Best if we get out of her scent field."

The men stood motionless, aware of the smells of hair tonic, tobacco, bay rum shaving lotion, shoe polish, and recently cleaned firearms, trying not to swirl those odors any more deeply into the air above Blossom's head than they already had.

"She's got something," Kevin breathed. "Let her go on her own for a bit, then stay back a few feet. Sometimes what she's following stops or turns around. She needs room."

Blossom didn't seem to be in a hurry. When Kevin held the glove to her nose again, she shook her head and gave a short explanatory bark. The scent she was following along the floor of the church wasn't the scent on the piece of leather he kept shoving at her. The scent trails were definitely mixed, though the woman smell was fainter. The woman smell had been strong along the seat of the pew, then nearly obliterated by the kind of scent Blossom had smelled only once before, as a young pup. She'd awakened in a heap of dead dogs, all of them smelling of that sickly sweet odor.

She'd crawled out and away in time to avoid the shovels and the pit, but only just. The rest of her litter hadn't made it to the safety of the streets.

Now the man scent cut through the other smell, enveloping the woman scent. Blossom wanted to tell Kevin that the woman had been carried someplace, but that was too complicated to communicate. Better to concentrate on finding the trail to where the man had taken her. Down the aisle, across the front of the church below the main altar, around a corner and past another, smaller altar. Blossom stopped and sat down in front of a narrow door set into an alcove. She didn't make a sound.

Remington once again in his right hand, Ned Hayes closed his left fist around the door latch, turned it, and pulled. Nothing. "Can you force the lock, Geoff?"

"Stand back." He pulled the set of locksmith's tools from his pocket, probed the keyhole, and cursed softly under his breath. "The tumblers are rusted; my picks aren't moving them." He straightened from the keyhole, tiny flakes of rust clinging to his pick.

"Do you think he's still in there?" Ned pointed to the word *Crypt* in flowing Gothic script above the door.

"Unless there's another way out." Geoffrey pulled out a thicker pick.

"Stay here and keep trying," Prudence said. "I'm going to the rectory to get a key that'll be strong enough to break through the rust."

"Ask one of the priests or the housekeeper about the monsignor we saw. We need to know who he is. And hurry," Ned urged.

Whoever had carried her down to the crypt would soon be back, Alice reasoned. She tried to remember what she might have heard or seen in those last few moments before she fell asleep, but could recall nothing but the overwhelming fatigue that had made her crawl onto the pew like a sleepy child.

The door was locked and she had no weapon with which to defend herself, nothing in the pockets of her coat but the Stations of the Cross booklet, her rosary, and one glove. Why would he have taken her glove? It didn't make sense. But nothing that had happened to her this afternoon was logical. She searched under the stand of votive lights for something she could swing at the man when he came to get her. Nothing, not even dust. The ladies of the Altar Society or Jerry Brophy must have added the crypt to their cleaning list. *Brophy.* Maybe he stored a broom down here. Maybe she'd find it leaning in a corner or against one of the marble coffins. Five minutes later she knew there was nothing. Jerry must carry all of his cleaning supplies with him. He probably never forgot any-thing.

Think, Alice, think! She said the Guardian Angel prayer again, the lilting rhyme pat-tern of it fighting off a growing sense of panic. Nothing bad could happen to you if you remembered to ask your guardian angel for protection. And if it did — well, that was God taking over because he had some-thing else in mind for you to do. Or be. Like dead.

If she could hide, she might gain a few precious moments while he searched for her, might even be able to dash past him and out the door before he realized what she'd done. Would he leave the door ajar when he came to get her? Joseph had left his bedroom door open because he'd been so angry and distracted that for once in his life he hadn't remembered to close and lock it. There might be the slimmest of chances.

They'd played hide and seek down there, she and other children whose mothers belonged to the Altar Society. Around and around the catafalques they'd raced, stooping to hide, leaping up to chortle and run again, barely evading each other's outstretched arms until somebody collapsed from shrieking laughter and was it.

There was something teasing the very edge of her memory, some bit of information acquired long ago that was trying to push its way through into the present.

Alice turned slowly in a circle, her eyes darting from light to shadow, seeking whatever it was her brain was telling her was important to remember. When her glance fell on the rectangular marble coffin of Baby Maude, she knew she'd found it. Like a sleepwalker, she extended her hands to the child's final resting place, pushing gently so as to make as little noise as possible. The marble slab that had never been plastered down over the little girl's wooden coffin slid aside. Baby Maude's tiny skull smiled up at her amid a shower of splinters. One of the children playing down there had discovered the hiding place and smashed the rotten coffin as she climbed in. One of the other girls. It hadn't been Alice. She would never have dared such a thing.

"Is there enough room for me inside with you, Baby Maude?" Alice asked. Like most other families, Baby Maude's parents expected to lose more than one child. They'd left room for Baby Maude to be kept eternal company by a brother or a sister. Perhaps several.

Before she climbed inside and pulled the marble slab back into place, Alice took several votive candles and a box of safety matches out of the carton where they'd been stored.

When she emerged, safe and sound, she didn't want to have to face only darkness.

Please God, she and Baby Maude wouldn't have to keep company for too many long hours.

CHAPTER 31

"Father Brennan is hearing confessions this afternoon," Saint Anselm's pastor said.

"The church is empty, Father. There's no one in any of the confessional boxes."

"I'm sure you're wrong about that. Father Brennan is punctilious about his duties."

"We need to get into the crypt." Prudence had already explained her suspicions. The only things she'd left out were Blossom and the guns Geoffrey and Ned had carried into the church.

"I've never heard anything so ridiculous in my life."

"Father Mahoney, if you can't give us a key or show us another way into the crypt, Alice Nolan's death will be on your head."

"What seems to be the trouble, Father?" The assistant pastor, Father Kearns, and Mrs. Healy, the rectory housekeeper, crowded into the hallway, drawn by Father Mahoney's increasingly agitated voice.

"She claims there's a murder about to be committed in the crypt." Father Mahoney's face flushed red with anger and bewilderment.

"Let's not stand here in the open doorway giving scandal to the neighborhood," Father Kearns said. "I suggest we send for the police to prove or disprove Miss Mac-Kenzie's allegation."

"There's a tunnel from the basement of the rectory into the storage rooms beneath the church," Mrs. Healy blurted out. "You can reach the crypt that way."

"A tunnel?" Prudence wasn't sure she'd heard correctly.

"For bad weather," the housekeeper explained. "Some of our priests have been older men. One of the pastors lived well into his eighties. The tunnel's been there for years."

"Show me," Prudence snapped. She turned to Father Kearns. "Explain to Mr. Hunter what Mrs. Healy just told me and give him the extra key. He's on *this* side of the crypt door, in the church. Hurry."

They left Father Mahoney standing in the front hallway, mouth agape. Father Kearns, not used to being given orders by a lay person, especially a woman, decided nonetheless to comply. He grabbed the key to the crypt from a hook on the coat rack and took off at a trot.

Mrs. Healy led Prudence along the central hallway of the rectory, through the kitchen, and down a stairway off the pantry.

"This goes into the basement of the rectory," she explained. "I store the canned goods down here and hang the laundry to dry." She paused for a moment. "You can't have the whole neighborhood staring at a priest's underdrawers, now can you?"

"Why did you decide to tell me about the tunnel, Mrs. Healy? I don't think Father Mahoney was at all pleased."

"They're all holy men, to be sure, but not a one of the three of them would help a poor girl who's been sweet-talked out of her virtue and gotten in the family way. They've got their minds so fixed on sin they can't see that being lonely and wanting a little love is what makes them do it. The girls get caught and the men walk away with their hands in their pockets and their pants unbuttoned."

"You're talking about Ellen Tierney, aren't you?"

"I've heard a word or two, enough to guess that she might have been in the family way. Too early to tell Mick McGuire, they say, but caught tight nonetheless."

Prudence decided that if women ran detective agencies there would be no more secrets in the world. Anywhere.

"And there's something about that Father Brennan I don't like. I've caught him coming up these stairs more than once. He always has a good explanation, but nothing you wouldn't wonder about afterwards. Sneaky, if you ask me. Doesn't want anyone to know when he's coming and going. Hiding something."

Mrs. Healy walked through the lines of drying wash, skirted the bulk of the furnace and the coal chute, smiled fondly at the shelves of glistening jellies, jewel-toned fruits, and deeply dark vegetables. More than enough to get them through the winter. All of them canned by her own skilled hands. No one ever got sick or died from eating what she put in her Mason jars.

"Jerry Brophy found a drop of blood on one of the kneelers in front of the altar rail. I saw him scrubbing away at it to beat the band, and I asked him why." Mrs. Healy handed Prudence a key. "I've thought about that drop of blood at night when I couldn't sleep. That's why I told you about the tunnel. That's why I'm giving you the key.

"I've been housekeeper in this rectory ever since my husband died, God rest his soul, and that's more than twenty years ago now. Did you know you have to be a widow to get hired on as housekeeper to priests? It's true. Something is wrong here, Miss Mac-Kenzie. I can feel it in my bones. And it didn't start until after Father Brennan arrived. Nothing you can put your finger on, but it's there. Like the banshee no one sees. You can't mistake the cry, but it comes out of nowhere. And then someone is dead. It never fails." She turned on her sensible heels, black widow's skirts stirring up the dust of the cellar floor. "I'll say a prayer," she promised.

The tunnel led as straight as an arrow from the rectory to Saint Anselm's. Prudence unlocked the door at the far end with the same key Mrs. Healy had used at the entrance. She stepped into a storage room filled with broken cane-bottomed priedieux, banks of iron votive candle holders, racks of moth-eaten choir robes, and stacks of damaged missals and hymnals. There was a clear path threaded through the debris into a narrow passageway that branched in two directions. One had to lead to the church, the other to the crypt.

The almost certainly useless derringer in hand, Prudence crossed an alcove toward the crypt. It was too far back under the nave of the church to be anything else. She used the key Mrs. Healy had given her, then laid a tentative hand on the door latch, took a deep breath, and swung the door open so hard it bounced off the wall.

She saw a small undercroft with a row of pillars holding up an arched roof, marble and polished granite sarcophagi marching in orderly rows down its length, six votive candles burning steadily before the small altar where special Masses could be said for those who lay there. The air smelled of old dust and older bodies. She thought it must be at least as cold down here as it was outside in the street.

The crypt, like the church above it, was empty.

"Nothing," Prudence said when she had rejoined the others in the church. "Someone has been in the crypt because votive candles are burning and it was locked, but whoever it was is long gone."

Blossom bounded down the stairs, Kevin following closely behind. Father Kearns cast one scandalized look at the huge red dog who bared her teeth at him, then spun on his heel, and stormed indignantly off to report this latest intrusion to Saint Anselm's pastor.

Ned Hayes was bitterly disappointed. He'd been so certain they would be able to step in before Sally Lynn's killer claimed another victim. He trailed disconsolately down the stairs to the crypt, following the noise of Geoffrey's and Prudence's footsteps, fumbling the Remington back into its holster under his arm. He had an unopened bottle of fine Tennessee bourbon at home, and cash money in his pocket. He'd stop by the Turk's, smooth away the rough edges of disappointment with the most expensive cocaine he could buy. Tyrus would hover disapprovingly, but he'd read his master's mind and know better than to try to stop him entirely.

Tomorrow, when Alice Nolan's eviscerated corpse turned up somewhere, he wouldn't care as much as he did right now. Or at least the caring wouldn't be as painful.

He stood at the bottom of the staircase, sorting out the sounds echoing around him. Listening to Blossom barking, then Prudence's voice asking a question, Geoffrey's voice answering. He could head in their direction or he could go into the candlelit vault directly opposite. Maybe what he needed was a few moments alone to begin to accept another in what he thought of as a string of failures that defined his life.

The crypt was dim and shadowy, fluted pillars reaching like unnaturally straight trees for the arched ceiling. Every available niche crowded with the marble tombs of the affluent dead. What was the word? *Necropolis,* that was it. City of the dead. Quiet, cold, smelling faintly of dry decay.

The votive candles caught his attention. One of them guttered and died; the others flickered wildly in pools of melted wax. He lit a rolled paper spill and touched it to as many unlit wicks as he could before the spill burned his fingers, lit another one and moved methodically along the rows of crimson votive glasses until all the candles were lit. A gentle wave of heat and light rolled over him.

"We found where he left. There's a cellar door at the end of the hall that probably opens onto an alley. It's barred from the outside." Geoffrey and Prudence stood in the doorway.

"What's the matter, girl?" Kevin Carney's voice could be heard just outside the crypt. "Do you want to go back in there again?"

Blossom pushed against Geoffrey's legs, nudging him from the doorway.

"I had the devil of a time getting her out of here," Kevin said. He'd figured out that the killer's scent had to be mixed with Alice Nolan's, but Blossom hadn't seemed in any hurry to pick it up. Maybe she'd known it would end at a cellar door barred against them from the wrong side.

Now she went straight to one of the marble sarcophagi, a child's resting place from the size of it, and lay down on the floor, head on her crossed paws.

"What's she doing?" Hunter asked.

"Wait."

Blossom raised her head, sat up, barked twice, then placed both front paws on the sarcophagus. Her nails scrabbled against the slick marble, throwing her back. Down to the floor, head on her paws, up again, this time flinging more of her body against the marble tomb, trying to wedge her nose under the overhanging lid, shoving with all of her might against it.

"Take the far side, Ned," Geoffrey positioned his fingers under the marble slab. Kevin crowded in, wedging a thin shoulder under the covering stone. A dreadful urgency spread like cold fog from one man to another.

The slab moved with surprising ease, sliding across the top of the marble sarcophagus with a scraping sound that sent shivers up spines and set Blossom to whining loudly.

While the men lifted the lid to the floor, the dog hooked her paws over the side of the marble box, and leaned her head as deeply inside as she could.

They all saw it at the same time, a slender white hand reaching up out of darkness to caress Blossom's muzzle.

"I prayed someone would come," a voice whispered. "I prayed to my guardian angel, and here you are."

They lifted Alice Nolan out of the tomb where she had hidden herself, where she had crouched in blackness amid Baby Maude's fragile bones until her would-be killer gave up the search. Prudence folded her into her arms, rocked her gently, shushed the raw sobs.

"I heard him leave," she told them, drinking in the brightness of the lit candles, gulping air as though it were a welcome drink. "But I didn't dare try to get out. I was afraid he was nearby, waiting for me to show myself. I heard the dog barking, then the noise of a lot of footsteps. Suddenly I knew he'd gone. I can't explain how. Just that something evil had been here and wasn't anymore."

"The dog's name is Blossom," Kevin told her.

"Blossom. How beautiful." Alice smiled at

the dog.

Blossom smiled back. This human was like the weakest member of a pack, the one most likely to end up in the belly of a predator. She had the same look in her eyes, as if she saw her fate and was resigned to it. Blossom felt sorry for her. Sometimes, she knew, the weak pup held on against all odds and managed to survive.

She hoped Alice Nolan would be that fortunate.

"Old Seamus Reilly has died," Father Brennan announced to Father Mahoney in the late evening of the day Alice Nolan was found hiding in Baby Maude's tomb. He took his time removing hat and gloves, hanging his heavy winter coat on the rack that stood in the rectory's front hallway. "I was able to get to him before the end, thank God." It was what every good Catholic prayed for, the grace of a happy death. "What's wrong, Father?"

"You've been gone a long time."

"One of Mr. Reilly's neighbors came to the rectory after confessions looking for a priest. I don't know where Mrs. Healy was, but there wasn't time to tell her where I was going. I hope she didn't worry."

"It doesn't matter now you're back. I told

them they were wrong."

"Who was wrong, Father? About what?" Father Brennan rubbed his sculptured white hands together vigorously. It was near freezing today, and he'd been out in the cold longer than he'd originally intended. He set down the leather satchel in which he carried the holy oils of Extreme Unction to souls on the brink of departing this life. It was larger and heavier than the bag most priests carried, but Father Brennan liked to be prepared for any eventuality. "I'll put this away later. Right now I'm perishing for a cup of tea."

"There was a bit of a mix-up this afternoon," Father Mahoney remarked when Mrs. Healy had brought the tea tray and left them to it. "One of our parishioners managed to lock herself into the crypt. Quite a panic until they found her."

"Who was it?"

"Alice Nolan. Joseph Nolan's sister, poor thing. You must have met her when the Nolan maid was killed. She's been pestering her father for years to let her go to the Visitations, and she's finally gotten her wish. A bit weak in the head, if you ask me."

"Why is that, Father?"

"She has an overactive imagination. Makes

up stories about things that never happened."

"What would these imaginary stories be about?"

Father Mahoney slurped his tea. "Women get hysterical, you know. It's worse if they read novels." He added another spoonful of sugar to his cup. He liked his tea sweet. "There are times in the confessional when I know a woman is making up tales that would curl your hair if you believed them. Right out of the pages of the kind of book that doesn't belong in a decent home. I don't argue or tell her I think she's lying. I give absolution and a nice, stiff penance. That does more good than anything else."

"I find it hard to believe someone would lie in confession. What's the point?" If the pastor had somehow learned that he'd been gossiping about Alice Nolan with Jerry Brophy, there'd be hell to pay. Even though he thought he could argue and win a case against having broken the seal of the confessional. Father Brennan poured himself more calming tea. He drank it plain, no sugar, no milk.

"Wait until you have a few more years on you, Father." Father Mahoney had to ask the next question directly, and he hated doing that, but Father Brennan wasn't being

555

cooperative. "Was Alice upset when she left the confessional?"

"I don't know that she came to confession today. I can't put a face to all the voices yet."

It was the answer he expected, no real answer at all. "There was something else odd," Father Mahoney said.

"What was that, Father?"

"Did you run into a monsignor this afternoon?"

"What would a monsignor be doing at Saint Anselm's?"

"That's what I said, but they insisted they'd seen a monsignor come down the street and go into the church. They described the red buttons and the piping on his cassock. He was wearing a biretta. They described that, too. And he had a scarf wrapped around his face against the cold. An unusually tall, slender man."

"I don't think I understand who saw what." Father Brennan put down his tea cup.

"Do you remember that Geoffrey Hunter who came with Miss MacKenzie asking about the Nolans' maid, Ellen Tierney, and the girl from Staten Island who was murdered?"

"I do."

"The two of them and an ex-detective who was forced off the Metropolitan Police a few years back came up with the idea that whoever killed those girls was connected to Saint Anselm's. They were hiding in an alley across from the church this afternoon, waiting for him to show up."

"The killer?"

"They had a vagrant and a dog with them." Father Mahoney sighed. It had been a trying day. "Apparently they also decided that Miss Nolan was the next intended victim, and when she didn't come out of the church after the monsignor went in, they ran across the street to save her. The crypt door was locked, so Miss MacKenzie came here to get the key. Mrs. Healy took her into the church through the basement tunnel. I had a few words to say about that, I can assure you."

"I'm certain you did."

"All because an hysterical woman dozed off in her pew and had a nightmare. Can you imagine? She said she woke up in the crypt with no memory of how she'd gotten there, and then she became frightened, so she hid."

"What about the monsignor?"

"No one seems to know who he was or where he went." Father Mahoney wished he had something stronger than milk to put in what remained of his tea. "That's why I asked if you'd seen him here in the rectory. I assume he was looking for me. If he exists at all."

Father Brennan shook his head regretfully. "I didn't come back to the rectory before going to Mr. Reilly's," he said, contradicting what he'd told the pastor earlier. "There was certainly no monsignor in the church."

"Well, then." Father Mahoney rested his elbows on his substantial belly and made a tent with his fingertips. "Reilly was still alive when you got there, was he?"

"By the grace of God. He was able to make a good death."

"The body's at Bellevue now, I suppose."

"Nowhere else for the poor man to go. He hadn't any family. Nothing put by for a burial. Or so the neighbor said."

"He's not the first and he won't be the last."

"May he rest in peace."

"Amen."

"Will the Visitations take her, do you think? This Alice Nolan?" asked Father Brennan. "After what happened today?"

"Oh, they'll take her all right. They're all a bit touched in the head, if you ask me. Soft. Alice wouldn't last a week with the

Charities, but she'll do fine with the Visitations. Out of sight, out of mind, I say. That's always for the best."

Father Brennan nodded his head in agreement. *Out of sight, out of mind.*
Out of reach. Out of danger.

Father Mahoney had a visitor that night after Father Brennan and Father Kearns had gone to bed. He tossed and turned and fretted over what he was told, then made an unannounced and uninvited visit to the archbishop's office the next morning. He impressed upon his superior's assistant the urgency of his request and the importance of avoiding scandal at all costs. Father Brennan was one of those odd priests who didn't fit in anywhere, who arrived at a parish with good recommendations, and left within a year or two under a cloud no one cared to penetrate too deeply. Sad, but too frequent an occurrence to cause much discussion. Fortunately, there were always empty slots needing to be filled, so no real damage was ever done.

The assistant agreed, and gave Father Mahoney ten minutes with the archbishop. It was all he needed.

"Priests lie to their pastors all the time about their whereabouts," the archbishop reminded him when Father Mahoney had finished stating his case in as much detail as he thought prudent and strictly necessary.

"They do," Father Mahoney concurred. Both men knew that it was usually about a woman, a love affair with the bottle, or the greed that comes from never having enough money. "But I think we have a more serious problem here than the usual."

"Can you be more specific, Father?" The archbishop wasn't asking for details, just confirmation that the situation, whatever it was, warranted swift removal and reassignment. He trusted that Father Mahoney, a priest for more than thirty-five years, understood that.

"He has to go, Your Eminence." Father Mahoney hesitated, then decided to wade a bit further into the deep waters of chancery business. "The police might become involved if he stays. The newspapers, also."

"We can't have that, can we?"

"No, Your Eminence. The scandal."

"I'll see what I can do," the archbishop said.

Father Mark Brennan's career in New York City was over.

His transfer came through less than five days after Saint Anselm's pastor requested it. Given that it was two weeks before

Christmas, the speed with which the archbishop's office moved was nothing short of
a miracle.

Seamus Reilly was buried from Bellevue
with no one but two city workers to shovel
him into the ground.

"But wasn't it a shame that the priest
didn't get there in time to give the poor man
the last rites," remarked the neighbor when
he came to Saint Anselm's to complain to
Father Mahoney the night Reilly died.
"There was plenty of time to receive the
Last Sacrament if he'd only come right
away. Seamus was cold by the time he got
there."

What was troubling the neighbor was that
he'd been waiting outside the building to
take the priest upstairs to where Reilly was
breathing his last, but Father Brennan
hadn't come from the direction of Saint
Anselm's at all. When he reached the steps,
he hadn't met the neighbor's eyes. And he'd
smelled like he'd been with a woman. There
was no mistaking that odor if a man was
careless and spilled over on his pants. If
Father Mahoney understood what he
meant.

The other thing that was bothersome was
that one of the women who lived in the

neighborhood had sworn up and down that she'd seen a monsignor walking along the street like an ordinary person. At first she'd thought it was Father Brennan rushing along, the priest was that tall, but then she saw the scarlet piping on the cassock. She'd leaned farther out her window thinking how grand it would be if a monsignor could be the one to ease poor Seamus out of this world. A monsignor, fancy that! But then the monsignor passed by and it had been Father Brennan who turned up at Reilly's apartment after all. Too late to do any good.

Did Father Mahoney know who the monsignor might have been? Who had sent him? And where he got off to?

CHAPTER 32

"There's a key hidden above the ledge," Davey said, trying to be helpful. The tall man who had asked about the maids who came to have their uniforms altered reached above the shop doorway. "No, it's the ledge over the window. Mr. Neil said it was safe there because everybody thinks it has to be on top of the door."

"That's very smart, Davey."

"Mr. Neil isn't dumb. Like me." Davey hung his head. He'd made another mistake. He knew it. Mr. Neil had told him to forget about the men who'd asked him questions, but he'd remembered the tall man as soon as he saw him peering through the window of the uniform shop. And he went right over to see what he could do to help. Davey liked it when people told him he'd done a good job.

"Have you seen Mr. Slattery this week?"

"No, Miss." The lady's voice was soft and

gentle, not like the screeching sounds made by women calling out their windows for children to come home. Or the raw pleadings when Mrs. Slattery was still alive and Mr. Neil had to go into the back room to fix things, shooing Davey out of the shop and locking the door behind him. But not before he'd heard. He hoped the nice lady would ask him another question.

"Davey, did you ever see Mr. Slattery, you call him Mr. Neil, dressed up like a priest?"

"Wearing a long black dress, you mean, Miss? Except that my mother told me another name for it, but I don't remember what it is."

"A cassock, Davey."

"Maybe I should write it down." He always carried a small notebook and a pencil in his back pocket. His mother said that was the way to learn things, write them down. "He had red trimming on his dress. And a funny hat with red buttons on it."

"When did you see him wearing the hat?"

"I wasn't supposed to, but I came early when he said he'd be needing me to mind the counter. Mr. Neil doesn't like loud noises, so I tiptoed in as quietly as I could and I didn't shout hello. He was in the private place, but he'd left the door open, so I peeked in. He had his eyes closed and he was praying. You're not supposed to interrupt people when they pray, so I sneaked out and went home for a while. When I came back he wasn't wearing the . . . cassock."

"Was this a long time ago, Davey?"

"A long time." He nodded his head solemnly. He wasn't sure what the difference was between a long and a short time because people didn't always count the same way. He hoped it didn't matter.

"Let's not stay out here any longer, Prudence. We don't want to attract attention."

The tall man thanked Davey for his help and gave him a dime.

The shop was silent, dim, and orderly. It smelled of the black and indigo dyes of the uniforms hanging in perfect symmetry along two walls.

"There's a lamp on the counter over there," Prudence said. "Shall I light it?"

"I'll turn the lock and pull down the door and window shades," Geoffrey answered. "If anyone knocks, we'll ignore it."

"What are we looking for?" A pale yellow light poured out from the gas lamp.

"Whatever he's left behind. I think his departure was unplanned and quickly accomplished."

"He left Alice drugged and unconscious in the crypt, then he panicked when he couldn't find her again."

"What we don't know is whether he went back to Saint Anselm's to collect incriminating evidence and just happened upon Alice or if he had already targeted her."

"We're not even sure he's our man," Prudence said. "You always tell me that circumstantial evidence is the least trustworthy."

"Which is true. Unless it leads to something stronger, more certain."

"Do you think he's gone for good, Geoffrey?"

"I think it's very likely."

"He's meticulous. There isn't any dust on the counters and the floor looks like it's recently been waxed. I haven't found anything out here in the shop."

"I didn't expect we would, but it doesn't pay to cut corners. Let's move to the back rooms." Holding high the lantern, Geoffrey led the way through the curtained doorway into the area where they expected to find a storeroom and perhaps some trace of where the late Mrs. Slattery had performed the illegal terminations sought by so many desperate young women. He set the lantern down on a scrubbed wooden table then took out his folding knife and began to scrape lightly along the crevice where the two halves of the table top met. "I'm looking for traces of old blood," he explained to Prudence. "We won't be able to prove that a stain was caused only by blood and not something else, but in my own mind it would go a long way toward certainty in identifying Slattery as a suspect."

"We already know that abortions were performed here," Prudence reminded him. "There's bound to be blood."

"We've been *told* they were done here." Geoffrey deposited splinters of wood onto the clean white linen of his handkerchief. "Let's look at these under the lamp," he said.

Prudence turned the wick up as high as it would go. The gas sputtered as it rose into the chimney; the light brightened, became less yellow.

Using the tip of his knife, Geoffrey nudged apart the fragments of pulp, including samples taken from an area that could be easily cleaned, where blood couldn't seep into the wood and escape the eye. Within moments it became obvious that there were very dark particles mixed in with shreds that were the same pale pine color as the table legs.

"There's an easily identifiable difference," he said.

"There's no way to prove the discoloration was caused by blood." Prudence touched one fingernail to the splinters resting on the handkerchief.

"It's nothing a judge would accept in a court of law," Geoffrey agreed, "but it's enough to make me think we're on the right track." He dribbled water from a half filled glass someone had left behind onto the dark splinters. The liquid that oozed out was too deeply blackish brown to be identifiable as blood.

Prudence opened what turned out to be a closet door where an ironing board leaned against one wall and shelves held irons and baskets of thread, measuring tapes, pincushions, and the thick braid used to protect hems that brushed all day long against stone floors and uncarpeted stairs. There were thick stacks of small pieces of material saved from alterations, set aside to use for patching, she supposed. Like every other place in Slattery's uniform and tailor shop, the closet was dust-free, organized, and contained only what one would expect to find.

"There's nowhere else to look down here, Geoffrey," she said, "though I find it hard to believe abortions were performed this openly."

"The front door would have been locked," he said, walking back to where the heavy black curtain hung in the doorway separating shop premises from the workroom they were searching. "The young woman would have been told not to make a sound, perhaps given a piece of wood to clench between her teeth, maybe even a dose of laudanum to calm her down. This is a neighborhood where people mind their own business. Even if some of the women knew what the Slatterys were doing, they wouldn't have said anything."

"In case one of them required a similar service in the future."

"Exactly. And my guess is that relatively few clients ended up in charity wards with infections from which they never recovered. Either accidentally or because they knew how to take precautions, the success rate must have been high. It's the only explanation for why they've been able to stay in business so long."

"How long do you think that's been?" Prudence asked.

"Big Brenda believed that Mrs. Slattery was active since right after the shop was opened. There was never a husband; she claimed to be widowed. A daughter and then Neil, who was several years younger, but probably about five or six years old when they arrived in this country."

"Can Brenda's information be trusted?"

"Gossip, rumor, maybe a grain of truth here and there. It's all we have."

"I'm ready to go upstairs to where they lived." Prudence picked up the lamp while Geoffrey folded the handkerchief carefully and put it in a trouser pocket.

"Let me go first," he said, one hand resting on the Army Colt .45 in its shoulder holster.

The staircase was narrow and dark, but the walls were recently painted and free of greasy finger- or handprints. A railing had been nailed to one wall, presumably to help an aging and ailing Mrs. Slattery make her way back to the apartment at the end of a long day. A single door at the top of the stairs closed off the living quarters.

"Is it locked?" Prudence whispered. They were the only two people on the premises, but whispering seemed more fitting than speaking aloud.

"No." Geoffrey turned the handle and stepped through the doorway into what Prudence's lamp revealed to be a comfortably furnished parlor. He lit two gas wall fixtures and another lamp that sat on a three legged table beside a cushioned rocking chair. "They must have been doing very well," he said.

Crocheted doilies rested on the backs and arms of upholstered chairs, brightly polished brass candlesticks stood on the mantelpiece, and two baskets on either side of the fireplace held ample supplies of coal and split firewood. The kitchen was at one end of the parlor, separated from it by a sideboard that held dishes, glasses, a tray of silverware, and precisely folded napkins and tablecloths.

"Stay here for a moment. Let me check the other rooms." He walked quickly but quietly toward closed doors that opened onto two bedrooms. "All clear," he said, coming back into the parlor, pushing the Colt .45 deeper down into its holster. "I'll take Slattery's room. You search the mother's."

Black dresses hung neatly in the wardrobe, pairs of shoes and boots lined up below. An umbrella leaned into one rear corner, and hatboxes sat on the single shelf. Prudence checked skirt pockets, the toes of shoes, the empty spaces beneath hat crowns. She ran a hand over the wardrobe's floor, feeling for a secret compartment, but found nothing. In two drawers at the bottom of the wardrobe, someone had positioned perfectly folded

571

nightgowns and undergarments. A warm, knitted shawl in stripes of black and gray hung over a ladder-back chair. The basin and chamber pot had been washed after their last use and stowed out of sight under the bed.

Prudence sighed, then attacked the tables standing on either side of the narrow bedstead. A rosary, prayer book, and pair of gold-rimmed spectacles were the first things she found. Nestled next to them was a clean, folded handkerchief and a small bottle of Lydia E. Pinkham's Vegetable Compound. Prudence opened it and sniffed. Enough alcohol to keep the herbal elements from spoiling for a long time to come. She held the prayer book upside down and fanned the pages. A shower of holy cards, commemorative funeral cards, and pieces of paper with prayers and intentions scribbled on them rained out. One folded piece of thick white paper looked official. It was Mrs. Pauline Slattery's death certificate; she'd been gone for three months. The cause of death was pleurisy.

Prudence ran her fingers beneath the mattress, from top to bottom of the bed and on both sides. Nothing. Hands on hips, she stood looking around her, searching for a place to hide something from the prying eyes of a son who was compulsively clean, neat, and organized. The bedroom's single window and the mirror in the door of the wardrobe had been washed with vinegar, the bed linens crackled with starch, the floorboards and the furniture gleamed with polish.

If I wanted to conceal something from him, where would I put it? Prudence asked herself. Her eyes raked the walls, but she'd already looked behind the few pictures hanging there. She stared at the wardrobe, willing it to give up its secrets, but nothing happened. Almost absentmindedly she tried to run a hand behind the bed's headboard, but there wasn't enough space. That was odd, to push a bed so close to the wall. She pulled it out an inch or so, struggling with the weight of it, then slipped her hand into the space she opened between the wall and the bedstead. Up and down, left and right.

The envelope had been tacked just far enough in so that a swipe of the dust cloth wouldn't reach it. Sitting on the bed, Prudence slit it open with a hatpin. Neil Slattery's birth certificate. Born 1855 in County Cork, Ireland. Father Unknown. Bridget Slattery's birth certificate. Born 1852 in County Limerick, Ireland. Father Unknown. Mrs. Slattery had in reality been

Miss Slattery, hounded out of one county into another when she turned up pregnant and unwed. America must have seemed her only escape.

"Prudence?" Geoffrey stood in the doorway, a carpetbag in his hand. "I've found something."

"So have I," she said, holding out the documents to him, fingering other folded papers still in the envelope.

"These may explain a lot." He read them through quickly, then returned them to her. "If his mother blamed him for being a bastard, and she made much of her living ensuring that other bastards didn't get born, it could have eaten at him through all the years of his growing up until he became twisted enough to think he owed it to her to continue the mission. Get rid of the evidence of sin before more unwanted children could be born with the stain of bastardy."

"What's that, Geoffrey?"

"I think it's the carpetbag Nora Kenny must have brought with her from Staten Island. It never turned up." He gave it to Prudence, who placed it on the bed and pulled open the handles.

She didn't recognize any of the clothing inside, but then she'd never seen the adult Nora Kenny when she wasn't wearing a maid's uniform. A lawn shirtwaist settled onto her hands, as light as lace and finely embroidered with a pattern of tiny shamrocks. Surely that was Agnes Kenny's work. Prudence had seen examples of it in her mother's linens stored in the attic between sprigs of lavender to ward off the moths. "I think you're right," she said.

Geoffrey picked up the carpetbag and turned it over. On the flat bottom someone had written *Property of Kenny, Staten Island.* The ink was faded, but most of the letters could be made out.

"Dear God," Prudence sobbed, one hand covering her mouth. "She must have come here because her uniform no longer fit around the waist. She walked in and Slattery pegged her for a whore who couldn't be allowed to bring a bastard into the world. He killed her, Geoffrey. He killed her and then performed some kind of macabre ceremony on her poor body."

"She might have come because she asked around and was told about a safe place to get rid of it. We won't know until he confesses."

"*I* know," Prudence said. "Nora would have cherished Dominic's child. And Dominic would have seen it as his way out of the future his father insisted he live. He would have taken Nora away somewhere safe. Out West perhaps, where they could begin a new life together. Where they didn't owe anything to anyone except each other."

"Let's take these with us." Geoffrey repacked Nora's possessions into the carpetbag and laid the documents Prudence had found on top.

He looked around Mrs. Slattery's bedroom and thought that something seemed wrong, off somehow, as if the walls weren't in the right place. But that was ridiculous. Prudence, carrying Nora's carpetbag, was waiting for him.

Geoffrey thought she had unerringly put her finger on exactly what had happened to her childhood friend. It must be unimaginably painful for her to remain in the place where Nora might have met her death. He'd take her home, and over restorative cups of tea they would talk their way through her grief. Prudence was fragile, he reminded himself, no matter how brave and stalwart a front she chose to wear in front of him.

He had helped see her through a difficult time not too long ago; he would do it again.

Neil Slattery choked back sobs of frustrated anger. He had torn the apartment apart looking for the document he had known his mother must have hidden there. The birth certificate that proved him the bastard she'd so often accused him of being, the filthy thing she had tried and failed to purge from her body. It was humiliating that the Mac-Kenzie woman had found it, and worse that it had been in so obvious a hiding place all this time. Now he'd never be able to destroy it.

He pressed the lever that opened the panel concealing his narrow hiding place and stepped out. His mother had insisted there had to be somewhere to secrete the instruments she'd used and the record book she'd prided herself on keeping. *"Who knows? One of us may have to hide there someday,"* she had said, leering the gap-toothed grin that was as good as a slap in the face.

She'd hated him. Had tried to kill him when he was no larger than her thumb. Tried again when he had stubbornly grown to be as big as her fist. She'd told him the stories of her failures so many times that they became his stories, and when she'd faltered in the retelling as she grew older, he prompted her as if he'd been there. On the outside. Mixing the herbal concoctions. Sitting in the boiling hot water. Probing with the crochet hook.

He held the record book in his arms and

cursed himself for not having gotten rid of Nora Kenny's carpetbag. But he had a weakness. He liked to keep souvenirs. For a while. Not too long. But for a few weeks or a few months. To stroke and remember. He listened, just to be on the safe side. His mother had put great importance on protecting themselves. He had let a good fifteen minutes pass before he left the secret cupboard. Counting off the seconds and the minutes the way his mother had taught him when he'd been a small, unruly child and she'd locked him in whatever dark closet was available. *"One hour. Count it off,"* she'd told him. It had kept him from screaming.

His thing hurt. He'd tied the string around it before he went to Saint Anselm's, exactly the way she'd done so many times. It would be a terrible sin to have it grow long and hard in a church. And he was inclined that way. All bastards were. They wanted to repeat the crime of their birth, and the only way to prevent that was to knot in the seed. It hurt, it throbbed, it swelled with no possibility of release, but it kept another bastard from being created, and that's all God and his mother wanted.

It was time to leave. Again. For the last time.

He knew someone down on the docks who owed him a favor.

CHAPTER 33

When Father Kearns proposed a farewell dinner for Father Mark Brennan, transferred unexpectedly to Boston, and wasn't that a shame, Mrs. Healy could find no good excuse for refusing to cook it. All she could do, because it was good riddance to him as far as she was concerned, was keep to the strict abstinence rules of the Church.

Brennan was leaving on the Saturday before Christmas, which meant fish on the Friday night of the dinner, so she'd bake a bony big cod for the three priests, and serve it up surrounded by mounds of boiled potatoes, boiled carrots, and boiled turnips. With grated horseradish on the side, hot enough to bring tears to the eyes and set the nose running. It was a meal beloved by the pastor, tolerated by his assistant, and decidedly not Father Brennan's favorite. Mrs. Healy had served it on many a Friday night. She'd seen the way Father Brennan took small helpings and moved them around on his plate, contriving to eat very little while seeming to consume enough so as not to give offense. Father Mahoney, bless his ignorant stomach, would think it a fine sendoff.

The potatoes were kept in a great bin in the cellar to prevent them sprouting more than was decently edible, the carrots and turnips buried in sand. It had been Father Kearns's idea to buy the rectory's staples in bulk to save money, though Mrs. Healy still went out to the shops every day. She enjoyed gossiping with the women who were buying supplies for family dinners. The rectory could be so dead quiet and gloomy during the day that she'd go out even when there wasn't anything to get.

For the last couple of days she'd taken jars of hot tea and slices of bread sopped in drippings over to Kevin Carney and Blossom, though she hadn't the foggiest notion why the two of them were still camped out in the alley across from Saint Anselm's now that all the fuss was over. Still, she supposed it never hurt to have one of Billy McGlory's runners keeping an eye out for you.

She'd picked up the cod early in the morning, always best to get it fresh before it sat out too long. You could trust the Fulton

Fish Market, but what was lovely in the morning could start to stink by mid-afternoon. Worse in the summer, but you had to be careful in winter, too.

The rectory was quieter than usual this afternoon, even though all three of the priests were in. Father Mahoney had gone off to his bedroom to lie down for a bit, Father Kearns was making entries in the big ledgers that had been haphazardly kept until he arrived, and Father Brennan was seeing to the last of his packing. Not that he had more than two suitcases, which was about right for a priest, but he could fuss over the smallest thing, like a handkerchief not ironed and folded with a sharp enough crease.

Having them all out of her way and busy on their own suited Mrs. Healy just fine. Basket in hand, she made her careful way down the cellar steps after the potatoes, carrots, turnips, and horseradish root, thinking through what she had to do next. She liked to plan out a task so there'd be no surprises and plenty of time to get it done right. Peel the potatoes and put them to soak in salted water, scrub the dirt off the carrots and turnips, but leave the peels on. They were good for the bowels. She'd grate the horse-radish and mix it into some dried mustard powder moistened with a few tablespoons of porter. Do it early so her eyes wouldn't still be red from the fumes when she served the dinner. She wouldn't want Father Brennan to think she was cut up over his leaving.

The smell she'd noticed down there was getting stronger. She'd have to mention it to Jerry Brophy. Strictly speaking, he was only supposed to take care of the church, but the man was such a fool for cleaning that he happily took on whatever extra jobs she could find for him around the rectory. He loved scrubbing floors. Maybe that was the problem. Something spilled that was starting to rot in the crevices between the flagstones that kept the cellar cool. Not as cold as outdoors, of course, but far from as warm as the floors above. Maybe she could sniff it out.

She'd look a real gorm if anyone saw her snuffling like a dog around the shelves where the Mason jars stood in perfect rows. Nothing there she could see, though the smell did seem a bit stronger. Not a stench yet but definitely enough to make her want to pinch her nose. The bins for the root vegetables had an earthy scent, not the slightest bit objectionable. Mrs. Healy couldn't understand it. The farther she got from the Mason jars, over by the coal chute and the furnace, the fainter the odor, but she could have sworn she'd looked carefully at every shelf to see if a jar might have cracked and leaked its contents.

One more try. She'd take another look and then tomorrow, after they'd gotten Father Brennan off, she'd send for Jerry Brophy and his mop and pail.

"I'll be back in a few minutes, Father," Mrs. Healy said as she slung her coat over her shoulders and grabbed the string bag she always took to the greengrocer's.

"Are you all right?" Father Kearns asked. He'd wandered into the kitchen for a cup of tea to take back to his desk just as the housekeeper came up the cellar stairs, her face as pale as though she'd had some great shock. He took the basket of vegetables out of her hands and set it on the table.

"I'm fine, Father. But I've got to get another horseradish for the dinner tonight. You know how Father Mahoney loves his horseradish."

"Isn't that what this is?" He held up a knobby root.

"It's gone too strong," Mrs. Healy replied, snatching it from his hand and tossing it back into the basket.

She didn't offer to put the kettle on for him, just marched out of the kitchen and down the hall like a soldier on a mission.

"I'll leave the cellar door unlocked for you, Kevin. I swear to God Almighty if it's what I think it is, we've got a murderer in the house."

Kevin unfolded himself slowly from his cardboard and newspaper shelter. He hadn't been able to explain to Mr. McGlory why he was reluctant to leave the alleyway across from Saint Anselm's, but the saloon keeper had slipped him a couple of coins and waved him off. He hadn't anything pressing for Carney to do at the moment; the final weeks before Christmas were slow for saloons. Gamblers, drinkers, and fornicators got religion at this time of year. It gave the card sharks, the bartenders, and the whores a chance to rest up.

"Tell me what you think it is, Mrs. Healy."

"I don't like to say it out loud, Kevin. Not till we're sure. But I can tell you I never put those bits and pieces in those urns, and I never hid the urns back behind what I canned last summer. The tops aren't sealed with wax. That's why the smell's been getting out."

"How bad is it?"

"I noticed it, and she'd be bound to," Mrs. Healy said, reaching down to pat Blossom's head. "But maybe nobody else, at least not for a few more days. Sometimes the laundry will leave a moldy smell when the weather's bad and the furnace is acting up. No one has any reason to go down there except me, and since Father Mahoney had Jerry Brophy put a lock on the door, I keep the key in my pocket during the day."

"What about at night?"

"Well, the key has to be in the door, doesn't it? In case of an emergency."

"There you are then. Someone's been down there at night when all he had to do was turn the key in the lock. I'll take a look for you."

"I wish you would. I'm that scared."

Dominic Pastore bought a first class ticket on board the *USS Augusta* as soon as Billy McGlory sent a messenger to tell him about the mysterious monsignor and what had been found in the cellar of Saint Anselm's rectory. There wasn't time for decent false papers, but first class passengers had the run of the ship and were rarely disturbed when anything untoward happened in steerage. He'd have to do the best he could and then disappear as soon as the boat docked.

McGlory ordered Kevin to burn the contents of the urns Carney brought to the back door of Armory Hall and never tell a soul what he'd found and what he'd done with them.

"Shouldn't there be a priest?" Carney asked.

Blossom knew instinctively that what she would normally have gobbled down with great gusto was this time so different that she risked not being forgiven if she set her jaws to it. Or even showed too much interest. She realized that the first time she caught a whiff of the parts and the tiny unborn pups the girls had left behind and decided not to draw her human's attention to the fragrant cache another human had so painstakingly hidden.

"Say a prayer if you want, Kevin. You're as good as any priest in the eyes of God."

So Kevin and Blossom bowed their heads over the fire he built in a small barrel behind the saloon. He shooed off the curious cats who slunk past and flung rocks at the few rats brave enough to venture out in the daytime. Blossom barked a quick explanation to the dogs; she was feared and respected, so even the fiercest curs turned tail without a snarl of disagreement.

When it was over, Kevin poured the flakes

587

of ash into a shiny wooden box Mr. Mc-Glory had given him. It was inlaid with mother of pearl, the prettiest thing Kevin had ever seen. He would bury the box and its contents in the graveyard of Saint Anselm's, right at the foot of the statue of the Blessed Mother. He thought the girls would like being close to her, especially Miss Sally Lynn.

On Mr. McGlory's orders, Kevin sent Blossom off to find a carcass somewhere; there were always dead things lying around in the alleys. She brought him back a rank and barely nibbled cat and the two rats it had killed before their bites brought it down. He skinned and gutted the bodies with great care. Then he told Mrs. Healy she'd been mistaken about what she thought she saw and smelled.

"It's probably Jerry Brophy's doing," Kevin explained to a disgusted Mrs. Healy, showing her the three small urns, a piece of cat liver, and the strips of meat he'd rolled in the dirt to put the appearance of age on them. "He caught the things and cut them up as bait for his rat traps, then forgot where he put them. The great *amadán.*"

"But why would he use the urns? Suppose someone found out? And what happened to whatever was inside?"

"They were empty. That's why he used them. You know how he is, always scrounging and cleaning and saving every scrap of this and that."

"What's to be done then?"

"I'll just clean the urns out in the rubbish bin and put them back in the crypt. I wouldn't bother mentioning it to Jerry at all, if I were you, Mrs. Healy. He won't remember, and you know how he gets when he thinks someone is making fun of him. The man has a temper, for all he acts so holier than thou." Kevin packed everything away in a piece of burlap he'd found rolled up behind the rack of Mason jars. She didn't ask what it was or where he'd gotten it.

"I feel like a fool, Kevin."

"We wouldn't want this to get out, would we? It's sure Jerry won't say a word and neither will I."

"I've a dinner to fix, and I'd better get on with it."

"We'll all be back to normal soon, Mrs. Healy."

"I'll have to say a prayer for thinking such a terrible thing about him, but I can't pretend I won't be glad to see the back of Father Brennan."

"Maybe he'll choke to death on some cod

bones tonight and save you the trouble."

"God forgive you, Kevin, for wishing the death of a priest." She snorted indignantly, then bent down and kissed his dirty cheek.

Blossom wagged her tail invitingly and got a pat on the head.

"So Father Brennan is leaving for Boston tomorrow," Ned mused. "He gave the last rites at two of the murder scenes, but no one saw him anywhere near Madame Jolene's."

"There's something about him that sets my teeth on edge." Prudence tried to smooth the frown from her forehead, but couldn't manage it. "I don't think I can put a name to it, but it's definitely there. Geoffrey?"

"Let's go over the whole thing one more time, starting with Joseph Nolan, who may not have killed anyone, but whose actions certainly brought about his own death." He knew that once the discussion began, neither Prudence nor Ned would give up until they'd tested and discarded one hypothesis after another. They'd examine every detail of the case until it all made sense. "I think Josiah needs to be a part of this."

"I agree," Prudence said, getting up from the conference table to ask the secretary to leave his desk and join them. "He was very brave at the Carousel."

Josiah brought his stenographer's pad, his pencils, and a tray of coffee, absurdly pleased to have been invited to contribute his perspective to this most puzzling case. Miss Prudence had made it clear that they wanted him to do more than just take notes.

"We know that Joseph Nolan believed he killed Sally Lynn," Geoffrey began, "and that he was prepared to kill Prudence and Josiah rather than have his perversity revealed to the world. He'd been going mad for years; when he finally broke, he lost all touch with reality."

"No loss there," Ned declared.

"The same hand mutilated all three women. Does anyone disagree?"

No one did.

"Then it couldn't have been Nolan because we know where he was the night Nora Kenny died."

"Could he have climbed out of bed, dressed himself, and gotten out of both Sally Lynn's room and the brothel without anyone hearing him?" Prudence sounded doubtful.

"I'm willing to agree that it's very likely he did not leave Sally Lynn's side that night." Ned didn't sound pleased with the concession.

"I saw Joseph Nolan die, and I don't regret for a moment witnessing it," Josiah put in. "I would have killed him myself had I been able to."

"He's dead, but he's unlikely to have murdered three women. He was just a bastard too tainted by evil to deserve to live." Ned turned to Prudence. "I apologize for the language," he said.

"According to the newspapers the case was declared officially closed when Nolan had the misfortune to be mauled by an unidentified dog," Josiah said. "Fahey and McGuire have been released."

"As far as we know, Blossom never recognized the killer's scent," Prudence contributed.

"Blossom strikes me as a dog who doesn't consider it necessary to inform her humans of every thought and discovery." Ned had once had a dog nearly as smart as Kevin's. A very long time ago.

"Let's move on to Jerry Brophy." Geoffrey didn't think anyone would consider his suggestion seriously, but it had to be made.

"Nothing for him or against him," Prudence said. "He lives alone, and apart from his cleaning mania, might be considered fairly normal."

"He killed his wife," Ned stated with absolute certainty. "His kind usually does, though they're rarely apprehended."

"She died of a fever," Josiah reminded him, paging back to earlier notes.

"He probably poisoned her," Ned continued. "But he was clever enough to do it when there was fever in the tenements and another death wouldn't be noticed."

"It wouldn't take much planning," Prudence conceded.

"I grant you he may have contributed to his wife's passing," Geoffrey declared. "From what we've learned about her, she didn't treat him half as well as she did her clients."

"They paid her," Prudence said. "Brophy's never been known to spend any of the money she must have earned. What happened to it?"

"Perhaps he scrubbed it clean," Josiah said. "Coin by coin."

"Brophy couldn't have killed them. He wouldn't have been able to tolerate blood on his skin or his clothing. Remember what we were told he did for his wife?" Prudence reminded them. "He cleaned up after her, scrubbed the table where the abortions were performed, settled nerves, and collected fees. Does that sound to you like someone who could slit throats and empty out bellies?"

"I agree," Ned said. "As strange and perhaps even as despicable as Jerry Brophy may be, and except for ridding himself of his wife, he doesn't have what it takes to murder in cold blood."

"Father Mark Brennan, who sets Prudence's teeth on edge," Geoffrey said. "We know Father Brennan is attractive to all of the women who go to church at Saint Anselm's."

"He may be one of those priests who gets moved from parish to parish more frequently than the average," Josiah said. "The lawyers who represent the archdiocese are closemouthed; their cases never reach the courts."

"An affair?" questioned Prudence.

"Something that won't bear scrutiny," Ned agreed.

"But I don't think he's our killer," Geoffrey said.

"He has something of Joseph Nolan in him," Prudence said. "Internal conflicts that pull him in several different directions at once."

"The pastors who get him transferred out of their parishes probably consider him a weak or even a bad priest, but obviously not weak or bad enough to do any more than move him along somewhere else," Ned agreed. "Nolan went mad. I don't see that in Brennan's future."

"A faceless, nameless killer who's still roaming the streets of the city," proposed Geoffrey. It was his penultimate proposal and they all knew it.

"The kills would have to be random then," Prudence continued. "All of the links we've discovered over the past weeks would have to be purely coincidental, meaningless."

"Not necessarily. We just have to admit that the killer is clever enough to hide his face and conceal his name. Perhaps forever." Ned tried to catch Geoffrey's eye, but Hunter was engrossed in the Pinkerton exercise of applying logic to crime. "No one is that smart. Or that lucky."

"So we finally come to Neil Slattery, owner of a tailor shop that supplies household staff with uniforms and does alterations. Whose mother performed abortions there. And who has disappeared." Geoffrey always brought them back on point.

"You found Nora's carpetbag in his apartment." Ned was ticking off the points against Slattery on his fingers.

"Slattery had to have been the monsignor we saw walking from the rectory into the church when Alice Nolan was supposed to become his next victim," Geoffrey continued. "What he was wearing distracted us. His disguise worked."

"Davey, the boy who sometimes minded the counter in the tailor shop, said he saw Mr. Neil wearing a cassock and biretta with red piping. He was clear on that, though not too much else," Prudence admitted.

"Alice Nolan never saw the man who drugged her and carried her down to the crypt," Ned contributed.

"Brennan and Slattery are both tall, slender men, though in Slattery's case all we have to go on is how the few neighbors who would talk to us described him. At a distance I imagine it would be easy to mistake one for the other. That's another thing that threw us off. When you see a man wearing a cassock, you immediately think *priest.*" Geoffrey shook his head ruefully at the deception.

"If it was Slattery, why did he risk going back to Saint Anselm's? He had to have known we suspected him," Prudence asked.

"He went to destroy what remained of his victims. Maybe he thought he could remove the contents of the urns from where he'd hidden them in the basement of the rectory."

"We interrupted him. He wasted time looking for Alice, and then he heard us upstairs. He fled out the cellar door into the alley."

"He's the only link we have between Saint Anselm's, the three killings, and the attempt on Alice Nolan. He's the only commonality that makes sense." Ned slapped one fist against the palm of the other hand.

"We've got men at the steamship offices and the railroad station," Geoffrey reminded them. "If he tries to buy a ticket, we'll have him."

"Even under another name?" Prudence asked.

"He needs papers to leave America for Europe, if that's the direction he decides to head. He'll have to chance using his own because he won't have time to buy false ones."

"He doesn't need papers to buy a train ticket," Ned said.

"My gut is telling me that Slattery has decided it's time to go home, back to Ireland. He can disappear there in a way that's not possible in this country. The neighbors all say he still has a strong Irish accent. That's not something he could hide once he gets out of the city."

"Excuse me," Josiah said. He disappeared

into the outer office and came back a few moments later, followed by a man dressed in the clothes and cap of a dock worker.

Geoffrey shook his hand and introduced him to the others. "Bill and I were Pinkertons together," he said, pulling out a chair for the new arrival. "Sit down and tell us what's up."

"Your man had a contact down on the docks, just like you thought. A clerk in one of the ticket offices. I was told there was some talk about the clerk's sister and a merchant seaman a few years back, but nothing ever came of it."

"Slattery's mother did abortions," Ned said. "We think he did, too, after she died."

"He's got a ticket on the *USS Augusta,* due to sail in two days. What's interesting is that he's not listed on the passenger manifest. I got a look at it and he's not there. My guess is that the clerk will add him at the last moment, just before the ship sets sail."

"Second class?" asked Ned.

"He'd be safer in steerage," Geoffrey said. "He could blend in with the other Irish going back where they came from."

"I couldn't find that out," Bill apologized. "Money changed hands, that much I do know."

"I don't think he'll attempt to pass as a first class passenger," Prudence said. "Second class would be a great deal more comfortable than steerage, and he could keep to his cabin during the day. Perhaps feign seasickness."

"I'll see what I can learn." Bill laid an envelope on the table. "I bought these as soon as I was sure. The *Augusta* is a decent ship, but she's not as fast as some of the newer ones."

"Seaworthy?"

"So I'm told. And her captain has a good reputation," he added. "Let me know what names you decide on and I'll have you added to the first class manifest." He hesitated, but Pinkerton training took over. "I'm not sure it means anything, but another first class ticket was bought around the same time I got these. It's unusual in first class for someone to decide to sail at the last minute. Just thought I'd mention it." He smiled and stood up. "Two can play at this game."

"Did you get the name of the late first class passenger?" Geoffrey asked.

"That's another thing that's unusual. My source wouldn't tell me. He's not the kind who frightens easily, but he was clearly at pains to hide the name from me. I didn't press him."

"Slattery will kill again, if he's really the one. He won't be able not to." Ned thrummed his fingers against the arm of his chair as Josiah escorted Bill from the conference room.

"I don't like it when a case gets away from us," Prudence said as Josiah returned to stack cups and saucers. She followed him to the outer office, sipping the last of her coffee as she went.

"It hasn't gotten away from us," Geoffrey said. "All but the last act."

"What is that supposed to mean?"

"Kevin was with us when Alice Nolan was attacked. Her brother was dead by then. We've known for a while that someone has been having us followed. If we had men watching the docks and the train station, he might have been interested, also."

"The way those families operate, the sons follow in the father's footsteps or else," Ned said. "I saw a lot of it while I was a copper. Dominic Pastore may have been willing to take a chance on getting out while Nora was alive, but not after she was killed. He had to make a decision. And maybe by then it was a choice he welcomed."

"Slattery won't make it to Ireland," Geoffrey predicted.

CHAPTER 34

Neil Slattery stayed on deck until the *USS Augusta* passed by Lady Liberty, sailed out of the mouth of New York Harbor, and entered the Atlantic Ocean where Sandy Hook Lighthouse had guided mariners into the New World since before America was born.

He'd been six years old when his mother dragged him and his sister Bridget aboard the *Utopia*. Sailors shoved them down into the bowels of the ship where they languished in the dark and the rancid smell of sickness for two weeks until the vessel made port in New York Harbor. He'd never smelled air as sweet or seen light as bright as when he stumbled up onto the deck to stare open-mouthed at his new country.

America. Where life had been brutally hard until the respectable widow Slattery turned her hand to saving young women from the stigma that had driven her from home and family and all hope of a decent life.

Twenty-five years. He'd done the best he could after Bridget and then their mother died. But it hadn't been enough. He'd come too close to getting caught to be able to stay. He didn't belong anymore. He never found the dream all of them in the *Utopia*'s fetid steerage hold had talked and sung about.

Neil had always known he'd go back, though his mother laughed at him whenever he asked about Ireland. She made fun of him because what he thought were memories were fairy tales. The grandfather he'd never met wouldn't allow him to set foot on the farm, being the bastard that he was. And the grandmother, the aunts and uncles, the cousins — none of them would welcome him with open arms. Not a single one would offer him a cup of tea.

She was wrong, his mother. He had money in his pockets, and as long as you had coins to hand out, you were welcome anywhere. But he wouldn't go to the farm right away, not until he was as rich and grand as everyone expected someone coming home from America to be. He'd set himself up in Dublin or Cork, open a nice little tailor shop on a quiet street in the kind of neighborhood where girls were likely to need his services. He'd wear his string, tied as tight as he could bear it. Not just at night when the dreams exploded in his head and the heat of them poured out of his body despite the string. In the daytime, too, but perhaps not as tight. He'd throw away his special knife, never use it again. Fling it into the ocean when they were well out at sea. Late at night when the decks were empty.

Eight days at sea before they reached the port of Queenstown. He would eat and sleep and plan for what lay ahead. Most importantly, he would keep to his cabin and only venture out when other passengers were unlikely to be on deck. He hadn't been able to bear the thought of steerage again. The clerk whose sister's reputation he'd saved had assured him that there were a few other Irish on the second class passenger manifest. But in the clerk's opinion, steerage would have been a better place for Neil to conceal himself, if that's what he was trying to do.

Neil had kept his intentions to himself.

The second class steward pocketed Geoffrey's bribe and set about supplying him with as much information as he could gather. Only one name on his corridor began with an S. He hadn't been sure whether it was Sullivan or Slattery; the clerk who'd filled out the manifest had bunched some of the letters together and it was hard to make them out. The gentleman in question, Mr. Slattery it appeared, never left his cabin; the steward brought him his meals on a tray and deposited the tray outside his door. When he came to pick it up, the food was eaten and there was always a generous tip, but the passenger himself remained invisible.

There was no night steward in second class, so the mysterious Mr. Slattery certainly could go for a stroll on deck without anyone knowing, but that was discouraged. The decks were slippery with spray that wasn't mopped up until morning. A passenger might lose his footing, even be thrown against the railing. Much better to take one's daily exercise when everyone else on board did.

From after dusk until well past midnight, Prudence and Geoffrey took turns watching the doorway through which Slattery would have to step to reach the second class promenade deck. Prudence insisted that their hours on guard be equal; she wouldn't allow it to be any other way. Geoffrey protested, and only reluctantly agreed when she argued him into submission. She flushed with pleasure when he told her she would make a splendid advocate in a court of law, but didn't weaken in the slightest. Fair was fair.

Four nights out, their steady observations finally paid off. At a little past midnight, as Prudence was on her way to relieve Geoffrey, Neil Slattery stepped out of his cabin and made his way quietly along the corridor toward the open deck. Prudence heard his footsteps before she saw him; she stepped into the shadow of a metal staircase and remained there until he had passed, Geoffrey following not too closely behind.

"He's carrying something," Geoffrey whispered in her ear. "It's wrapped in dark cloth, so I can't tell what it is. He may intend to throw it overboard."

Their plan was a simple one. Wait until Slattery left his cabin, then pick the lock while he was on deck, let themselves in, search the place, and confront him when he returned. From what the steward had told them, their prey couldn't be induced to open his cabin door to anyone. This was their only hope of getting inside. There was always the possibility they would find nothing incriminating or that Slattery would turn on his heel and call for help when he spied them in his cabin, but it was a chance they had to take.

"Wait," Prudence murmured. "Let's make sure he's doing more than stepping outside for a quick breath of fresh air." She listened to the sound of retreating footsteps, straining to hear them through the crashing of the ship's hull against the waves. When all was silent again except for the sea, she squeezed Geoffrey's arm. But instead of setting off toward the doorway, he turned to face her, pressed his body against hers, and laid a hand over her lips. She froze.

Whoever else was out on deck with them was approaching so stealthily that only a Pinkerton trained ear could have heard him. He glided by the unlit space where Geoffrey had covered Prudence with his bulk, paused for a moment as if sensing he wasn't alone, then moved on.

The moon passed from behind a cloud, bathing the deck briefly in brilliant white light. The last time Prudence had seen that face had been beneath the Carousel in Central Park. Despite herself, she trembled. Geoffrey laid a hand on the back of her head and pressed her face gently against the strength of his chest. Gradually the quivering ceased. What was Dominic Pastore doing here? Had he followed them? Or had he had his own sources of information all along? It flashed through her mind that Geoffrey might have known the man was aboard and not told her. If so, it was a deception she couldn't deal with now.

She pushed to signal she was all right, and Geoffrey released her.

No question what they would do next. They followed behind Pastore as he paced silently and steadily in Neil Slattery's wake. His gloved hands hung loosely at his sides and a brimmed hat hid his face. He looked back over his shoulder just once as they passed through a ray of light coming through a porthole. One glance and then he continued on his way. Prudence had no idea whether or not he had seen and recognized them. When Geoffrey stepped into a patch of moonlight and no longer hunched his shoulders to conceal his height, she realized that Pastore knew perfectly well they were there. He probably even knew their cabin numbers, Prudence thought. *Settle down. Settle down and concentrate on what you're going to have to do next.*

Slattery had reached the starboard bow as far forward as the second class railing would allow him to go. He seemed to be waiting for the moon to show itself again as he gazed upward at the thin clouds obscuring the stars. Just a peaceable passenger unable to sleep, breathing in the fresh tang of the salt air.

Dominic Pastore moved quickly, but as he lunged for Slattery, the tailor whirled and slashed out with a broad bladed knife that flashed a dazzling silver beam.

"No!" screamed Prudence. Before Geoffrey could stop her she hurled herself between the two men, pushing Dominic backwards as Geoffrey bounded forward and reached for her.

As his arm snaked around her waist, Slattery brought the knife down with ferocious strength. It slashed through the thick wool of Geoffrey's coat sleeve; blood that was black in the moonlight sprayed out and onto the deck. His wounded arm fell to his side and Prudence felt Slattery pull her against him. The knife was at her throat.

"Don't move, either of you," he snarled.

Geoffrey swayed on his feet. Dominic stood close to catch him if he fell. Neither man said a word.

Prudence thought frantically. What could she say, how could she convince this madman to let her go? To let all of them go. What guarantee would make him believe one of them wouldn't persuade the captain to have him ambushed by too many sailors to fight off? Could she promise to stay with him in his cabin until they landed? Accompany him down the gangplank?

He was breathing rapidly and heavily, occasional sobs breaking through the labored respiration. "If you take one step toward me, she's overboard," Slattery promised. "If I go, I'll take her with me."

"No one wants to hurt you," Geoffrey soothed. Using his uninjured hand and his teeth, he'd managed to tie his handkerchief around his arm above the knife wound. Thick black liquid continued to ooze out onto his sleeve, but it was no longer the heavy stream it had been.

"Who's the other one?" Slattery asked, nodding toward Pastore.

"I'm the man who's going to kill you," Dominic promised smoothly. "You murdered my Nora. Your life is forfeit, now or in the future. There is no escape from me. I'll come upon you at a time and in a place where you least expect it. *Bastardo!* Bastard!"

Prudence stared at Pastore, willing him not to continue, imploring him with her eyes to allow Geoffrey to talk this crazed killer into submission. He could do it, she knew he could. Geoffrey could persuade anyone to do anything. But it took time to work his magic, and she was afraid Dominic would rob them of that.

Step down hard on his instep. Jab your elbow into his stomach. Go limp so he has to hold you up. Use your knee where it will cripple him. How many times had Geoffrey gone over the ways a woman could save herself? Dozens, Prudence thought, ever since she had decided they would be equal partners taking equal risks. Being on a ship in the middle of the Atlantic Ocean changed everything. She was barely keeping her balance on the deck that was now thinly coated in Geoffrey's blood as well as the treacherous sea water.

"*Andiamo,*" Pastore said.

Geoffrey didn't waste time answering.

Both men were on them before Slattery could react. The knife flew out of his hand and clattered onto the deck, but his arm around Prudence's waist tightened. She could hardly breathe. Her feet were lifted into the air as Slattery pressed them both against the rail, bending her backwards so the spray coming from below soaked her hair.

"I'll take her with me!" he screamed. "Throw me over and she'll go, too."

If there was a moral choice to make, Geoffrey didn't debate it, not for a fraction of a second. He fought his way past Pastore, who seemed determined to destroy Slattery no matter the danger to Prudence. With the small knife he pulled from where it was strapped inside his boot, Geoffrey stabbed Slattery in the arm that imprisoned his partner. Over and over again, until the arm loosened and Prudence fell free.

And almost over the railing.

Geoffrey held on to her as she flung her arms around his neck and struggled to bring her upper body to safety and her feet to the deck again. She staggered against him as he dragged her away from the railing, both of them near collapse.

An agonized shriek made them turn. Dominic Pastore, with what had to be the superhuman strength of pure rage, had lifted Neil Slattery above his head.

There was time to reach them, time to try to wrestle Slattery from Pastore's deadly grip, but neither Geoffrey nor Prudence moved to stop it. This was justice in its purest, most elemental form. They would never breathe a word to a living soul of what they knew was about to happen.

He was alive when Dominic Pastore hoisted him over the railing and threw him into the Atlantic Ocean. Alive and screaming. But no one heard him over the roar of the waves and the wind, the pulsating

611

clamor of the ship's engines.

For a few moments Neil Slattery was a white face bobbing in a dark sea.

Then he was nothing.

EPILOGUE

"I wouldn't wish London in the winter on anyone," Prudence said, climbing into the carriage Kincaid had warmed with hot bricks wrapped in layers of soft wool.

"But the sea voyage home wasn't too bad, I hope." Josiah floated a Clan MacKenzie tartan blanket over her knees.

"Geoffrey walked the decks every day while the rest of us cowered in our staterooms or the card parlors."

"The seas were rough?"

"We sailed into gale force winds," Geoffrey explained. "The deck chairs had to be stowed and ropes were strung along the railings and passageways." He flashed a smile of pure delight.

Josiah stared at him in horror. Any body of water larger than the placid seven-foot-deep lake in Central Park filled him with dread.

"There were times Geoffrey chose to be

on deck when even the sailors only ventured out if they had to." Prudence touched her partner's arm lightly. "I told him he should have been a naval officer instead of a Pinkerton."

"I'm assuming everything was quiet here," Geoffrey said. He'd expected a torrent of telegrams from their often excitable secretary, but Josiah had been remarkably silent during their month-long absence.

"Tim Fahey is back on Staten Island. Agnes Kenny wrote a note to you, Miss Prudence, which I opened as per your instructions. Just in case they needed anything. She said Tim is fishing again and mostly healed from the beatings he got during the third degree. You'll be glad to know that the Kenny family is continuing to take care of Windscape." He wondered if she'd ever feel comfortable in that childhood summer home that held so many sad memories of her mother.

"Did she mention anyone else?" Prudence asked.

Dominic Pastore had disappeared as swiftly and completely as Neil Slattery. They'd caught a glimpse of someone who might have been him descending the gangplank when the ship docked at Southampton, but nothing definite. It was as though what had happened that night in mid-Atlantic vanished with him. There was no report of a missing passenger. When Geoffrey gained access to Slattery's cabin, it had been cleared of all his belongings. The steward wasn't sure he remembered him.

Prudence didn't doubt that Pastore, too, had returned to Staten Island. Like Tim Fahey, he followed the path he'd been born to walk. If he and Nora had ever made plans to escape into a new and different world, that future had evaporated with her death. He had sealed his fate when he took the vengeance his culture expected him to exact.

"Detective Phelan has been promoted," Josiah said. "He's Chief Byrnes's fair-haired boy now."

"We could have predicted that." Geoffrey's experience had taught him that recognition and reward often had nothing to do with competence.

"Mr. Hayes had a setback, but Tyrus reports that he's on his feet again." Josiah wasn't sure how Miss Prudence would take his next bit of news. "Kevin Carney and his dog are sleeping in the stables. Kincaid says the horses love her. Blossom, that is."

Prudence's peal of laughter filled the carriage. "I told him they were always welcome. Blossom saved our lives, Josiah."

"Yes, Miss."

"What about our friend in the saloon business?" Geoffrey asked. Like everyone else who talked about him, he avoided using Billy McGlory's name.

"They're closing in on him, Mister Hunter. The reformers have him in their sights and I'm not sure he's going to be able to walk away this time. I've saved the papers for you."

"A month of newspapers to get through?"

"I did some clipping."

"Much appreciated, I'm sure."

"What about the Nolans?" Prudence asked.

"The house is for sale. Miss Alice is taking to convent life like she was born to it, but the rumor is that Mr. and Mrs. Nolan have separated."

"Geoffrey, do you believe madness can be inherited?" Prudence asked.

"I've seen it run in bloodlines," he answered. "In the South, before the war, a woman could be hidden away in an upstairs room, tended by a slave day and night, and kept quiet by laudanum. The men drank too much, shot at anything that moved, rutted like hogs, and generally lived short, vicious lives. That was a kind of madness. People believed it came from cousins repeatedly marrying cousins, but I'm not sure it's entirely due to our peculiar marriage customs. Victims frequently grow up to be abusers. I think it likely Francis Nolan was more responsible for his son's madness than we'll ever know."

"And Father Brennan?"

"My contact in the archbishop's office informs me that he's settled in nicely to his new parish," Josiah informed her. "There are a lot of Irish in Boston. He should feel right at home."

"Until he has to be moved again," Geoffrey said. But that was the Church's affair. There was no proof of wrongdoing of any kind. He'd have to let it go.

"I don't know which city is worse, New York or London," Prudence said, peering out at the crowded streets, the multitude of horse-drawn vehicles jockeying for position, the piles of dung swept against every curb by hordes of ragged urchins. It was a little better as they approached the MacKenzie mansion on Fifth Avenue, but only by degree.

"I wouldn't live anywhere else," Josiah said. A staunch and loyal New Yorker, he was convinced there was no other place on earth that could rival his beloved metropolis.

Prudence smiled. She shared Josiah's feelings, though she'd never put them into words. It was a case of being New York born and bred, she decided. Unlike the masses of immigrants who hoped to move on through the city to something better, she knew she belonged here. Her bones sensed it, even when they were being rattled around in a carriage lurching its way across cobblestoned streets.

New York was exciting and dangerous, beautiful under a blanket of snow or garlanded with the green of springtime, ugly in the tenement districts, brutal when the gangs rich people never saw set out to maim and kill each other. She and Geoffrey had a foot in both New Yorks. They lived in opulence and safety, but the nature of the work they had chosen to do carried them into the darker city where life was raw and passions flared to killing intensity with the speed of a Lucifer match striking fire.

"Kincaid," Prudence called into the speaking tube that connected the interior of the carriage to the driver perched high above them outside. "I've changed my mind. You can drop the baggage off at home later. Right now I'd like to go to Wall Street. To the office."

Geoffrey touched one hand to his forehead in mock salute.

Josiah knew he'd been right to lay in a new supply of German pastries and freshly ground coffee this morning. There was nothing momentous on the horizon for the firm of Hunter and MacKenzie, Investigative Law, but there were a number of inquiries that might prove promising.

Prudence wondered if anything could match the challenge of the case they had just solved. *When you think you've seen it all, something entirely new comes along,* her father's voice reminded her. Judge Mac-Kenzie had never underestimated the depths to which human wickedness could sink.

His daughter was learning the same lesson.

ACKNOWLEDGMENTS

Somewhere amongst the many drafts of this novel I needed a new character. Thanks to Eileen Brady who provided me with just the person I didn't know I was looking for.

No book ever springs to life entirely on its own. Many voices contributed to the telling of this second of Prudence MacKenzie's adventures, but none with greater fidelity than those of my Tuesday Critique Group. Thanks to Joyce Sanford, Louise Boost, and Betty Barry for being there with editorial pens at the ready.

As always, editor John Scognamiglio and agent Jessica Faust saw what all the rest of us missed and pointed it out. Just when you think you're finished, it's time for a few more revisions.

ABOUT THE AUTHOR

Rosemary Simpson was born in New York City and almost immediately began roaming. By the time she entered college she had traveled extensively throughout the United States, the Far East, and Europe where she found a second home in France. After returning to the United States she earned undergraduate and graduate degrees in French language and literature. She currently lives near Tucson, Arizona.

Rosemary's favorite novel has always been Anya Secton's classic work of historical fiction, *Katherine*. (She's read and reread her way through three editions that were usually held together with tape and rubber bands until another could be bought.) The fascination lies in an inherent conflict between what we know actually happened and the frequent and gaping holes in the historical record. Sometimes there are only a few verifiable facts on which to build a story and recreate a past event. That's the writer's greatest and most enjoyable challenge. She can only make up what can't be proven and cannot violate the integrity of what is known. Writing historical fiction often means wandering through the most obscure, wonderful, and frightening byways of time and geography,